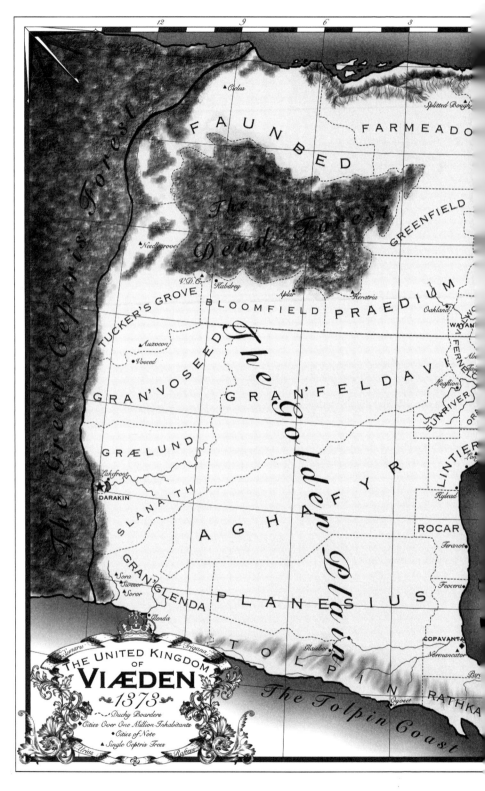

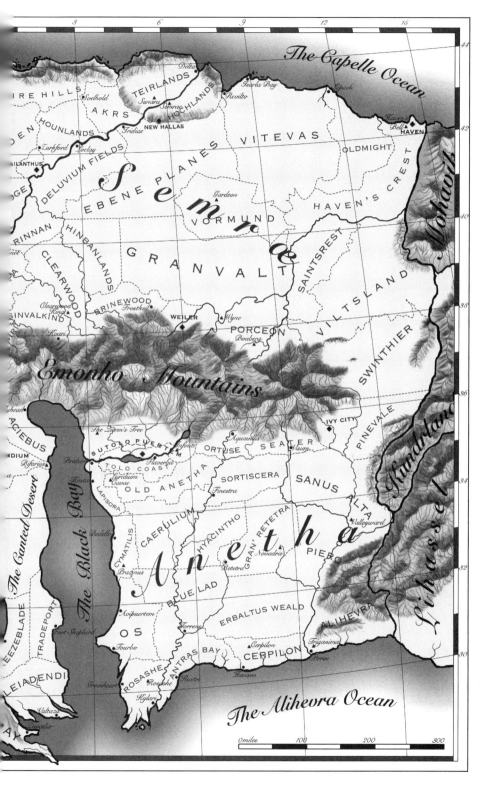

# PROGENY OF GODS

## TOME I

## VERTUÉM DESTINY

GEOFFREY STORM

*Progeny of Gods: Vertuém Destiny*

Library of Congress Cataloging-in-Publication Data is available
2015908028

ISBN-13: 978-0-9963780-0-0

First Edition — First Print

Book design by Geoffrey Storm
Printed and bound by Edwards Brothers Malloy, Ann Arbor, Michigan
Typography by Georg Duffner and Geoffrey Storm

©

*Mom, thank you for sharing the stories
that gave my mind wings.
And Dad, thank you for bringing me back
down to earth again.*

*This one's for you.*

# Part I

# A Land of Truths and Legends

# 1

# VIÆDEN

Greyson took another step into the light, not quite sure what he was looking at. The busy sounds of the ship's bridge faded into muted shuffles of feet and soft chirps from the radar. The sun's warmth rose up over his legs and body as he entered the pool of light upon the wooden floor. The bridge's front window was a glowing panorama, ignited, golden-white before his eyes could adjust. But, with one more step, Greyson's green eyes were unveiled.

Of course he'd heard stories, tons of them. And he'd seen pictures too. But every picture of this place just looked like the edge of any old forest. Nothing compared to the spine-tingling world before him now. This wasn't any old forest. It was a kingdom of trees, draped in the sun. The scale of which . . . made him feel like dust. But he wasn't dust. He was still standing in a wooden ship, flying thirty thousand feet off the ground. And those trees were damn-near seven miles tall.

The Great Ceptris Forest looked like an unkempt hedge, forgotten, way out on the lawn. Like a lumpy, green wall, grown for millennia to keep out the unknown beyond. It spanned forever to his right, curving down into the haze of the northern horizon. And the same to the south, eventually meeting the sea, somewhere, far out of sight. But dead ahead, right at its edge, stood the forest's crowning gem: a tree, shaped like a broadsword, aimed at the sky, threatening the blue to stay where it belonged, or spill its black guts across the land. Greyson had seen pines before, but this was something altogether different, the only one of its kind. And while it stood one mile shorter than the forest behind it, the trees closest to it seemed to bow in honor of its needled branches, creating a bright, flourishing canvas for its dark bristles to pop against. In the kingdom of trees, this pine was its capital. Darakin, they called it. An entire city carved from its heart.

Greyson's breathing deepened, abs tightening as his lips stretched into a nervous smile. This new world reflected in his eyes, and sparked something inside him. He could feel his heart stir, and stretch, like dawn had finally come to rouse it from an endless sleep. He rubbed his chest, taken wholly, and unexpectedly, by a feeling he thought he'd outgrown. Something his life had been missing for way too long. But what it was exactly, he couldn't say. It was almost like wonder, but deeper than that. Older than that. Something that stretched far back into his childhood, when his mom would tell tales of a far away land.

"So this is Viæden." Just saying the name gave him chills, flashing back to a thousand bedtimes, and a thousand different stories his mom tucked him in with each night. Legends of trees seeded by gods, forests rife with faeries, and blades crafted by angels. All taking place here, in this enchanted realm, way back when.

He'd heard so many stories, he almost thought this place was fantasy. And seeing it now, he still wasn't sure. Scared he was still dreaming, Greyson turned to his friend Tay, to make sure he saw it too.

Tay was a bit shorter than Greyson. Five inches shorter, to be exact. Though if you asked Tay, he'd say four-and-a-half. And his real name wasn't Tay, it was Taymes. But nobody called him that. Except for Tay's mom. It was one of those old names, back when names had meanings. It meant "guardian of happiness," and his mom thought it was the cutest thing. Safe to say, it was not a popular name to grow up with. Especially when you're also the fattest kid on the playground. Not that he was actually *fat*. Just chubby. But it was plenty more than enough to be dubbed *Tubby Taymie* by the kids back home in Wellington.

"Look at these ladies." Tay pointed to the lake below, shimmering as it mirrored the forest on its waves. He had his nose smashed up against the glass, staring at two figures that stood on the shore, facing each other on either side of the capital. Greyson hadn't even noticed them until now. They looked like trees, only a mile tall. But their trunks had been molded into womanly figures, arms held up to Darakin on display, foliage like windswept hair all down their backs.

"Please don't do that to the glass, Mr. Hooker." A stern voice came from behind.

Tay peeled himself off the window with a sharp glare, like those childhood bullies had followed him here. The only thing he hated more than his first name was his last name.

Greyson and Tay both turned to find that the captain of the ship—or in this case its general—had entered the bridge through its sliding doors. General Brown stood in the center of what would have been a perfectly symmetrical control room. That is, if there was such a thing as symmetry in Viæden. Every one of the bridge's control panels was carved of redwood and polished, smooth as glass, finished with a glaze that shined like it too. Keys and monitors glowed in grids of yellow and green from each panel's flat top. There were no signs of exposed wires or circuitry like the machines the boys were used to back home, and not a single straight line to be found.

The ship's crew hardly matched the organic bridge at all, wearing bland, navy jumpers with brown boots and a dull, metal pauldron over each of their left shoulders. And General Brown matched even less, wearing a black and gold dress coat, with tails that hung down to the backs of his knees. But it was more than just what he was wearing. He held himself differently. More casually than the rest of his men, but still clean cut. Not stuck up at all. Pretty welcoming, actually. His uniform was clear of any sort of decoration, even though he must have won a thousand medals to reach the highest rank in the whole Kingdom Guard. But the fact that he displayed none of them meant they weighed on him with humility instead of pride.

It made Greyson feel extremely underdressed, having just woken up and wearing only a wrinkly, white tee and his work pants, which were sort of like jeans but beige and more durable. "General Brown," he greeted with an eager hand, stepping forward to meet him beside the helm in the middle of the room.

"Good to see you again, Mr. Wight." Brown gripped his hand, much firmer than he'd expected.

Greyson was quick to match his strength. Or at least try. He couldn't tell, losing feeling in his fingers. Pretty strong for an old guy. He had to be in his late sixties, at least.

"How has your flight been so far?" he asked, releasing Greyson's hand to shake Tay's. "Apologies for my absence. Bad memories in those mountains. Not in a very social mood passing through."

Greyson nodded. "That's alright. We slept most the way anyway."

It was a nine-hour journey from Wellington to Darakin, most of it spent traversing the tallest mountain range on the planet: the Biazlé Mountains, which surrounded Wellington completely, and served as the Kingdom of Viæden's eastern boundary. They were so tall and unforgiving that not even a high-tech ship like the one they were on—a Viæden bark ship—could fly over them. Let alone the lesser tech of Wellington. The only way to cross them was through one of only two known passes. Which was nerve-wracking because the weather was *always* terrible, and the valleys were so unnaturally narrow. Greyson couldn't blame the general for locking himself in his cabin, given what he must have been through. Brown was the man almost solely responsible for the liberation of the Biazlé Mountains during the War of the Commonwealths, like thirty-five years ago. And, from the stories Greyson's dad used to tell . . . It was a nasty war.

"I imagine this past month has been very exciting for you both," said Brown.

"Painfully," Tay squirted out.

Last month, the whole of Wellington was in a curious frenzy because one of Viæden's bark ships had arrived. It was such a rare thing to see one leave the kingdom, mostly only to bring goods and supplies from a strange and distant land where machines were made of wood instead of steel. They looked like living works of art, and flew just as gracefully, with no wings to carry them. People would line the streets of Wellington whenever a delivery arrived, for a chance to see the massive, flat-bottomed, bark ship glide overhead and dock in the cradle of Wellington Tree's branches. But there was no delivery scheduled for that day, which instantly sparked all kinds of excited rumors through town. Mostly it made everyone uneasy, and had them all thinking that another war was about to start.

Luckily its purpose was not so . . . malicious.

"It's one of Viæden's officers," Greyson's dad had said to him on one of Wellington Tree's balconies. The tree was massive, much larger than all the rest in their valley, almost a mile high, and home to the most affluent buildings in town: the Duke's manor, guard house, mall, and of course, the banks. The

4

rest of the city sprawled out beneath the shade of its leaves, encircled by miles of farmland, and mountains beyond. "General Brown," his dad said.

Greyson and his dad stood together, and alone, sky veiled by Wellington's leaves, a single wooden door behind them, which led to an interrogation room. Guards had been disappearing within all day, and now it was Greyson's turn. "He's looking for the best of our guards to take back with him, to become part of the king's Royal Guard."

Greyson's eyes locked with his dad's. He was an inch shorter than Greyson. Stout, and fatherly. His hair was blond like his son's, though darkened with age, then lightened again by grey over his ears. "Dad, I—"

"You're going to do your best."

"You need me here."

"No. I don't. Not as your captain. And not as your father."

Greyson cocked his head at that.

"Greyson. You know I only want the best for you. And I know you think it's your responsibility to stay and protect us. But there is nothing to protect us from here. So you've grown comfortable, in this paradise. This sanctuary of light." He waved his hand over the balcony. "But this is not the life I want for you." His brown eyes sharpened. "And this is not the life you want either . . . I can't watch you stay still and limit yourself—*cripple* yourself by passing up a chance to leave, and experience all life has to offer . . . You belong out there, son. Forging a life of your own."

Greyson was silent, feeling his dad's words passing through him, lifting him. His lungs filled with air. A deep and freeing breath. He loved his family, and would stay with them all his life if he had to. But in the back of his mind there had always been a tiny voice screaming out for escape. And finally, with his father's blessing, that quiet voice turned to a roar. A battle cry, both inspiring and terrifying. He would finally leave the walls of his valley, and discover what worlds lay beyond.

"You're nineteen now. And Tay's twenty! You boys need to get out of here. And this is your chance."

Greyson collapsed into his dad, wrapping his arms around him without a word. Just trying not to cry. Then, finally, after another breath, he managed a "thank you."

His dad pushed him back and looked into his eyes again, arms still on his shoulders. "Do good." He shook him once for emphasis. "Be good." Then he turned Greyson toward the door, and pat him on the back.

Greyson didn't know if his father had anything to do with it, being captain of the guard and all, but General Brown took an instant liking to him. Chose him almost immediately. Luckily they were hiring in pairs, and Greyson suggested Tay as his partner. A month later, Brown's bark ship returned to collect them.

"Yes, sir," Greyson assured the general. "Thank you again for choosing us. It'll be an honor to work for you."

Brown nodded. "The job's not yours just yet. The king still has to have a look at you both. And there is the matter of Berinhard and Riese. He has to see for himself which of you is best suited for the position, in his eyes." He leaned in close, making the grey in his dark hair, and faint liver spots, hard not to notice. "But, between us, the only thing the king really cares about is loyalty. Assure him of that, and you'll do fine."

*Loyalty* popped in Greyson's ears, exciting him even more. That was something he was in no short supply of. He'd lived in the same house all his life, on the hills outside town, where the sun would set over the mountains, and shine through their front window, right through to Mr. Trout's strawberry fields out back. But his dad was right. It was too much like paradise. And downright boring at the best of times. His loyalty was what kept him there. He felt he owed them all to stay, because they'd given him so much. Such a privileged life compared to some of the other kids he knew. So he became a guard like his dad, and accepted the monotony of handing out traffic violations and circling uneventful patrols on repeat for the last full year of his life.

"We're going to meet the king?" Greyson asked heavily, not knowing that was part of the process.

"Yes. He tries to have as much to do with the Royal Guard as possible, including their hiring. Which reminds me. Your previous captain told me you were one of the best pilots in Wellington."

"He did?" Greyson's nervous lips bent into a smile. *Well that settles that,* he thought. His dad *had* said something to the general, knowing Greyson'd never advertise his own strengths without plenty of coaxing first.

"Yes. And if you are given the position, you'll be granted a ship like this one. Have you ever flown anything this large before?"

As far as bark ships went, General Brown's actually came up pretty short. But it was still much larger than the huvs Greyson was used to piloting.

"Oh. No. I haven't."

"I have," a voice called out, so deep it tickled Greyson's gut like heavy bass. The two other recruits had arrived on the bridge. Big-ass guys . . . more giants than guys, really. They needed to duck just to pass through the doorway. Greyson hardly ever felt short at six-one, but these guys were at least a foot taller than him. They'd been picked up from Mohavik earlier that morning, where apparently their diets consisted of pure steroids, because one had arms so thick around, the leather he wore looked like it used up the whole bull just for one sleeve. And the entire pelt of some other furry animal for a collar.

Greyson locked eyes with him immediately, a malicious glare fired back at him. He tried to return the favor, but only squinted his eyes instead. Apparently giving dirty looks was an art form he was not particularly versed in.

"Very well then, Riese. You'll land the ship." Brown turned away from Greyson and Tay.

"Okaaay," Tay dragged out with a bitter look, swinging his head to lock eyes with Greyson, like he'd already blown it.

And right then they realized, this was going to be a fight.

Riese stepped up to the helm, separate from the rest of the bridge's controls. The chair that accompanied the wheel was way too small for his bulbous ass to fit in, so he slid the tiny thing back a few clicks, out of his way, and slouched so his sausage fingers could reach the U-shaped helm.

"What's with you?" Tay whispered. "We gotta get this guy."

"I know!" Greyson barked under his breath, searching Darakin's branches for a game plan. Now that he knew how much his dad wanted this for him, he couldn't mess it up. How the hell did Riese even know how to fly this thing? "These ships hardly ever leave Viæden," Greyson whispered. "And when they do, they sure aren't piloted by guards looking to take 'em for a joy ride." He looked to Tay. "He lied."

"That shit."

Just then, a ship emerged from Darakin, twice the size of theirs: a tanker, long and flat-bottomed, asymmetrical, and ridged on its sides, where it'd been mined from its tree. The bark ship flew from the cover of the branches toward them, faster than Greyson even knew these ships could go.

"Um . . . General," he said, not too sure if this was a big deal or not.

Brown turned his attention to the glass, but from where he was standing, near Riese, he couldn't see the ship below them, arching straight up like a breaching, wooden whale.

"Look out!" Tay screamed as the collision bell rang.

Finally spotting it on the radar, Riese jerked the helm back and spun hard to starboard.

"What are you doing!?" Brown yelled as the ship swung out of control, and the whole crew hit the deck like the rug got pulled out from under them. Evading just in time for the oncoming ship to blur past the window in a wall of bark and engine-fire.

The control room shuddered as it passed, and Riese leveled the ship out with a jerk.

Not exactly the maneuver someone who had experience piloting these things would pull, Greyson thought. He could have just hit the brakes. And he *should* have checked his radar, first thing.

"Everyone alright?" Brown climbed to his feet, supporting his weight on the edge of a control panel.

His crew grunted in response as they stood too.

"God, Riese," said Tay, still on the floor. He'd been thrown all the way across the room. "Did you at least get the guy's number before we start smashin' our ships together?"

Greyson pulled himself up, facing a monitor that just happened to be displaying a flashing I.D. "Actually, we did."

"You're kidding." Tay stood to look for himself.

"No. We must have gotten it when it flew over us. The number's VBS-22137." He turned to the general. "Should we go after it?"

Brown hesitated to take the wheel himself, but stopped short, acting like he'd only meant to brush his jacket off. "No. Just land, Riese. The king will be expecting us."

"You can manage that, right, big guy? Or do you need us to take over for you?" Tay wrapped his arm around Greyson and posed with a stupid grin on his face, like the two of them were on the cover of a cheesy pamphlet for how much fun being a guard was.

Greyson couldn't help but smile at that.

"I got it," Riese growled through his teeth, taking the ship in as delicately as his burly hands allowed.

The prickled limbs of the king's tree reached out to their ship like spiky arms looking for a hug. They grew like rungs from the trunk, forming shelves of deep green, with dark caverns in between. And these branch-caves were so long and dark they needed lanterns to light their insides. A few streaks of light did make it down through the dense spikes of the branches, but there were so few it hardly made a difference. The lanterns did their job just fine, big as houses, partitioning off the flow of traffic in and out. And it must have been rush hour or something because the place was packed. The bark ships all lined up like logs sent down a river to be chopped. Some were smaller, most were bigger, and there were even a few monsters out there: giant freighters taking goods in from the very corners of the king's realm. There were also a fair amount of tiny ships, not commercial or military, zipping around from branch to branch, each one unique in its own organic way, but all unified by their common ceptris hulls.

It was an entire mile until they reached the trunk, where a colossal hollow awaited them: a hangar, spanning almost the whole width of the tree's core, which at that height was almost a thousand feet across. Its floor looked metal, to better withstand the relentless traffic of a military landing bay: the weight of ships, the heat of engines, the shuffling of cargo, the spilling of various fluids, and the endless march of men.

General Brown's ship was only about a hundred sixty feet long, and could easily maneuver through the hangar with plenty of room to spare. Still, part of Greyson wished Riese would graze a wall or squash someone with the landing gear to prove just how incompetent he really was. But, no such luck. Even though the hangar was lined with bark ships and crowded with workers, there was an open patch of landing pad saved just for the general, and a hurried worker waving glowing rods to guide him in. Riese dropped the landing gear and rotated the ship ever so slightly toward the hangar's core: a thick wooden tower, a hundred feet across, supporting the roof of the bay like a lofty circus tent. And as soon as he was in position, the ship gently came to rest within docking bay three of Viæden's capital city.

# 2

# Eyes of a Demon

Greyson and Tay stepped from the bridge into the ship's main hallway, Berinhard and Riese right behind them. The hall was curved from floor to ceiling, tangled roots jutting from its walls. It looked almost like an ant tunnel, with many other tunnels branching from it, sealed by rounded doors. The entire thing was carved of wood, mined right from the ship, but intricately, leaving all those roots in the walls, whittled down into a woven lattice that emanated a warm light from between its grains. Everything Viæden built had this same look, a mix of organic and synthetic, but with the synthetic bits hidden to make it all look to work like magic.

Their room was the very last one on the left, right across from the giants'. It was pretty small inside. Just two lumpy, old beds with rough blankets, and a tiny cabinet in between. All carved right from the wood.

"Ugh." Tay stretched, tussling his messy, brown hair. "I'm finally starting to feel like a real person again."

Greyson took a good look at him. His face was young and animated, slightly goofy, but he could wrangle in the ladies just fine. "Maaaybe you shouldn't have spent all night out with the guards yesterday." Which he knew would happen.

"Well *excuse* me for taking a bullet for the both of us." Tay picked up his sandy-colored duffle bag from the floor and put it on the bed. "That party was for both of us, you know."

"I went," Greyson winced.

"For like, an hour."

"Yeah, 'cuz I knew we had to get up at *five* in the morning to come here."

Tay sat on the edge of his bed and stared blankly into the reminiscent void. "That was the last time we were gunna see any a them. Is an hour really all they meant to you?"

Pulling his white tee up over his head, Greyson paused, blond hair floating in the static, confused at Tay's sudden sentiment for home. "Oh, shut up. You didn't care about any of them. You just wanted an excuse to get trashed." He threw the shirt into his bag and pulled a crisp, grey button down from the cabinet, sliding it over his bare shoulders. His body was lean and fit, and even though Tay had lost most of his baby fat, Greyson was in much better shape.

"I'm so offended right now," Tay said. But he wasn't.

Greyson shook his head and smiled, concentrating on lining up his buttons.

Tay looked over to the open door. Across the hall he could see Berinhard and Riese gathering their things too. They barely fit in that room together, bumping into each other like two cruise ships trying to dock in the same harbor.

"So what kinda 'roids you think they're on?"

Greyson glanced at the men across the hall. They were both very pale, with very light hair. Might have even been brothers if their last names weren't different.

"All of them," he said as he finished with his buttons, then looked back to Tay. He was still sitting on the edge of his bed with a zoned-out stare, wearing a wrinkled, green tee and jeans. "Are you not getting ready?"

"I am ready."

"You can't wear *those*." Greyson pointed dramatically to Tay's bright green high tops.

"Why not?" They were, after all, his favorite.

"Please tell me those aren't the only shoes you brought." Greyson's eyes widened in horror.

"Calm down, I brought my red and black ones too." He slid his sick kicks out from under his bed. So proud.

"Taymes! We're going to an interview with the *king* and you look like you just slept in the clothes you went out in last night."

"I mean, I did."

"You're changing. Now."

"Fiiiine." Tay reached for his duffle and opened the top flap, which was already unzipped. "Oh." He stalled out. "Holy shit."

"What?"

"I remember that now." He frowned.

"What?!"

"I puked in my bag."

A laugh farted through Greyson's lips as he slapped his hand over his mouth. "Oh, gross!"

"God dammit."

"Oh, you're so disgusting," Greyson choked through a laugh.

Tay picked through his bag and pulled out another green shirt, crusty chunks of half-digested something stuck to it like a moist macaroni painting. He dry heaved at the sight of it and dropped it back into the soiled bag.

Greyson couldn't help but fall back onto his bed in crippling laughter.

"It's not funny."

It really wasn't, seeing as now Tay had no choice but to sit through an interview smelling like a pub floor. But Greyson could not stop laughing. Literally rolling on his bed. "This would *only* happen to you!"

"Of course. I'm so funny," he said dully. "I probly did it on purpose 'cuz I thought it would be funny later." He shook his head. "I have problems."

"Enough for the both of us." Greyson dried his eyes and stood again, reaching over his bed to pluck a long, black weapon from between his mattress and the wall. Its woven hilt was worn and weathered from the many years and hands that had graced it. He slid its wooden scabbard back an inch to see the mirrored blade beneath.

It was an heirloom of his family's. The same one his dad had used in the War of the Commonwealths. Now handed down to him as a token of faith that he would find the greater purpose he left home in search of.

"Speaking of which, what was the scream about earlier?"

Greyson's skin chilled suddenly to iron, and goosebumps rose from his flesh like five thousand nails forcing their way out from within. His grip on his dad's blade tightened, and a rot grew in his stomach as darkness, fangs, and blood flashed through his mind. "Bad dream."

"I thought you were over those."

"So did I."

Greyson had had bad dreams all the time as a kid. Nightmares about being chased, or hunted . . . or worse yet, sometimes *he* was the one doing the hunting. And the worst of them always ended bad, and bloody. It was never monsters that chased him though, always people. Other kids. Which wasn't surprising to him. Hard to call them nightmares really, when they were more like flashbacks than anything.

"This one was different though," Greyson said. "I wasn't me." He paused to think. "At least I don't think I was . . . I was up in space . . . looking down, and . . . I think I was an *angel*," he said carefully, trying not to make Tay laugh.

It didn't work. "What? That doesn't sound like a nightmare."

Greyson turned to him. "Well, it ended with my heart getting eaten out of my body while I watched, so, it kinda was."

"Oh, gross! By what?"

Greyson shivered. "I don't know, some alien, demon thing."

"You're not bringing that, are you?" Tay pointed to the sword, bringing a swift end to the thread.

"Yeah." Greyson tied it to his belt.

"You're gunna make us stick out like a bent dick."

"Deal with it." Greyson grabbed Tay's jacket from the back of the door and threw it at him.

"Seriously." Tay pulled the jacket off his face. "Swords are for, like, ceremony and stuff. Nobody uses them anymore, except for all the weird kids at the lunch table."

"Just drop it, Tay. You know why I have it." He took his own coat from the door.

Both of their jackets were the same, military green, almost like a biker jacket, embroidered with the yellow chevron of a Wellington Guard on their sleeves. Only difference was that Greyson's fit him better.

The boys stepped into the hall, Tay paying careful attention on how exactly to hold his duffle bag without getting gastral slime all over him. And just as they did, the giants stepped out in front of them.

"Hey, valley-fucks," Riese called out. "Judge my flying again and I'll lift you by your neck 'til you stop wiggling." He got right up in their face. Apparently all the 'roids made them super aggressive too.

Greyson recoiled, taken off guard. But Tay reacted instantly, puffing up and stepping toe-to-toe with him, like a dog, oblivious to its own size. "What's your problem, man?"

Riese was tall enough to stand chin-to-chest and look straight down at Tay. "My problem is there's only two spots open in the Royal Guard, and there's *four* of us. And I'll be damned if we get beat out by some pansy-ass, Wellington brats too young for the job."

"Whoa! Whoa! Who you calling a pansy, you ugly fuck!" Tay pointed to the giant's mug and reared back with a balled fist.

Quickly, Greyson slapped Tay's arms back down and held them as he struggled. "Tay! Tay. Tay. If we mess this up, we're going back home," he said very clearly. "He's doing it on purpose."

"Don't worry." Tay shook Greyson off him, and straightened his jacket. "I'm not fallin' for any a his shit. I got this. Nice try, shovel-face," he said as they turned to head down the hall. His face *did* look like a shovel, now that he mentioned it.

Tay was always on the defense, always looking for a fight. More often than not for the right reasons. That was how they met actually, way back when.

Though Wellington was a paradise, it sure didn't seem like it when they were kids. Everyone they grew up with really made it feel like hell half the time. Their favorite game to play was always *Hunt the Demon*. And Greyson, being the only kid without brown eyes, was always forced to be the demon.

"Green Demon! *Grey* Demon! Demon Greyson! *Get him!*" they'd chant and charge. A dozen nine-year-olds tearing through the wheat fields to find him. But, one day, the kids took it too far, tracking him down to an old tree that bent over the field, like it'd grown sideways across the sky. "*My* mom says he was hexed by a witch!" the ringleader shouted—the tallest and oldest of the bunch. His name was Bail. "She poisoned his eyes and turned him mad! He'll come after us all when he's grown. We gotta get him now before he gets his powers." Bail bent to clutch a rock. A big, jagged thing he could barely fit his fingers half way around.

Greyson cowered, hugging his knees, crying against the tree. He was really small for his age, and couldn't hope to defend himself, even if he wanted to. "I'm not a demon!"

"Oh yes you are!" said Bail, marching closer.

Then, out of the tree falls Tubby Taymie, too fat to keep up with the other kids, but just the right weight to knock old Bail out cold. "Leave him alone!" he shouted to them as they ran, screaming back into the wheat.

Tay was never allowed to play *Hunt the Demon*, because he could never keep up with the rest of the kids. So he'd climb that tree to escape their cruel game whenever they played, and as fate would have it, that day Greyson chose the crooked tree for refuge too. They'd known each other before then, but never really understood how similar they were until right then. Never understood how much they needed each other. Tay protected Greyson until Greyson struck a growth spurt and didn't need protecting anymore. Then, at eighteen, they both joined the guard, where handing out a very liberal serving of parking tickets to those stamen suckers that'd picked on them became Tay's favorite pastime . . . along with maybe slashing a tire or two to go along with it.

General Brown stepped from the bridge to greet his recruits as they approached. To his left was the only patch of wall in the entire hall that wasn't curved or woven with glowing roots. And as they arrived, that piece of wall fell away, opening like a drawbridge and blasting them with the cool breeze of the outside world. The air had layers to it here, fresh with pine up front, but with a greasy aftertaste behind it, like oily tools baking in the heat.

Greyson and Tay followed their general down the loading ramp to the metal floor of the docking bay, Berinhard and Riese right behind. Always right behind.

The hangar was massive, overwhelmingly vast, and so tall that it looked like clouds were forming at the crux of its domed ceiling, or at least a little layer of fog way up there. It messed with Greyson's perspective. Like he'd been shrunken down, or that the sky had suddenly hardened into a wooden shell. It made his stomach feel like it was in free-fall for a second, worried gravity would flip any moment and the enormous dome would suddenly become the floor and drop him to the ceiling.

"Welcome to the castle tree, boys," Brown announced over the hangar's commotion.

A wave of heat rained down on them as another bark ship glided overhead, its four ventral engines glowing hot like molten disks glued to the corners of its underside. It flew in from the hollow's wide open entrance, which was way too big to be sealed by any door. Instead, the hangar was protected by the expansive limbs outside, reaching far out into the sky to provide a prickled blanket of cover.

"This tree is home to not only the castle in its upper levels, but also its namesake, the City of Darakin," Brown continued. "It is the largest vertical city in the kingdom, at over one thousand levels." He led them beneath his ship, toward the hangar's solid core.

The ship's underside was busy with many of the hangar's personnel running hoses to the engines and spraying them down with some sort of watery solution. Maybe to keep them from overheating? Or maybe to keep the bark streamlined? Or was it as simple as cleaning off all the dead bugs? Greyson didn't know for sure, but it fascinated him. The runoff flowed down to an open pit in the floor, covered by a huge and squeaky metal grate, at least ten feet across, which was apparently safe to walk on, though Greyson and Tay did so quickly.

Beyond a ridge of crates and cargo piles was a string of splinter ships, arranged side-by-side like interlocking zipper teeth. They were much smaller than bark ships, and way more agile. The fighters of the fleet. Room inside for only one pilot, sometimes two. Greyson gave a giddy shiver, seeing so many in real life. He'd had a poster of two splinters in a dogfight hanging over his bed since he was twelve. They didn't have wings either, not really. Instead they were *shaped* like a wing, or an arrow head, very thin and flat, much more streamlined than a bark ship, but still looked like wood.

The core itself was an immense wooden stem, like a tree within a tree, reinforced by steel, but artfully so, molded in the shape of squiggling roots up to the dome.

"The tree's core acts as the city's highway." Brown led them into one of the core's cardinal entrances: a high fissure in the wood. It opened into a wide hall with no visible ceiling, running the circumference of the core. But instead of walls, the round hall was lined by chains of elevators. Greyson couldn't see all of them, but he guessed there must have been nearly a hundred on the outside ring, and maybe eighty on the inner.

"The inner ring will take you to any of the tree's eighteen districts, and the outer will take you to each level within that district," Brown explained dryly. "Provided you have the clearance." He stepped into the first available carriage on the inner ring. "And we're going to the very top." He pulled a gold badge from his pocket and waved it in front of a scanner as the rest of them got onboard, then pressed the highest glowing button on the lift's touchscreen.

Loosened by nerves, Greyson's guts were in a free fall to his toes as the elevator took off. It finally occurred to him that he was about to meet the most powerful man in the whole world: the King of Viæden.

He felt like a kid again, flashing back to his mom's stories. She had tons of them, enough to settle his nerves every time he woke up screaming. But his favorite, above all, was the story about the ancestors of Viæden's kings. And, oddly enough, the first time he'd ever heard it was on the same day Bail tried to kill him.

Tay'd taken him home immediately afterward, and he'd cried the whole way. Then straight up bawled when he finally reached his mom. She was in the kitchen, just starting dinner when she heard him wailing.

"Greyson, what's wrong?" She spun to face him, hands dripping wet from the sink. "What happened?"

He wrapped his arms around her waist, and hid his tears in her blouse.

She looked to Tay for an answer.

"The other kids tried to hurt him." Tay scratched his head nervously, hoping he wasn't somehow in trouble.

Then Greyson looked straight up at his mom's welling, brown eyes. "I'm not a demon," he tried to say.

He could feel her breathe deeply against him. "No, baby. You're not." She knew right away it was about his eyes. "C'mon, let's go lie down." She pat him on the back and aimed him toward his room. "Thank you for bringing him home safe," she said to Tay as she saw him to the door. Then she joined Greyson in his room, and climbed into bed with him. Nine was a bit old for bedtime stories, but this really was a special case.

Greyson brought the tears down to just a sniffle, knowing she was about to make it all better.

"You're not a demon, baby." She ran her hand along his back to coax his face from the pillows. "That's not what your eyes mean."

He came up for air, and lay his ear down on the pillow, gazing at her through glazed eyes.

"There was once a boy just like you, who lived in a kingdom, long ago. Before Viæden was ever thought of. And his kingdom stood at the edge of a vast forest. The boy loved to run through those woods each day, and catch the light as it flickered through the leaves over his brown eyes. And each day that boy would run further, and faster, as his legs grew strong, and his breath grew long. And one day he'd run so far into those woods that he'd found a secret place, where no one had ever been, and no trees grew, only a meadow of white flowers. And in this sacred grove there stood a woman, waiting for him. Waiting for the day he became strong enough to find her. She was clothed in white and green sparkling light."

"The goddess," Greyson whispered.

"Yes." She smiled. "Light's daughter, Trigana. She knelt down to the boy and smiled like the sun, so bright and beautiful that the boy began to cry. But instead of tears, what shed from his eyes was their color, like two muddy streaks rolled off his cheeks. And his eyes were left a dazzling green."

"Wow," Greyson said, so soft, eyes widening.

"She blessed him, Greyson. Because she knew his kingdom would one day be attacked by extremely powerful swordsmen, with evil magics in their blades. And she knew he was special, so she blessed him with green eyes, so that those evil men could not hurt him . . . And do you know what happened to that boy?"

"No, what?" He had to know.

"He survived. He lived on. And he founded Animallia. The city from which all of Viæden was built."

Greyson rolled to face her fully.

"Your green eyes don't make you a demon, Greyson. It means you're destined for greatness. Just like that boy who would be king."

Tay's ears popped for the dozenth friggen time as the lift finally came to a stop on the top floor of the castle tree. He was surprised Brown, Riese, Berinhard, Greyson *and* him could all fit in that tiny elevator, considering Berinhard and Riese were actually as big as a cow, put together. And probly just as dumb.

The lift doors opened, and they all herded off the elevator into fresher air, following Brown around the elevator core, into the castle halls. And man, were they some *fancy* halls. 10, 12 feet wide, and at least 3 stories high, easy. Fancy moldings, fancy paneling, fancy lights strung up on the walls, and fancy paintings hanging in between. And so much gold. Gold everything: Tables that had no use other than decoration, and antique chairs that nobody sat in. And it was *damn* crowded up there, crammed with government people and . . . *aristocrats*, Tay guessed the right word. All dressed in the same white coats, tails down to their knees, brown-leather shoulder pads, and either a high collar, or a draped hood. Each one of them, man or woman, had a different color vest underneath, decorated in whatever symbol represented the ministry they worked for. They'd look pretty badass if they didn't all have a funny, white, ascot thing wrapped high and tight around their necks too, frilly in the front, draped just a little ways over their vests. Completely ruined the look. Stupid traditions.

"And this, is the Hall of Kings," Brown said as they came to a T in the hallway, with a big round room for a junction, whose far wall was all windows, floor to ceiling. The branches outside must've been pretty sparse this high up 'cuz it was nothing but blue sky and sun pouring through them. In the center of the junction was a bronze statue of what Tay guessed was the king. He'd never actually cared enough to find a picture of him before.

"These halls are filled with the offices of our law makers and duchy representatives," Brown explained. "Right leads to the council hall, and left to the throne room."

Greyson was being awfully quiet. He looked spaced out, wide eyes fixed on the floor. Nervous as hell. He was probly starting to second-guess himself, as usual. But Tay was certain they had nothing to worry about. They'd *finally* managed to escape Wellington, and he was *not* about to get sent back for losing to these two idiots.

Tay gave him a nudge to root him back in the moment.

Greyson shook his spell and flashed his green eyes at Tay before following the general left toward the throne room.

The hall was curving slightly with the curve of the tree trunk, windows to the right, more paintings of old men to the left, and at the end, a pair of tall, glass doors.

Brown led them through into some kinda waiting room, stuffed with guards. It had sparkly stone walls, as tall as Riese, and dark green wood the rest of the way up to a ceiling slotted with thick crossbeams. A huge, crystal chandelier hung down from the center beam, a good 6 feet across. But the room's main attraction was the biggest set of doors Tay had ever seen in his life. 30 feet tall, 14 feet wide. The thing hardly even looked like a door at all, it was so big and busy with engravings. All kinds of old symbols, carved between silver vines that curved their way all down its green face. But one symbol stood out from the rest, literally. Raised from its surface, in the very center, was the

Emblem of Viæden, which Tay knew was taken from an even older symbol for the Goddess of Earth.

He could only guess at what was behind those doors. This waiting room alone made the Duke of Wellington's house look like a shack down by the river.

General Brown returned from somewhere in the mob of guards. Tay hadn't even realized he'd left, eyes busy darting every which way. "You can leave your things here with Ms. McBride," he said. "Berinhard, Riese, you will see him first." Brown stepped away again, to the green doors, giants following. "You must treat him with respect. But do not kneel. Only bow your head. Remember that kings are no longer regarded as divinely chosen to lead."

"Wait, why?" Greyson squeaked, but it was lost in the chatter of the room.

Good question, Tay thought, but didn't feel like screaming it to get an answer.

The doors broke down the center and opened out onto the freaking surface of the sun. Tay didn't realize how dim the waiting room was until the pure white light of the throne room stabbed him in the eyes. And before he could adjust to see what was in there, the doors closed again.

"Are you freaking out as much as I am?" Greyson asked in a high voice.

"Just breathe," Tay said. "We'll be fine. Those guys are dumber than rocks."

"Yeah but General Brown said the king liked loyalty best, and that's not exactly your strong suit."

Greyson was beyond nervous at that point, verging on terrified. Tay could see it in his face. "I'd rather suck up to him than go back home," Tay assured him. "So as long as you're not hyperventilating in there, we're fine."

"Do you think all these guards are here for the same spot?" Greyson eyed the dozens of navy jumpers around them.

"I don't know. Why don't you ask them?" Tay added a little sass that time, 'cuz it was a stupid question, and Greyson was just looking for another excuse to freak out even more.

They did all seem to be staring, though. But maybe only because him and Greyson were dressed like civilians in comparison. And hopefully *not* because they could all smell the puke-bag.

Greyson shuffled away from him, finding a desk to the side of the room, real big and outlined in gold. "Hi, sorry. The general said we could put our things here?" He dropped his bag in front of it.

"That's fine." The secretary smiled.

Tay stepped closer and leaned out from behind Greyson, locked onto her face. She looked exactly the same age as them, brunette, with kind of a sexy, I-don't-give-a-shit bob haircut.

"Are all these guards here for the same thing we are?" Greyson asked.

"No, only the four of you are interviewing for that position today. The rest are all domestic guards here for their weekly meeting."

"What do you mean domestic?" Greyson asked.

"Um." She paused, like she'd never had to explain it before. "When it comes to hiring Royal Guards, the king likes to select from foreign soil, for some reason. These guards here are all born and bred in Viæden—Can I help you, Mr. Hooker?"

Tay blinked out of his daze. Flattered, almost. "Do you know me?!"

Greyson gave him an awkward look, but Tay didn't care.

"I know everything about you." She sounded underwhelmed.

"How?" He was hooked.

"I have your papers right here." She opened one of the thin, green files on her desk. "Taymes *Hooker*, born in Wellington, 1353. 5'8", 180 pounds."

"Those are old numbers," he dismissed. "And it's 5'8-and-a-half."

"Passed secondary school by a snake hair, and barely made it through Academy," she continued.

"Written tests don't mean shit in the real world."

"M'hm. It says here you are combative and *unyielding to authority*. I can't imagine where they got that."

"Free spirit, baby."

She looked up at him. "I have no idea why you're here."

"'Cuz I'm damn good at what I do. And I'm a lot more than words and numbers on a piece a paper." He grinned. "You should let me show you sometime."

"Confidence only gets you so far." She leaned in close. "And you're not the only one that comes through here wanting access to more than just the throne room."

Tay's jaw dropped open like it had a rusty hinge. Partly shocked, mostly turned on. "You know, your mouth might be sayin' fuck you, but," he tapped on her desk, "your eyes are sayin' *fuck me*."

Then *her* mouth dropped. Her phone also started ringing.

"It's okay, I get that a lot. Right, Greyson?"

"Please don't involve me in this." Greyson covered his eyes.

"Megan," another secretary called from across the room. "When you're done flirting, it's for you."

"Shut up, Steph!" She ripped the phone from its receiver. "This is Megan, how may I help you?"

Tay and Grey both turned to the other secretary, blond, curly hair framing her face, and bright blue glasses framing her brown eyes. She flashed a welcoming smile and went back to work. She seemed nice enough, but kinda also seemed like a lesbian, so Tay wasn't interested.

Then, finally, the Viæden doors boomed and cracked open again.

# 3

# EYES OF A KING

Greyson watched as Berinhard and Riese strode by them like icebergs, staring them down with stoic confidence.

General Brown stayed in the doorway and waved for Greyson and Tay to enter the nearly blinding light. The boys stepped forward through the threshold, and into an extravagant hall, built brick-by-brick out of luminous, white marble. It was the length of a playing field, five stories high, crowned by a dozen chandeliers strung from gothic arches. Stained glass windows ran from floor to ceiling along the room's right side, tickling their eyes in hues of red, blue, green, and yellow as they walked past each one. Smooth pillars stood high between each window pane, mirrored down both sides of the great hall. A long carpet, green as a forest at twilight, carried them to the king. It was something right out of his mom's stories. Greyson never knew places like this still existed. It was built just like a temple . . . or at least, what Greyson imagined a temple would look like. He'd never actually seen one in real life.

But as nice a view it was, Greyson was too focused on his nervous stomach to fully enjoy it, fixated on how bad that secretary said Tay's record was. He knew Tay wasn't the best subordinate but . . . Did they even really stand a chance against Berinhard and Riese? What the hell did the general see in them in the first place? *Were they really only chosen because his dad suggested them to Brown?* Whatever the reason, they had to stand out now . . . or this fairytale would be over. Greyson just hoped Tay would keep his mouth shut, and let him do the talking.

The king stood as they approached, adorned in an unnecessary number of robes. As a base, he wore white: a white shirt, white vest, some white breeches that made his thighs look weird and swollen, white slippers, and one of those ruffled neck scarves. Then over that was what looked like a robe of purple, just a sliver of it showing underneath the largest robe-cape-thing, which had a dark green base and raised texture of swirly black designs that looped and knotted on repeat. The collar was big and fluffy, white with gold flecks here and there. It looked *real* heavy, almost overwhelming for such a petite man.

"Dude, I want that cape," Tay whispered.

Not surprised.

The king smiled, like an actor whose sole purpose was to perform, day in, day out, raised four steps up on a dais, three green banners hung like curtains behind him. That genuine smile surprised Greyson. He figured a king with such a wealthy realm and responsibility wouldn't be bothered with every new addition to his Royal Guard. But he looked like he absolutely loved it, wielding a proud smile. His face was thin, younger than General Brown's, but not by much. And his short, grey hair was crowned by a simple golden twine circlet, absent of any gems or character . . . Weird. That's the one thing Greyson imagined would be more epic than it was.

As they arrived, the king motioned for his audience to sit in the fine chairs that faced him, flanked by servants wearing tight, green doublets.

Tay was way too underdressed for this.

"Your Highness, I present the two recruits from the Commonwealth of Wellington," Brown announced. "Boys." He gestured to the king. "His Highness, H. Huey, King of Viæden."

The boys lowered their heads in respect, as the general had said.

"Yes. Greyson Wight and Jaymes Hooker."

Greyson flicked his eyes at Tay to make sure he didn't try and correct him. Tay's face scrunched, a little insulted, but he kept his mouth shut. Good.

"Please, be seated," the king offered, sinking back into place. He sat so gently in his chair, gripping its armrests, and breathing easy. The throne was as tall as the king, and looked almost as old as those green doors, made of thick and rigid oak, coated in gold, which was chipping and peeling at the grains.

"I understand you boys were *amid* the best new guards in Wellington.

And I'm sure it's no *revelation* to you, but that was just a small tree-colony. You'll have your work cut out for you here, I assure you." His voice seemed kind of light for someone his age. And he spoke oddly, putting emphasis on all the . . . *big* words. Like he was bragging that he knew them.

Huey leaned in to have a good look at them. And as he did, Greyson noticed right away that his eyes were a murky, old green.

Greyson's mouth dropped, and he literally gasped, which had never happened to him before in real life. But then, he'd never seen another green-eyed person in real life before either. His body wasn't sure whether to be frightened or elated, rippling with a tingling sweat.

"I see you have a sword, Greyson. A brave thing to *wield* in this age of bullets and lasers," the king said.

Greyson'd forgotten he'd even brought it, which doubled his nerves. He'd meant to put it down with the rest of his things, but got distracted by Tay embarrassing himself—*Wait, did he call it brave?* Tay was wrong! Maybe this was the advantage they needed. "Thank you, sir—Your Highness. It's tradition in Wellington for the officers of the guard to have—" he stopped short, confused by the king's sudden look of fear. Maybe he wasn't as into the sword as Greyson thought. "I'm sorry, Your Highness, I shouldn't have brought it," he stammered, trying to untie it from his belt.

"No. No, it is not the sword." Huey stopped him. "It's your eyes."

Greyson looked up again.

"Your eyes are green."

"Yes," he said carefully. Then it all made sense. Why the general had picked him. Why the king's eyes were green. Why Viæden used the goddess, Trigana's symbol as their insignia . . .

Maybe it really did mean he was blessed by her.

But the king's response was not at all what he was expecting. "Do not think that just the color of your *eyes* makes you any *better* than anyone else," he snapped. So suddenly. Flipping his act entirely. Defensive, like Greyson's irises had just insulted him.

"Um, no, Your Highness. I don't," Greyson said with all sincerity.

"Now that you are in Viæden, you must know that we no longer believe in such *fairytales* like *Vertuém Destiny*. No more than we believe in *deities*. Worship of any kind is—*illegal.*"

The boys both cocked their heads at that.

Religion was never a big part of their lives in Wellington. Most everyone did believe in the Goddess of Light, and a handful believed in Her children too, especially Trigana, but it was a very unspoken thing. There weren't any temples or fancy cathedrals, and nobody really brought it up, ever. It was one of those real private things that people kept to themselves, and only learned about from their parents, or whispers on the playground. It didn't make sense why something like that would be made illegal.

"Excuse my ignorance, Your Highness. But what is Vertuém Destiny?" Greyson asked. But as soon as he did, an aide carrying three fine water glasses on a tray appeared from behind the throne. He was young, Greyson's age or younger, with short black hair and a bloody bit of tissue stuck to his right cheek where he, no doubt, cut himself shaving. The poor guy was so focused on balancing those water goblets that he didn't notice the first step of the dais right in front of him. He tripped and stumbled like a juggler that missed his mark, letting the tray crash to the marble, splashing the throne with the finest mist.

"Xander! How dare you!?" Huey flailed his arms like he'd walked into a spider web.

"I'm so sorry, Your Highness!" he pleaded, rushing to wipe the  chair down. But before he could lay a hand on it, the king snatched the cloth from his fingers and backhanded him across the face with a *clap*.

*Wow.*

"*Do not* touch my throne! *Never* touch my throne!"

Xander recoiled in shock, clutching his cheek as the king vigorously dried the side of his armrest. Greyson and Tay shifted awkwardly as the aide ran for the back door again.

Then, when Huey was satisfied with the aridity of his throne, he sighed and turned back to them with a forced smile. "First day."

Greyson smiled and nodded, pretending that was a completely reasonable outburst.

But Tay just stared at him, clearly not donning the same facade. Greyson knew that look. Tay had a hard time respecting anyone, especially bullies. Greyson could see him wanting to pick a fight, searching the room for anything to verbally slap the king right back with. He found it hanging on the wall behind the throne. A green banner with the golden symbol of a goddess on it.

"Excuse me, Your Kingliness."

Greyson cringed, dreading whatever was about to come out of Tay's mouth. Likely the last squirt of gas before this bundle of sticks they called an interview went up in flames.

"Totally on board with the no god thing, but why do you still use that symbol?" Tay pointed to the flag.

The king bit back immediately. "That is the *Emblem* of *Viæden*. At one time it was the symbol for the Goddess of Earth, *yes*. But no god stands behind it now. It is the kingdom's *insignia*, and nothing else." He stared Tay down, almost egging him on. But thank the gods—*er whatever*—that Tay stayed quiet for once. "My father believed in gods, and look where it got him," Huey added, leaning back as if he'd just dropped the mic on them.

But the boys stayed silent, lost again.

"You do know of my father, don't you?"

The sweat really started to flow now. So unprepared. If Greyson had known he was going to meet the king he would have at least brushed up on his history first! "I'm so sorry, Your Highness."

"*I* do," Tay butt in.

Greyson looked to him slowly, trying to blink in code: *Shut the fuck up!* But Tay wasn't getting it.

"Let's hear it then, Mr. Hooker." Huey crossed his arms.

"The old king . . . uh, Goddy?"

"Godfrey," Huey corrected.

"That's the one. He's famous for the whole Stick Man thing. Right?"

"Perhaps I should tell the story," Huey insisted.

"Please," Greyson snapped his eyes back to the king.

Tay gave a little scoff only Greyson could hear.

"My father's name was Godfrey Huey, the twenty-seventh, and he died, protecting *me*, his only son, from a *man* calling himself *Stiqula*. That's Sti-Q-la, Mr. Hooker. Not Stick Man."

*Stiqula.* The name ran through Greyson's mind. He'd heard it somewhere before . . . But where?

"I then *renounced* religion because in our history it has brought nothing but *war* and was the *presumptuous* reason the monster attacked in the first place. I *installed* a ban on worship of *any* kind to *save* lives and *prevent* further wars."

Greyson nodded, only half listening, running back through all his dad's war stories, and his mom's stories too, searching for the name. But Stiqula never came up. *Where the hell had he heard it?*

Then, it clicked.

It wasn't in their stories. It was much, much more recent than that.

His dream.

His nightmare.

A scream, a hiss, a roar, echoed in his ears as the dreaded memory crept forward from the darkest reaches of Greyson's mind. The king, the light, the throne room, all began to fade and melt away as the vivid dream took hold. And suddenly he flew, ripped from his feet by silken wings that uncurled from his shoulders and shot him to the sky. He was an angel, soaring into space, past the trees, past the clouds, into the darkness that lingered always overhead.

Then, just as the stars began to form, he slammed into a pane of glass that kept him from them. Trapped.

Greyson banged against the window, suddenly taken by a primal fear. But the crystal surface would not budge. And the stars beyond offered him no sympathy.

"*Please!*" he screamed. "*Oyopa!*" he called out to the Light Goddess and struck the glass again. "My Lady." His voice wavered, but the words were not his own. Greyson was a bystander to the horror wreaking havoc within the angelic body he possessed. "Pray, do not punish me, for I am innocent. I am *innocent!*"

Then the seething hiss returned. From behind. A cry so vile, and distinct.

Greyson spun to face it. But behind him lay only a white, pillared hall, dressed in a long green carpet and stained light.

"Now." The king cleared his throat, tearing Greyson down from space.

Greyson shivered, rooting his feet on solid ground, and turning back to the green-eyed king upon his throne.

"Back to business." Huey nodded.

Greyson felt his breathing, his heart, pumping way too fast, sweat chilling like he'd caught a sickly fever. *What the hell was that? What the hell did he just see?*

The nightmare he'd had on the way to Viæden just leapt back into his conscience like it had a goddam mind of its own.

He shook his head. He couldn't freak out. It was over now. And for the interview's sake, he had to ignore it. Whatever it was.

"As of late," the king started, and Greyson tried to follow. "I have been recruiting a *plethora* of guards from neighboring provinces, due to the increase of crime the past few years. It seems, in this *modern* age, my people need an example of loyalty and respect to follow. And that is why I make it *imperative* that each one of my Royal Guards is an *epi-tome* of loyalty and respect." Huey leaned forward in his chair. "Jaymes, let's start with you. What makes you loyal to me?"

*Oh fuck, oh fuck, oh fuck, oh fuck. Tay, you better come up with something good.* Greyson watched his friend think for a moment. His face was hard to read. Blank. But at least it wasn't pissy . . . But now it was taking too long! *Say something!*

Tay looked to Greyson like he'd heard him scream, then opened his mouth. "Well—"

Just then, the secretary's voice came over the intercom. "Your Highness, I'm sorry to interrupt, but I have reports of a stolen vehicle."

The king let out a breath. And so did Greyson.

"Why are you bothering me with this, Ms. McBride?"

"I'm sorry, Castle Command is looking for an order from the general. The ship was stolen from the military bay, and was carrying a large quantity of astrolite. The ID number is VBS-22137."

Greyson blinked. "That's the ship from earlier."

"Astrolite?" the king asked. "What is *astrolite*?"

"A very explosive liquid," Brown answered as he stood. "I'll need to take care of this. Excuse me, Your Highness." He headed for the door.

"Wait," the king called to him. "Send the recruits." He gestured to the boys.

"Huey, given the severity of the matter, I don't think it's wisest to send them by themselves."

Displeasure struck the king's face like a bag of shit. "Then you will go with them." He bobbed his head back and forth. "Find that ship for me and the positions are yours," he said, without giving the general a say in the matter.

*What?* Greyson thought. That easy? *Too* easy? He didn't really care at that point, looking to Tay in anticipation. "Yes, sir."

Both of them stood and turned down the green carpet again, nearly breaking into a run as they passed by the general. The intricate doors opened as they approached, and they entered the dark lobby in a full-blown frolic.

"Ohhh, too bad. Look's like we're gunna get the job, guys," Tay announced to Berinhard and Riese, who were huddled in the corner together, craning their heads at Greyson and Tay like two startled bucks. "Nice try though."

"They will be joining us, Mr. Hooker," Brown announced as he entered, striding across the room.

Tay let out the longest, guttural scoff, flinging his head back to really sell his disappointment.

That got a chuckle out of Megan, seeing him so annoyed. Which in turn brought a smile to Tay's face, her paying attention to him. He threw a determined finger at her as he followed the general into the hall. "We're not done here!"

She eye-rolled hard as he and Greyson disappeared, Berinhard and Riese following after.

# 4

# The Vertuém

Trying to beat Berinhard and Riese, Greyson and Tay raced back to the general's ship, almost tackling a crewmember as they hit the bridge.

"What the hell!?" he sputtered, staggering back.

"Sorry!" Greyson blurted.

*I am innocent.* The angel's voice echoed in his head.

That stopped him dead. Greyson stood there, staring at the guard with his mouth open, awkward and speechless.

Then Tay grabbed him and pushed him toward the open pilot's chair before he could say anything else. "You better drive this time."

"Right, yeah," Greyson nodded. He had to focus. He had to prove to Brown that he was better than Riese, and this was his chance.

The U-shaped helm slipped into his fingers as naturally as lover's hands. But they felt like they had rigor mortis. "Fire up the engines!" Greyson ordered, jiggling the unresponsive wheel. "We've got a ship to follow."

No one moved.

Tay waved at all the frozen men. "Hello? Let's go!"

A guy in a uniform, kinda like the general's, but an ugly brown, walked right up to Tay, eyes as dark and angry as they came. His hair was peppered with hints of ash, though he couldn't have been much older than the two of them. "We aren't taking any more orders from recruits."

Greyson grunted in building anxiety. They didn't have time for this. That stolen ship already had a huge head start. But of course some prick officer had to choose *now* to whip his dick out.

"Is that right?" Tay asked, looking to the nameplate on the officer's chest. "*Lieutenant Knight*," he mocked, pressing his index finger into the silver tag.

Knight snatched Tay's arm. "Get off my ship."

Like two stubborn rams, they butted heads, neither one about to back down, both waiting for the other to make a move first, to avoid any repercussions for beating the shit out of each other. But before any shit could be beaten, General Brown stepped onto the bridge.

"What is this?"

His men scattered instantly, bringing the ship back to life.

Knight spoke to the general without breaking his death-glare. "These men think they can order us around for some reason."

"For now, they *will* be running the ship, Knight. They need the practice. It's just a routine recovery mission. Stand down."

Knight gave Tay his arm back and stormed off the bridge like a five-year-old, passing between Berinhard and Riese as they arrived.

"I see you've found the controls just fine," Brown said to Greyson. "I was going to suggest you take the lead, since Riese already had a chance to show his skill."

"Yes, sir." Greyson smiled.

"And, Taymes, you may take the radarman's position, here." He pointed to a control panel against the port-side wall.

"Oh. Okay." He accepted it like an ugly sweater.

"The forward cannons are just to your right, if it comes to that."

"That's more my style," he said, wiggling his fingers over the controls.

"Very well, Riese will take radarman. Berinhard, you're on communications."

The silent giants slipped to their stations.

"Bay Command just gave us a go," the com-guy said as he left his station and handed the headset to Berinhard.

The ship hummed, vibrating up through Greyson's feet as the engines warmed and the helm loosened in his hands.

"We have lift," said the engine master as the ship wobbled and rose off the ground.

"Good," said Brown. "Now clear the bridge. None of my crew is to enter for the remainder of the flight."

"Yes, sir," the crew responded, leaving none but the general and his four recruits in command.

Greyson shifted the helm to port, and the ship rotated in the hangar, letting the glow of the afternoon sun beam in through the forward glass from the mouth of the tree-cave, a mile away.

"Alright. Easy, Greyson. Let's not get too excited," Brown cautioned.

"Yes, sir," he agreed, even though his excitement was hard to hide. He reached over to retract the landing gear without even having to look very hard to find it. All the controls were in pretty much the same place as they would have been in a huv, except that the accelerator wasn't on the floor, but a lever right next to the wheel. Seemed pretty stupid to have to let go of the wheel to speed up, but, as Riese had discovered earlier, this huge ship couldn't maneuver nearly as well as a huv, so the acceleration had to be more constant and calculated, rather than knee-jerk. He gripped the accelerator to his right and eased it forward. But . . . nothing was happening . . . So he gave it a bit more of a thrust. Instantly the hum of the engines swelled to a roar, and the bark ship shot out of the hangar like a friggen bullet.

"Greyson!" Brown yelled, falling back into a seat.

"Whoakay," Greyson cringed and arced the ship above oncoming traffic, weaved through the hanging lanterns, dove below the roof of the pine-cave, and finally flew out into the open sky.

Tay let out a long breath, and dropped his head to his control panel.

Greyson gave a quivering sigh too as his pulse recovered from the quick spike.

"I think I should drive, general," Riese said, like a real dick.

"I'm sorry, sir. I wasn't used to the ship. But I'll be fine now."

Brown stood, straightening his jacket. "This ship doesn't have the best reaction time. I'm surprised we made it out of there at all."

Greyson wasn't sure if that was an insult or a compliment.

"If memory serves, the ship we're looking for was headed east . . . perhaps by northeast," Brown continued. "Let's head that way until the radar picks up its tag."

Fifteen thousand feet below, the sparkling sunlight of Darakin's lake swept beneath them, and in a moment was replaced by the surrounding greenery blanketing the earth, as far as the eye could see. But it wasn't really green, the afternoon sun had turned it all to gold, just like it did at home. Though there, the grass was just regular height, and here, it grew as big as trees. Greyson could see their golden blades, mixed in with the moguled canopy of a carpeting forest below. And hidden down there, nestled in the trees were tiny streams of silver, catching the sunlight at rare angles as they snaked their way into the lake. Blooms of canary flowers followed those streams, all throughout the wood.

Then Greyson remembered, those weren't just ordinary flowers. Nothing was ordinary here. They were cities too. Sprawling villages, fabled the world over for their technicolor makeup. Greyson felt fully immersed inside one of his mom's stories now.

He lifted his eyes past the horizon, and into the darkening sky. The sun was still an hour from setting, but even so the sky began to turn an unnatural shade of purple. And as his mind lingered on the fading light, an alarm rang inside of him, growing from the nothingness, into a blare. A siren, pulsing through his head, as sharp as demons' claws.

"Pray, do not punish me, for I am innocent. I am *innocent*!" the angel cried through the wailing siren, calling out to the distant light of the stars beyond the glass.

But their pale light could not help him here.

Greyson saw it all again. Even more clearly this time. Hearing every word. Feeling every heartbeat. He was standing in a room whose walls were made of crystal, held together in patterned shapes like stained glass. But the window was smooth and flat, making up an entire wall of the dark room at his back.

And this time he saw that the angel prayed into his fist, from which dangled a diamond chain.

"*Stiqula* is the one who should be punished. *He* is the only reason we transgressed. The only reason we left our place. To *find* him and be certain that his darkness was gone for ever. Punish *him*, my Goddess, I beg. Not us!"

Then a scream, a hiss, a roar echoed from behind. And the angel spun in terror to the dark, pressing his silk wings against the glass and peering into a long hallway, rippling with crystal walls, blackened by a veil of shadows.

He knew that sound. Every angel did. It was the cry of demons.

Greyson breathed deep and fast, vision clearing again, bridge and sky beyond, returning.

*Stiqula.*

That's where he'd heard the name. He spoke it in his dream. His nightmare.

Again he tried to hide his fear. Still very aware of where he was, and understanding a psychotic break was not going to win him any points with General Brown. But so much terror swam in him. That angel's mixing with his own. It was hard to bear, gripping the helm, clenching his jaw until it hurt.

*Why was this happening to him? Now*, of all freaking times.

Why was he dreaming of something, so vividly like this, in the middle of the day, wide awake? It was almost like a memory. It sure *felt* just like one. But the only thing he knew of angels was the stuff in fairytales: guardians of light, teachers of good morals. Nothing like the weak and frightened creature that he'd seen. And he was certain he'd never heard the name Stiqula before he dreamt of it. That's why it had stuck out so much when the king had said it. Like it'd bled right from his nightmare.

But as shocking as it was to hear, it was only the second strangest thing the king had said.

"General." He tried to aim his words behind him. "The king never explained . . . about my eyes."

Greyson noticed Riese's ears twitch back at the question, whipping his head around to see those eyes for himself, like he hadn't noticed them before. Their color. And when he saw them, it made his nose wrinkle in disgust. But it was fear that played in his brown eyes.

"He just doesn't want it to go to your head," Brown said simply.

"But why would something like that ever go to my head? I used to be the butt of every joke in Wellington."

Brown stepped forward so that Greyson could see the dumbfounded look on his face. "You . . . Have you never heard of Vertuém Destiny?"

Greyson's mouth opened in search of what to say. "I . . . no, sir."

The general's brows raised high as he looked off into space to think. "Well. As I'll assume you know, all children are born with green eyes. And over time they fade to brown. But, on very rare occasions, a child keeps his or her green eyes. And those children are said—*were once believed*—to be deeply connected to the gods and their Grand Destiny."

Greyson's eyes got all wide, like it was his mom's voice he was hearing, not Brown's. Maybe he *had* heard this story before, though with a slightly different twist.

"It's called Vertuém Destiny," Brown continued. "And those with green eyes are the vertuém. Up until fifty years ago, your eyes would have been celebrated as a symbol of a paragon. A hero, perhaps. Only the most brilliant people were ever known to have the eyes of a vertui. The best of humanity."

"The *best*?" Greyson repeated. He certainly didn't feel like the best.

"Stronger, smarter, luckier. It's hard to say. No two were alike." Brown walked to the bridge window, arms clasped behind his back. "But you can see why the king has decided to make this sort of elitism illegal."

"*I guess*," Greyson said to himself. But it would have been nice to know sooner.

While his favorite story of the green-eyed boy who would be king stood out in his mind, it was really the only story he'd ever heard of a green-eyed person . . . a *vertui*, being special. Nowhere near enough to counter the years of abuse his eyes had caused him. So he'd grown to assume that his mom's story must not have been true, and she only told it to him to make him feel better . . . That is, after all, the only thing his dad said those stories were good for anyway.

"I don't really get it," said Tay. "Why would the king flip out on Greyson like that? His eyes are green too."

"Yes. I can't always speak for the king's actions," Brown stated.

That made Greyson look at him funny. And Brown turned back to him, silently staring, for just a moment. Then the general looked away again, brushing his chin with his hand, as if he'd said too much.

Greyson didn't know what to make of it, returning his gaze to the sky ahead.

Did Brown believe it? Vertuém Destiny? Even though it was illegal? . . . That would explain why he took such a liking to Greyson so quickly . . . But how could a general believe in something like that? A man who's seen life's brutality up close, just like Greyson's dad. And his dad didn't believe a word of his mom's stories. Because it was a waste of time to believe in something that could never help you.

Greyson's dad was as military-minded as they came. Cutting out every inefficiency from his life. Focusing only on what it took to keep his valley safe. And that did not include vain prayers to silent gods . . . And he'd raised Greyson to be just the same. With one exception. He'd let Greyson's mom tell him all the bedtime stories she wished. And only explained to him later that none of them were real to begin with. But if that was true, why even let her tell them in the first place? Just to prove he shouldn't believe everything he heard?

Or did it mean . . . there was actually some truth hidden in those stories after all?

# 5

# DARKNESS WITHIN

Just over an hour's journey northeast from Darakin, at nearly eight hundred miles an hour—which was as fast as Greyson dared push Brown's old ship—they'd reached the heart of one of Viæden's ancient realms. A region known as Semræ. Named for a powerful kingdom that once dwelt there. On the bend of the bowing earth, a ceptris tree formed from the darkening sky. But it was different from the rest Greyson had seen. The sun's light did not halo it like all the others. It did not reflect the sun's glow at all. Instead, this tree consumed it. Its leaves were so dark and purple that what light hit them died instantly, leaving nothing to shine back onto the world. A dead, brown soil surrounded its trunk for twenty miles in every direction, like a plague. And as they approached this seven-mile tree, their radar fixed onto it.

"Gardeón," General Brown said heavily. "If the radar wasn't leading us there, I would not dare go near it."

Greyson hesitated. "Why?"

"Guardian's the one Stick Man's in, right?" said Tay.

"As the legend goes," Brown answered.

His words slapped the back of Greyson's head like a block of ice, and the helm slipped in his hands as he shivered, jerking the ship slightly starboard.

*Stiqula?* he thought. *No way. No fucking way!* First he dreams about Stiqula before ever knowing about him, then he learns he may or may not have some kind of deep connection with destiny, and *now* he's flying right to Stiqula's door? This was too much. *Way* too much.

The sense of wonder Viæden gave him had long outstayed its welcome. He didn't want to be inside this fairytale anymore. It was getting too real.

"But it's not true, right?" Greyson asked the general, afraid of what the answer would be.

Brown moved to the glass, looking down at Gardeón's ancient roots. "When Animallia was lost, we were powerless to Stiqula. Our fleet, our armies . . . our king. All fell to him. He was unstoppable. The whole of Viæden at his fingertips . . . And then he vanished." Brown opened his hand, like he was letting a caught fly go free. "*That* is not legend. I saw the flames myself. Heard the screams and silence. Younger than you are now."

Greyson groaned a little. "Animallia?" The fabled city from his favorite story. The one his green-eyed idol founded.

"Our former capital," said Brown. "Called by a different name now . . . And the Dead Forest will forever stand as a monument to Stiqula's lust for death."

His mom never mentioned that part.

The general was not helping his nervous stomach. "When he came, he claimed this tree as home. And after his war was won, we once believed that he returned here to find the Goddess of Light, Herself, waiting for him. And She locked his evil away, as only She could."

A high ring pulsed once throughout the bridge and startled them all..

"Ship's up on the radar," said Riese looking to the bridge window. "Straight ahead. Five miles."

Greyson searched for movement on the tree, realizing how hard it was to find a bark ship against the ceptris branches. Its trunk was bare for a mile before the branches began, twisting outward in a sort of spiral before stretching wide with purple leaves.

At three miles out, Brown's ship slipped under its canopy. The tree's underside was like a hollow dome of leaves, as if they sprouted from the tips of thick black veins that rose up from the planet and divided into obscurity.

Then he spotted it, right where Riese said it would be. Two miles off the bow, slightly starboard as they approached. "They're headed for the tree."

"Why haven't they reached it yet?" Tay asked. "They had a huge head start."

"Tankers are much slower than our military ships," Brown explained. "We've caught up with her just in time."

As they grew closer, the details of the ship came into focus. It was undoubtedly the same one Riese had almost hit. And its engines were firing at full, glowing bright yellow, with a trail of orange behind. They were headed straight for the trunk, only a few thousand yards away, with no signs of slowing.

"What are they doing here?" Greyson asked, wiping his sweaty palms on his jacket.

"I don't know. But it won't matter soon. Come in alongside them. Berinhard, try to hail them on the com."

"I've already tried. There's no response, sir."

"We're maxed out, general. And they're not slowing down," said Greyson.

"Trying to get away with their loot," Riese said.

He seemed convinced. But it didn't take much to convince an idiot. That ship was approaching way too fast, and that tree was way too wide for them to still have time to bank around. If that stolen ship didn't slow down in the next ten seconds, they were going to slam right into that tree.

*Stiqula's* tree.

Then suddenly darkness crept forward from behind Greyson's eyes, and his vision narrowed to a tunnel. *No, no, no, no, no, not now!*

His tunnel vision closed, and he saw nothing before him but a shadowed, crystal hallway. From which echoed a vile, seething, hiss. Wings pressed against the window to the stars, the angel screamed, terror burning through his blood as a demon leapt forth from the black. A horrid, unnatural figure Greyson could see in all its unholy glory. As big as Riese, but so thin it was skeletal. Black, glossy skin looking just like bones. Dark, starved muscles strung from them like the creature's skin was inside out.

Its long arms stretched wide to seize him as its tattered leather wings heaved back, body uncoiling from a crouch, stretching over seven feet long. It had no purpose but to kill, crafted for that sole reason. Its long head had no eyes, no nose, no ears, only an unhinged jaw, spread wide with two hundred silver fangs. A monster by every meaning of the word. It collided with Greyson, and sank its silver teeth into his flesh.

Greyson screamed this time. He couldn't help it. Feeling those wild fangs in his chest.

He didn't know what the fuck that was, he didn't know why it was happening, but Stiqula was connected to that nightmare—that *demon*—somehow. That much was crystal clear.

And if Greyson really had a destiny great enough to be protected by a *goddess*, then he was *meant* to be here. Meant to see this. Meant to do *something*. But those visions made him too terrified to think, and there was no time left to spare.

"Tay, shoot them down!" he screamed.

"What?" Riese sputtered.

"Greyson." Brown demanded an explanation.

"They're still at full, sir! That trunk's too wide for them to divert. They're going to crash. They're going to free Stiqula!"

"He—" Brown looked from Greyson to the ship, eyes spread wide in panic. "Taymes, fire. Now!"

Tay slammed his fingers down on the controls.

A shudder resonated from below, and a yellow light shot from the ship, followed by a stream of grey smoke. It flew toward the tree, closing the distance between the two bark ships, curving in the wind. The rocket struck the stolen ship, right on target, exploding in a perfect sphere of flame against its aft. Then its explosion was engulfed by another, larger, as the astrolite ignited. The tanker ripped itself apart, astrolite spraying out in a flaming cloud. The bits of ship that survived slammed into the bark of Gardeón, and showered its flaming payload all over its face. Then the golden cloud dissolved into a rich black smoke as the flames sank their red teeth into the tree.

Brown and his recruits could only stare, mouths agape.

"It's okay. It's gunna be okay, right?" Greyson asked, breath quickening, then clapped his hands over his mouth, as if to stop his air from escaping all at once.

"Oh, fuck." Taymes fell back into his chair, eyes pinned to the smoke and flames before them.

Lieutenant Knight burst back onto the bridge, "What . . ." He focused on the smoke outside. "What happened?!"

Brown was stoic. Petrified . . . *Did they have any other choice? Was that ship really planning to crash? Or did they just fulfill their own prophecy by pulling the trigger themselves? It all happened so fast. There was no time to see reason beyond fear.*

But now they needed answers. Starting with Stiqula.

There was a chance he was still left unaffected. And also a chance he was never there to begin with. His disappearance *was* truly nothing more than rumor. He very well may have died in the war, but become such a legend that whoever'd witnessed his death exaggerated his story to say that the Goddess trapped him here . . . The tree *had* been thoroughly scanned and searched innumerable times, to no avail . . . Could it be that the monster they all believed lived here was just a myth?

There was only one way to know for certain.

"Greyson," Brown finally spoke. "Take the ship in."

"Wait, what?" said Taymes.

"You've doomed us all," said Knight.

"I thought you guys didn't believe in any of this crap anymore?" Taymes sputtered.

Knight shut his mouth and growled.

Brown knew the feeling. Unable to explain how deeply Viæden still feared their legends . . . regardless of what laws the king imposed. Millennia of faith was hard to abandon in just a few short generations.

"Greyson," Brown urged again.

Greyson pushed the ship in closer to the fire. The tanker's flames had taken root where three branches diverged from the trunk, forming a cradle for the debris to rest within. Two of the branches grew out at steep angles, but the middle one stuck out at a perfect ninety degree angle, and was wide enough to land Brown's entire ship on. At the very edge of the flames.

"Let's go." The general turned to leave the bridge.

Greyson and Tay stood to look at one another as they left their posts.

A very nervous, uncertain stare. Tay un-holstered his two glowing pistols: wooden, with wide open grains from which shined an amber plasma beneath.

The boys followed Brown into the hall, dreading every moment.

A group of guards lingered by the loading ramp. Brown was the first one standing at the door, and the boys joined them as it lowered. The deep chill of the coming night swallowed them up as the ramp reached the bark of the tree and they all filed out. The sky appeared as dark as Gardeón's purple leaves as the last remnants of sun evaporated into night. The wind at that height was so furious, it was pushing even *Riese* around like a drunk, unpredictably whipping from one direction to the other as they shuffled forward in a tight mob of a dozen. Each guard with a rifle, and a flashlight at the end of it.

The flames ahead were so bright they stung Greyson's eyes in contrast to the dark around them. But as they neared, the extent of the damage became clear. The air glowed in reds and yellows as tree and ship together burned. The tanker had come apart, nearly disintegrated in the explosion. But its steel skeleton held two separate halves of it together to form a flaming valley down which the team trekked, between the upright branches on either side of them. Metal bones protruded from the wreckage, moaning as the hungry fires were fed by the wind. The constant shift and flicker of the flames made it impossible to see if anything was watching them from beyond. It sure felt like something was.

Greyson unsheathed his dad's sword as dread crept through his gut. And, upon the ring of its release, the uneasy guards around him lifted their rifles to the flames.

Then, they saw it. Through the smoke. The trunk: a wall of charred bark ahead of them. And a hole, stretched wide like fiery, fanged jaws.

The tree was breached. Opened like a bleeding sore. And fire was its blood.

They all stared upon the gateway to oblivion and did not move, a hellish bawl echoing from it as the wind rushed through its open mouth, casting cinders to the air.

Greyson's blood went still and cold, frozen in fear. He couldn't move, arms gone limp, dropping his sword's tip into the bark as the guards shuffled around him.

*He* had done this. It was his order.

His fault.

Instead of saving the world from a terrible fate . . . he'd caused it.

The guards' lights shined upon the darkness, but could not enter, and nothing could be seen within.

Silently, General Brown strode by Greyson, grazing his shoulder as he did.

No one spoke a word. The general made his way to the front, to the very edge of darkness. Greyson almost expected him to reach out and touch it. But he didn't. Instead, he disappeared within. His men following after. Each one vanishing from sight. As if that darkness were a fog.

Greyson and Tay were the last to enter. And did so together.

The air was thinner inside, so thin it seemed to suck the oxygen right from their lungs. And so cold their breath looked like ghostly souls escaping from their mouths.

The guards' lights traversed the hollow like spotlights, patching the room together with every pan of their aim. It was cavernous and tall, yet with a flat floor beneath them, and alcoves in the walls, rising high out of sight. It reminded Greyson very much of the throne room, though not as deep, and windowless. Like its evil counterpart. A cathedral of shadows.

"It looks clear, sir," one of Brown's guards made the call.

Soothing words to Greyson's ears, though he could not fully accept them. There was a darkness here, stronger than just night and shadows. This place was stained by it. Evil. He could feel it. As though the deadening silence between each heartbeat was lengthening.

He clutched his chest from the sting.

"General," said Knight, light fixed on a corner of the room. He had wandered deeper in than all the rest.

Brown looked, and his guards separated to let him pass, to let him see what clue Knight had discovered. But the general did not move immediately. He stood there, motionless, eyes pinned to the ground, unwavering from what Knight had found.

Greyson stepped closer to the general to see what struck him still as Knight moved toward the object.

"Knight. Don't," Brown urged, like he was saving him the burden. He stepped forward to take his place.

Brown knelt to retrieve it from the ground: a black sword, nearly four feet long in full, with a two-handed hilt, and hardly a handguard at all.

"His blade," Brown whispered, "was never found."

Greyson swallowed as the guards shifted uneasily.

Brown's gaze faded from the blade, drifting up, as if he were slowly working out how the blade could have ended up there, cast aside like some worthless thing. He blinked and dragged his eyes higher, to the ceiling, fifty feet overhead. And Greyson's eyes followed. The wood up there was grey and poxed, poisoned by some putrid brew. And in the glow of the guards' lights, was a charred inscription. The Signature of Darkness:

Half a heart, marked by the cross of angels, crowned by the horns of demons. But within the heart, a smoldering crater, no larger than a body.

"He's gone," Brown said. "He's free."

# 6

# MAN OR MONSTER

The throne room had a more menacing glow to it at night, barely illuminated by torches on the walls. The throne was missing from its stage, and taking its place were three dark figures, anxiously awaiting the presence of their king, dreading his reaction to the grave words they would bring him.

Greyson stared down at his dad's sword in the failing light, drawn across his open hand. He could see his green eyes in its shine. And hear his dad's voice in his head.

"Mom wants to shield you from all the dark realities of the world. But that's . . . impossible. The world is dark, as much, if not more, than it is light. And pretending that's not the truth can leave you ill-equipped to handle such darkness when it inevitably comes." Greyson could remember every word, so clearly. It was just the day after Bail and the other kids had attacked him. And instead of filling his head with more stories, his dad put a sword in his hand.

"Everyone has darkness in them, Greyson. Ignoring that truth is more dangerous than embracing it." His dad took up a pellet rifle, and aimed carefully for the tree in their backyard. Then fired. The gun clapped as the powder charge was struck. And a pitiful yelp cried out from the tree before a black ferret fell from its limbs to the grass.

It was still very much alive, squirming, trying desperately to climb back up into that tree as they approached. But his dad had struck it in the spine, paralyzing its hind legs. It dragged itself a foot up the trunk, legs and tail dangling after it, then lost its grip as they arrived and rolled down to the grass again.

"Everyone has darkness in them. But some more than others," his dad said. "And some have such little light that life is nothing but suffering. It takes true strength to recognize this. And even more to help them." He unsheathed his sword, its polished steel shining in the morning sun. At twenty-seven inches long, it was enormous for a nine-year-old to hold. But not heavy, not a burden. Sharpened only on one side, like a cleaver. He knew what his dad wanted him to do.

"But *you* gave him that darkness!" Greyson teared up, refusing to be part of it.

"And it is irreversible. That fate is settled, come and gone. Our only remaining choice is what to do about it now. Will you let its suffering continue? Let the darkness slowly creep into its soul until it dies? Or will you kill it now, and end the suffering that I have caused?"

Greyson looked down to the ferret, lying still. It knew running was no use, and it was in too much pain to try. All it could do was blink its beady eyes at him and pant as quickly as a speeding heart. He poked it with the sword's tip to make sure it was still alive, and it lashed out at the blade, clinging to it with its claws, biting at its steel.

"You see this aggression? There is hardly any light left in it at all."

"It's afraid!" Greyson cried. "It doesn't want to die!"

"And what is fear, but darkness?"

Greyson took in a deep and quivering breath as tears fell from his eyes. He hated his father in that moment, and raised his blade to show him just how much. With a frustrated scream, he swung down into the ground, severing the black ferret nearly in two behind its shoulders, leaving a red and purple valley in its fur. All four legs went rigid, and its eyes blinked slowly once more.

He struck again quickly, cutting it lower down its back in haste, then one last time at its neck. Each swing stung his hands as the blade came to a halt, and stung his heart as the ferret's light blinked out.

Greyson threw the red sword at his father's feet and ran. Back to the house. Back to his mother's light.

But he couldn't run from it. Not really. That day changed him. Just as his dad intended . . . The world's light seemed a little less bright for every day after. And his mom's stories faded with it. Because they could never feel as real as anything his dad told him, or as visceral as the red blood and purple organs he was made permanently aware of floating around inside of everyone . . . instead of a soul of light and a glowing heart like his mom had him believe . . . And eventually he came to realize life reflected his dad's stories almost completely, and nothing in his mom's.

"What is fear but darkness?" Greyson said softly to himself.

If that was true, then his heart had just turned black as night.

Greyson never understood why his dad believed in darkness and light, but not anything else from his mom's stories. He never prayed to either, but he spoke of them as if they were real forces, things to defend, or protect from. Was he just being metaphorical? . . . Or did it mean there really were gods out there that played with men like dolls moved by fate's strings?

"So what do you think?" Tay broke the silence. "How much trouble are we in?"

Greyson looked at the dim silhouette of General Brown, arms folded, haloed in torchlight.

"I cannot begin to fathom." Brown was furious beneath his calm exterior. You didn't need to know him well to see it. He spat those words from his mouth, like the two of them weren't worth the breath.

"Well, say Greyson's idea was right, and that ship *was* headed to free him. At least now we know about it. Whereas before, he woulda had the upper hand."

Brown looked at Tay like he was a child. "He will always have the upper hand."

Tay winced at him. "Then I must not be getting it." He turned to Greyson. "Am I missing something?"

Greyson didn't have an answer for him . . . Just as lost.

Why was Brown so scared? How could he be? After seeing so much blood and brutal tactics in the War of the Commonwealths . . . And that was against an entire country.

But Stiqula's just *one* man . . .

Tay turned back to the general, as if he'd read Greyson's mind. "He's just a man," he said, without much confidence.

"A man?" Brown locked onto him, unfolding his arms, letting a little of that rage flash to the surface. "Trapped in a tree for fifty years with no food, water, or escape?"

His words echoed through the empty hall, and silence lingered after.

"Well," Tay stumbled, trying to make sense of it the only way he knew, the only rules he knew the world to run by. "How do we know he was even in there to begin with? We left right away after we found that sword."

"That was for our own safety," Brown assured. "Regardless of what you've been taught, I have seen this creature. And he is no man."

Greyson rubbed his aching chest. That sting, like demon's fangs, had not left him yet, swelling and receding in waves. He had to know . . . He had to know what it was this veteran general feared so absolutely. "What is he?"

Brown turned to Greyson, contemplating what to say, breathing deeply, on the brink of explanation. But before he could respond, a door behind the dais finally opened, and an aide appeared in its archway. The sting in Greyson's chest bit harder, imminently closer to the king and his punishment.

"His Highness will see you now. Follow me, please," the boy said meekly, disappearing behind the door again.

The three followed. Each with much reluctance.

The small wooden door led them to the entrance of King Huey's royal chambers: a grand staircase with black and white marble flooring and glossy wooden rails, lit by clusters of electric candles.

"Kind of late to see the king. This must be important," the aide said.

Greyson looked at him again. It was the clumsy aide from earlier. "You're Xander, right?" His voice sounded more tired than he thought it would.

"Yes." Xander smiled.

"Let's just say you're not the only one that screwed up on their first day."

Xander laughed, then quickly swallowed it.

At the top of the stairs, a window to their right cast moonlight onto another marble floor and stairs beyond, curving up out of sight. And to their left, two guards stood at attention in front of golden doors, textured with a few scenes from some old story Greyson felt too sick to analyze. Xander pushed through them, into the king's chambers, where they found yet another grand hall, though quite a bit smaller than the throne room, and lined with doors instead of windows. Gold and earthy pastels everywhere. Portraits and pillars lining the walls. Rugs and tables with flowering centerpieces between every carved door. It was all very uninspiring at that point.

They were brought to the first door on their left. The king's office.

Knight, Berinhard, and Riese stood in a line against the wall next to the door, having already given their side of the story.

Again, Riese's eyes locked with Greyson's as they entered . . . which would have been getting pretty old if Greyson hadn't fully thought that he deserved it right then.

The office was dark, lit only by moonlight spilling onto an old desk from a grand window behind. Bookshelves lingered in the shadows at the edges of the room. And above a blackened fireplace hung the painting of a man, standing behind a seated woman and child. The green-eyed man wore a clean beard, and a robe much like the king's. The woman wore her hair up, dressed in green gems and a golden gown to match her husband. And the child, who couldn't have been more than nine, had on a pleated, white shirt beneath a tiny black vest, embroidered with all the intricacies of Viæden design.

"He made me stay up all night," Xander said kindly. "That wasn't so bad. Maybe he'll go easy on you too." He pulled the doors closed as he left, like he was locking them in with a wild animal.

Instantly, another door swung open, and the king glided into the room, adorned in beige sleeping robes, only slightly less ornate than his formal ones. They quickly turned to face him as he sat heavily behind his desk and stared the two boys down.

"How? How could you do it?!" His voice was sharp, and loud. Startling, even though they knew it was coming.

Greyson and Tay bowed their heads without an answer.

"Brown!" He faced the general. "I would *never* have expected this from you. *Exspecially* with your history of this monster!"

"It was not our plan, Your Highness."

"Oh, *no*? Tell me, what *was* your plan then?"

"It's my fault, sir," Greyson admitted.

"So I hear," Huey bit.

"The tanker had its engines at full, Huey," Brown stepped forward, "too close to Gardeón. We believed it was on a crash course, in an effort to release Stiqula. We were attempting to intervene."

Was the general defending him? Greyson strained his eyes to see without turning his head. It sure sounded like it. He wasn't expecting that. And even though he knew he didn't deserve it, a fraction of guilt lifted from his chest, like he was trapped under a fallen tree, and to help lighten the load, Brown had taken away a single branch.

Huey took a moment to comprehend, than a breath to respond.

"I had the final say," Brown finished.

The king exhaled. "Your lieutenant seems to think that if the tanker had crashed, it would have brought the entire tree down. And no matter *what* sort of creature he *claims* to be, he would have *never* survived." Huey lurched forward, slamming his fist down on his desk with a deep wooden crack. "The only thing you've successfully done is doom us all!"

Greyson's heart jumped at the king's screams, beating so fast it felt like it was boiling. And right then he knew why. Not from regret or guilt, or even the fact that he was being screamed at. His heart seized because it came to understand the truth faster than his brain: the general was right. Stiqula was no man. He couldn't be. No man could instill such unnatural fear like this. Even the king was taken by it, the very man who purged his kingdom of religion in the first place, precisely *because* of Stiqula. And the fact that a creature such as this existed did away with his dad's logic, and did away with his mom's stories too, because apparently she'd been cutting out all the bad parts of those legends. And just like that, the only world he knew was swept right out from under his feet. He felt just like a child again, sheltered and lied to about the true color of the world.

"You will fix this!" Huey screamed. "Or I will kill you all, *myself*! Before that monster has a chance to kill *me*, like he did *my family*." His last words wavered, passing from anger into pain for a fleeting moment.

The king's threat of death echoed in Greyson's ears. And all the blood drained from his head, like his body was trying to kill itself before the king had a chance.

Greyson stared at him, stewing in the wise light of the moon, face more wrinkled than ever. Greyson stared like he didn't understand. Couldn't comprehend how little his life meant to the king. He almost seemed like a different person from the man he'd met earlier. The smiling actor on a stage. That man was gone. The king who would give Greyson everything he'd ever dreamed. Replaced by this man, who'd stripped him of all he had.

"You were not the only one hurt by him, Hero," the general uttered.

"Be silent, Theodore!" The king slammed both his fists this time. "You're lucky I don't kill you where you *stand*."

Brown took in a deep and silent breath, chest swelling and receding again.

"Now get out." Huey waved them off quickly, before his eyes could let go of the tears they'd been growing. He leaned back and covered his red face with his hands.

It was over. Judgment passed. Sentence final.

Execution.

Greyson turned to leave. Empty. Floating to the door.

This day . . . he'd been so nervous for this day. His meeting with the king of everything. A man with the power to change his life. He'd been nervous for the worst possible scenario, worried himself to death over it, the chance that the king would reject him, and send him home with his head hung low.

But this . . . this scenario he never could have thought of. This wasn't even an option. Like some horrible nightmare he'd stumbled into . . . hung by his neck from the castle's branches.

Brown opened the door for them to exit, but stayed as Greyson and Tay passed into the hall, closing the door again.

*He turned back?* Greyson thought. Was he fighting for them? Arguing that it was just an accident? Greyson turned his ear to the door in tense anticipation, hope swelling in his chest, peering into the crack of moonlight. General Brown knew it was an accident.

"Your Highness, I feel you should know. I've recovered his blade."

That wasn't what he was expecting to hear.

There was a long silence before the king uttered anything in response. "What will you do with it?"

"I plan to hide it. Lock it away somewhere it can't be found."

"Is it here? Now?"

"My ship, yes."

"Get rid of it. Get it away from here. I don't want it anywhere near my city."

"I'll take it to the VDC then."

"Yes. Better to risk the convicted lives than my people's."

Suddenly, Greyson was kicked to the ground, yanked up again, and slammed into the wall next to the door.

"Who the fuck you think you are? You fucking green-eyed demon!" Riese thrashed him against the wall again as Knight and Berinhard watched.

"Get the fuck away from him!" Tay lunged for Riese. But with one swing of Riese's arm, Tay was floored.

"You *grunbicks* always get the special treatment. *You let him out!* And they give you the spot anyway. You are not special. *You are the devil's shit that stains the world!*" he slipped back into whatever fucking accent his fucked up country sounded like, shutting up only when the sound of Tay's gun charged in his ear.

"I said, get the fuck away from him." Tay put the ringing barrel right up against his ear-hole, just in case he hadn't heard it.

Riese let up on his shirt, and Greyson slid down the wall to his feet.

"That's right, big guy. You're gunna talk with your fists, I'm gunna talk with my guns," he said as the giant moved away from his friend. "Now why don't you go shovel some shit with your face."

Just then, Berinhard grabbed Tay from behind and pinned his arms down against his sides. The two struggled for only an instant before General Brown opened the door into the hall.

"Guards!"

Berinhard let go of Tay, and they all stood at attention.

Brown looked to his lieutenant. "You're just letting this happen? In the King's Hall!"

"I'm sorry, sir, it—"

Brown turned for the exit before Knight could find an excuse. "Berinhard, Riese, you are to report to Colonial Vermilion in Cantidium for your new position as city guards." They followed after him.

Greyson and Tay stayed behind, completely unacknowledged. But Greyson couldn't let the general go without knowing what came next. They had to help somehow. After all, the king said it was *their* responsibility. "What about us, sir?"

Brown stopped at the end of the hall, his men diverting around him. He stood there for a moment, as if the man in him wanted to keep going, but the general held back. He turned, outlined in the azure light, defined only by a shadow.

"What's our next move?" Greyson took a few cautious steps forward.

Brown didn't seem to like that. "*We* aren't doing anything," he said as the rage that he'd been hiding climbed to the surface. "My men and I will handle this. You can go back to Wellington for all I care."

Greyson's hope scattered, all at once. Fast and painful as a firework going off in his heart, leaving nothing but a darkened, fleshy pit behind. Rejected by the only person that could help them out of this forsaken mess.

Instead of fighting for them, Brown had abandoned them. Like a burden.

Whatever it was he saw in Greyson died in that tanker's flames.

"But, what about my eyes?" he uttered.

But Greyson's final plea only triggered all that was left of Brown's rage. He lurched forward, clenching his fists. "It is illegal!"

Greyson had forgotten already, cowering in the general's screams. He crumbled as Brown turned and stormed off with Berinhard and Riese. He couldn't support himself anymore, slumping against the wall where Riese had pinned him, staring at the floor to make sure he wasn't bleeding from the gaping hole in his chest where his heart used to be.

Tay watched him as he slid to the floor. Defeated to his core.

Helpless. Hopeless.

"Well, I'm not going back home," said Tay.

Greyson didn't move, still burning a hole in the decorative rug. "Why not?" he asked, barely louder than a whisper, voice dry and broken. "What makes you think we belong here anymore?"

"Fuck them, what about us? What about what *I* want?"

"You can't just say fuck everything, Tay! People could die." He rested his head against the wall behind him. "*We* could die."

"That's not what I mean. I mean, fuck them, we'll figure it out on our own."

Greyson was quiet, thinking.

What chance could they possibly have? How the hell could they ever hope to win against something capable of wiping out entire cities?

He looked at Tay like he was an idiot.

But Tay just smiled, and gave him a hand. "Let's go after this guy."

But Greyson didn't take it.

Tay was still an idiot. So blatantly unaware of anything he did. There were no repercussions in his world, just shit happening. But Greyson couldn't live like that. He couldn't help but worry himself to death over every little thing. Every drop of darkness he'd spilt on the world.

"Would you just stand up." Tay jerked his hand closer. "So we let one guy outa jail. So what? We've put five times that many people *into* jail, so it totally balances out."

Greyson took in a huge breath, finally giving Tay a hand. "I don't think it works like that." Tay pulled him to his feet. "Something tells me this guy's a little different."

# 7

# A DARK DISCIPLE

Darkness.

Darkness was all he knew. For ever, and for always.

He did not exist but for the faint and quiet grain of light, buried deep and hidden in his heart, which let it beat but once a day.

*Boom.*

The only sound to ever echo through that chamber since its closing.

It was a cell. A cursèd prison built by gods.

*Boom.* It came again. A thunderous echo in the pitch.

Then, *light.*

Fire's light, exploded in upon this once-eternal night.

Spreading, swirling, crawling, burning, all throughout the wooden hollow: the volume of a black cathedral. The fires rose to fill the space, fifty feet high, whipping at the arched and wooden ceiling.

And at a body that was clung there.

He felt it. The heat. The warmth. The pain. It woke him. And he stirred.

His first movement in half a century.

He screamed. He cried.

Then broke free of his burning chains and fell through the cloud of flame.

But when he struck the cell's hard floor, the fire washed away in his dark wake.

The room was cold, and quiet.

Dead.

All but for his quivering breath and beating heart. Now come to life again.

He crawled at first, then rose and stumbled, stepping forth from the only thing he knew. Into the light of roaring flames. They were warm against his skin, and hypnotic in his fragile eyes, glowing, squirming, raging, filled with so much energy he could not follow them. On the wind, they crackled and whipped: a million yellow flags strung up from the earth. It stunned him still, perceptions shocked, suddenly excited after half a century of sleep. And in the rapture of his senses, his body gave way, and he fell from the tree, into the open air. He had been asleep so long that he knew nothing but despair, feeling only pain in the darkness between dreams and awake. He began to think that he was birthed from darkness. And now, new to the world, everything felt momentous, as if he'd never felt the breeze before, rushing past him as he fell, or the tickle in his belly, loosened by a lack of gravity.

He slammed hard into the bark, landing on the lowest bough of the tree, feeling the pain he knew again. He felt weak. Broken and weak, resting on his back, taking great effort just to breathe. Then, he opened his black eyes, and wondered at the world. He saw nothing that he knew. He did not know where he was, or how he'd come. He was lost in the place he saw before him. Lost in the splendor of his eyes.

The leaves rustled softly in the wind, and soothed his ears, mixing with the quiet song of insects in their branches. He could barely see them in the night, the leaves, so dark against the sky, framed in points of shimmering light. The stars—sparkling beauty by the thousands. Like martyrs, they held the darkness back, so brilliantly, away from the world. But somewhere up there was something that his old heart searched for.

There was one star among them, different from the rest, far to the east. It was cradled in the ashes of a star long gone, a pink nebula, like wispy clouds stretched across space, with a glowing heart, and arms like a god's, reaching to protect the lonesome light. A light that did not twinkle as the others. For it was much closer than a star. Yet, so far away.

"Nn—" he tried to speak, tried to remember.

The spell cast on him blocked his thoughts, stole his memories, and kept him dark. But he fought to remember, strived to speak, longed to evoke the name.

"Nn—nae." That was it. He nearly had it. If he could just remember the name, he could remember everything.

"N—Nævah." Home.

That was his home. Nævah.

But that was all he could remember. Nothing else.

"Where am I?" he spoke, strength returning. And soon he could stand.

He felt something behind him, something dark and familiar. The cold finger of the devil pricked him as he turned, shivering to face it. As he watched, the bark of the trunk behind him disappeared. A shadow, cast by nothing in the night, grew up from the branch, two hundred feet high, and nearly half as wide. Another hollow had appeared before him, and evil echoed from within. He knew Darkness well. And It tempted him to find It, to return to Its embrace, from a world so strange and bright.

The hollow was enormous, too dark and vast to see its ceiling, nor its far wall. But Darkness drew him further, like the whisper of a ghost, calling from the deep. With one thousand blind steps, he found the back wall of the hollow, and a crevice that grew crookedly in its grey wood, large enough to step through. And without hesitation, he did.

The crack turned and split into many paths, descending and rising up again, making it impossible for light to follow after him. But his once-holy eyes could detect forms of light outside the visible spectrum, allowing him to see where men could not. And what he found there in the dark surpassed all that he knew of fear. Fear was so powerful in this place that it became the air he breathed, taken down into his lungs, infusing with his blood, and cutting at his veins like shards of glass. Stronger, and stronger his terror grew, pumping his blood faster, harder. The fear filled each chamber of his heart with razor shards, slicing them at every beat until his old heart tore itself apart. But still he continued, for It beckoned him to find It.

But the fear in his blood only worsened, the shards growing larger, heavier, as thick and strong as diamonds. Blood oozed from his holey heart and filled his chest, pressing hard against his lungs, like stones, squeezing them until he whimpered. Then his whimper grew into a scream. A cry of anguish and trepidation, silenced as his lungs were emptied—pressed up against themselves, tight as retching stomachs. He stumbled, unable to abandon what he fought so hard to find. But his tortured corpse could not continue. He fell, forced down, flat against the ground under the suffocating weight of diamond blood.

And that is when He came. Up from the depths, Refsiel appeared to take his soul. His body tingled, muscles twitching from asphyxia. And his bleeding heart slowed to a quiver. The Darkness filled him as what little life remained began to fade.

Such *fear*! Such *hatred*! It felt as if all the evils of the world were in him, and could not be released. This was his end. The end of a life he could not remember. And the birth of a dark disciple. As if his diamond blood were ice, his heart began to freeze into a crystal. And Darkness raised him from the ground, and plunged His evil hand within to grasp his crystal heart, and break it.

Instantly he was released, fallen to his knees. His splintered heart was free, beating loud and strong to expel the dreaded crystals from his blood, which left him through every pore. Pooling on his skin, the liquid crystals hardened into armor, charged with power. And the weight was lifted from his lungs, filling them with chilling air again.

*"You gave Me your heart once. It is time I give you Mine,"* a hellish voice echoed in his head.

"Please—" It pained him to speak. "Please—t-tell me who I—am." His voice was so loud, booming in his mind. Darkness had not left him fully. He could feel It in him, like the swelling of his brain, pressed out against his skull. Then suddenly the agony erupted from his head in flames. He cried and twisted at the devil's feet as the fire turned from red to black, and the last of his nerves died. His body's pain was ended.

His screams faded into gasps as he realized his suffering had gone, though the fear within his heart remained unquantifiable. His mind now felt clear. As if some curse had been dispelled, now burning from his head in lightless flames.

*"You are Stiqula. Once an angel, now no longer."*

Stiqula. That was his name. He remembered having heard it.

*"You are to become this world's savior against the Tyranny of Light."*

"This world is not my own," Stiqula spoke softly, trying to recover from his torment. "Where am I?" He rose before a figure he could no longer see. Even His voice, though still terrible, was lessened. Weak.

*"Vínesíri."*

Viæden. Stiqula saw himself plummet from the sky within a burning meteor.

*"Yes,"* said Darkness. *"Recall. Remember. Lift the curse once placed upon you."*

But he could remember nothing else. "How?"

*"Upon this world lie relics of your past. Find them all, and your true self will be known. Your true quest will begin."*

"How am I to find them?"

*"Follow your heart, as you found Me."*

He lowered his head in understanding, expecting the amorphous fear before him to recede. But it stayed, black and mighty. The Darkness had one final gift for him.

*"As token of My faith in thee, a gift. A power given only to one other. The power to grip the wind."*

Stiqula's arm was plunged into the blackness, out of his control, scorched and tortured as if wedged between the devil's jaws and six million razor teeth. He was certain he would lose his hand to the venom if he did not pull it free. But try as he might, he was powerless to Refsiel. He screamed again and was released, just as suddenly.

*"Her pale Light comes."*

Stiqula cringed, clinging to his arm. Then at his right, the tree-wall burst inward, hurling him across the chamber in a cloud of wooden splinters.

When the dust cleared, a crooked, white line shone through the dark, illuminating the room in dawn's pale light. Stiqula did not know what to think of it. He rose again, and inspected his hand in the bright, thin beams, which halved the room's darkness, top and bottom.

His skin was ashen-grey, veins barely showing dull blue-green beneath. And upon the back of his right hand, strokes of charred burns aligned into a symbol. The Symbol of Air.

Stiqula remembered Viæden's gods, and the one this symbol belonged to. Eir Semræ Sunaru, Lord of the Sky. But he did not know fully what it meant . . . Had Air's Power now become his to command? How could that be? He would have voiced his confusion if he'd still felt Refsiel's fear near, but it had vanished with the light.

A few steps from him, the floor dropped off, plunging down into the dark, a bottomless chasm to hell itself. Leaning over its edge, he could still sense the God's evil far below, and dared not stare into the void any longer, feeling the hunger of Death's eyes upon his mortal flesh.

Across the chasm was a great mirror, hanging from the wall of the old hollow, set within a golden frame, blessed by two dozen ancient symbols at its edges. It was unreachable across the void, but in its reflection he could see the horizontal plane of light coming from the fissure, dissecting the dark around him. And standing in the white beams was a monster.

Stiqula slumped to his hands and knees.

And his reflection followed.

"Who am I?" He touched his face, bony and ridged, decayed and dying. His chin was pointed and his cheeks were sunken. His brows were fire, his teeth were sharp, and his eyes were dark and cold.

He looked just like a demon should.

"I was an angel," he cried, tearless though it was. While his mind was cleared of the curse, needing only to be filled with memories again, his body was forsaken still, demonized to reflect the blackness of his soul, and forced to contain all the anguish of his heart. Unable to ever feel the relief of tears, or joy of happiness again.

Stiqula reached up to his shoulders, for at his back, his mind expected to see two glorious wings . . . But there was nothing. Only darkness.

"What happened to me? Why can't I remember? Who has done this to *me*?!" He threw his hand across the ravine at his monstrous reflection, eyes flickering yellow. The symbol on his hand shined brightly the same color, and a glorious wind ripped through the air, shattering the mirror into a warped web of clouded glass, without him ever touching it.

*"Oyopa,"* Refsiel whispered, one last time.

Stiqula watched the Symbol of Air fade from his skin. "Oyopa . . . *She* has done this?" He looked to the gash of dawn, like horizontal lightning running the length of the room. "But She is all things good and bright. How could She forsake me? What have I done? What darkness have I wrought, and now forgotten, that She may curse me so unforgivingly?"

Stiqula stood and staggered back down the winding path he came from, to the great hollow, and the light. Still gripping his blesséd hand, he emerged adorned from neck to toe in armor: thin and ribbed, hugging every muscle like a second skin, black, with muddy grey accents to fool the eye into thinking it was bone. The only place it curled away from his body was at the shoulders, creating sharp, broad pauldrons, from which hung a tattered cape.

With his head clear, he now recognized the old hollow. Once filled with his followers, bustling between massive ships ripped from the limbs of ceptris trees. Not bark ships, no, a perversion of Viæden's fleet. Stick ships: giant branches, a thousand feet long. They gave him a strategic advantage over Viæden. Larger in volume, but not mass. Mostly empty space between their tangled limbs, they were much harder to hit. The targeting systems of the time could not lock onto such a detailed shape, rendered useless.

A single stick ship still remained, small enough to fit within the hollow, smaller than all the rest he could remember. Just nine hundred feet. Its nose was rough, torn from its tree with haste, smooth only at the visor of its bridge window. Its core was thin and cylindrical, branching off into smaller spires as it wound its way to stern, all layered in a thin, grey coat of bark that peeled at its joints.

He knew this ship. But not its name. He felt connected to it, as if he looked upon a part of himself he'd once forgotten. But his mind was blank as a starless night.

Stiqula walked from the hangar, out onto the branch, wind tearing at his cape with jealous claws. The sky was getting brighter through the leaves, still absent of all color in the young light of the morning. The sun was not yet risen, but Her glow still lit the sky, brighter in the east. He could now see the globe, a mile beneath him. A wasteland encircled his tree, for nearly twenty miles. And beyond that the curving world turned green, bare of any landmarks but for the north, ahead of him. There, at the edge of his vision, high cliffs rose from the earth, and twin ceptris trees rose higher still beyond them.

A strong blow from the wind swept through Gardeón's dark leaves, and thrust him forward, nearly launching him from the tree. Stiqula spread his stance to remain on his feet, and closed his heavy eyes to let the wind vent its frustration on his cape.

"I know," he spoke to the Air. "I know that you are angry. But this dispute lies with your Father. Not with me. It is no fault of mine you've fallen out of favor. And while my angel heart should dread His interest in me . . . well, as He said, I am no longer angel."

The wind blew only stronger. And Stiqula opened his eyes to steady himself again.

"Is it out of envy that you wail? That your power is now mine? Or is it fear? That whatever move He's planned for me leads to your demise? I could never keep up with your vacillation, Eir. Your actions were never clear enough for any angel to seek counsel in."

But he did not come to taunt the sky.

"Refsiel wants something from me. What that is I do not know. But just like when my heart was pure, Her Light will guide me." Stiqula closed his eyes again and breathed deep. For he knew that in a moment She would rise to meet him. He had come to see the sun.

While his body had fallen victim to the curse of time, his mind was like a newborn to the world: bits and pieces were returning, but any sense of law or reason still was blank. He knew, as every creature did, that Light was good, and Refsiel, evil. But still uncertain to him was if Oyopa's goodness was learned or forced upon him at his birth. Was She deserving of his love? Or was he Refsiel's only chance to end Her *tyranny* . . . as it was put. His mind clashed with itself, for he knew Darkness was also King of Lies, and could be playing him a fool. But his heart knew the answer. While his mind was unreliable, the stains of his past remained woven in his heart's brittle fabric. And he would know the truth by its reaction to Her.

The morning rose over the mountains at his back, and shone upon him. Its waves were warm and loving, like atonement . . . A mournful embrace for keeping him locked in the dark, so long. He looked over his shoulder at the rising light, and stared upon the glorious disk as it leapt from the mountains to the sky. Its rays bathed him, absolved him of all sin, and welcomed him into the world again.

He hadn't seen the sun in . . . millennia it felt like. He had forgotten the bounty of its power . . . Its infinite beauty. And though the vision was euphoric, his heart knew instantly it was a lie. The sun was Light, and life-giver, but it was also Light that stole his life away, the warden that imprisoned him, and transformed his heart to none but pain and dust.

He turned his night-stained eyes from Her.

"Don't try to sway me, Oyopa. I've made up my mind," he said coldly to the sun. "As I did before . . . Though I wonder just how long ago it was." He looked to his body. So long he was held captive and immobile, his body had decayed. The armor he wore restored his strength and flexibility, but his appearance still disgusted him. "You cast me into darkness, just as You did

Refsiel, all those millennia ago."

He headed for the hollow, and to the stick ship that remained. But in the rays of dawn, his memory returned. That ship was his. He'd built it, carved its halls himself with brawn and toil. It was a relic of his past. One of which Refsiel had spoken. And suddenly he felt the others. More that must be found to regain every memory he'd lost.

He looked to the west, far beyond the curve of the horizon. He could not see it, but he knew a forest towered there, unlike any other. A once-proud and flourishing city, capital of Viæden. "Animallia," he said. Where his siege of the world began, and ended. He attacked that city with such ferocity it set ablaze. Their king, their commanders, could do nothing against him. Nothing but watch their city burn . . . It seemed only the Goddess Herself could stop him. And in the end, She did.

But what would make him do such a thing? What would make him commit such crimes against all order and reason? An angel's purpose was to keep man from being conquered by Darkness, not to conquer them himself.

Giant spans of time were missing. The most important parts, it seemed. He needed his relics to complete them. And if he was to find them, that is where they'd be. Across the world, in Animallia. He could feel them, pulling on his heart. Like echoes across time.

Stiqula continued to the hollow, but stopped one step outside its shade. Before he left Light's grace for good, he had one last thing to say. "You taught us to love Light, for You love us: Your progeny. But You do not love us, do You? . . . You made Him and me the same. Created us as Your antithesis, such that we have no other fate. And for this reason alone, You punish us, though we are as You made." He blocked the bright sun with his arm. "You are cruel, Oyopa. This my heart knows. And with my relics, my mind is soon to know to what extent Your madness goes."

# 8

# Relics of a Faded Past

General Brown hadn't slept that night. Tortured by the choice he'd made to listen to Greyson, and fire. Astrolite was one of the most explosive compounds known to man. And if it had struck the tree directly, it *would* have destroyed that dark cathedral completely. Greyson's heart was in the right place, but still so young and naive to the world . . . He jumped too quickly.

*Why did I listen to him?*

Because he's vertui?

Because there was no time to think?

No time to see reason beyond fear.

After their meeting with the king, Brown did exactly as he said he would, and flew to the Viæden Detention Center, where Stiqula's blade would be locked away in one of its many vaults. Among all sorts of ancient and forbidden things. However, on his journey to the VDC, alone in his cabin, he inspected the sword, carefully. He knew it well. More than he cared to admit. And while its surface was scorched a shimmering black from whatever curse was lain upon it, an ancient inscription could still be made out at the base of its straight blade. Four symbols made up a phrase, each one standing for a single word: *Death, be not proud*.

This hieroglyphic language had passed into the histories long ago. But being such a keystone to Viæden's myths and legends, there were certain symbols everybody knew. These included. It was the epigram of a forgotten empire, one that believed themselves mightier than Death, Itself.

"So naive they were," said Brown. "To believe that anything but death awaited them." He breathed deep. "Or perhaps they knew their fate, and accepted it instead of cowering. Perhaps *we* are the naive ones, running from death in fear." Rotating the blade in his hands, something triggered in his brain.

In fifty years, many memories had dulled to grey, but this blade shone brightly, everlasting. Though . . . the vision he had of it was not the same. Something was wrong. Something was missing.

Instantly, he stood and hurried to the bridge, and ordered a diversion from their course, to land at a city very near the VDC, on the outskirts of the Dead Forest.

Kabdrey was a flowered-city. Built during the exodus of those that survived the destruction of Animallia. It housed the only memorial to honor the fallen metropolis.

He set the ship down in a nearby city port and walked the streets with his men to the museum at the city's center. At six-forty in the morning, Kabdrey had just begun to wake. Its street venders were the first to appear, bright and early, to heckle those on their way to work, and try to talk their way into a sale from anyone who'd listen. Though most of them shied away from the blade-wielding general, and his twenty armed men, marching through town.

The atmosphere was quite different from life in a vertical city. Here, the buildings were spread out traditionally, side-by-side, instead of carved and layered in a tree. But unlike traditional structures of the previous age, the majority of Kabdrey's buildings were not built, but grown. Occasionally a stone and mortar structure could be found, but the vast majority of its buildings were made of leaf-mould.

Leaf-moulding allowed craftsmen to bend the giant leaves of ceptris trees, or native flora into a desired shape, and inject them with an enzyme that would harden its organic properties, hard as stone. This technique resulted in every leaf-moulded building being quite unique and beautiful. Clovers, flowers, ivy, trees, some folded into spectacular shapes, others frozen as nature intended.

The Museum of Animallia was one such building, with a green facade of leaves, overlapped and molded into a traditional rectangle, three stories high. The leaved walls were further covered with much smaller, living ivy vines, leaving dark trails of green and golden blooms all across its face. Spaced along its front were tall glass windows reaching every floor. And from its roof stemmed five green towers, lofting bright pink and purple tulips high above the city.

The museum's curator was waiting for the general as he arrived. Brown met her on the front steps, leading up to wooden doors, as intricate as the facade. She was skinny and pepper-haired, in her work dress, white sneakers, and a brown, puffy jacket to ward off the brisk morning.

"Thank you for meeting with me on such short notice, Andiel." Brown took her hand in greeting. But she did not meet his eyes in response. She could not take them from the blade he carried.

"Is this . . . really his?" she stumbled awed by the sword's appearance, glistening black against the dawn. But not only that, its legend was far more stunning. She appeared almost frightened of it, as if it still posed a threat to her, even in the general's hands.

"It was discovered last night," said Brown. "In the very place Stiqula was believed to have disappeared."

"And where was *he*?" She finally pulled her eyes up to Brown's.

But the general had no answer for her. Closing his mouth and biting down in frustrated silence. "I don't know."

She breathed in sharply.

"He may be dead," Brown continued. "Or he may not be. But either way, we must secure this blade in one of the detention center vaults."

"But you said I could have it." She squinted.

"Do you really want to be the one he finds with it if he comes looking?"

She swallowed. "Then why have you brought it here?"

"Something is missing. Another part that . . . works with the blade. A simple trinket, seemingly harmless. But it could mean all the difference. Perhaps misidentified as Animallian jewelry?"

"What makes you think we've misidentified something?" She drew her keys from her jacket pocket and turned to unlock the doors.

"Because I've seen it. I visited this museum years ago to pay my respects. And I remember seeing a necklace on display that resembled the chain. I thought it merely a coincidence until I discovered it missing from the sword. I don't yet know what significance it plays, but—"

A shadow crept over the doors as they opened, growing to encompass the entire building. A tangled shadow, darkening the keeper's face as she turned toward the sun in curiosity.

But Brown stayed, staring up at the museum, blackness draped across it like a dead and barren tree, stretching its foul limbs to steal the sun. The chill of its darkness struck deep to his core, resonating with his heart, in just the same way it had before. His heart quivered, speeding up so suddenly it leapt through time, back to when he first set eyes upon that vile shape. Just eighteen years old. When the city he called home had burst into flames, and his life was changed forever.

Now, an old man, frightened as a child, turned slowly to face the sum of all his fears, counting the seconds as if they were his last.

The *Aliqula* had come.

Greyson and Tay sat silently across the table from one another, stuffing their faces with a Viæden breakfast: scrambled cosabro eggs, two boar-links, red-hot planesious peppers, toast, tots, and Ozberry syrup, which tasted something like blueberries, but sweeter, and turquoise.

They'd had a rough night.

After leaving the king's office, they'd tried to collect their things from the secretaries, but Megan and Steph had already gone home, and their bags were gone. But, judging from the lingering perfume of puke, it smelt like Megan had locked their bags up in her desk for safe keeping. Super helpful.

With hardly any cash, and no place to stay, they had to ask directions to the cheapest hotel in the tree. And they ventured all the way to the roots to find it. Turned out it was actually outside the tree. On the ground, beneath the branches—not on the lake side, on the forest side. The run-down part of town, where they found a crummy room, just thirty hueys for the both of them. It only had one bed, shared between them and whatever the hell else was living in the mattress, poking at them all night.

After a few terrible hours of sleep, they checked out of that cesspool and went looking for something to eat. Only problem was, they'd just spent all that was in their pockets on that itchy, three-hour nap. And then they realized they couldn't even *get* back up to the king's secretaries or any of the guard-floors because they didn't have the clearance.

Finally, Tay'd had enough bullshit and tried his luck loitering in the elevator core of docking bay three, to sneak onto one with some unsuspecting guards. That bit worked. And by the grace of the Goddess, they were actually headed to breakfast themselves in one of the guard cafeterias.

Nice people too. Greyson and Tay stood in the breakfast line behind them, and when the boys got to the register and realized they needed to scan their nonexistent badges to get their food, the two guards stepped in and scanned their badges twice. Ellis and Lawson were their names, guy and a girl, not in that order, royal guards themselves. Feeling guilty, Greyson explained their situation to them, minus the Stiqula bits.

The boys sat down next to them to eat, in hopes of finding some way to get back into the game, instead of going home defeated, or staying there to die.

The air in the cafeteria was filled with many different breakfast aromas, which, all together, weren't that appetizing. But most of all, there was a sense of calm floating over their heads. Word of Stiqula must not have broken yet. Neither of them knew how to even *start* bringing it up, or even if they should . . . But they didn't have a choice. If anyone was likely to help them out, it was these guys.

Nearing the end of their meal, Tay threw his head in their direction, signaling to Greyson to strike up the conversation. Which was odd because Tay was the more talkative one, but he was smart enough to know that in a sensitive situation like this it was better to have Greyson do the talking. So Greyson took in a big breath and looked to the guards next to them.

*Hey, so you know that Stiqula guy?* Greyson tried to formulate the approach in his head. *Yeah . . . Is there any way we could maybe take your ship to go stop him?* Wait, that wasn't even how it worked. These guys weren't captains. They didn't have their own ships. So . . . *Hey wanna ask your captain if we could take his ship? . . . or like, come aboard?*

Greyson deflated, closing his eyes tight to help him think. A sharp kick hit him under the table, and he looked up to Tay flailing his head at the guards again. Greyson took in another breath, looking at them, even opening his mouth this time in hopes the right words would just fall out.

"You have beautiful eyes, Greyson," Ellis said, just noticing.

"Oh." His breath escaped him all at once. "Thank you."

"Are they real?" she asked.

"Yes?" *What?*

"Well, you never know. Some people wear contacts to change their eye color. As if that somehow makes them a better person."

"Really?" *That's a thing?*

"Oh yeah."

Tay rolled his eyes.

"Do they believe in Vertuém Destiny where you're from?" She brushed the straight blond hair from her face to see him better.

"Mm, n'I don't think so." He looked to Tay for approval.

Tay raised his eyebrows and shook his head to confirm a no.

"I just heard about it for the first time yesterday." He looked back to her, sitting diagonally from him.

"Well, I believe in it."

"Ellis!" Lawson snapped.

"I do," she asserted, not sorry about it.

"C-can I ask why?" said Greyson. "I mean, I literally don't know anything about it."

In the air behind his sentence, a quiet alarm grew louder and louder, silencing the chatter of the canteen and springing every guard to their feet. "Let's go!" Someone shouted. All the room scattered, some sprinting to their dorms to grab their gear, others, fully dressed already, headed for the elevator core.

"What's that? What's going on?" Greyson and Tay stood with Ellis and Lawson.

"Somethin's up!" Ellis answered.

"Red bell. It's an emergency," Lawson explained in a hurry.

"Get to your ship. Your captain'll meet you there."

"We don't have a ship!" Greyson stammered before they could leave.

"Sorry then." Lawson turned to join the flow of traffic to the core. Ellis started walking backwards to follow, shrugging her shoulders at Greyson.

"Well, can we come with you!?" he shouted after.

She waved for them to follow as she turned to join the march.

Greyson looked to Tay.

"Let's do it." Tay skipped into a run.

"Is this allowed?" Greyson asked finding their new friends in the crowd.

"Yeah, our captain's cool. He'll let you on," Ellis answered as the alarm disappeared.

It was replaced by a stern voice over the intercom. "Attention, Royal Guard."

The room silenced but for the shuffle of feet.

"We have just received word from General Brown that at six-fifty this morning, the City of Kabdrey came under attack from an unknown enemy. Brown's fireteam was completely wiped out in the assault, and the target is now en route to the Viæden Detention Center."

Greyson's face went white.

"The following fireteams are to report to their ships for immediate departure to the VDC. All other guards will remain in the city on red alert: the *Ion*, *Centripetal*, and *Chordata*. Repeat: *Ion*, *Centripetal*, *Chordata*, report to ships. All else: red bell. Red bell."

"What the hell?" "Are we under attack?" The guards speculated around them.

"That's us. We gotta go," said Lawson. The mass of guards had all jammed together, slowing to a stop at the entrance to the elevator core.

Greyson looked to Tay again, near nauseous, knowing that his actions had now begun to spread, and propagate, to punish completely innocent people . . . An entire fireteam . . . gone.

"It's Stiqula," Greyson said quietly.

But loud enough for Ellis to hear. "What?!" She spun back. "Why would you say that?"

"Oh, he's just fuckin' around." Tay laughed and nudged him not to answer.

Greyson flashed his eyes at her. "Just a feeling."

"Let's go! Move it!" she shouted to the crowd.

Once to the core, they caught a lift down to the hangar, and as they approached the three bark ships lined up along the hangar opening swarmed with men, Ellis turned to Greyson. "A'right, just hang back a minute. I'm gunna gage his reaction, then I'll wave you over."

"Okay, no problem," he said as they separated.

Greyson watched as Ellis and Lawson joined the crowd around the bark ship in the middle, *Centripetal* written on its side. As a military ship, it was much larger than General Brown's, by five or six times. And spiked out from its edges were all kinds of guns, cannons, and antenna.

Another pack of guards unloaded from the elevators and streamed into the hangar, colliding with Greyson and Tay, standing right in the middle of their path. Getting kicked around like a dead bird on the sidewalk, the boys were pushed from the traffic, and onto one of those big, squeaky drainage grates that collect all the sludge when ships are being cleaned. So they decided to wait there and spare themselves the abuse.

The *Centripetal's* captain stood at the foot of his loading ramp, counting his men as they boarded.

"Captain!" Ellis shouted, stepping from the line. "We've got two recruits that don't have a fireteam yet. They wanna come with us."

"That's not my problem, Ellis."

"Oh, come on, sir. You just let your own kid on board last week."

"That's because last week we were making rounds, not headed into battle. If they get hurt, it'll be my ass on the line."

"Please, sir. One's a vertui."

Her captain sighed as the *Chordata* began to rise right next to them, engines firing down at full in an emergency takeoff. The sheer power of its thrusters sent a steady vibration throughout the entire hangar. Greyson and Tay looked down at the grate, quaking beneath them, edges squeaking, bending. Rusted as shit. *Fuck.*

The boys tried to dive away from each other, to either side of the grate, but in the added force, it snapped beneath their feet, swinging wide like a trap door, plunging them down into the dark below.

"Fine, where are they?" her captain reluctantly agreed.

She smiled and turned to find them. "They're right over . . ." Her smile faded. "Where the hell'd they go?"

"We don't have time for it, soldier. Get on." He pushed Ellis aboard.

*How could he find us so quickly?* General Brown gripped Stiqula's sword tight.

The *Aliqula* had come. Limbs slicing through the sunbeams like bladed tentacles.

His men stood with him on the steps of the Animallian museum, staring up to the stick ship in wonder, like a nightmare, broken free from the stories their grandparents would tell by firelight. No amount of training could combat the power of the *Aliqula's* legend. But Brown had seen this ship before, and could separate legend from truth by strength of his courage.

He was the only thing left standing between Stiqula and his blade.

And he could not have it. Not at any cost.

"His weapon reserves are empty," Brown broke the silence.

"How do you know?" Knight replied.

"Because we're still here." He backed into the museum, ordering his men to follow. "Get in the building! He's here for the blade."

Brown's guards filed in, rifles drawn. There were only twenty of them. "He knows he's outnumbered. He won't charge. Be vigilant. And do not fear his legend. Truth will keep us alive. He has been defeated once. He can be again," he spoke, still facing the blinding sun as two of his men closed the doors and locked them tight in front of him.

Stone staircases flanked either side of the symmetrical lobby, leading to the upstairs exhibits of Animallian art and culture. To the general's back was a ticket booth in a half-moon shape, behind which the curator cowered. And beyond that lay a cafe, looking out onto the building's courtyard, containing a model of the forest-city before the fall. The whole of the museum echoed in their fearful footsteps as they awaited whatever fate was to come.

Brown scanned the room. The first and second floor doors on either side of him, the front door, and the courtyard glass were a lot of angles to cover. A lot of directions Stiqula could strike from. But it was better to keep all his men in one place than to split them up to cover each wing.

"Do *not* leave this lobby. No matter what," he ordered. "Two of you, up stairs, guard that exhibit door. And two on the other side as well." He pointed high. "Five of you, in back. Watch the courtyard. The rest of you, stay here. And watch these doors." He pointed to the three choke points around him.

"What about the chain?" the curator asked.

Brown turned to Andiel poking out from behind the front desk. "Where is it?"

"Well I don't know exactly which one you want. *The Fall* exhibit is in the northwest wing. But there is jewelry scattered throughout the whole museum!"

Brown took in a deep, frustrated breath.

*What was it worth? His guard's lives?* He debated its importance.

It could be nothing. Or it could be everything. And if ignored, Stiqula would claim it and kill them all anyway.

Brown clapped his hand over his eyes, bared his teeth, and grunted.

It was a decision no officer ever envied making. "*Fuck!*" he screamed, uncovering his eyes again. "We'll search each wing. Together!" He marched to the north wing, and the guards he'd sent off quickly made their way back to him. "It's the only way we stand a chance." He arrived at the north doors: two wooden antiques, inscribed with ancient carvings. "But if he gets that chain before we do. He may very well become invincible." Brown cracked the door open and peered inside as his guards gathered behind him. The north-wing exhibit was two stories, the second consisting of only a railed-off walkway along the walls, lined with paintings and busts. In the center of the room stood an iron statue of a bare man wrestling three monstrous wolves, each tearing at his limbs . . . It was a shooting gallery of windows and blind spots.

Brown turned back to his men. "Six of you, upstairs." He spotted the curator, still behind the desk. "Aren't you coming?"

Andiel had no desire to leave her cover, but she was safer with them than hiding on her own . . . Brown hoped. Plus he needed her help to find the chain. She hobbled quickly over to the group of armed men and women as they began, carefully filing into the exhibit hall.

Light poured in from the eastern windows, creating five veils of golden dust across the whole of the exhibit. But it was clear of any movement. Dead silent.

Brown spotted a few display cases on the far wall, filled with jewels and artifacts, as one of his guards checked the first window.

"He still hasn't moved, sir. Ship's still stuck right where it is."

"What does the chain look like, general?" Andiel asked.

Brown tried to remember. Quickly. Every second mattered. If Stiqula hadn't struck yet, then he was likely hunting them. Watching carefully within the glare of the sun, sizing them up to single out the weakest from the troop. "Thin. Long. A dark . . . silver, I think. With black gems."

"Why the fuck is this important?" asked the last man to enter the room as the rest of the group passed through the first window's light, slowly, cautiously, letting their eyes adjust to the shade again.

"Shut your mouth, soldier," Knight barked from Brown's side.

"Black gems," Andiel repeated. "There's two that come to mind. One is there." She pointed to the case Brown was inching toward. "A piece found in the city . . . I can't remember where."

"And the other?" Brown asked as the troop shuffled through the second window's light. He looked upstairs to his six men, who had split, three and three on either side of the room's upper railing.

"Yes, it's in the opposite wing, I . . . wait, no." She stopped herself. "No, we just moved it, I think."

"Think harder," Brown urged, passing by the statue in the center of the room, and through the third light ray.

"Did anyone see that!?" the last guard shouted.

The whole team spun back at once to see.

"That light!" He pointed to the first window. "It flickered!"

"Keep your head!" Brown ordered.

"He's here!"

"Was it the ship's shadow?" "No, too fast!" his men chattered.

Brown glanced back at the display case, only a few more yards away. "Quickly!" He picked up the pace, passing through the fourth window's beams. And his men followed, fanning around him in a ball of raised rifles that faced every direction. Every window.

They could all feel that monster closing in.

One last veil of light remained between Brown and his prize. But as he entered it, another shadow flickered past the second window. And in the last guard's fear, he screamed, firing a shot, and putting a bullet through the glass. The team all spun toward the sound, faster than before, and even more on edge.

"He's out there!"

"Don't shoot until you . . ." Brown spun back to the display case, right in front of him. The chain Andiel spoke of was inside, along with many others. None of which matched the one in Brown's memory. The case stood before a north-facing window, one that the dawn could not reach. ". . . See him," he finished as a pure black, armored body glided into view, as though all the world had slowed to a still. Only Brown could see him over the case, standing a few feet lower than him on the street outside. *He* did not match Brown's memory either. Only a shadow of his once-angelic beauty, now decayed and rotten-grey, with hair like fire . . . It *was* fire, burning black. His onyx eyes were all that Brown could recognize, still fixed with cold determination. But then, they changed, irises appearing from their darkness like two golden rings, glowing brighter as Stiqula raised his right hand to the glass.

A flameless explosion erupted from Stiqula's open palm, shattering the window and the case, blowing Brown right off his feet, back through his guards, which were all rocked to the ground with him in a cloud of sharp and glittering debris.

Stiqula leapt into the building, through the cloud, right over the pile of guards, landing opposite them and digging his black nails into the last guard's chest. Stiqula slid across the marble floor, dragging the guard with him, then pinned him up against the statue in the center of the hall, kicking his arm and snapping it back around the corner of the statue's base. Stiqula then ripped the guard's rifle from his broken arm and spun to unload it into the three guards on the upper level. And as they fell, he disappeared again, smashing through the third window, into the sun-glared streets as quickly as he'd entered.

Andiel screamed for her life as she scampered to her feet and made a run for the lobby, sprinting past the armless guard as he gasped his final breath.

"Andiel!" Brown coughed, rolling to his front and rising to his knees. The wind had been knocked right out of him. "The other chain!"

Brown's guards rose around him, faster than he could manage. Frantically they panned their rifles in every direction, not knowing from where the monster would strike next.

A spray of amber bullets beamed in through the fourth window, dropping two more guards. Brown's men quickly pivoted to fire back into the dawn. But they were still blind to what was outside, striking only glass and stone.

"Andiel!" Brown screamed, clutching the sword as Knight helped him to his feet.

She'd reached the wooden lobby door, finally looking back to find Brown shuffling toward her as fast as he and Knight could manage.

"Where!?"

She put her fist to her mouth and looked west, to another door on the second floor labeled *The Fall*. But before she could respond, Stiqula fired again, landing a headshot on a guard right in front of the general.

Brown stared in shock as his guard fell before him. "Retreat! To the lobby!"

Andiel opened the lobby doors for Brown, and the ten of his men that remained on the first floor. Six of them ran for it, but four remained vigilant, striding back to the entrance with their eyes on the windows.

But, either out of bravery or boredom, Stiqula was done playing a coward's game. He burst through an upstairs window, tackling one of the guards up there, and in a single motion, swept the man up into a headlock to use him as a shield, and took hold of his rifle, spraying its light upon the two others before they could react. With the guard's finger still on the trigger, Stiqula wrenched the gun up to the man's head and made him pull that trigger on himself. His brain turned to vapor as he slumped from the monster's grasp. All before the four men on the first floor could leap for cover.

One guard slid along the floor beneath the upper railing, firing up at where Stiqula stood. The light bullets beamed through the wood floor all around him. But before any of them could hit their mark, Stiqula flipped over the railing and grabbed hold of it to swing himself under the ledge, planting his armored boots in the guard's chest, crushing his ribs like a red, rotted pumpkin.

By then, Brown, Knight and the six guards that followed them had made it to the lobby, and turned just in time to see the three guards that remained in the exhibit blown away by some violent blur of air, sweeping up all the room's debris in its wake and smashing them against the walls.

Brown couldn't tell if his men were still alive. Nor could he spot their bodies before Stiqula stepped out from behind the center statue to meet his gaze again. The blade in Brown's hand tingled, like it resented the stranger that held it, craving its master once again.

The general screamed in fury as his men took aim. But he knew it wouldn't be enough, ripping an entire string of grenades from the belt of the guard closest to him, then activated them all with a whip of his wrist, and hurled them at the monster.

Stiqula saw the string and dove back behind the statue, just before they struck its front side and exploded. Brown and his guards slammed the exhibit doors on the blast, but were still thrown back into the lobby by the wave of heat and sound.

"General!" Knight screamed as he watched him fall back into his men, half of them falling with him.

Brown felt like he'd gotten the sense knocked out of him. Room spinning, blurred out of focus. But he could feel Knight clutch his arm, which steadied him slightly.

"Could he survive that?" his lieutenant asked.

"He's alive." Brown managed. "But we don't have much time before he realizes that, himself." His guards helped him to his feet. "This blade is calling to him somehow. I can feel it." He looked to Andiel. "The chain must be calling to him also."

"It's on the second level, northwest wing." She pointed to the north-wing stairs, above the doors they'd just escaped from, smoke floating from the open archway at their peak.

"Is there another way?"

"Yes, the museum loops around the courtyard. Up those stairs." She pointed to the opposite staircase.

He nodded, attempting a step in that direction, but stumbled, being caught by his guards again. That first blast must have taken more out of him than he'd thought.

"Sir." Knight held him. "We won't make it."

Brown turned to his pale face.

He was right.

Brown had never seen such power before. Those yellow eyes. That *force* he used against them. Like he could call upon the wind for help. He'd killed fourteen men in an instant. Good men, each one of them. Brown looked to the faces of his guards that remained. Frightened also, but attentive, waiting for their orders.

"If we leave now, we may still have a chance to hide the blade," Knight said.

"Go, general. We'll buy you the time you need," one of his guards assured.

Brown breathed deep. Accepting that there was no other way. He took his guard's hand. A fearless woman, ready to die for her kingdom. "Go in strength."

"*Sumensaru.*" She repeated the sentiment. An ancient expression, wishing luck to those who most needed it.

Brown released her and turned for the front door. Knight and Andiel followed quickly as his guards sprinted up the stairs.

Stiqula's ears rang shrill as he lay on the floor of the exhibit, gasping and dizzy from shell-shock. He rolled to his back and panted until his lungs could inflate fully again.

"That hurt," he coughed, then breathed as deep as his aching ribs allowed. "What are they doing here?" Like they were waiting for him. He strained his stomach muscles to sit up. "They must know about my relics."

Moved to find them before the guards, he struggled to stand, cloudy room still spinning. He shook his head to try and steady himself, and surveyed his surroundings. The door the old man had left through was destroyed and inaccessible. No doubt they were waiting for him on the other side. He'd counted each one as they entered the building. There were nine left, including the civilian. Not impossible odds, but he had expended much of his energy taking out the others. His old body ached, bouncing around inside that armor. He felt weak, muscles atrophied, even though the armor Darkness had given him surged with power. He needed to watch himself. Surprise was the only way he would beat them. But, beyond that, he needed to spare every life he had the chance to. Still uncertain of Refsiel's plan for him, he did not want to give Darkness any added strength, such that He would receive from the deaths of these men. Stiqula had a purpose other than Death's soul reaper. And focusing to find it, he felt a tug upon his heart, like a string threaded to its core, yanked forward.

He was close, drawn to the upper corner of the hall, and an open doorway facing west, entrance still clear of debris. Quickly, he leapt to the second floor and entered a separate exhibit labeled: *The Fall.* A memorial to all those he'd slain in days long past.

This hall was long, with tall windows on either side, and displays between. Divider walls were placed throughout to snake a visitor's path, creating more wall-space for pictures and descriptions, which limited his view.

Hung from one of those walls was a painting of Animallia in the dead of night, red with fire. Its eight-mile-high trees like flaming pillars, chimneys billowing cindered smoke into a moonlit sky . . . A very romantic version of what actually had happened.

Movement flickered in his eye. He looked out the window next to him, across a courtyard to the other side of the building. The guards were on the move in search of him. It would only be a few moments before they found him.

Then he felt it. The draw of his heart. His hidden memory. Right in front of him. A glass case stood between two windows and their dusty light. Within it lay a white bust without a head or shoulders. And strung twice around its neck was a low-hanging necklace, ornamented by a simple crystal shard, only an inch long, black as Refsiel's heart. The chain was only slightly brighter, busily woven of a familiar alien metal, and sharp obsidian gems. It was labeled as a trinket of the dead queen's, one of only a few recovered from the ashes of the former castle tree.

But this trinket belonged to no queen.

It cried out for Stiqula, begging him to take it. Pulling so strongly at his heart it would burst from his chest if he waited a moment longer. Charged by untamed emotion, the Symbol of Air on his hand glowed yellow and fired a sharp gale from his palm to shatter the glass. By reflex alone, he snatched the necklace before it fell, and was instantly taken by its memory, stolen away to another place, another world entirely.

All was white, all was soft, and silent. Winter snow upon an endless plane. Stiqula stood amongst the light abyss, searching this way and that for any sign of life. But there was none. Nothing but the quiet, and a dulling pain within him. His splintered heart. It felt like it was healing. Regressing back in time, to the peaceful life he had forgotten. Then from his heart bloomed something he had thought impossible: the glowing coals of love. And with its coming, his healing heart split once again, separating light from dark, like oil and water. This old, white love could not mix with his black soul. And like the wrong side of a magnet, they repelled. The goodness left him, flung straight from his chest, haloed and pure. The light grew into a figure. And soon Stiqula looked upon the face of beauty.

An angel. A true angel. Aliqula.

She glowed before him, perfume wrapping 'round him like the embrace of her wings. His light looked upon him with the greatest joy and kindness that an angel's eyes could hold. But his eyes stung in bitter pain. It hurt to stare at such beauty, knowing it was once a part of him. And just as she was filled with every goodness, he filled up with every kind of sorrow. Two halves of a heart, now sundered into separate entities, never to be joined again. His eyes burned in her reflection, in need of healing tears that would not come.

This radiant being, Aliqula, stepped forward to him. And he tried with all his might to raise his arms and take her. But he couldn't. He couldn't move. Encumbered by the weight of darkness and a broken heart. Then, by some miracle, as if she knew it was the only way to soothe him, she cried. Tears streamed from her sapphire eyes and filled her heart with sadness too. She raised her hand up to his face, and at her holy touch, his curséd guise was lifted. He took an angel's form again. Smooth and pale, with wings of silver, and hair as black and straight as iron thread. She brushed the iron from his eyes to find them, arctic blue. And then, as if to share his grief, or steal it from him, her sadness grew. She traded their emotions, and bliss and rapture took him. But forced upon him, they felt empty. And seeing her again, so sad, he could not smile. She grew weak, destroyed by sadness, collapsing into him. But still he could not catch her. She struck his chest and disappeared, splashing into brilliant dust, a million gleaming particles that rolled from his breast. They could not find their way back to his heart. Instead they showered him in light, and were lost to the snow.

As she left, so too did his ecstasy, and the bright world around him.

He collapsed to the floor of the museum, a hideous beast, and wailed into his hands with the fever of a shattered soul. His corpse burned with a passionate regret, paralyzed by emptiness.

She was gone. And he would long for her evermore. Every drop of his burning blood needed her. He would not live long without her. She was everything. She was his heart, and he, an empty corpse. She was his morality, his meaning, all his happiness, and sorrow. Without her, he was nothing. A bloody shell of darkness and despair. *She* was the reason he burned Animallia. He did it to prove to man the might of angels. To force them help him return to Nævah. To be with her again.

But why were they separated? Why was he cast from Her kingdom? What was her fate!?

"*Where is she!?*" he cried.

"He's here!"

"Don't move!"

The guards had found him.

He was in no condition to fight. Heart fixated on its missing part.

His morality was gone. He opened his eyes, now crazed and bloodshot without tears. An unbearable pressure growing behind them.

Two were at his left, the rest to his right, snaking through the exhibit.

From a nearly lying position, he launched himself into the air, spinning to face the ceiling. And as his left arm swung beneath him, he fired a maelstrom of air down the cluttered hall, catching all the guards and artifacts in its wake. Still in the air, his right arm came over him to wrap his chain around the guard that stood too close. It caught her 'round the neck. And as Stiqula landed, he tore her down, planted a foot in her back and pulled the chain straight up, severing her head like a bladed noose.

The final guard opened fire and riddled his chest with a dozen glowing craters. Most of their energy was absorbed by his demonic armor, but their sheer number launched him from his feet and through the window at his back.

The pain, inside and out, was unrelenting. And he could not release it. It coursed through him like flaming lithium.

The pressure that had begun in his eyes now spread to every inch of his body as he fell, as if the courtyard were the sea, and he sank to the very bottom.

He struck the ground, hair singeing the grass around his head. He hardly felt the blow over the swelling agony within him. He had to release this *suffering*! He had to free his body of its wrath or die this very moment.

Six more shots struck his gut from above, multiplying his discomfort. Stiqula opened his eye just a sliver, fearing their pressure would launch them from his head if opened fully. He would rather lie there to die drowned in misery than be taken out by the likes of man.

He thrust his arm to the sky, fingers spread as wide as his cramped muscles could allow, swollen veins ready to tear. And from his palm he expelled a flood of air, stronger than he'd ever summoned. It collided with the guard in the window and hurled him into the ceiling, which was swept up in the gust as well, torn right from the building. And for a brief moment his arm felt sweet relief. But it did not last. Like a splash lost from a river. But a more crucial discovery was made. This power, this gift from Darkness, *was* his release. A cure to Light's curse. He clenched his fist and bore inside himself, collecting every ounce of agony upon Eir's glorious wind, and released it all at once.

His entire body erupted in a shockwave of energized air, obliterating his armor, escaping him with such force it caused friction in the open air and sparked a sphere of lightning, which grew outwards at the speed of sound and turned the courtyard into dust. The museum's windows and walls shattered all at once, exploding out into the streets. And the flowered towers crumbled down around him in a cloud of verdant stone.

Brown and Knight ran as fast as they could, back to their ship. And the moment it was in their sight, the shockwave hit them. A wall of sound that shook their bodies, then went silent as it passed. They both spun to see the museum's towers fall into the street, half a mile back.

It hurt the general, as deep as any cut, to watch and know that none survived. His guards . . . Most he'd known for years. As close as family. All of them dead. Killed for no reason other than his own incompetence.

He screamed for them. He wailed, striking the sword down into the street, in the hope that it would shatter. But the sword held true, clanging against stone and biting at his grip.

Knight turned Brown away from the smoke and ruin, and led him back to their ship. But Brown was in a haze. Only coming to at the sound of Knight's voice.

"Orders, sir?" They'd made it to the ship's main hall, loading ramp closing behind them. Knight wanted to know if they should turn and fire on the museum's rubble. But in Brown's mind, there was no use. If Stiqula could survive whatever that just was . . . he could survive anything. And bombing the rest of the town would only end more lives than he already had.

"You have your orders, lieutenant."

Stiqula gasped and sprung to his feet, then stumbled and fell back against a crumbled piece of wall. He looked to the sky, streaked with smoke and dusty clouds. The museum lay strewn all around him, unrecognizable.

He could not control his shallow breathing, exhausted of all energy, body prickling like every limb had fallen asleep. The slightest pressure was amplified by the dead weight of his arms and legs. But his chest hurt most of all. A mix of empty lungs and bullet holes.

At least the anguish of his heart had passed, for now.

His armor was gone, grey, naked body exposed and bleeding. Three entrance wounds, or clusters of wounds, seeped blood down the canals of his wrinkled torso to the dirt. It was still red. That surprised him. Though it was darker than he remembered.

He had barely survived, emptied of all energy, and trembling. Hardly hanging on at all. What his armor could not absorb of the plasma, his bones could, much stronger than a man's, as the good Goddess decreed. He'd certainly be dead if not for that.

Or would he? . . . Perhaps the only reason he'd survived was because

Death still had a use for him.

A glint of movement caught his tired eyes, and he turned his heavy head to face it. At first he thought it was a slug, slinking over ash and rock at the scent of his blood. But then he noticed the slug could not hold its shape, black and glistening, like ink, rolling along the ground toward him. The ink slug was met by others, pooling together as they progressed, joining their bodies to form one dark, roaming puddle. The darkness splashed against him, thinning and hardening as it traversed his skin. It felt cold, and familiar. Stiqula raised his hand to watch it crawl along his arm, stopping at his wrist. And there the liquid froze into the ribbed structure of his armor once again.

Regenerating armor. Curious. But Stiqula had no time to dwell on it, for from his hand dangled the chain, and his mind was taken by it: a prayer chain.

Every angel had one. And this was hers . . . Her *diolance.*

"Where is she?" he managed to say, laying his head back against the wall.

He could not remember her fate. He could not see it through the fog of his mind. All he could see was her smile. And her tears. He searched the sky for where he'd seen Nævah the night before, gazing long and deep to find the only light in his black world. But there was nothing beyond the clouds. Nothing to echo back against his heart. Not a whisper. Not a sound. He could not feel her anywhere.

Perhaps she was too far away, he thought. He prayed. He could not bear to think of life without her. The only reason his heart still beat.

Was she alive? Was she with Light? Or worse yet, Darkness?

He had to know. Nothing else mattered.

Stiqula stood, weak, but able. He turned to a distant bark ship rising from the city. It was headed for a tree, sprouting out of the horizon, illuminated in the sun. The tree was much smaller than the ones around it. Only a sapling compared to the old trees of Animallia.

Something was there. On the ship, or in the tree. He felt it. Something called to him, just like the chain had. He'd felt it before, all along, blended with the call of her prayer chain, now obviously different.

The old man with the sword. He was not among those that Stiqula had killed.

*That sword.*

That sword was his.

His final relic. His final memory.

# 9

# A Chance Encounter

Greyson and Tay splashed down at the bottom of the pit. A pit filled with frothy, foamy, dirty, greasy, water. Tiny chunks of bark and gods-know-what bounced against them in the gritty, lukewarm, slime filling up their ears and brushing past their lips and eyes before they emerged at the surface.

Tay screamed and flailed like a cat in the bath, certain he was dying.

Greyson could feel the bottom of the pool with his feet, and grabbed Tay to make sure he was okay. "Tay. *Tay*! You're alright. Just stand up!"

Tay couldn't form any words, just unintelligible cries.

Greyson spotted a ladder built into the wall and leapt for it, dragging Tay behind him. "Here, grab it!"

Tay couldn't control himself, driven insane by the brown water suffocating him.

Greyson grabbed his arm and yanked it from the water for him, wrapping it around one of the ladder's metal rungs, then caught him by his shirt and pulled his whole torso out. From there Tay was able to find the ladder with his feet and support himself.

"Dammit, you're heavy," Greyson gasped.

Tay trembled, saying nothing, terrified to his core, only panting, wheezing in panic.

"Are you okay?" Greyson saw his emotions collapse further into tears.

"Are you crying?"

"Sh-shut the fuck up!"

Greyson cocked his head, starting to feel bad for him. He knew Tay hated water, but had no idea he was a full-blown aquaphobe. "C'mon man, let's get outa' here. Can you climb?" He tugged on his jacket again to signal he should go first.

Tay was hesitant to let go of his rung to reach a higher one, but the fact that he was still half submerged pushed him to try. Slowly, he climbed past Greyson, dripping down onto him as he took the lead. It was only about a twenty-foot climb, but it seemed like two hundred for them both.

By the time they reached the hangar floor again, the fleet was long gone.

"Shit," Greyson sighed, staring at the blank space where their only hope used to be. He brushed the irritating water from his face and hair and turned back to Tay. "What do we do now?"

Tay looked like he was about to puke, holding himself to keep from shaking.

"This is our only chance. We have to follow them!"

Tay was in no mood to discuss it.

Greyson sloshed back toward the core, looking past it to the back of the hangar, searching for anything they could use, flicking his arms to dry them.

There looked to be a whole other section of the hangar, walled off and sealed by a few huge industrial doors. In front of that was a smaller bark ship, under repair, with scaffolding attached, and a chunk of its bark missing, metal bones exposed to the air. And next to that was an even smaller bark ship, just barely larger than a Wellington school bus.

"C'mon." Greyson started for it.

"I'm so wet," Tay choked like he was crying, but he wasn't. Just extremely uncomfortable, weighed down by his freezing clothes. "My shoes," he whined, starting to act like himself again. "Completely ruined."

Greyson let him vent, even though he sounded like a wounded cow.

As they approached, they saw a blue logo on the side of the ship that read: *O'Nasi Corp*. And a greasy man slid out from underneath it.

"Should we ask him, or?" Greyson slowed down to speak softly to Tay as the man turned his back to search for his next tool.

"Let's just take it. He's not looking." Tay nudged Greyson with his shoulder.

"Don't you think we're already in enough trouble as it is?" Greyson stopped right outside the ship's open door.

"How much more trouble could we possibly get in? Just get on, ya pansy." Tay pushed him. "It's a company ship, no one'll even notice."

"Except the guy working on it," Greyson screamed in a whisper.

He pushed him again. "I didn't almost fucking drown for nothing."

Greyson threw up his hands in defeat and jumped the two steps onto the ship. It looked even smaller on the inside, with only the helm, some controls, and a few places to sit along the walls.

Greyson took the pilot's chair and started up the engines as fast as he knew how.

The man outside looked up from his tools at the sound of the engines and spun around to see his ship climb and speed off.

"Hey," he yelled after it. "Not again!" He threw his wrench to the ground.

"You know where you're going, right?" Tay braced himself behind the pilot's chair.

"Um, I was hoping we could follow those ships," said Greyson, speeding from the city's branches. "But of course I can't find them now." He scanned the skies. A few ships dotted the green horizon in every direction, like dust drifting on the breeze, but they all looked the same, so far away. He had no idea which ones to chase.

Just then, a door at the rear of the ship slid open.

Tay turned at the sound to see a meager man in a white lab coat, accompanied by a rather determined looking woman. "Uh-oh."

"What the *hell* are you doing?" She strutted straight for Greyson. "Turn this ship around!" She punched him right upside the head with something hard and heavy in her hand. Felt like a fucking bullet went through his right temple, knocking him clear out of his seat. As he fell, he yanked on the wheel and jerked the ship down, dropping it from the sky, nose first.

She wasn't expecting that, frantically leaning over the chair to switch on the autopilot and right the ship again.

But Greyson was too busy screaming on the floor to notice. He couldn't even open his eyes. But he was definitely crying. Very loudly.

"Settle down, lady!" Tay pulled her away from Greyson.

"Don't touch me!" She pushed him off, aiming whatever she'd hit Greyson with at Tay. It was a gun. A small black pistol she leveled at his nose.

"Whoa, *whoa, whoa*! We're guards!" Tay yelled.

"So that gives you the right to steal my ship?"

"Gah," Greyson moaned, squirming on the ground, heartbeat in his head. "I'm sorry," he tried to say, opening his eyes. But all he could see was a blur in the shape of a woman in a white coat standing over him.

"Ugh. Damn my conscience," she said, kneeling to make sure Greyson was okay, still keeping the gun on Tay.

Greyson rolled to look at her fully, vision clearing. Her hair flowed like a rich silt river after a rainstorm high up in Wellington's mountains, waving down into loops over her shoulders as she leaned in closer. Her cheeks flared red in frustration, standing out against fair skin. And her eyes . . . were just as bright and green as his.

"Are you okay?" She didn't sound too concerned.

But suddenly his pain was gone, numbed in the sudden surge of endorphins charging through his body. "You're a vertui," he uttered.

She looked oddly at him, just noticing his eyes, tilting her head to align their gaze. "You are too." She softened.

"So we're all chill?" Tay gestured to everyone. "We can put the gun away?"

"Not yet," she said, taking Greyson under the arm to help him stand.

Standing was a rush. He had to support himself against the control panel, holding his head as she released him and took a step back.

She lowered the gun a bit, but still bounced it back and forth between them. "Why did you take my ship? Which is super illegal, by the way."

"Nuh-uh," Tay wagged. "Guards can *commandeer* whatever they want in an emergency."

"Not if it involves endangering a citizen," she swung her aim back to his head. "And I'm still on board, if you haven't noticed."

"We're sorry. We didn't know," Greyson panted. "We needed to go with the fleet."

She looked back to him, keeping the gun on Tay. "Well, why did they leave without you?"

"Why you asking so many questions?" Tay squawked. "We don't need to answer these."

"Because if you're just irresponsible, then you're taking me back," she said to Tay. "But, if you have a good reason." She looked to Greyson. "Then I might as well go along with it." Her brow raised inquisitively, waiting for an answer.

"We missed them because we were never assigned a ship."

"Greyson!"

"Would you put your dick away please, Tay? We don't even know where we're going."

Tay grunted, leaning back and zipping up his metaphorical dick.

"We don't have a ship because we're new. And we need to follow them because the king might kill us if we don't." He pressed his hand against his head where she'd hit him, closing one eye from the sting.

"And why exactly would the king want you dead?"

"Because the fleet is headed for Stiqula. And we're the ones that let him out."

Her jaw loosened, eyes widening as her aim sunk to the floor. "Dear gods. That was *you*?"

"It was an accident," he said. But how the hell did she know already?

"You can explain on the way. Where are you headed?" she asked, hiding the gun under her jacket at last.

"The detention center."

"It's north." She pointed to her left.

"Thank you." Greyson spun back into his seat, turning the nose of the ship to the Dead Forest. "Hold on." He punched it. Only the very tips of the Dead Forest's trees could be seen over the curve of the world, faded in the atmosphere.

She moved to the side of his chair and pointed out the window. "It'll be the smallest tree, right here at the southwestern edge."

"Thanks." Greyson slid his eyes from the window to the lavender blouse beneath her coat, then quickly threw his eyes forward again. She was tall, probably almost as tall as him in those heels. And she was beautiful. But she dressed like she was too busy to care. "I'm Greyson by the way."

"Sam." She looked at him cautiously.

"Sorry again, Sam."

"It's alright. It's turning out to be a much more exciting day than I had planned. Just don't get us killed."

"Uh, and I'm Tay," he introduced himself, taking a step toward her to make sure she heard.

"Pleasure." She hardly looked at him.

Tay sank a little at her unwelcoming salutation, then turned to the so-far silent man to take out his frustration. He was skinny and pale, with short, black hair in contrast. "Who's this guy?" he asked, as if he couldn't speak for himself.

"My name is Jacob Cain. I am a biologist for the O'Nasi Corporation."

Tay was taken aback by the man's awkward, uninvited recital of his resume. "The what?"

"Where are you from?" Sam asked, like they were stupid for not knowing.

"Wellington," Greyson answered.

"Hm," she acknowledged. "That explains the accent."

"We have an accent?" he said delicately, trying to identify it in his voice.

"There's a little Biazlen in there, yes. The O'Nasi Corporation is one of the largest aeronautic and assorted technologies producers in the kingdom. You can't fly anything in Viæden without at least a part of it coming from our company."

"Our?" Greyson asked.

"My father is Nash O'Nasi," she said like it was no big deal.

"A'right then, what does an aeronautics company need with a biologist?" Tay asked, glaring at Jacob.

"That would be my personal department. A hand-selected group I've chosen from the smartest minds in the kingdom."

"Chosen to do what?" Tay prodded.

She glanced at him, and then to Greyson. "Why are you all wet?"

Tay waved his hands at the back of her head, obviously dodging his question.

Greyson looked down at himself, almost forgetting. "I—" he cleared his throat. "We fell."

"Those fuckin' water dungeons you got in there are *not* safe!" Tay screamed.

"Water dungeons?"

"The drainage wells in the hangar," Greyson clarified.

"Oh. You *fell* in one?" She nearly laughed. "What, you didn't see a giant hole in the ground?"

"The grate snapped." Tay crossed his arms.

"Yeah. Anyway." Greyson moved right along. "How much have you heard about Stiqula?"

"Not much. The king hasn't released anything yet. The only reason I know is because I'm friends with one of his secretaries."

"*Megan?*" Tay said abruptly.

Sam looked at him, startled. "Yes . . ."

"Tell her I said hi." He grinned.

"I'll be sure to," she said dully, returning to Greyson. "How did it happen?"

"We were sent to find a ship, stolen from the castle, headed right for the Guardian Tree. It was on a collision course, so I took the risk of firing before it had the chance to crash and disturb Stiqula."

"Looks like you were wrong," said Jacob.

*I know*, Greyson screamed in his head. "Thank you, yeah," he said. "I really think I made the right decision."

"Asshole," Tay added.

"Oh, *I'm* the asshole?" Jacob pointed to himself.

"Howbout, I put an asshole in your forehead?" Tay pointed his fingers like a gun at Jacob's face.

"A'right, enough," Sam stopped them. "It happened. It's over. Now we have to deal with it."

"You're taking this a lot better than everyone else," said Greyson.

"Yes, well. It was bound to happen sometime . . . Can I ask more specifically what happened? The devil's in the details." She was intensely interested in all this, borderline excited by the news.

"Um, okay." Greyson wasn't too sure what else to explain. Of course bringing up the fact that he'd been seeing visions was way off the table. "I saw the ship, figured out what it was trying to do, and told Tay to fire."

"Which then you did?" She finally took an interest in Tay.

"Yeah. After the general gave the okay."

"And what is your relation to each other?" She pointed to them both.

"Friends?" Tay answered.

"For how long?"

Greyson was starting to feel like a test subject, riddled with side effects and unrelated questions. "Since we were little. What does that have to do with it?"

"It has everything to do with it," she answered quickly. "Which general was it?"

"Brown," said Greyson. "He's the one that called the red bell on the detention center."

"He's there now?" A hint of fear bent her tone, and she looked to Jacob with determination.

He shook his head in response.

"What's going on?" Tay asked.

"It might have been a good thing you didn't get onboard with that fleet."

"What, you think Brown's a bad guy?" said Tay.

"No, that's impossible," Greyson assured.

"Maybe he just doesn't know it yet," said Sam.

The Viæden Detention Center was a strange little tree. Its trunk only reached a half-mile high before it split into three branches, which continued to grow vertically. And all of the smaller branches that sprang out from the main three stood straight up as well. As if it envied the height of the Dead Forest next to it, stretching its boughs up to disguise its young height. The highest branch stood in the middle, stretching two miles from its trunk. Its second branch grew very near the first, though not as high or thick. And its third was the shortest, only a mile and a half or so, opposite the second. All three branches housed Viæden's prisoners, but only the third housed its vaults, which were inaccessible from the rest of the prison, except by ship or hovercraft.

Knight at the helm, Brown's bark ship pulled up to the highest vault of the third branch, slowing to a hover.

"Be sure he follows you," Brown said from the doorway of the bridge. "And if he doesn't, don't come back." He turned away without a reply.

In the hall, the loading ramp was down, open to a ledge carved from the third branch. His ship wobbled in the wind-stream, but it was close enough to leap without great risk, even though a fall would have meant a two-mile plunge to the forest below. Brown jumped down to the ledge, and planted his back against the trunk. Not too bad for a sixty-eight-year-old.

Knight pulled away as he watched, jetting across the sky in his small bark ship. From this height Brown could see Kabdrey, far away, a lighter patch of green, encircled by the darker forest. A steady plume of smoke rose from the city's center. And a crooked stick ship rose up beside it. The *Aliqula*.

Brown deflated, exhaling all his air. Overcome by a strange sort of acceptance.

He'd lost. And he knew it. Watching his own death approach. He had hoped to escape this alive . . .

What a cruel thing hope could be sometimes.

Stiqula's ship was not diverting. Not following after Knight as Brown had intended. He knew his sword was here. And he was coming for it.

Brown looked left, to the Dead Forest, towering above him: prickled trees, eight miles high, green only at their tapered peaks. They were dark and grey like Stiqula's flesh, huddled close to one another. The only patch of blight in all the realm. They were so deformed and barren it was hard to tell what kind of tree they ever used to be.

He could not let their fate befall the kingdom twice.

His end was inescapable now. But there was still a chance to save the kingdom.

The ledge he stood on wrapped the circumference of the vertical branch, a short distance at this height. The entrance was not far, a circular door, the thickness of a vault's. Within was a round room, thirty feet across, with walls of steel, completely bare but for some glowing tube contraption in its center, and a man that stood before it.

"Luteus," Brown called.

The man, in his mid fifties, wore a uniform much like Brown's, but a dark green. "General." He turned to greet him. "Why so urgent?"

"Stiqula is coming."

He choked on his breath. "Coming . . . back?"

"Coming here, now."

"W—why!?"

"Because of this." Brown lifted the blade.

The colonel swallowed in its presence. He was commander of this detention center. And he knew it meant the blade was his responsibility now.

"Is everything in order?"

"The vault is prepped. And my men are waiting below."

"You'd better call for them now. He's just outside," Brown said to him, fearless, and tired.

But Luteus had enough fear for both of them, not expecting this to go so wrong so quickly. "He—?" The colonel pulled his gold officer's badge up to his mouth. "Get up here, now!" he ordered his men.

"This is it?" Brown looked to the blue tube, large enough for a man to fit in. At first glance it looked like glass, but standing closer to it now, he saw that it was some amorphous fluid, held in place by powerful magnets on the roof and floor.

"The ultima-vault." Luteus swallowed. "Once something passes through its field, it's never coming out. Unless by my hand alone." He nervously wiggled his fingers in front of him.

"Good. How does it work?"

"Just insert the blade, and be sure not to touch the field."

Brown slid the sword into the translucent, blue solution, and it instantly reacted, sparking tiny streaks of lightning all throughout the tube. It felt thick, like cutting through a fatty steak. As half the blade became submerged, the rest was pulled inside automatically. Brown released it, and it floated to the core, blade frozen upright.

A 3D replica appeared on a screen in front of the colonel, and the gelatin began to solidify into crystal where it met the air, slowly deepening toward the blade.

"Do you think we can stop him this time?" Luteus asked carefully.

Brown didn't answer. He didn't have one. This monster was different than the one he'd faced before. Stronger. More aggressive. And far more unpredictable.

"General?"

"A battlegroup from Darakin is on its way. I plan to hold out until they arrive. He is alone. A single ship, with no weapons. He'll be no match for them. And by the Goddess' grace, we'll take him down." That fleet was the only hope he had left. But they were still at least fifty minutes out. His only chance to save the kingdom was to slow Stiqula until they arrived.

*Had he truly done all that he could?* . . . Did he even have a choice at all? If the world was ruled by fate, how much of his own life did he decide? If played out a million times, would he have listened to Greyson and fired every time? . . . Because some god willed it so? If that's true, then what meaning did life really hold? Why even create an illusion of choice at all . . . if every move we make amounts to nothing in the end?

Then Luteus asked, "How was he freed?"

Brown turned to him, studying the concern in his colonel's expression. More than just colleagues, they were friends, and had been for more than a decade. He deserved the truth.

But before Brown could speak, Luteus' eyes were stolen from him, and his concern regressed to fear.

Brown turned. There, in the doorway, was Stiqula, calm as stone, threatening as a thundercloud. And Brown looked upon the fallen angel like a long-awaited fate. It was a strange thing to look at him. Same height and imposing stance as he had had before, just over six feet. Shoulders broad, and muscles tight. But his skin had died, turned grey as ash. Encased in armor that made this once holy thing look cursed.

"It can't be," Luteus gasped.

"I'm sorry to disappoint," the monster spoke as he entered. His voice was still remarkably human. Again, almost identical to Brown's memory, unmistakably magnificent as it had ever been, though now with a deeper tone of apathy. "I know you've worked so hard to keep it from me. But I must have it."

"I can't let you," the colonel whispered.

"It's not up to you." Stiqula's calm was eaten by his rage. "I want. My. *Blade!*" He lunged for Luteus, bashing Brown out of the way with his left arm, hard enough to break bone. The general was flung across the room as Stiqula latched onto Luteus' face, digging his thumb deep into his eye and smashing his head against the crystal vault. Screaming, his claws sank into the colonel's skull and Luteus' body was ignited in a shimmering darkness, that chewed through the vault. As the colonel's body turned to vapor, the tube exploded, sloshing to the floor in liquid form.

The slush washed up against Brown as he pulled himself up against the wall, and watched Stiqula claim his prize.

He grasped hold of the ancient hilt, and snapped it free of the few blue shards that remained, then turned to Brown, complete. "Finally," he said as the vault door slammed shut. But as the lights turned red and sirens cried, Stiqula doubled over. He clutched his head in a brief bout of agony, as if a sudden lightning storm played through his mind.

At first Brown thought the alarm was too loud for him, or maybe he was infuriated to come all this way just to be trapped again. But then his fit ended, too quickly to be either. Stiqula regained himself and looked to Brown with new eyes. Still black and terrible, but with a wiser gaze, as if he only just remembered the regal being he once was.

"You'll never leave here now," Brown threatened, empty as it was. His left arm was certainly broken, maybe a few ribs too. He wasn't fighting anyone. He wasn't going anywhere, lying in a heap against the wall.

"I remember you," Stiqula said between alarms. "Only a boy then." Stiqula's face changed, anguish disappearing. He looked almost pleased, though nowhere near a grin. But even a blank expression looked elated on the body he had now. "You know this blade well." He stepped forward. "And you know this vault cannot hold me. For this blade has another form, beyond this one." He wrapped his chain carefully around his hilt and fist, and drew the alien metal to Brown's neck. "The lerité." The siren cried. "Though mine was cursed long ago."

Stiqula's face flashed anguish again as he activated his curséd lerité. The air around the sword grew darker, heavier, collapsing inward on the blade and striking it with a shrill metallic clang, igniting it in darkness, just like Luteus had. But instead of disintegrating, the blade remained, throwing off a molten heat as the vault's light dimmed to black.

# 10

# V.D.C

Stiqula stepped from the ultima-vault, black against the morning sky. A siren echoed through the branches. But it was no concern to him. He was complete.

His dormant blade glistened in the sun, obsidian, forged of otherworldly metals and the bones of his progenitors. Aliqula's prayer chain dangled from its hilt. And he remembered all. Nævah and the ways of angels. His youth, and his journey across a sea of stars. He knew everything that had happened to him on this wretched ball where life began. He knew everything. Except her. She was still a shadow. An artificial blankness, extracted from his memory, and all that remained in its wake was an emotion, strong as love.

He grew tired of these games. But was it Light, or Dark that played him?

He looked up from his weapon, to an adjacent branch, largest of the three, nearly six hundred feet away. Something was still out there. Calling to his heart, much fainter than his relics had, yet undeniably clear. What could it have been? All of his relics had been found. Yet something dwelling in this place was still tied to him, woven into Refsiel's plot.

"Freeze! Don't move!" a guard shouted, sprinting for him along the ledge, rifle drawn.

*When will these people learn to shoot first?*

Stiqula activated his blade, and the curséd lerité materialized, haloing his sword in a blurred cloud of ionized air, which collapsed into a single rod of darkness with a clap. Stiqula lunged and sliced the man clear in half, right through the gut, lodging his sword in the branch as it exited his body. His torso slumped and fell away from the tree, revealing more guards behind it, rounding the curve of the tower. But as they drew to fire, they were fired upon by an even larger gun, reducing them and the bark around them to plasma in an explosion of red light. Stiqula traced the shot back to the tallest tower. Two anti-aircraft cannons had come online, a few hundred feet above him, discharging their shells in pulsing beams to either side of him. He wouldn't be able to withstand a single one of those strikes. And as they converged on his location, he took a leap of faith that Refsiel's gift of the wind could do more than take down his enemies, but carry him as well. He flew into the sky, twisting to avoid the deadly fire, and braced himself as he approached the highest tower. He slammed into the tree with too much force to catch himself, tumbling down the valleys of its bark until his claws latched hold of something.

His head was bleeding, pumping dark blood from a gash above his left eye. But at least he was safe from those cannons, directly below them, out of reach. Thirty feet below him was another ledge, where three guards stood, looking across to the vault branch as it was bombarded by cannonfire.

"Where'd he go!?"

He'd leapt so fast they hadn't seen him.

Stiqula reversed the blade in his hand and released the tree, falling, blade-first, straight into the back of the guard standing between the other two, replacing his spine with the plasma of his sword. Then, in two swift strokes, Stiqula slashed through the others before they could react. But as soon as they fell, a fourth guard came running out from an entranceway directly behind Stiqula. Unfortunately for him, his only weapon was a captain's sword. He struck Stiqula in the back with all his strength, which only amounted to a slight shift in Stiqula's weight. Such a pitiful swing. Stiqula almost smiled out of pity.

As the guard recovered from the tumultuous vibrations resonating down his sword, Stiqula dropped his blade into the wood. As he released it, its leretic plasma disappeared at once. Then he spun in a full circle, grabbing the man's arms and swinging him to the floor, snapping his wrists as he stole his own blade from him and drove it straight down through his heart. Still holding the blade, Stiqula leaned in close as the guard took his final gasps.

"Should have had a gun," he said, activating the man's sword with the same black light that clung to his own. But the feeble steel of men could not withstand the heat of his cursed plasma, and melted into nothing as it burned a sizzling hole in the guard's chest.

Stiqula stood and retrieved his ancient blade, turning to face the tunnel to the tree's interior.

An automatic door granted him access to a security room, with only a small control panel and another, larger metal door in front of him. The first door slammed shut behind him as he entered, and the room's lights dimmed to red.

"Foreign body detected," a computer voice said. "Access denied."

Stiqula sneered at the machine, bashing it with the blunt side of his weapon, then activated his lerité and stabbed it into the metal door. The blade sliced through its steel with ease, leaving a trail of molten goo behind as he cut a circle large enough to enter.

The cut-out slammed to a wooden floor on the opposite side, leaving a trail of steam behind. And as Stiqula stepped through, he found a massive chamber beyond. The entire core of the tree had been hollowed, creating a misshapen panopticon. A crooked spiral of catwalks, like flattened roots, wound their way above and below him, over thirty stories in all. And along its walls were hundreds of cells, each glowing silver-blue with forcefield walls. The shield-walls averaged twenty a floor, and were transparent, revealing two, three, sometimes four prisoners held behind each one.

"This is a prison," he said aloud. "Interesting."

The guards were ready for him, collecting on the catwalks in their riot gear: all black with silver bracers, pads, and helmets. One story up, across the voided core, five men took aim. Their glowing visors gave them stats on what they saw, distance to target, and where was easiest to land a blow.

Without fear or hesitation, Stiqula aimed the tip of his blade at them.

And the guards opened fire, sending five amber streams of light at the intruder. But each one was refracted, bending from their path, spiraling into his blade, absorbed like a black hole.

Once they realized their non-effect, they held, lowering their guns, dumbfounded. Unharmed, Stiqula leapt for them, up and across the forty-foot void, slicing two of them clear in half as he landed on their catwalk. He brought the blade up over his head and cut down the single guard to his left, then spun the blade around again to aim it for the last two on his right. The sword was so fast and colorless that it could only be seen in the brief moments it was still between blows. But they could certainly feel it as it drove through them, skewering them both against the wall, where the catwalk turned to cross the hollow core.

Two more guards, one wielding a riot shield, the other firing from behind, marched down the catwalk to him. Stiqula pulled his sword from the wall, and held the hilt level with his head, blade down the side of his body. He turned sideways to be as thin as possible, using it as a shield of his own to advance up the slightly inclined catwalk. But Stiqula only managed to take one step toward them before the riot shield lost his nerve and stopped, taking a step back, bumping into the gunner behind him. Stiqula was nearly to him, and, unable to run, the man swept his shield at the monster in an attempt to bash him from the narrow path. But instead, Stiqula sliced right through the polymer shield, and the guard's hand behind it. He screamed from the loss of an entire limb, and Stiqula palmed the guard's open mouth to shut him up and cast him from the path.

The gunner turned to run back up the catwalk, to some sort of control room: a bulging lens of glass in the wall of the hollow, with doors on either side. Stiqula twitched his left hand, and a focused gale struck the guard's legs, sweeping them out from under him. It was just about all the power left that he could muster. But it was enough to trip the guard, slamming his head on the catwalk and scrambling to latch onto anything as his body slipped and pulled him over the edge.

Stiqula smirked at the comedy of the guard's attempt to save himself. Then he realized his grin, and swallowed it. It was strange to feel such joy. Especially since it was death that caused it. Which made it seem unnatural. . . Hollow.

The power Refsiel had given him was exhilarating. After an eternity of immobility and powerlessness . . . it felt good to flex his skill. To lay his mark upon the world again. But this power was not his. It was Darkness' . . . and could not be trusted. He had to keep it in check. He could not let it consume him. He must take no joy in death, or else become the monster Refsiel clearly wished him to be. Refsiel could not be trusted, for the reason he bestowed Stiqula with this strength was still unknown. Stiqula could not let himself forget he did not fight for Him, he did not fight for joy, he fought to find her.

As he thought, seven more guards emerged from the control room to surround him, hugging the pathways that ran the circumference of the core, another level above him. Three fanned out on each side of him, and the last stood between him and the control room, taking aim with a colossal rocket launcher, able to fire three shells at once.

*That* was not good. While his lerité could save him from laserfire in one direction, surrounded, it was useless. And he stood *no* chance against the firepower that monstrosity of a launcher could unleash. He turned to plunge into the void, but as he did, his wrist was caught, latched on to by an iron tether. The sudden jerk of his arm, and squeeze of his tendons, freed his sword from his grasp, and sent it spinning to the air.

Five more tethers fired from the guards that surrounded him, latching onto him and wrapping around his arms, legs, and neck. Then they tightened and electrified, stringing him up over the void, stunned and immobile, legs tied together, left arm pinned against his side.

His body screamed, staring down the barrel of a rocket. But, surging with electricity, his muscles seized, and he could not open his mouth to release his cries. Instead the building pressure was so great one of his vocal cords ripped right from his throat, and darkened blood sprayed from his closed teeth.

"What are you waiting for!?" A guard screamed to the rocketeer. "Do it!"

The cold-hearted bastard wanted to watch Stiqula suffer, unable to writhe, unable to release. An exemplar of all men. Believing himself righteous when in truth he reveled in the cruelty. *You vile creatures*, his scrambled mind screamed. *Claiming your souls as light, denying the truth of what you are, violent and savage, far more interested in darkness than the light! So ignorant and proud! Well you may* **have** *your darkness then!*

Stiqula fought the current, uncurling the fingers of his right hand, and letting them snap shut around the tether bound to his wrist. His lerité instantly appeared upon the iron, shining black and melting through it, snapping the cord. In the sudden release of tension, the thick metal cord whipped back into another guard's face, cracking his visor. The guard fell and dropped his tether gun, setting Stiqula free of a second restraint. The last guard to Stiqula's right now could not hold his weight against the pull of the three guards opposite him, and his tether-gun ripped from his hands.

Stiqula swung down to the opposite side of the hollow, just as the rocketeer fired and its glowing shell blurred past. Stiqula slammed into the wall below the three guards struggling to hold him, just as the rocket exploded against the wall next to him sending a plume of smoke and fire rolling up the rough interior.

The fire sprinklers activated, showering the entire chamber. And as the rocketeer took aim again, Stiqula rooted himself in the wall, jerking on the tethers, tearing all three guards from their catwalk, and into the fire of the second rocket.

Stiqula plunged with what remained of the guards' bodies, past jutting roots and bridged paths, on his way to the chamber's floor, fifteen stories down. Ripping free of his restraints, he used his pain as power, summoning the rage that swirled within him, casting it out of his body in a blast of air. A hemisphere of Eir's power fired down against the chamber's floor to cushion his fall. But as he struck, hard and heavy, the glass floor shattered all at once, and he dropped down another story to his final resting place in a hail of glass, rain, and charred bodies.

Greyson pushed the tiny ship as fast as it could go, which was only about six hundred thirty miles an hour. Any faster than that and he was afraid the engines would explode. He could hear them moaning the whole way. A forty-five minute journey north from the capital, across nothing but green plains, patches of gold farmland occasionally swathed throughout.

In the distance, the Dead Forest grew, higher and higher as they approached. Like pillars of the sky. Its trees were the tallest and oldest in the world. At least two miles taller than the Great Ceptris Forest. And very different in appearance. Something resembling the way Darakin looked, but its trunks were all so much thicker, and its branches so much shorter. Barren of any green at all, but for their very tips, so high above the world they grazed the edges of the atmosphere. So high they were fueled by starlight in place of the sun . . . Their bark though. It looked like their only source of nutrients *was* starlight, dead and grey. They'd been standing for thousands of years—*hundreds* of thousands, maybe. Greyson didn't know. Already miles tall two thousand years ago, when the green-eyed boy in his mom's story founded Animallia deep within them. Disturbing to think such massive, enchanted things could be destroyed. Let alone by one being . . . one monster. The same creature Greyson was responsible for unleashing onto the world again.

The small ceptris tree that made up the detention center was straight ahead, just six miles away, dwarfed by the dead trees around it. And looming with an unsettling aura. He could see the *Ion*, *Chordata*, and Ellis and Lawson's ship, *Centripetal*, had already arrived. The *Ion*, hovered near the forward-most branch, docked with the VDC. It was close to six hundred feet long, average for a military-grade bark. The furthest ship from them was the *Chordata*, long and thin, seven, maybe even eight hundred feet. It hovered on the far side of the tree. And the last, in the middle, was the *Centripetal*, the same length as the *Ion*, but distinguishable by its branching engines. Its body separated into three sections, each tipped with the yellow glow of engine fire. It was hovering just next to the tree as well. Just hovering. Nothing else. None of them were firing, or fighting, or . . . in *any* sort of urgency at all. Which should have been a relief, but . . . no matter what his eyes saw, Greyson's heart couldn't shake the feeling that something was wrong. And that feeling worsened with every quiet second that ticked by outside.

There was something else out there. Unseen. Waiting.

"Don't get me wrong," Tay spoke for everyone, "but I thought there'd be a little more action by the time we got here."

"Don't be so sure there's not." Greyson rubbed his chest.

"I feel it too," said Sam.

Greyson looked up to her in surprise. The corner of his mouth twitched, hinting at a smile before he looked back to the window.

"I don't feel anything." Tay crossed his arms.

Greyson took the ship in closer, shifting his vision to the gruesome bark of the Dead Forest again. Being such a legendary city, Greyson had always wanted to see Animallia, in all its glory. Though he never thought it would be like this. "So this is Animallia?"

Sam looked up, shifting her perspective back to take in all the forest they could see. "What's left of it."

"I never knew it was destroyed."

"Really?" Sam looked at him. "Is Wellington *that* isolated?"

"No, I knew," said Tay.

"Of course you did," said Greyson, less sarcastic, and more disappointed this was just one more thing to add to the list of horrible things his mom never told him about. "How did Stiqula do that to the trees?"

"Fire, mostly." Sam's gaze returned to the glass. "Because the trees are so large and far apart, there was plenty of surface area to burn, and oxygen to fuel it. But the trees are also so wide and dense, the damage never got very deep. They're still alive a few feet beneath the surface. So they stay standing. Very eerily. There's one tree inside that's actually still burning."

"Why don't you just put it out?" Tay asked.

"The king wanted to leave it," Sam explained. "An eternal flame, for everyone that died there."

*Wow*, Greyson thought. That was actually quite a beautiful way to honor them all. He'd seen how the king got when he'd mentioned his family, and that they'd died there. Were murdered there. Greyson couldn't even imagine how he'd feel, what he'd do, if that had happened to his own family.

"So what's our plan, here? We gunna dock with Ellis and Lawson er what?" Tay asked.

"That's what I was thinking," Greyson nodded. He'd been heading straight for the *Centripetal*. Nearly there. That's when he noticed another ship he didn't recognize. It was docked just on the other side of the tree, at the junction of the detention center's three main branches. It was a bit smaller than the rest, but still obviously military. Maybe it belonged to the prison? Or came from a nearby precinct to help? Greyson was about to circle to check it out when he noticed out of the corner of his eye, Sam turned to look at him.

He could feel her eyes on him like two curious hands.

*Was she checking him out?* Just in case, he bit down and flexed his jaw, wizening his gaze, trying to look as heroic as possible.

"What's that?" she said.

He looked to her again as she pointed out the window, somewhere across the controls. She'd been looking through him the whole time. Feeling stupid, he flew beneath the *Centripetal* and turned the ship to give her a better look at whatever it was she saw outside.

They were only about a mile off the ground, the earth was clear below them, a grass forest as far as they could see. But, about fifteen miles east of the tree, the green of the forest changed color, lightening to more of a grey, artificial green, with a canopy of clovers and purple flowers, sprawled out like a city. A thin column of grey smoke rose from its center. And almost a perfect circle was cut from the green, four hundred feet across.

"Is that Kabdrey?" Sam gasped.

"They did say he attacked a city," said Tay.

"But there are no craters, no fires . . . The patterns in the earth . . . I've never seen this before. It's as if it's all been . . . *blown* away. How did he do this?"

"I don't know," Greyson said in just as much shock.

She reached across him to the control panel. "Let me get a picture."

He pressed himself as far back in his chair as he could, trying desperately not to accidentally touch her and seem like a creep.

"There." She stepped back again.

A muffled boom came from somewhere outside the ship.

That sure didn't sound like a picture snap.

"What was that?" she sputtered.

Jacob and Tay crowded to the front of the ship. Everyone leaned as far as they could over the control panel, scanning the ground for any sign of an explosion, listening intently for another.

Stiqula's body was a wreck: cut, electrified, shot up, strained, and splattered. His breath was short and shallow. Everything hurt. Even though his power had saved him, it was just barely. His bones were damn near unbreakable, but such strong and heavy things wreaked havoc on his muscles, bouncing around inside of them like iron blades in spongy sheaths. He no longer had the strength to breathe deeply or gasp, even though his body needed it. His bones were too much of a burden for his lungs . . . At least lying on his stomach they were.

He staggered to his hands and knees, cool water running over his neck, and down beneath the armor on his back. Refreshing . . . mostly. The siren sounded far off now. He would have at least a little time before the guards could find him. He spotted his sword, not far, fallen down here with him, to the bottom of this pit. He tried to reach for it and stand at the same time, but couldn't manage those two things at once. He grabbed hold of its hilt and stumbled back against a control panel.

The rain drizzled along his face as he looked up to it, opening his mouth to soothe his ailing throat, and clean the dark blood from his chin. The water collected in the gutters of his eyes, like tears, as he closed them and imagined they were real. It gave him solace . . . just the thought that he could feel . . . an emotion most found undesirable.

If only they knew the torture life could be without it.

He opened his eyes again, to be certain no guards were near, descending to find him. There were none, as of yet. But they would be here soon. He sighed one final breath as his body neared as close to recovered as he could allow. Which was not as much as he would have liked . . . Perhaps Refsiel had not made him as powerful as he had thought. Darkness' power, like everything in this world, had its limits . . . and so did this rotten body.

How long had it been? How old was he now? The last age he remembered being was eighty-four . . . And he felt far older than that now . . . But had he even aged trapped in that tree? Or was this just Oyopa's curse that did this to him? There was no way to know. But he knew that old general, and men could only live a tenth the lives that angels could. So it could not have been so long.

This room had a smaller circumference than the cell block above him. A choke point in the tree, left for lateral stability. It was a small control room, with a metal door at one end, and a shielded door at the other. Wiping his hand over the glass floor, he could see the blue glow of shield walls below. Another cell block lay beneath him, just like the first. As he made ripples in the thin layer of water, he heard the quiver of a breath come from behind him. He craned his neck and ducked down to see a guard curled up beneath the control panel. He tried to curl up even tighter when he saw Stiqula's face.

"Hello in there," Stiqula greeted, hoarse and tired. He reached for the man, who whimpered and screamed as Stiqula dragged him from hiding, plowing the debris along the floor. He only wore a navy jumper for a uniform. No riot gear. He was young and meek, yet wise enough to hide instead of throw his life away by attacking.

"Please don't kill me!" he squeaked.

"Oh, no. I think I'll keep you with me." Something to bargain with. Or at least another shield.

"No! No! *No!*" he screamed as Stiqula pulled him from hiding, took his right hand and crushed it, bones grinding together like jagged stones in a coin purse. Only a precaution to protect himself. The man cried out in torment as Stiqula took his other arm by the wrist and stood, dragging the man behind.

"Come now. You don't need two of those." Stiqula pulled the squirming guard toward the shield door, just as Stiqula was pulled toward it by his heart.

He lifted his blade to the shield, and as its tip neared the glowing field, he activated it, warping the flat surface of the shield, pulling it into his black blade until its generator-frame sparked and died.

A hall lay beyond, dead-ended at thirty feet, lined with smaller shield doors, six feet tall, three feet wide, twelve of them all together. And held behind each one was a man, in cells much smaller than the rest Stiqula had seen. Not much larger than the dimensions of their doors. This was a cell block of the highest security. Clearly home to only the most dangerous of Viæden's criminals.

He was drawn to the very end, to the last two cells, facing each other. A man came to his door as Stiqula approached. Old, but strong, with clear definition of his body beneath the grey jumper he wore. The only patch of hair he had grew on his face, a thick grey beard. And his eyes shined emerald in the light of his shield door.

"So these are the vertuém cells." Stiqula turned to face the opposite shield.

Its prisoner did not greet him at the door like the others. Instead he lingered in the shadows, huddled at the back corner of his tiny metal box.

"You," Stiqula spoke, having found his heart's connection.

The man turned to look, then stood and stepped to the front of his cage. He was a beast, shirtless and swollen, bald and dark. His skin was not fair like the rest of the kingdom's people, instead he was the color of the night sky at twilight's end. Almost too dark to see the tattoo woven between the muscles on his chest, a symbol Stiqula did not recognize, and one more, a sun on his right shoulder. His knuckles were scarred, ground to the bone, and over his heart there was another scar, as if he'd tried to dig the emotional organ from his body. But his face was untouched, wide, and heavy. And his eyes: dark, forest green, with black lines that formed the shapes of crosses on his irises, like darkness crawling from his pupils.

He was too large for his cell, unable to stand without curling his spine. And his heart . . . so powerful it bent ripples in life's fabric, pulling darkness in like gravity.

"You are different from the others," said Stiqula. "But I do not know you. You are no relic. And yet you are the reason I have come. Your darkest heart, calling out to mine. Refsiel, it seems, has bound our fates together."

The man said nothing, only staring.

"Do you speak, vertui?"

He nodded.

"What is your name?"

"Itxaro." His voice was deep and loud, with an accent foreign to this land.

"Do you understand what I have said, Itxaro?"

Again he nodded, slowly.

"Then you will be free."

"No! Not him! You can't free *him*!" The guard kicked his legs.

Stiqula looked down at him. "Are you worried what he'll do to you?" He wrenched him off the ground, hanging by his arm. "What your cage has done to him?"

Stiqula lifted him higher still, releasing his arm and catching him by the neck before he fell, pinning him against the wall between Itxaro's cage and the next.

"When a heart is locked away, it freezes, stunted as the world spins on. This is the very antithesis of life—of Light, what keeps you fools *alive*, safe from Refsiel's End. Chaos is the agent of rebirth—regeneration. Without chaos, there is no hope, and without hope, life dies. It is your reckless caging that has loosened the divide between His world and ours. It's no wonder Darkness has the strength to speak to me. Your disregard for life will bring it to its end!"

He threw the man back down the hall.

"He will be free. And if you wish to go on living, you will free them all." Stiqula slashed at the frame of Itxaro's door, and with a spark, his shield door dispelled.

Itxaro stepped from his cell, stretching his back. He stood six-foot-nine, a whole eight inches higher than Stiqula.

And just as he was free, the prison's rocketeer arrived through the metal door across the control room. He spotted his fellow guard trying to stand, and positioned himself between him and Stiqula, launcher locked on target.

Stiqula and Itxaro faced the threat with worry playing on both their faces. There was nowhere to run. And that guard hadn't come to talk. He came to pull the trigger. So he did.

The rocket lit the back of its launcher and flew forward in a trail of smoke down the shielded hall. There was only one chance to save their lives. And Stiqula raised his hand to take it. Eir's power slowed the rocket soft enough to keep it from detonating, reversing its trajectory and flinging it back at the guards. The rocket flipped past them as they watched, colliding with the control panel on the far wall with a fearsome burst. The men disappeared behind a cloud of booming flame, and the launcher slid from the explosion to Stiqula's feet.

Stiqula bent to pick it up in his left hand, and walked to the smoking control room to inspect the damage.

Itxaro trailed behind him.

Miraculously, its glass floor was not destroyed, only littered even more with rubble than before, but the control panels were a flaming, useless mess. "Now, how do we release them?"

Itxaro touched him on the shoulder, and pointed straight up, thirty stories, past a tangle of roots and raindrops to the ceiling of the chamber. It was a bare patch of wood, seemingly unremarkable. But as Stiqula watched, Itxaro smashed a glass panel on the wall with his elbow, and pulled the lever inside. The ceiling cracked and opened, like the petals of a flower, revealing a blue glow within. The glowing object descended from the ceiling like a chandelier, the shape and size of a human bug-zapper.

"The shield generator. Yes, of course." Stiqula looked down to the launcher in his hand. Three rockets still remained in their chambers, and he took aim to fire them all at once. The three hell-fire flares shot from the control room and spiraled around each other as they rose. One exploded on a catwalk, another caught by a root. But the last of them met its mark and impacted on the generator, blowing it to bits in blue flames and red sparks.

Then, floor by floor, Stiqula watched each cell lose power. Like darkness approaching.

A muffled boom came from somewhere outside the ship.

"What was that?" Sam sputtered.

Jacob and Tay crowded to the front of the tiny O'Nasi ship, everyone leaning forward as far as they could to the windshield, scanning the ground for any sign of an explosion.

Then from the sky fell a fiery ship, long and thin. It was *half* the *Chordata*! Cutting a black line through the sky, plummeting uncomfortably close to their little craft.

"Whoa!" Tay yelled.

Without a word, Greyson yanked back on the controls as it fell past, and followed its smoke trail up, nearly taking the ship into a backwards loop before the sparse leaves of the detention center came into view above them. And there, from its highest limbs, a barren branch detached from the tree and fell, stem first, unleashing a barrage of missiles onto the unsuspecting *Centripetal*, directly above them. The rockets tore through the feeble ship, shredding it to pieces, which rained down on them like metal meteors.

"No!" Greyson cried. *His friends were on that ship!*

But there was no time to mourn, all that fucking metal was about to crush them if he didn't get the hell out of the way. The *Centripetal* broke into halves, pumping out a black cloud of debris between them. Heart pounding, Greyson took the ship straight into it, their only hope of escape from the gigantic pieces falling on either side of them. The O'Nasi ship was pummeled with bits of wood and flaming steel, one large enough to fracture their window with a piercing *crack*. Their tiny ship trembled as they cleared the haze, just in time to see that barren branch level out above them. *It was a goddam ship!* He'd never seen anything like it. It looked just like a dead stick, floating right in front of them. A *stick* ship, suspended by magic. It was so thin and twisted, there was no room for engines. At least not as Greyson knew them.

"That's the *Aliqula*!" Sam screamed.

"The what?" Greyson yelled back, still trying to comprehend. The thing just *looked* evil, wreaked of it, bathing in the death-clouds of its victims.

"Stiqula!" she yelled again.

The *Ion* detached from the tree and fired on the stick ship in a red hail of lasers, striking it only a few times before the *Aliqula* shot into the distance at top speed. The *Ion* arced to follow. And the nameless fourth ship rose up from below.

"We'll get him now!" Greyson shouted, feeling a rush of confidence with two barks on his side and Stiqula on the run.

But no sooner did his confidence arise, was it completely decimated again.

The nameless ship opened fire on the *Ion's* belly, rockets exploding through the bark, plumed like flaming mushrooms from its top. Then *Ion* disappeared altogether, engulfed in flames.

Greyson stared in shock as Sam gasped, and the fireball fell from the sky.

"Oh fuck me," Tay uttered.

They never stood a chance. None of them. They were slaughtered. Without mercy. Without heart.

Shallow tears formed in Greyson's eyes as the back-stabbing ship took off after the *Aliqula*.

This was his fault too. These countless soldiers. Countless ashes. None of them would have died if he hadn't released that monster in the first place.

"Go after them!" Tay screamed, shaking the back of Greyson's chair and snapping him out of it.

Greyson wiped his face and fired that ship's engines at full.

# II

# THE ROCK

*Viadeis, Zaphiel 27, 1373.*

Stiqula read the alien letters, printed at the corner of a folded newspaper. The date.

His jaw bit down, sharpened teeth fitting tightly together.

"Fifty years," he spoke. Should he be relieved it was not longer? No. For look at what he had become. Far too hideous for just time to have changed him. An angel aged at half the speed of man, yet retained fair beauty well into their second century.

The paper slid from his hand to the floor as he looked to the sun through a glass ceiling. Light had done this to him. Changed him. Cursed him . . . So much so that when he and Aliqula meet again . . . she would not even recognize him. He was no longer the angel that she knew.

"And for that, my Lady, You will pay."

He looked from the sun to the blown out entrance of the building he was in. Two buildings in reality, built of desert stone, rising a few stories on either side of him. This room was just an atrium between them. With nothing but a guard kiosk in its center, now a smoldering pile of rubble.

"What were you doing here?" He turned to the guards next to him. Three of them: two male, one female, all in uniforms that matched the desert sands outside. They were on their knees, cut and dirtied from his explosive entrance, restrained behind their backs by his new men.

"We were just guarding it, that's all!" one of the guards whimpered.

"Guarding it? From whom?" Stiqula asked, still exhausted from his exertions in Kabdrey and the prison.

"Everyone."

He leaned down to the outspoken guard. "What have you taken from me?"

"Nothing! I swear! This place was shut down fifty years ago!"

Stiqula saw the truth in his weak eyes, standing again and looking to the back of the glass atrium, at a wall of rippled night outside. "Hold them." He walked to the glass.

Itxaro was waiting for him there, standing at the window, looking out onto a crater and . . . *the Rock* . . . the guards had called it. Though Stiqula knew it by a different name. The *deor anxelus*. It sat, two hundred feet from the building, rising from a murky pond that had formed at the bottom of its crater, five hundred feet deep. The stone measured thirteen hundred feet across, only slightly smaller than the crater it had made. The jagged ember of a star that'd lost its will to live. A piece of Refsiel's space, used to punish, to exile only those who had committed the most egregious crimes. There was no greater penalty. Not even death.

Stiqula activated a small terminal against the window, causing the glass to wobble and slide away, bringing a wave of dry air through the atrium as a thin, metal bridge extended to the *Rock*. Itxaro followed him across the bridge, into the *Rock's* shadow, trailed by a dozen of his men. It was instantly cold, out of the sun, growing colder with each furthering step. Ahead, the bridge ended at a crude hole in the *Rock's* surface, nearly indistinguishable from its obsidian face. And Stiqula stopped just before its black veil, men piling behind him.

"This place." He swallowed. "I hate this place . . . And it hates me just the same." He aimed his words for Itxaro, not taking his eyes from the blackness in front of him. As if staring at it was the only thing keeping it inanimate. "You feel it, don't you? The darkness here."

Itxaro said nothing, staring just as deeply.

Finally, Stiqula entered the frigid black. The desert heat could not penetrate these shadows. And an air of fear caused him to activate his cursèd lerité, before his heart stopped altogether. As if it could protect him from the traumas of his past.

The room began to form out of the shadows as his eyes adjusted. It was long, and pillared, carved rawly from the black stone, chipped and jagged.

"My blade," Stiqula spoke. "It hungers for your soul." He stopped and turned to Itxaro, holding the glowing rod up to his chest. "It craves the light within your heart."

"Dare iss no light in my heart," said Itxaro.

Stiqula inched it closer to his chest. "It is faint, yes. But there is life in you, and therefore, also *light*." Stiqula pointed with his sword into the shadows, down an adjacent passage. "Within this Rock there are two more weapons like this one. Their blades have long gone, but their chains remain. Find them, bring them to me, and their power shall be yours." Stiqula picked up two flashlights from an old work cart and handed them to Itxaro. "Take your men, and follow that dying light in your heart."

Itxaro moved at his direction, without a word, and the men behind him followed, emptying the room of all but Stiqula and the Darkness.

He closed his eyes, and breathed deep, chilling his lungs.

His blade deactivated as he calmed and exhaled.

He had to be brave. He could not let this fear defeat him. He had to know . . . the truth he most desired. Stiqula opened his eyes, and turned to a pillar at his side. In the faint light he saw many marks upon it. Scratches, deep as nails.

He traced his fingers down their ancient grooves with a shudder. "As You've commanded. I have my relics once again. And every memory but one." His voice was humbled, somber. He had nowhere else to turn but Darkness to remember what he sought. "I can see her. Remember every detail of her form. I can hear her voice as clear as my own, smell the sweetness of her skin . . . But I cannot feel her, anywhere. She has left my heart . . . My mind. And all I'm left with is a shadow of her love." Stiqula's sadness grew to rage at the thought of all he'd done culminating in the ghost of an emotion. "You promised I would remember everything, and I have not." He panted, terrified to threaten the Dark by name. "*Refsiel!* Where is Aliqula!?"

And like a static shock within his mind, the darkness cleared. He remembered all in that instant. One hundred glorious years, down to the day, bathed in the light of love. Such an explosion of emotion dropped him to his knees for want of breath. His splintered heart felt like it boiled, burning hot with a hundred years of life unleashed. But this string of happy memories came to a sudden end when the vision of his love became engulfed by flame. She lay immobile on a crystal alter, lain across his arms, ring of fire drawn around them.

He screamed, launching from his knees and falling down against his back. He screamed. Like the single shred of heart that remained within him had suddenly been torn by Refsiel's claws. He screamed. And writhed in agony. Then what was left of his vocal cords were split, and hemorrhaged in his throat. Yet on and on he cried, making no noise louder than a squeak of his tense lungs, gargled through his blood, and the thrashing of his body on the floor.

His heart was gone.

His love was gone.

Aliqula was dead.

And he could do nothing to save her. He could not even mourn her loss with tears. Only tarnish what they shared with hate and wrath.

*"She is with me,"* Refsiel's voice echoed in the dark.

Stiqula's body lay suddenly still, encumbered by despair.

*He* took her from him . . .

*He* had her.

*Refsiel.*

He truly was the King of Lies.

He truly was the devil.

Stiqula could feel the cords of his throat mending. What damage done by him, reversed by Refsiel, so that he may speak. Though all he longed to do was tear them infinitely ever more . . . To scream his heart's full anguish could only take so long.

Stiqula flew from the ground, to his feet in an instant, taking up his blade and activating it, aimed straight back at his heart. "Then I shall shed this bloody corpse and send my soul into the dark with her!"

But Darkness boomed, *"You will not be with her! For this realm is Mine, and I will not allow it."*

Stiqula's heart broke again.

*"You shall be joined when I see it fit,"* the Dark proclaimed. *"When I have wrung you dry of all I need."*

What spark of will Stiqula had now left him, and he dropped his sword to the ground.

For all the strength Darkness had given him, he still was just a pawn. A puppet in His ever-constant war against the Light.

What a fool he was to ever leave Her graces.

And now he could not return, even if She'd take him. He had to stay here in this darkness, until he knew her soul was safe.

"What would you have me do?"

*"Bring Me into life."* He spoke each word slow and clear.

Stiqula did not understand. "But. You are Death. Death cannot live."

There was no reply.

"How?"

*"Send souls to the dark, graceless angel. And Darkness shall cover the land once more, veiling all paths but one: To thy love. To My fate."*

Refsiel's voice echoed for a time, but His power was used up. And as the echoes faded, the room returned to light, desert heat creeping through the doorway.

Stiqula took his sword and turned immediately for the door, striding toward its light like a child coming home . . . But in his mind the Light was tainted still. Warped by the knowledge that it was She who trapped him. Stole all those years away from him . . . And if it was just to punish him—stop him from his actions fifty years ago . . . was She not also architect of his fate? Did She not write his destiny long before his birth? Did She not know that he would fall? . . . Did *She* take Aliqula from him?

As Stiqula stepped from his *Rock*, he gazed upon a world that was no longer light and shadows, but endless, swirling grey. A world where no question could be answered, and no answer could be known. He was lost without her . . . Aliqula. And freeing her from Refsiel's chains was all that mattered.

"Great, we lost him." Tay had already given up. "We should have never taken this piece a shit ship."

"We didn't have any other options, Tay." Greyson started to show his frustration behind the wheel of the O'Nasi ship. They'd been flying for almost a full hour now, and lost sight of that bark ship like forty minutes ago, shrunken into infinity. "Do you have any idea where he could be going?" he asked Sam.

"I'm not sure. Jacob, where are we?"

Jacob fiddled with a screen on the wall next to Tay. "We're just passing by

Cantidium now, headed southeast."

Sam searched the earth below for any distinguishing features. The natural green that painted the landscape dulled in front of them, fading to a sickly beige, gently sloping upward as it reached into the horizon. A two-trunked ceptris tree stood far off at the world's edge.

"The Canted Desert," she said. "I know where he's headed. This is where his Rock crashed down, fifty years ago."

An enormous black stone came into view as she spoke, half buried in a crater that was just barely big enough for it. The dead branches of a stick ship rested at its rim. Right next to the mysterious fourth bark ship.

"Whoa, what?" asked Tay. "*That's* Stiqula's Rock? I thought that was just some religious symbolism crap."

"No." Sam shook her head. "It's very real."

"We found him," Greyson said, not really relieved as the Rock crept closer.

Tay frantically searched the small room for the weapon controls. "Doesn't this ship have any guns?"

"This isn't a military ship," Sam said obviously.

"Well, what are we gunna do?" He threw his hands in the air.

"Call for backup," Greyson answered.

"With *what*?" Tay asked, very loudly.

"I've got it." Sam pulled an old blackwood flip-phone from her jacket pocket.

"What, are you calling the guards?" Tay mocked.

Greyson turned from the controls to watch her dial.

"No. Megan." She put the phone to her ear.

"Oh." Tay's eyes smiled at her. Then he leaned in to whisper to Greyson.

Greyson was expecting him to say something stupid about Megan. But he didn't. "Guess Stiqula really was trapped in that tree after all."

Greyson looked at him, just as seriously. They'd both been thinking the same thing for the past hour, played on repeat in their heads: the destruction of the battlegroup. The death of their friends, Ellis and Lawson. And an endless string of questions about the monster that had done it . . . But at least they could be certain he was, in fact, a monster. And he was, in fact, as dangerous as General Brown portrayed.

How the hell were they ever going to stop something like that?

"Megan!" She finally picked up. "It's Sam."

"You can tell her I say hi, if you want," Tay snuck in.

*There* it was. Greyson rolled his eyes.

But Sam ignored it. "I know you're at work, just listen. We've tracked Stiqula down. He's—"

Then, out of absolutely freaking nowhere the door behind Sam warped in with a flash-bang, like the room behind it and everything in it, including the engines, suddenly exploded with a sound so loud and shrill it almost killed them on its own. Greyson could feel the compression wave punch each of his organs as it passed through his body.

Sam, Tay, and Jacob were launched forward, piling onto him as the whole ship was rocked so hard it did a front flip, tossing everybody around like loose change in a loud, metal pocket. Greyson was the only one that managed to stay still, already seated. And by instinct alone, he spun to grab the wheel and pull it back as hard as he could, ship dropping from the sky. The rear engines were completely gone, but he could still feel some push from the ventral ones. They flipped again while he pulled, Tay and Sam screaming falsetto behind him, trying to keep their feet on the ground, gripping the back of his chair for dear life. On their third flip the engines caught, and the spinning slammed to a stop, dropping everyone to the floor again. But they were still aimed for the ground, and the *Aliqula* was rising to meet them, dead ahead.

"Holy *shit*!" Greyson screamed, weaving through the dead limbs of the stick ship, nearly clipping them all as it flew beneath the passing ship.

The dry earth was not far below, and getting a lot less far every second.

Greyson slammed back on the accelerator, hoping to reverse, but it was no use. They were dead in the air.

"We're fucked! We're fucked! We're gunna die!" Tay wailed.

Sam grabbed him by the shoulders. "Shut up!" She pushed him away from her, launching herself back as well. They fell into wall-mounted seats across from each other, which sensed their presence immediately, slamming safety bars down over their shoulders, and blasting them straight up through the roof. Immediately after, Greyson's chair did the same thing, strapping him in and blasting him off into the thrashing wind and blinding light of the desert sky.

Through squinted eyes, he could barely make out the smoking ship tumbling down to the ground. Jacob was still in there. A parachute deployed from his chair, jerking him upright, and all his organs squashed down onto his bladder at once. His head whipped back too, banging against the thin padding of the chair. That didn't feel too great.

The ground wasn't far below him, a sprawling beige, sprinkled in dark rocks and pale vegetation. And literally right before the ship crashed into it, Jacob's seat ejected, popping its bright yellow chute half a second later as the crash came to his ears.

It sounded like Sam was screaming Jacob's name. And someone else was screaming too, but he couldn't tell if it was Jacob or Tay. He'd never heard that scream before, so it was probably Jacob. But then again, he and Tay had never been this shit-out-of-luck before.

Everybody hit the ground at the same time, strung out along the path of their dead ship's descent. But the wind still dragged Greyson's chair along the ground for quite a ways before his chute got caught up on a weird, thorny tree-bush and finally stopped. He unstrapped himself just as Sam sprinted by him, toward Jacob and the crash.

"Are you okay?" he asked, which was kind of a stupid question since she was in a full-on sprint.

"Jacob!" she screamed as she neared him.

Greyson stood, a little dizzy, looking back to where she'd come from to find Tay, crawling from his chair. He moaned and collapsed to the sand. But Greyson could tell by the way he moved that he was just being dramatic. "You good?"

Tay gave him a shaky thumbs up.

Then Greyson turned to see what had Sam so scared. Jacob had hit the ground way harder than anyone else, landing right in one of those thorny plants. And as Greyson neared, he saw one of its spikes had snapped off in Jacob's shoulder. There was a lot of blood all over that white lab coat. The thing had to have been almost an inch thick.

"Gods, are you okay? Can you breathe, Jacob?" Sam unbelted him from his seat, lying on its side in the middle of the bush.

"I think I'm alright, Samantha." Jacob stared at his shoulder, hardly fazed at all by it. Like a friggen robot. If that'd happened to Greyson or Tay, it would have been the end of the world. But this guy . . . didn't seem to care at all. Greyson couldn't tell if it was badass or just plain disturbing.

"And you can move your arm?" she worried, pulling him to his feet.

"Not very well, but yes." He stood, wiggling and squeezing his left hand to make sure it still worked.

"You're just going to leave it in there?" Greyson asked.

"He'll bleed out if we remove it," said Sam, way more emotional about it than Jacob.

"Oh, dude." Tay came up behind them, covering his mouth at the gruesome sight. He pointed with his free hand, trying to say something, but dry heaved instead.

"Nice," Sam scowled.

Greyson looked to the blue sky. The *Aliqula* was just a speck in the distance. They'd missed Stiqula completely.

He took a breath, a little disappointed, but honestly relieved. "Let's see where we are." He looked to a small rampart of sand next to them, climbing it to find a blinding desert in every direction but one. Across an empty patch of rough terrain to the south was an enormous, black mass, cresting from the sand like a misshapen, onyx sunrise. In front of it stood a shattered building, riddled with men in black jumpsuits. Realizing what he was looking at, he dropped to the dirt for cover. Stiqula might have left, but he also left all his guys here for some reason.

Recovering from his gagging fit, Tay threw himself down next to Greyson, peering over the hill. "That's a lot a bad guys."

"Yeah, where the hell'd he get them all from?"

"The prison?" Tay wondered.

"*Shh!*" Sam snapped.

Tay whipped back around. "Don't *shsh* me! That was a perfectly reasonable guess." His eyes bulged when he saw what she was shushing him for.

A wasp had just buzzed in, landing on the grey plant that had stabbed Jacob, looking for its flower. It was striped, red and yellow, to match the desert glare. The size of a fucking barn owl.

"Ho, shit!" Tay drew his gun, faster than Greyson'd ever seen him do before.

"*No!*" Sam yelled.

Too late. He pulled the trigger, firing a beam of light into the thing's abdomen. It exploded in a shower of yellow guts, thorax and head parts plopping to the ground.

Sam was stunned, arms stretched out to the bug like it was her kid. "You idiot!" She unfroze with a temper.

Tay winced at her. "What? Pretty sure I just saved your life."

"It was a red hornet," Jacob explained. "When one of them is killed, it releases a hormone that agitates the others. Which you've just showered us in."

"Oh," Tay said without closing his mouth.

Sam looked to the smoke of their ship, a few hundred yards away, kicking off her heels and darting for it. Greyson wasn't about to stick around to find out why, leaping after her. Tay and Jacob trailed behind.

"Are we taking cover?" Greyson yelled.

"That won't stop them!"

The ship was a mangled wreck, ass-end missing, main cabin wide open to the air. Sam leapt aboard like a hurdle, diving into the smoke in search of something that could hopefully save their lives.

Greyson stopped himself against the hot and sandy bark of the ship, turning back to see Tay right behind him, Jacob straggling to catch up. And even further behind them both was a rising tidal wave. A fog of buzzing wings. The frenzied swarm of a thousand giant hornets.

"Sam!" Greyson screamed for her to hurry, pushing off the ship, and sprinting back to Jacob.

"Fuckyougoin'?" Tay wheezed as they passed in opposite directions.

Greyson drew his sword as he met Jacob. They were wide out in the open. And that horde was coming fast. They had nowhere to go! The hornets swept across the desert like a coming sandstorm. Each *one* of them probably able to eviscerate you with those serrated stingers.

Just then, Sam leapt from the smoke, cracking two blue flares in her hands as she hit the ground running, trailing a bright, blue fog behind her. "Greyson, no!" She saw he was about to take a swing, and threw one of her flares ahead to cloak them in its fog, just as the swarm engulfed them. The buzz of wings grew to a roar. Hundreds of them blew past in a red and yellow blur that dimmed the sun. But none of them attacked, each one diverting around them, away from whatever fumes Sam's flares emitted.

Greyson couldn't move, he barely even breathed, praying the blood-starved creatures would not find them in the fog. This fear. He knew this fear. A strange, primal sensation, praying the deadly animals he knew were all around him would not attack. His trembling heart was beating at exactly the same speed it was in his nightmare, just before that demon leapt from the black to bite him. Then, from the fog, a hornet dove at him, cracking against Greyson's head, so hard he flipped to his back. But the hornet was totally unfazed, jumping off the ground and returning to its flock as the sky lightened again.

The sound of wings faded. Replaced by the racket of gunfire and screams.

Sam turned to the building in front of the Rock, which was now overcome by the deadly yellow cloud. "They're killing them all," she said, more saddened than relieved.

Greyson stood again to see the convicts running in a frenzy, some firing their weapons to the sky, others falling from the weight of the insects clinging to their bodies. Most scrambled for the loading ramp of the bark ship—now clearly a stolen VDC ship—parked to the left of the building, and sealed themselves inside.

With no one else to kill or eat, the hornet cloud dispersed.

"Okay. I'm over this place," said Tay.

Sam turned to Greyson. "Are you okay?"

He turned to her, feeling the side of his head to make sure there wasn't any blood. "Yea—I. Yeah. Evened out that punch you gave me," he cracked. But her lack of amusement quickly told him this wasn't the time for jokes. He cleared his throat. "So how do we get out of here?"

"Pray that there's a working phone in there somewhere." Sam nodded to the building.

"Great," said Tay.

Itxaro's dark heart lured him through the unlit tunnels of the Rock. At first he ignored Stiqula's advice to follow his heart, not understanding what it meant. But after a full fifty minutes of wandering through hall after endless hall, all carved sharp and crudely from the glistening black stone, he soon found his mind and eyes were failing him. And it was then his heart reacted, tightening the closer he came to what treasure Stiqula spoke of, as if it was afraid. But even then it took time to find, only able to feel its proximity, and not which path to take.

Then, finally, at the dead-end of a hall, his heart flexed so tightly it could hardly beat.

But the men he led could not feel it like he could. And they'd had more than enough of his mindless wandering. "Another dead-end? You got no idea where you goin', do ya?"

Itxaro turned to the man behind him, taking a heavy step forward, towering over him.

He rocked his fist into the inmate's gut, stealing the wind from his lungs. The man gasped and doubled over, meeting Itxaro's knee to the face. He lurched back against a wall, where Itxaro caught him. His broken nose sprayed blood all over himself as Itxaro shook him like a dog, back and forth against the wall. The flashlight dropped from the man's thrashing hands, illuminating the other prisoners' terrified expressions from the floor. Itxaro punched him again and again, endlessly until his hand hit stone and he threw the lifeless body to the other side of the hall with a cracking slush.

The other men stared in silence. They'd seen many terrible things as criminals, done many terrible things, but none of them had ever seen something so sinister before. Itxaro attacked him like a wild beast, as if he reveled in the blood.

He flicked the slush from his scarred fists, then shined his light at the bloodstained wall. There was a fracture in the stone amongst the dripping red, no larger than a fist. And stepping toward it, he reached inside, seeing something within. A lever.

The dead hall sprang to life, showering them with steam before the wall lowered into the floor with a slam. And as the steam cleared, Itxaro gazed upon his treasures.

The weapons that had been calling out for him to find, mounted in this secret place. Two chains, one matching Stiqula's exactly, the other darker still, strung out, parallel to each other. The shimmering chains drew him nearer as his men's lights reflected off their bejeweled pattern and flickered onto his grinning face. He reached out and touched the rippling metal, warm beneath his fingers. He grabbed hold of them both and ripped them from the wall with a shudder.

Greyson's eyes darted all around in search of any straggling hornets as they approached the stone building, very cautiously. On the lookout for any leftover convicts too. But he didn't think he'd find very many. The desert had become a battlefield from one of his dad's war stories. Bodies in black and bloodied jumpers littered the dirt outside the three-story structure. Two structures, really. Big, tan cubes, connected in the middle by an atrium of glass, whose entrance had been shattered by . . . a grenade, it looked like.

"What was this place?" Greyson asked.

"A research facility," Sam answered. "Investigating Stiqula and the Rock for just a few months before the king shut it down."

"Why would he do that?"

"You know religion's illegal here, right?" she said. "He shut down or destroyed anything even remotely supernatural. This included."

"Oh, right." Greyson hadn't forgotten, not after Brown had screamed at him about it. He just figured something as tangible as this *Rock* wouldn't have been considered supernatural.

Yet, entering the blown-out building, he was starting to see why.

He couldn't take his eyes off of it, almost hypnotic. All he could see of the Rock was a narrow sliver of its surface through the alley of the atrium . . . so dark it looked like space itself had fallen to the earth. "And what is it, exactly?"

Sam flashed a confused glance at him. "Well, I don't know what the king's told you, but this is the meteorite Stiqula came here in, fifty years ago."

*Meteorite?* Greyson thought. He came from *space*?

The stars of his nightmare ignited in his mind again, echoing with a blaring siren, and a demon's hiss.

"He's, an alien?" his voice cracked.

"Sort of." Sam nodded. "But it might be more appropriate to call him an *angel*."

She did *not* just say that. Greyson felt sick. Light headed. Ripped from his body once again. Flung far out into the stars and darkness.

With no purpose but to kill, the demon leapt for him, a black and skeletal, *unholy* union of wings, claws, and teeth. Terror took Greyson again, hitting just as hard as that demon collided with him, crashing into the starry glass at his back.

Those silver fangs cut deep into his chest, biting down like they never meant to let go. And its claws latched onto Greyson's shoulders, digging just as deep. Greyson screamed with pain, fear, and adrenaline, taking hold of the demon's long head and flexing his strong wings to push off the glass.

But the demon had wings of its own, and taloned feet it dug into the floor, fighting to keep Greyson pinned against that window. Greyson had only gained an inch, but it was enough to pivot the demon's top-heavy lunge, and spin *it* into the glass instead. The monster struck the window, biting down even harder into Greyson's flesh.

He screamed again, moving his hands to the creature's rubbery neck, holding it back from taking another, deeper bite. Their strength was matched, neither budging. It had latched onto him like a parasite whose life depended on it. But *his* life depended on its death. Greyson swept his wings forward to pull the demon from the glass, then instantly swept them back to push against the air and slam its body down again. This time its claws slipped from his shoulders, cutting down his arms as the demon slid away from him. But its powerful jaws still refused to open. Instead the flesh within its mouth ripped free from Greyson's chest, heightening his pain tenfold as the air attacked his freshly-exposed sternum.

With his left hand, Greyson held the monster pinned, and with his right, he drew a long and crystal sword, which ignited at his touch, as bright as sunlight in that darkness.

"May the Goddess have no pity on thee, demon!" he cried as he drove the blade into the creature's heartless breast. And its fangs finally stretched wide again to give one final hiss.

Greyson breathed relief as the demon's wings fell, its whole body going limp upon his heavenly blade. All was quiet again but for the strobe of the alarm. A warning that still not all was right upon his space ship.

The glass behind the demon suddenly fractured in a crooked web. His blade had pierced it through the demon. With a sharp inhale, Greyson withdrew his sword and kicked off the glass, wings heaving down to help lift him as the window shattered, sucking the demon out into the stars.

But space's vacuous claws showed no prejudice toward evil, and pulled Greyson back upon a torrent of escaping air.

Greyson broke into a silent sweat, looking up through the atrium's glass roof as if he'd see the crystal ship that angel was on, and that demon falling from it toward the earth.

"I thought angels were . . . just stories," he said, without much confidence. Because if Stiqula really was an angel . . . then that meant there was a great and terrible chance the angel in his dream was real too.

Sam gave a reluctant chuckle. "Don't tell me you believe everything the king tells you."

He was afraid she'd say that.

He could feel it. Feel it hanging over him like a dangling chandelier, ready to crash down at any moment. That dream wasn't just a nightmare. It was a goddam *vision*. Some cataclysmic event linked to his destiny.

His Vertuém Destiny.

Even though he still didn't know exactly what that meant . . .

But if it really was a vision, was it of the future or the past? He had no idea how this worked! "At this point, I have no idea what I believe."

"Well. Call him what you will, angel or alien, he's certainly not human. And I believe he's from Nævah."

*Nævah* . . . Greyson knew it from his mom's stories. The white planet. Home of angels . . . But his dad said it was uninhabited. A gas dwarf. "Why do you say that?"

Sam looked at him for a moment, as if she didn't like him not agreeing with her. Or was she just contemplating whether or not she should tell him the whole story?

"My dad used to have a friend in the guard," she said finally. "He was here, the day Stiqula came. The first to crack this Rock open and step inside. And of his entire fireteam, he was the only one who came back out alive."

"Whoa," Greyson said quietly.

Sam reached up to touch her shoulder. "He said that Stiqula had two bloody stubs protruding from his shoulder blades. And the weapon he used to kill them all was made of light. Somehow turned black."

Greyson saw his angel's blade again, like crystal wrapped in starlight, flashing out in front of him and splashing the walls of his ship in their light before plunging deep into the writhing demon. He could almost feel the heat of it still on his skin.

And now Sam was saying that Stiqula had one of those things too? But black? How does *that* work?

"Which would lead me to believe that he is some form of winged humanoid," Sam continued. "Exiled from his homeworld for one horrific reason or another," she pronounced the words very clearly, like it was way over Greyson's head.

"There is also the possibility he did that to himself," Jacob added, still standing in the broken doorway. "Coming here to enslave humanity, and fulfill some angelic superiority complex."

"Right," Sam hardly agreed. "My point is, in an effort to disprove the supernatural, the king ignores substantiated proof by labeling it conspiracy and rumor when it's nothing of the sort." She moved to the remains of the kiosk in the center of the atrium, stepping over the bodies and rubble with bare feet.

The king's anger over Greyson's eyes made even more sense to him now. And Brown's interest in them as well. The king didn't like it, but there really was some truth to the legends. "Like Vertuém Destiny?" he asked.

Sam looked up from the broken kiosk, right into his eyes. "Yes."

Her eyes broke away again. "This radio's dead. I'm out of ideas."

"How are we gunna get outa here?" Tay asked.

Greyson's head was too all over the place to concentrate on a rescue plan, spinning with a million more questions. So he took a breath to ask one more.

But a noise outside made him bite his tongue.

Jacob, still standing just outside the shambled entrance, looked quickly to his left. "That ship's door is opening." He hurried inside.

Of course. The stolen VDC ship. Filled with convicts.

"Shit, really?" said Tay, pulling his guns out.

"Get down!" Greyson ran to join Sam, ducking behind the crumbled kiosk. Tay and Jacob following. "They don't know we're here yet."

"You sure? You want me to ask?" Tay said, starting to stand.

"Don't!" Sam yanked him back down. "We don't know how many there are, but they'll *all* hear you fire."

Tay rolled his eyes. "So what do we do!?"

Greyson looked to the Rock's extension bridge out back. "Sneak around to that ship."

"And what if there *are* a thousand guys still on it?" Tay asked.

"Then we're dead either way." Sam took off in a crouch to the bridge.

"Your girlfriend's gunna get us killed," Tay jabbed.

Greyson looked at him in loud embarrassment and pushed him after Sam.

It was a real different story out back. The building was perched on the very edge of the Rock's crater, as big and deep as a stadium. There was only a tiny path of land, barely six inches wide, between the stone wall of the building and the five-hundred-foot drop down to a muddy moat in the crater's bowl.

"I'm not sure about this, Samantha." Jacob hesitated, looking at the length of the building. A good sixty-foot scoot.

"You don't have a choice, Jacob." She gave him an encouraging push.

He slid a ways down the path and Sam hurried after, hugging the wall as close as her body would allow. Greyson put his friend before him and barely got a toe on the path after Tay before the cliff crumbled under Jacob's foot and he yelped, pulling back to regain his balance.

"Jacob, you're fine!" Greyson shouted under his breath, crouching to hide from the convicts he knew were about to enter the atrium.

"If you don't keep moving I'm *going* to shoot you," Tay explained very clearly.

Jacob worked up the courage to step over the break just in time for Greyson to slip behind the corner of the building, just catching the outline of two convicts in his peripheral before he did. And if he saw them, then they'd seen him too. But even though he was hyperventilating, Greyson did his best to keep his breaths to tiny gulps at most, terrified an inflated chest would push him off the wall and over the cliff.

Jacob was moving excruciatingly slow, inching along that wall like his life was *not* depending on it. And that's when Greyson noticed something. Movement. Where the connecting bridge met the Rock's rippled surface. *There were prisoners in there too!*

"Shit, Jacob, move!" He yelled under his breath, pushing on Tay, who fell into Sam, who sent Jacob flying the little ways left down the wall to solid ground, falling on his face as the Rock prisoners spotted them and opened fire.

Greyson ducked under a spray of red beams and exploding rock as he turned to jump the rest of the way, rounding the building, out of sight from the convicts on the bridge. Tay, Sam, and Jacob took off toward the nearby bark ship, Greyson drawing his sword and following after. But as Tay broke past the front corner of the building, an arm latched out and snatched him from the group, throwing him to his knees with a gun to his head.

"Oh, piss," he said, three convicts closing in around him.

Greyson, Sam, and Jacob froze as two of the convicts aimed their guns at them.

Sam returned the favor, drawing her gun in an instant, making it a stalemate. But Greyson could hear footsteps clattering up the metal bridge. The prisoners from the Rock would be there any moment to end this standoff. And they were *all* gunna die if someone didn't do *something* before they arrived.

Sam had done her part, drawing the other two convicts' complete attention. And Jacob was absolutely useless. Which meant it was all up to Greyson. But what could he do!? The prisoners were too far to hit with his sword!

Unless . . .

Greyson reared back with his blade and whipped it forward again, letting go of the sword completely. It flipped through the air like a tomahawk, piercing Tay's captor right in the heart. Immediately, the other two men swung their aim to Greyson, but before they could pull their triggers, Sam pulled hers, hitting both of them, one in the thigh, dropping him to his knees, the other in the shoulder, which laid him out on the dirt.

Greyson was hypnotized by the guy with his sword in his chest, still standing, just starting to tip back. His hair was long and matted. His face was rugged, scruffy. Middle aged. Someone's dad. And his eyes . . . were brown, and blank. Already dead.

Greyson didn't notice the guy on his knees raise his gun to him again. But Tay did, instantly tackling him to the ground and wrestling him for it.

Greyson's kill finally fell next to them. And Greyson focussed back on the footsteps echoing through the atrium. "Tay!" Greyson's body jerked forward, going for his friend and his sword. But he froze as soon as the first convict stepped from the atrium.

Sam fired at the man, and he dove back inside. But it wouldn't be for long.

Tay's wrestling match was taking forever, finally ending with him giving up on the gun and punching the guy's lights out instead, just as a mob of jailbirds filed out of the atrium, guns blazing.

Tay scrambled to his feet and joined the others, sprinting past exploding sands as fast as their legs could carry them, up the ramp of the bark ship, into cover.

Greyson turned right down the ship's main hall, to the bridge, and decked the lone convict standing there before readying the controls for takeoff.

Jacob turned left and looked down the hallway to see dozens of convicts with the same surprised look on their faces. And without even looking, he reached down to tap the controls next to him. A metal door slid from the wall, slamming shut just as the prisoners rushed for it, hammering at it with just their fists.

The ship lifted as Sam, Jacob, and Tay entered the bridge.

"Just so you know, this ship is full of really pissed-off prisoners," said Tay, taking the seat to Greyson's right.

"I was afraid of that," said Greyson, steering in the direction of the castle tree.

"Yes, let's just hope they don't have any guns back there. Or any other means of disabling the ship," said Sam.

"No! God, why?!" Tay cried, finally noticing his once-green shoes, now caked with dirt and sand. "They're dead!" He threw the now worthless hightops against the wall and released a plume of sand.

"Good. Maybe now you'll get some boots like a real guard," Greyson said.

"At least you *had* shoes," said Sam, lifting her dirty foot to inspect the damage.

"Oh, are you okay?" Greyson asked, just remembering she'd been barefoot this whole time.

Sam lifted her other foot and dusted the bottom of it with her hand. "I'm fine," she said simply.

Jacob lingered behind them, just now inspecting his wound for the first time too.

"Oh, Jacob," Sam said, taking a step toward him, concerned. "Has it stopped bleeding?"

He pulled his head back to take a look at the giant spike in his shoulder, red seeping down his white lab coat. "Not yet. Not with all this excitement."

"Right," she said, pulling out a wad of clean, but wrinkled, tissue from her coat pocket to dab at the dripping spike. "Sorry, I don't have anything else. You're sure you have no problems breathing?"

"I'm alright, Samantha. We'll get it looked at once we're home."

"Alright, but will you at least sit down?" She placed him in a chair against the back wall, stepping back to look him over one more time with guilty eyes.

"I'm sorry to put you both through this," Greyson said, glancing from the windshield to her. "I know it's not every day you see someone killed, or—have to run for your life." He was doing a bad job masking how shaken up he was.

Sam sat in the chair to his left.

He could feel her eyes on him again. But this time they felt like two curious hands, exploring the landscape of his young face. He looked at her to make sure he was right this time. And their eyes locked. They shared an awkward moment, green eyes connecting like two forest worlds, noticing each other for the first time. But nervously, he pulled away again, returning his eyes to the windshield.

"I'm not your average engineer, Greyson. I'll be okay," she said. "But *you* don't sound like it."

He cracked a smile at his own transparency, looking down at his dirty clothes, glazed with fresh dirt, dried hangar-pit juice, and yesterday's sweat. "That's because it's not every day *I* have to deal with something like this either."

"You can't beat yourself up about it. If you didn't kill him, then they would have killed all of us."

His eyes widened, still looking outside. Not realizing his transparency ran so deep . . . And that's when the regret set in. But not for leaving his dad's sword behind . . . rather *how* he'd left it . . . Greyson could still see his long hair, jostling as the sword hit him, disappearing six inches into his chest. The scruff around his mouth as it fell open from the shock of being struck. And his eyes . . . brown and blank as he tipped over backward.

"My dad says it's best not to think about it," said Sam, but as soon as she did her face tightened like it was a mistake.

Greyson nodded, processing her words for a moment. "What?" He looked at her again. "How would he know what this feels like? I thought your dad was a businessman."

Sam hesitated for a moment, then turned to Jacob with flared cheeks. "Among other things."

# Part 2

# A Heartless Angel

# 12

# A NEW SHIP

"While I would have preferred Stiqula was the one you brought to me, I suppose a ship full of escaped prisoners is . . ." The king searched for the right word. "*Commendatory*. Well done, boys," he addressed Greyson and Tay from his throne, Sam at their side.

Greyson didn't really know what that word meant, but nodded anyway. "Thank you, Your Highness."

"I believe you have proven yourself worthy to me. *Thus*, I hereby pronounce you both Lieutenants of the Royal Guard."

Xander and another of the king's aides stepped forward to present them with their badges. A small, gold disk, with the Emblem of Viæden raised from it, and the rays of a sunburst filling in the background. The words *Viæden Royal Guard* and *Lieutenant* were engraved along the rim.

That felt good. Actually doing something right for once. If only General Brown was there to see it. So he didn't have to regret choosing him and Tay anymore. At least not completely.

Even Xander beamed with excitement as he placed the badge in Greyson's hand. Rooting for him, one misfit to another.

"These badges may also be used to communicate with each other," the king explained.

Greyson flipped his over to find a few numbered buttons on the back, as well as a small speaker and microphone.

"Now, I believe you need a ship of your own." He looked to Sam. "As luck would have it, you have stumbled upon the daughter of Nash O'Nasi. Samantha, I think it would be very *suiting* if you were to design a ship for these two."

Sam looked at him with hesitation. "Yes, Your Highness . . . I'll get started right away."

"Wonderful." The king flashed a smile. "*But*, boys, do not forget—*accident* or not—Stiqula is still *your* responsibility."

"Yes, Your Highness." Greyson nodded. As impossible as the task still was, he welcomed it. He needed it.

"You may go." He waved them off.

They turned and walked back to the lobby.

"The king expects you to kill him all by yourself?" Sam whispered.

"We're still the ones that let him out," Greyson said.

"Don't defend him, that's ridiculous. Just because it only took two people to release him doesn't mean that's all we'll need to take him down." Clearly she was not a fan of the king.

"That's what I been *tryin'* to tell him," Tay agreed.

"Well, compared to being put to death, I'll take it." Greyson knew how impossible it sounded, but in order to have any sort of closure to all this, he had to be the one to fix it.

As they entered the lobby, Megan was just dipping into her seat, but as soon as she saw Sam, she shot straight up again. "Sam! What happened to you?" She ran over to her friend. "I tried calling you back a hundred times."

"Megan." Sam fell into a hug. "We were shot down in the desert."

"For Fyr's sake! Are you alright?"

"I'm okay. Thanks to them." She gestured to the boys.

"Yeah, we saved your friend *and* captured a shipload a bad guys," Tay bragged.

"Congratulations," Megan said heavily. "They wouldn't have broken out of prison in the first place if it wasn't for you too."

He raised his hands in defense. "Minor detail."

Just then, a balding man limped in from the hall on a blue, metallic cane. What hair he had left was a cloudy grey, and the glasses he wore were as outdated as the rest of his frumpy get-up: brown slacks and a beige turtleneck.

"Samantha!" he hugged her. She was pretty popular.

"Dad!? What are you doing here?" she said between his squeezes.

"Megan told me you were in trouble." He pulled back to have a look at her.

"I'm fine."

"What happened?"

She hesitated for a moment. "Jacob and I were . . . shot down . . . by," she paused, knowing the name would knock him off his feet. "The *Aliqula*."

O'Nasi released his daughter.

"The *Aliqula*?" he repeated carefully.

"Yes."

He tried to process her response. "Please tell me it was some low-life treasure hunter that found it and felt like opening old wounds," he said, as if he already knew the answer.

She took in a deep breath. "Stiqula—"

He waved his hand to stop her, closing his eyes in acceptance. "How?" He sounded way more familiar with the situation than just any old businessman would. Like it was personal.

Greyson had to come forward. "It's our fault, sir."

The man looked at him with eyes as wise and green as his daughter's.

"They were also the ones who saved me," Sam added.

O'Nasi looked him over intently.

Greyson felt another scolding coming on, cringing in anticipation.

"Thank you," he took Greyson's hand, "for saving my daughter."

Not quite the response he was expecting.

"What are your names?" His tone was suddenly much lighter, giddy almost.

"Greyson Wight."

"I'm just Tay."

"Nash O'Nasi." He released Greyson, eyeing the swordless scabbard at his side. "Greyson, I see you carry a blade—normally. Where's it gone?"

"Oh." He'd only just remembered it was missing. "I lost it. At the Rock."

"That's too bad. A good sword is hard to come by nowadays. And even more so: a good swordsman."

"I wouldn't exactly call myself a swordsman. The only real lessons I had were from my dad." Greyson looked down in thought. "It was his sword I lost, actually."

135

"Well, you'll be going back to get it, won't you?"

"I don't—have a ship."

Nash raised an eyebrow at him.

"The king has commissioned for us to build one for them," said Sam.

"Oh, good." Nash nodded. "But in the meantime, you'll take mine."

"What?" He couldn't possibly have heard that right.

"I can't just let you sit around while an heirloom-blade is swallowed by the desert. You'll take my ship to go and get it. I have plenty."

Sam gave her dad a sideways look.

"Really?" Greyson asked again.

"Yes," Nash said simply, and handed him a small, blue keycard.

"Wow, uh, thank you, sir. I'll bring it back to you."

"Do what you will." He turned to Sam. "Have you shown them the plans?"

"No," she said through her teeth. "I haven't drawn them yet."

Nash's inviting smile sank suddenly. "What's wrong with *your* ship, dear?"

"Nothing. I'm just not sure it's right for them."

"Nonsense." He lifted his arm and slid his woolly sleeve back to reveal a thick, black bracelet. He uncoiled it from his arm and began to type on its touch-screen face, pulling up a file to show the boys. "You'll have to give it away sometime, Sam. You can't pilot it all by yourself," he said as the file loaded.

"Well, how do you know *he's* such a great pilot?"

That hurt. Letting her ship get shot down wasn't the best display of his ability, but he thought he did pretty damn well, given the circumstances. And she was completely fine and friendly with him a minute ago . . . Had he missed something?

"Because he carries a blade. Something that takes great confidence and skill to wield in an age of bullets and lasers. Surprisingly similar to the skill and reactions of a worthy pilot."

*Confidence*, Greyson laughed in his head. Yeah right.

Even Tay *and* Sam rolled their eyes at the old man.

Nash presented his bracelet . . . computer-thing to them. And on its glowing screen, in black and blue, were the schematics of a ship. The largest, most advanced piece of technology Greyson had ever seen.

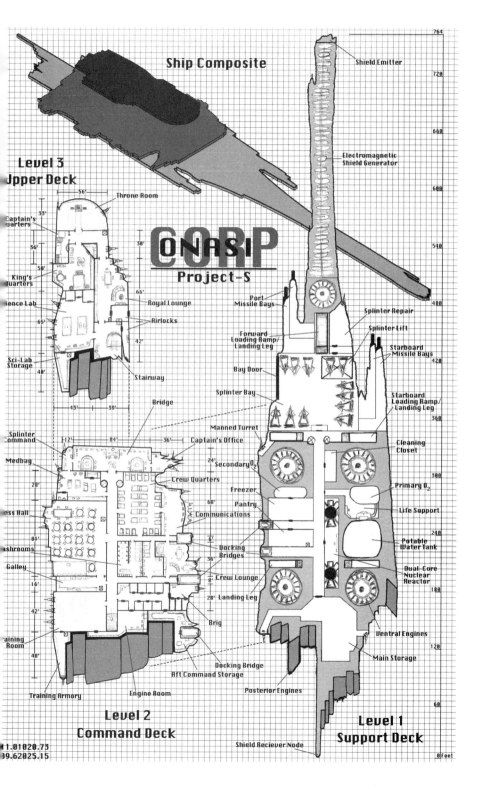

Ship Composite

Shield Emitter

Electromagnetic
Shield Generator

Level 3
Upper Deck

CORP
Project-S

Throne Room

Captain's
Quarters

King's
Quarters

Science Lab

Royal Lounge

Airlocks

Port
Missile Bays

Splinter Repair

Splinter Lift

Starboard
Missile Bays

Sci-Lab
Storage

Stairway

Forward
Loading Ramp/
Landing Leg

Bay Door

Starboard
Loading Ramp/
Landing Leg

Bridge

Splinter Bay

Manned Turret

Cleaning
Closet

Splinter
Command

Captain's Office

Secondary O₂

Primary O₂

Medbay

Crew Quarters

Freezer

Life Support

Mess Hall

Communications

Pantry

Potable
Water Tank

Washrooms

Docking
Bridges

Dual-Core
Nuclear
Reactor

Galley

Crew Lounge

Landing Leg

Brig

Ventral Engines

Training
Room

Docking Bridge

Main Storage

Aft Command Storage

Posterior Engines

Training Armory

Engine Room

Level 2
Command Deck

Level 1
Support Deck

Shield Reciever Node

Feet

It had a splinter ship bay, both ventral and posterior engines, a laboratory, royal chambers, training room, quarters to house a small army, and to top it all off . . .

"Is this . . . a shield generator?"

"Bullshit." Tay pushed him aside to have a look. "Ships can't have shields. They're too small to house the generators."

"Not this one." Nash smiled.

Taking a closer look, Greyson noticed that each room was detailed, with shelves, furniture, showers, everything a long-distance ship would need. But the details were drawn differently than the schematics, like they'd been sketched in by a nine-year-old, trying to give the cold outline some life.

Greyson looked from the gadget to Sam. She looked pissed, flexing her jaw and everything. He didn't know what to say, other than, "It's beautiful."

"Thank you." She nodded, but looked away like she didn't mean it.

"Good, it's settled then," Nash said. He had to know he was pushing her buttons, but he didn't seem to care, smiling through it. "And I'd like to take a look at that blade once you retrieve it, Mr. Wight. Perhaps I can teach you a thing or two."

Sam scoffed, garnering her dad's attention.

"Ready to go then?" He asked like she was a moody teen. "Jacob is waiting. Good-day, boys." Nash walked back to the glass doors and pushed through into the hall.

Sam watched him leave, like she was waiting for the space between them to grow before she followed. She really did not want him to have that ship, for some reason. And her dad knew it, almost teasing her about it. It made Greyson not want to take it from her.

"Sam." He touched her arm. "If you don't want me to have your ship, I—"

"It's not that." She gave him a glance, breathing deep. "I just . . . need to think about it."

She took a step away from him, flipping her tone back to professional. "It should be ready in a week or so. I'll see you then." She flashed a fake smile and followed her dad into the hall.

"See you then," Greyson said quietly, watching her leave.

"She got weird all of a sudden," Tay said while she was definitely still within earshot.

Greyson fired a *whatthefuck* look at him, gesturing loudly at Sam as the glass doors closed behind her.

"Here's your room assignment." Megan thrust some papers at them.

Tay turned to her with a grin, taking them. "Ooooo. Now you know where I live."

"And I'll be sure to avoid that part of the tree."

"Hey, c'mon. You really think I'm that bad?"

"Yes."

"Don't you think it'd be nice, dating a hero?"

"I don't know, is it?" She nodded to Greyson.

"Ouch." Tay's eyebrows sank.

Greyson laughed out loud. "C'mon, Tay, leave the lady alone."

Slowly, cautiously, Stiqula ventured into the dark of his hollow, to the place where Refsiel had first spoken to him. After learning the truth of Aliqula's fate at the Rock, he'd returned to Gardeón Tree, in search of clarity. To discern how much of what Darkness said was true, and what of it was cursed.

Aliqula was with Him, reduced to leverage in a malevolent blackmail.

He'd lost much of his faith in Darkness, no longer certain where his allegiance lay. No longer certain on which side of the line he fell . . . But, perhaps there was no line at all, contrary to everything he'd been taught to believe. Now, having been betrayed by both sides, he could see that there were far more forces in this world than just good and evil. Far more truths that neither Light nor Darkness could reveal. And perhaps he did not need to align himself with either of them . . . as alien a thought that was, for an angel to have no allegiance . . . Then again, he was no longer angel. He was free. His destiny was not bound by some creed, or other being's will. He was free to serve himself. And carve a destiny, all his own.

If he still had hair, it would have stood on end at this new found revelation. He had become an agent among men. And he would act as he saw fit . . . He would do whatever it took to see her again.

Even if that meant the world's destruction. For he cared not for the world, if Aliqula was not part of it . . . And perhaps by doing Refsiel's bidding, they would be reunited in His all-consuming Darkness once again.

But how? He needed answers. And he had come to the mirror room in search of them.

The mirror had been healed. In its reflection shone a monster once again, searching the darkness for its god.

"How does one bring Death into life?" he spoke. "As an angel, this I was never told. Only that Darkness always longed to live. But never how it could be done." He waited for a voice to echo his. "Darkness acts within us all, as evil to the human spirit. But for this evil to break free and crawl upon the world . . . I do not know." His eyes fell from the mirror down to the endless chasm. "I can remember . . . the Door to Darkness. It gave way to me, once. But *how*, was never certain. All that anyone has ever known is that Light sealed Refsiel and all His darkness behind that door long ago. But, how can He be freed? How can I open a door that was only meant to close?"

Fed up with the silence he called the dark by name. "Refsiel. How may I bring You into life?" He waited for the devil's tongue, but no such terror came. "Is it even possible to birth a god? To birth something that cannot live?" His questions journeyed down to the abyss in search of answers, but no such light awaited them there. Instead they died, never to be heard again, strangled in the silence of the dark.

Stiqula looked to the long crack in the wall, at the midday light that trickled through. Refsiel had spoken to him here, but now the room was stained by light. He may no longer have the strength. Stiqula knew that Light and Darkness shared the world in balance. And when One chose to act, the other swiftly countered. Thus was the way of the universe. Thus, Death could never speak for very long without the Light to come and mute Him. He could never claim souls for Himself without more souls of light to be born and replace them.

But. If that balance were outweighed by other means, say the actions of a dark disciple . . . then *Darkness* would become the greater power . . . Then He would surely have the strength for any feat. To speak, and act, unhindered. If only for a time. Perhaps even strength enough to rip free from the chains that bind Him to His realm.

Refsiel must have recognized Stiqula's freedom, bound to no certain fate. And that was why He'd taken such an interest in him. So that he may spread a wake of death across the world, such that Light could not counter on Her own.

Stiqula looked behind him. On the opposite wall of his sanctum hung old, tattered papers, curled by ink and time. He stepped to them, reading their faded contents. They were sketches, guidelines of a claw-like machine. He placed his hand against them, sweeping back their curled edges to see clearly. "Perhaps more death is what it takes to rouse You." He looked to the abyss. "And if souls are what You want, then souls You shall receive."

# 13

# EYES OF A KILLER

Alone in the quiet night, a child slept. Not yet old enough for school, and still too young to know the terrors of the world. Everything to her was beautiful, every day a gift, wrapped in her mother's love.

A distant boom roused her from a nestled sleep, and the shadows of the room yielded to her emerald eyes.

"Momma?"

Another thunderous rumble came, echoed from far away.

The little girl sat up and called for her mother again. "Momma?" She slumped out of bed and shuffled to the light of her cracked door.

Again the resonance came, louder now. Her room trembled in its wake.

Then a new sound rang from behind her door.

"Momma!" She pushed open the door to see her copper-haired mother standing in the open archway of their home, screaming out into the night. The girl ran to her mother's side. Their town was glowing. Their town was burning. And in the sky, a tangled ship rained fire on it from above.

Greyson put the O'Nasi Corp. ship down on the dry earth at the edge of the Rock's crater. He and Tay hopped from the ship into the night, freshly washed, and freshly clothed. At the guard supply store, Greyson had bought a new jacket while Tay shopped for his boots. It was a light charcoal color, with rings of white at the cuffs and collar, darker at the shoulder pads and elbows. The symbol of the Kingdom Guard was embroidered on the back, with the words: *Sunaru. Trigana. Urius. Raftem.* hemmed at its edges. The motto of the Guard, written in ancient Viædonic: *Strength. Protection. Courage. Justice.* Greyson always loved those words. His dad had them framed on a wall in his office back home.

"I already have a blister from these fuckin' boots," Tay whined.

Greyson ignored him, preoccupied with finding his sword. He knew exactly where it would be, though part of him still hoped it wouldn't be there, to save himself the grief of finding how he'd left it.

They searched the sand with flashlights, keeping an ear open for the buzz of hornets' wings. And sure enough, a few steps from the blown-out building, Greyson found his man, just how he'd left him, sprawled and bloodied in the sand, Wight family sword lodged in his chest.

The blood was dried, hardened, like his sword was plunged into cold lava. But something else was there too, splattered on the blade like inky sludge. Something only Greyson could see. Or maybe it wasn't even there at all. Maybe it was just an illusion that his guilty mind made up, fooling his eyes into seeing the thing he feared, above all else.

It was darkness. The prisoner's dark soul, released when the blade had pierced his heart.

Greyson's own heart resonated at the sight of it, rattling like a cage with a wild animal within. The vibration spread from his chest, across his body, making his hands tremble.

He clenched his fists to keep them still.

Two, brown, regretful eyes flashed through his mind. He twitched at the prick of the memory, clenching his eyes tight to try and erase them from his sight. But on they stared, seared into his mind like two bronze disks, branded to the inside of his eyelids. This vision, this lingering darkness was much older than his nightmare . . . and much more powerful.

The eyes of a bully. The eyes of a pitiful, dead boy.

"Death, by any means, is never beautiful. And to bring it to another should never be celebrated." His dad's words bounced in his head. "That is not the duty of a guard. Guards do not kill. We protect . . . But, if you have no other choice, if you have to kill to save your life, or someone else's, a crime as grave as death should not be taken lightly. It should be as darkening on *your* soul as it is your victim's. And such a deep connection cannot be made from the vantage of a gun . . . Darkness is most dangerous when it affects you, unaware. But if you stare into its eyes and know it well, then you can learn to manage it: keep it in check. Keep it from destroying you."

It was almost a year ago now, on the first of Raphael. Greyson only had one month to go before graduating from the guard academy, and he was starting to lose focus, preoccupied with how he and Tay were going to spend their next month off, instead of keeping his head on duty, where it belonged. That day he was stationed at the Bank of Wellington, a place he and the other guards unceremoniously dubbed the most boring post in town. But that day was different.

The bank was one of the few buildings built into Wellington Tree, a half-mile off the ground. Greyson was standing at the back door, nodding to a young woman with blond, curly hair that blended with the floral vines of her white sundress. She smiled back at him as she passed through the doors and onto the street: a balcony that wrapped the whole of Wellington's canopy.

Not a moment later, the muffled *pop* of a gun came through the door. Greyson rolled off the wall and pushed through the bank's door just in time to watch the girl fall to the street. A boy was standing over her. A gun in one hand, and a few bucks in the other. He was looking down at her, wide-eyed, like he hadn't meant to do it. Like he hadn't realized how fragile her life really was.

Greyson recognized those eyes. And came through the door with his amber guard's pistol drawn at them. "Bail!"

Bail looked up at him, buzzed, brown hair, beady brown eyes. He hadn't changed much since elementary school. "Greyson," he said. He whispered.

Life hadn't been good to him. He had a scar over his lips, and he looked scrawny against the balcony's blue sky. He had to be at the end of his rope, driven to this. Pathetic.

Greyson felt bad for him, his initial reaction was pity, not fear. This was a boy he knew, one far less fortunate than he was. And Bail hadn't raised his gun yet, arms still hanging low. Greyson could talk him down before he did anything else he was going to regret.

But then he said something that scared all Greyson's pity away.

"You gunna kill me now, demon?" Bail's eyes began to well. The reverse symmetry was undeniable. Greyson had grown tall and strong. And Bail had not. Now *he* was the weak one, scared and crying, backed against a railing. The only difference was that now they both had weapons. Far more dangerous than rocks. "Just like I said you would."

Greyson's certainty vanished. The boy he knew in school had not grown at all, had not changed into a reasonable man. He was reckless, ignorant, and scared. Not in the mood for words.

Bail twitched, trying to draw as fast as he could.

And Greyson pulled the trigger, hitting him in the thigh, just like he was taught. It wasn't fatal, by any means. But his reaction to the shock of being hit was strong enough to fling him back over the railing.

Those eyes . . . They locked with Greyson's as he tipped back, desperate to make one last connection with another human being. Even if that person was the one who'd pulled the trigger. Greyson watched the final moments play across his face as gravity began to win. His eyes bent from fear to regret. An ultimate regret for every choice he'd made throughout his life that'd led him here, to this moment, to his end. Too late.

Bail disappeared over the ledge, and had another nine seconds to reflect on each year of his life before he struck a jutting root and smeared along the bark for another hundred yards, 'til his dust and sixty dollars sprinkled to the earth.

Bail had been erased from the world. And Greyson had pulled the trigger. He was a killer. A murderer. And part of him died that day with Bail. Filling his life with as much grief and regret as he'd seen in Bail's brown eyes.

But the worst part of it . . . as much of an accident as it was . . . Part of him was glad.

And as horrible as that gladness felt . . . Bail got what he deserved.

At least that was what a quiet darkness whispered throughout Greyson's heart. No matter how much he hated if he felt that way . . . that feeling was still there. Undeniably clear.

That same day, his father handed him the blade again. For good this time. "Death is the enemy. And this blade will ensure that such an accident like what happened today, will never happen again. This blade is death, harnessed and tamed, and it shall only kill another by your conscious hand, unlike the chaos in the fire of a gun. With this blade, each kill you make shall feel as brutal as the first. It will slow the numbing of your heart to death, and keep you human. For it is better to feel pain than nothing at all. That is how you know you are still living . . . still fighting for the right reasons."

And now, he'd killed again, here in this canted desert. With his father's sword. And it cut him just as deeply as intended. Just as brutal as the first.

Greyson looked to the sword. What blackness he believed was there had gone. Either absorbed into the blade or never existing in the first place. He closed his eyes and pulled his sword quickly from the corpse, trying to ignore the scrape and pressure of the bones that it was lodged between.

"Whoa, Greyson, look," Tay gasped.

Greyson looked across the night to where Tay pointed. There was a glow, far off, across the dark desert sands, and in its red shine hung the *Aliqula*.

The grip on his blade tightened.

# 14

# The Red Streets of Rock Town

Stiqula's men encircled an elder in the square of his burning town. He had nowhere to run, cut off from the screaming masses outside the circle of armed criminals in black jumpsuits.

Then from outside their ring and flame, a monster, cloaked in black, stepped forth. Believing him a fire demon, who'd come to raze his town, the withered man dropped to his knees and whimpered.

Stiqula wrenched him from the street and spoke into his dull, watery eyes. "Jeremiah Amarine. Of all the darkness of my mind, your face I do remember. Though when we met before, your eyes were filled with dreams. And now it seems those dreams have all but passed to memory."

The man squirmed in his claws, trying not to meet the demon's glare. "Wh—who are you?"

"Look at me, Jeremiah," he enticed with a jolt. "You know who I am."

The man flashed his eyes at the monster, then looked again in recognition, becoming even more afraid. "S—*Stiqula*?"

"Why so surprised? Is it my face? My hair, perhaps? Or is it these eyes? These cold. Dark. Heartless. Eyes." Stiqula dropped him to the brick. "I have come to collect, Jeremiah." He circled his prey. "Where is the machine you promised me?"

"We served you so well," the man choked. "Why do you reward us with death?"

"Death?" Stiqula repeated. "Because death is what I require," he said solemnly. "Now, you give me that ship, and I shall let your village be."

"Dad!" A woman screamed from outside the circle. "He lies! You can't give it to him!"

Jeremiah lifted his gaze to the young woman screaming at the top of her lungs. His daughter. His eyes began to fill with tears, knowing her good heart would be the death of her.

"It is where you left it. Just as you said," the old man cried. "Now please, let us go."

Stiqula looked to a tall stone building at the square's edge, sealed by large, stone doors, blessed by the Symbol of Fire. "Of course." He cast his gaze back to the copper-haired woman. Both of their hearts were so bright . . . He could feel them, almost see them glowing in the remnants of his once-holy eyes . . . The loss of their hearts would be a great blow to the Light.

Stiqula felt for them, almost disheartened by the fact that these purest of things, these hearts, not unlike the one that held such bearing on his own, he now must end.

He looked to the man. "But unless you can tell me where the Door to Darkness is and how to open it, this is the only way."

Jeremiah looked up into the demon's eyes, lips quivering, not a single thing to scream but: "*Run!*"

Stiqula dug his talons into Jeremiah's shoulder and stood him on his feet, then reached inside his chest and sent his soul into the dark.

"*No!*" his daughter shrieked.

Stiqula laid him down upon the street as the convicts crowded in around her.

Greyson and Tay's ship soared over the glowing carnage of Rock Town, street after street, scorched by flame, coursing with people, flowing like blood cells through stone veins. The *Aliqula* hovered in front of them, now ceasing its fire, floating on the city's smoke like a net, catching the souls of its victims as they drifted to the sky. But Greyson and Tay's little transport had no way to attack the *Aliqula*, leaving them no choice but to land to be of any use at all.

Greyson put the ship down in an open road, diverting the stream of people around it like a blood clot. They leapt off, into an air dense with smoke, and roaring engines, floating on the chill of crying lungs. The streets were overrun, people sprinting off in every way, no purpose, no escape. Trapped like ferrets in a flaming maze. But they weren't running from nothing. Sprinkled in the crowds were black shepherds in prison jumpsuits, driving them from any sense of order, scattering them all into chaos, just for the fun of it.

A family of five sprinted past, running nowhere in particular except away from the prisoner chasing them. Out of instinct, Greyson checked the man as he ran by, knocking him to the ground, then drew his blade and drove it through his thigh. The convict screamed as blood squirted from his jumper. He wasn't chasing anyone now.

"Greyson!" Tay screamed.

He turned just in time to see another convict lunge for him, knife in hand: a nasty serrated thing, almost a friggen sword, swung right for his throat. Greyson lurched back to dodge the steel, less than an inch from his skin. Then as the man reared up for another strike, he twitched and dropped, Tay standing right behind him. Greyson looked down to see a singed hole, glowing in his spine. Tay'd shot him without a second thought.

He was so quick to kill . . . He didn't have to do that. Greyson was just about to block and handle it himself. Tay's death count more than double what Greyson's was. No real way to know for sure. He never talked about the ones he's killed, he hardly ever thought about it at all. And Greyson never asked. But you'd never know he was a killer, just looking at him. He was numb to the true gravity of what he was doing, the wake of darkness left behind him. And even though his dad warned him against that very thing, Greyson almost envied his apathy for death.

The two came together, standing back-to-back to cover every angle of attack.

"Did you have to kill that guy?" Greyson yelled over the mess of sound.

"Um, unless you really felt like getting turned inside-out, yeah!"

"You could have gone for the leg or something."

Just then, the first man Greyson had stabbed reached for a pistol strapped to his leg. Tay was first to spot it, jabbing Greyson out of the way with his elbow, right before the shot fired between them. Tay leveled his gun to the man's chest and pulled the trigger.

"Yeah, how's that working out for you so far?" he spat.

Greyson breathed out quickly, writing off the obvious slap in the face on the heat of the moment. They had two very different approaches to being a guard, rarely seeing eye-to-eye.

Greyson looked to the sky, red with the fire's glow against a blanket of low clouds. Three bark ships hovered just above the city, a safe distance from the *Aliqula*. They looked like they belonged to the city guard, lowering to help their people escape. He looked down to the crowd. The family of five had stayed next to them, hovering close to Tay, for safety.

"Let's get them out of here!" Greyson pointed behind them, to the nearest ship.

"Got it." Tay turned and ran through the family. "Let's go!" They hurried after.

Greyson trailed behind them down the street, shouting and waving for anyone who'd listen to join them, trying to add what order he could to the scattered confusion. A few people did join them, mostly stragglers, looking for some numbers to improve their odds. They grew into a mob of fifteen or so, hard to tell from where he was, but the more he could save, the better. Every life he saved eased the guilt on his heart.

As they ran, Greyson spotted an older man, wrestling with a convict around the same age for control of a rifle. Greyson broke formation to help solve their struggle, landing a blow on the back of the inmate's head with the butt of his sword.

"Thanks," the old guy said. He had pepper hair, and wore the uniform of a guard, but tan.

"Come with us!" Greyson waved him along as he shuffled after the group.

The old man hurried to catch up.

"What happened here?" Greyson asked as they jogged along at the back of their growing party.

"That stick ship came out of nowhere in the middle of the night and started firing on us. They hit the guard houses first. Made sure we were unable to fight back. Then they lowered and unloaded a few hundred men, breaking down doors, stealing people from their houses, gunning them down in the streets. It's madness! Absolute forsaken madness."

"I'm sorry." Greyson didn't know what else to say. "Is your family safe?"

"I don't have a family. I was with the mayor's detail. We were headed this way before we got separated."

The road opened up into a city square, judging from what was left of the inward-facing buildings and brick-laden streets. The nearest bark ship dipped low enough to graze the roofs of the two-story buildings at the far end of the square, front loading ramp open, ready to take in all the civilians it could. A shot rang from the ramp. There was a sniper standing at its edge, picking off any convicts he could find terrorizing the crowds below.

Taking a second look, Greyson realized this square was actually a rectangle, extending a good ways to their left, ending in a tall, stone building that looked like the keep of an old castle, with towers for walls, and crenellations on its crown.

Not watching where he was going, Greyson bumped up against the people in front of him. The whole group had come to a halt. But they were still too far from the ship. Greyson pushed his way in to see what the hold up was. And as he neared the front of the pack, he saw that the square ahead of them was firmly in control of Stiqula's men. Nearly a dozen of them, mostly armed, standing between them and their rescue.

One of them was gigantic, carrying a massive rod of rusted metal, with a heavy knot of bolts at one end, slung over his shoulder like a club. His grey jumper was ripped at the sleeves and open at the chest, revealing a sickening amount of muscles beneath tight, black skin.

"*Stiqula.*" His heart leapt to his mouth.

Suddenly their short standoff ended, and the convicts took aim at the crowd. The thin line of people in front of Greyson caught the first wave of lasers in their chests and hit the ground. The sniper in the bark ship opened fire again, taking some of their heat. But he could only take out two of them before he was taken out himself. The crowd scattered again, much faster than it'd come together, fleeing helplessly from the ringing pulse of laserfire.

Only three brave souls remained: Greyson, Tay, and the old man firing back. But they were defenseless out in the open. Dead men. Or at least they would have been if the old man's rifle didn't also have a thermal round left in the chamber. He fired at the base of an obelisk in the middle of the square to their right. The stone tower crumbled at the base and fell flush with the ground in a cloud of dust, making the perfect cover for them, five feet high.

The tip of the obelisk was only a few feet short of striking a large fountain, another of the square's centerpieces, closer to the keep. And standing on

PROGENY OF GODS

the fountain's rim was a copper-haired woman holding a gun in one hand, and a golden sword in the other. She fired her last bullet into an incoming convict and leapt from the rim to cut another down, close behind.

"That's the mayor's daughter," the old man said as Tay ran up to the obelisk and fired over the top. A few of the people from their group quickly followed him to cover.

"M'lady!" the man shouted, waving her over. She was way out in the open, two more men closing in on her. One had a thick, industrial chain, the other a crooked sword.

Lucky most these prisoners had such shitty weapons.

"Fyren!" she yelled back, glad to see a friend.

"Come with us!" Fyren pleaded as the bark ship swung around behind them, away from the action, where they could safely board.

"I can't!" She planted her feet firmly in the ground, back to the fountain, blade bouncing back and forth between the two approaching inmates.

Fyren raised his rifle to take aim and help her. But before he could pull the trigger, he was hit. Greyson couldn't see where the bullet had struck, but its light moved slow enough to see where it came from, over the fountain's pool, behind the woman.

Fyren fell back from the blast, launching his rifle through the air as the woman screamed.

"Fyren!" Greyson fell at his side, pressing his hand down on his bloody chest. He was still breathing, but he couldn't to speak. Three light beams had burnt through to his lungs.

The mayor's daughter could no longer focus on her fight. Her swing was blocked by the crooked sword, and with one blow from the chainman, she was disarmed.

As the air left Fyren's lungs, Greyson looked across the fountain, and to the shooter's eyes. Lightless, brown. They looked just like Bail's. And he wanted nothing more in that moment than to add them to the growing collection in his mind, and send his soul into the dark where it belonged.

Tay was right. Why should he bother sparing his morality on these *immoral* men?

"No!" The woman fought against them as they dragged her by the arms toward the shooter and the keep. "Stay!" she screamed. "Hide! Hide!" she repeated over and over again at the top of her lungs, as if her heart depended

152

on it. "*Hide!*"

Greyson stood, clenching his sword, preparing himself for what he was about to do. He didn't know who she was screaming at, but he knew it wasn't him. "Tay!" he shouted.

Tay crouched down again after firing a shot over the obelisk, looking to Greyson as he stared down his mark.

"Get them out of here!" Greyson barked, trying to salvage what lives he still could.

Tay looked at the few people cowering next to him, and even fewer still lingering in the square, then to the bark ship, safe at the square's edge. "C'mon!" He launched from cover, waving for them all to follow.

At the same time, Greyson charged. In six bounds he was at the fountain, leaping up onto its rim. His mark turned at the sound of his heavy footsteps, but it was too late. With a scream Greyson leapt from the fountain's ledge, sword like a spear, fixed to the shooter's heart. Before the convict could even raise his gun to fire, Greyson collided with him, piercing him against the ground.

The crooked sword and chainman turned back at the commotion, releasing the mayor's daughter into the arms of the black giant. They ran back to help their friend, too late. He was dead. And they were next.

Greyson pulled his blade from the man's body to block an incoming swing from the crooked sword, then parried it and ducked low, lunging forward beneath the sweeping strike of the metal chain to lodge his sword in the chainman's hip like an axe in a trunk. But Greyson's center of gravity was so far forward that he fell on his shoulder and rolled to his back, sliding a few inches, un-lodging his sword from the man's bones. The crooked sword swung down fast to take advantage of Greyson's vulnerable position, but was denied again by the mirrored blade.

Unable to stand without getting hit, Greyson rolled away from the swordsman, and to the wounded chainman, who still had a little fight left in him. As Greyson rolled to his stomach to push up and stand, he took a hard blow to his back, which flattened him again. He felt every link of that goddam metal chain as it bounced off his spine and muscles. Now he was really pissed. He launched from the ground, holding his arms up to protect his face, blade down to protect his body. Both on their knees, the chainman swung into Greyson's block, but the limp chain bent around his blade and cracked against the unpadded bones of his forearms. Greyson couldn't tell if they were broken or not. But he had too much adrenaline to care. As the chain fell from his arms, he swung with all his strength at the one place he knew would knock the guy out for good. His blade hit under the chin, instantly snapping his jaw and slicing open his face all the way to the nose. He was done. Falling back to choke on his own juices as he bled out.

Meanwhile, Greyson had lost track of the swordsman at his back. He had no time to look, jumping to his feet and spinning, pulling his blade around with the full force of his body. Their steel struck with such force it bent that shitty sword even more and left the convict wide open to attack. Greyson checked him, shoulder to chest, laying the man out on his back, then straddled him and pressed the flat of his blade down hard against his throat. He felt something snap in there as he watched the man's eyes fill red from exploding blood vessels.

Then, in the reflection of his blade, he saw his own eyes, green and terrible. The green eyes of a killer. A demon.

"*No.*" Greyson pulled back, shooting to his feet as the man gasped for air, coughing with life. Then something in front of Greyson caught his eye. A flicker of movement at the side of the keep. The mayor's daughter was being dragged, kicking and screaming down a thin alley.

He had forgotten all about her in the blurred haze of revenge. He leapt to chase after her, seeing the giant yank her into a side-door below the keep. And he flew down the wall to them, only to find a thick stone door slam shut in his face.

"No!" he screamed, beating his fist against the rock. There were no locks or handles anywhere. Nothing. No signs of opening it at all. "*No!*" he cried again, this time with more feeling, on his way to realizing that if he hadn't stopped to feed his rage, he would have reached her in time. "Can't I save *anyone*!?" He hit the door again. Almost breaking his damn hand. But he didn't care at that point. Disgusted with himself. He fucking deserved it.

He stood back from the door, checking it again for any lever that he might have missed around its edges, or on the walls next to it, above it even. But there was nothing. Nothing but the Symbol of Fire carved into its stone.

Greyson rubbed his hand against his side to dull the pain and looked back to the square. Maybe he could find a grenade or something to blow it open. He jogged out of the alley again. The square was almost emptied now, no signs of any convicts left, none living anyway. Only a dusty fog and rubble, enclosed by smoldering buildings.

Maybe Fyren's rifle had another round left in it, he thought, setting off for the obelisk. But as he passed the fountain, something stopped him.

He swore he heard a sound that fountains didn't make.

The sizzling crack of the fire was dulled by the fog, and the hum of engines also faded into the background as he focused on the water. It trickled from the stone blossom at the center of a shallow pool, like normal. But he knew he'd heard something. Like the quick squeak of a cry cut short.

Taking a step toward the pool, he saw the ripples moving strangely, not just coming from the center where the water fell, but from right near him at its edge too. He bent over the rim to see that there was an alcove carved under its ledge, making a lip over the pool, just large enough for someone small to hide beneath. Bending even further down, he saw her. A little girl, huddled up against the rim, curled as small as she could get, only her head above the water line.

She saw Greyson poke down and gave a pitiful cry, clutching her legs tighter to stay small. She must have been who that woman was screaming at to hide. She was the reason she couldn't leave the fountain. She was protecting it. Protecting her.

"Hey," Greyson said lightly. "Hey, it's okay. I'm not gunna hurt you."

She didn't believe him, crying louder.

"It's safe to come out now. All the bad guys are gone," he assured. "Come see." He dangled an open hand over the lip.

It took her a moment, but his patience and kind, upside-down eyes, softened her tears a little. She reached for his hand, hardly the size of his palm.

"That's it," he said easily. "You're okay."

She was cold. Lord knows how long she'd been in that water for. He grasped her tiny hand and pulled her from hiding, sheathing his sword to pick her up with both arms and pluck her from the freezing water.

"I've got you."

She couldn't have been more than three years old, wearing only a nightgown, all white, with green flowers at the fringes. Soaking wet. Her hair was half dry, from the neck up, and looked like it'd never been cut. She had a hint of freckles on cold, red cheeks, and the biggest, greenest eyes he'd ever seen, meeting his emerald stare with uncertainty, puffy pink from tears.

But suddenly her uncertainty faded, and her eyes widened into terror, looking past Greyson at some great beast charging from behind. He tucked her in close and leapt to the side as a massive pipe swung down to crash against the fountain's lip. Splinters of stone fired into the air as Greyson turned to land on his back and protect her from the fall.

They both looked back to see the black giant retrieve his weapon and lift it back to his bare shoulder.

Instantly, Greyson rolled the girl off of him, and set her on her feet, pushing her in the direction of the rescue ship. "Run!"

She did as he said, running off into the fog as he regained his feet and drew his blade.

*Fuck*, this guy was big. Like he'd *eaten* Berinhard and Riese. A wave of fear flashed through Greyson, like his body knew he was in way over his head. But he wasn't about to run. He'd lost too much today to finish off his dignity too. And if this really was Stiqula, he had no choice but to face him. His heart would never forgive him.

"Stiqula," Greyson choked, not knowing what else to say. "What'd you do with her?"

"Stiqula?" the beast replied in a voice so deep it shook Greyson's insides. "I am Itxaro."

"Wha?" He wasn't sure how to respond. "Okay, well, what'd you do with that lady?"

"She is gone," he said slowly. He had an accent that was angry and hard to understand. Or maybe it only sounded like that from the depth of his voice. "Now you are too." He grabbed his pipe with both hands and swung it down at Greyson with an incredible reach. The metal struck the bricks and split them with an echoing clang as Greyson leapt away.

This guy was big. But he was slow.

He unstuck the pipe from the ground and swept it around his body with a seven-foot reach. Greyson almost didn't make it out of there in time.

*Okay, maybe he wasn't as slow as he thought.* But either way, there was no way he could parry something like that. Just one hit could crush half the bones in his body. His only option was to be faster than him.

"Come here!" Itxaro boomed, lunging forward to swing down again.

The pipe, more like a sewer drain up close, hit the ground as Greyson leapt again. He wasn't going to miss this opportunity. Rolling forward beneath the giant's arms, he slashed him once across the side of his torso. Itxaro let out a guttural scream, and as Greyson recovered from his roll, Itxaro reached back with his free hand to catch Greyson by the jacket. The jerk back was so powerful it knocked the wind out of him, but without a second thought, he dropped his sword and threw his arms back to slide out of its sleeves. Free of the death-grip, Greyson dropped to the ground and bear-crawled to his blade as Itxaro barked in frustration.

The giant threw the jacket, flexing his entire body. His battle-cry echoed through the streets, chest, neck, and biceps bulging with veins, like a viscous wrath flowed through them. And then that wrath escaped him. The pipe in his hand erupted in what looked like lava, glowing dim at first, then a brilliant red, sizzling like a live wire, throwing off blurred waves of heat.

Greyson stood slowly, red light reflecting in his eyes. He could feel the heat from there, tickling his skin like static. He stepped back instinctively, as if his body knew not to go near it, whateverthefuck it was. He didn't want anything to do with it.

"Okay, I'm out." He sprinted for the obelisk so fast he thought he'd rip right through his pants. "Taay!" He leapt on top of the monument, skipping over the cracks as he ran down its back. "Help!" He skidded to a stop at the end of the statue, using his five-foot-higher vantage to search the square for any way to beat this guy.

*There!* Fyren's rifle, just a few feet away.

"Watch it!" Tay yelled, running out of the fog.

The obelisk shook beneath him, and he spun to face Itxaro sprinting up behind him like a wall of muscle, heavy, glowing chunk of iron dragged behind him. It sliced through that stone like melted wax. Greyson fell back as he approached, and Itxaro swung his pipe forward, up through the stone, nearly skimming Greyson's face. The blaze of heat burst by him like fire dragged across his skin.

Greyson fell from the statue, and as his back hit the ground, Tay opened fire.

Itxaro stood no chance now, on the wrong end of Tay's lasers.

Of course, to *all* of their surprise . . . Every. Fucking. Laser. Missed. He must have shot at him *thirty* times, and not *one* hit? *He was standing ten feet away!*

"What the fuck?" Tay said in a high-voice.

"You're the *worst!*" Greyson yelled, scrambling from the ground.

"It's not me!" Tay banged his guns together.

Itxaro smiled, completely unharmed. But the pipe in his hand began to droop, unable to hold its shape anymore. He wound back and flung the whole thing at Tay, spinning and breaking apart in the air in a hail of molten iron.

Tay looked up from his guns and saw the band of red-hot rain fan out as it approached, turning sideways to try and slip between the breaks in its spread. But he wasn't that skinny. A glowing nugget struck him in the shoulder, and a giant chunk grazed his back as it passed, immediately lighting his jacket on fire. "Ah!" He tore out of his coat, whipping it to the ground in a stream of smoke. "Fuck, that's hot!"

Itxaro laughed as Greyson found Fyren's rifle and took aim. One round left.

"Think that's funny, you overcooked motherfucker!?" Tay took aim at the same time. But this time Itxaro evaded, dropping down behind the obelisk, just as Greyson pulled the trigger and sent a stream of smoke zipping over the giant's head, exploding on a building at the edge of the square.

"Tay!" Greyson shouted, dropping the rifle. "I had him!"

Tay grunted, frustrated with himself, then started for Itxaro. "I got him."

Greyson ran for the obelisk too, flanking the other side of it as Tay rounded the corner, firing.

"He's coming to you!" Tay shouted.

Greyson raised his sword as he reached the pointed tip of the monument, waiting for Itxaro's bald head to poke around. *Finally* they had the upper hand!

Except that Itxaro never poked his head around. Instead, he climbed the thing in one bound and leapt right over Greyson, kicking his sword clear from his grip. The weapon splashed down in the middle of the fountain as Itxaro crashed down beside him like a booming shadow. Greyson was dumbfounded, lowering his open hands, unsure what to do. He couldn't believe that just fucking happened.

Itxaro stood, looking over his shoulder at Greyson. And their eyes finally met. Both as green as light through leavéd canopies, though Greyson's eyes were like dawn, and Itxaro's were nearly night. His mouth dropped. He'd heard so many fabled things about them, it never occurred to him that a vertui could be evil.

Their stare broke as they both searched for a weapon. Greyson leapt into the fountain, water barely reaching his knees, as Itxaro lunged for the mayor's golden blade, looking more like a knife in his hands. Tay rounded the obelisk just as Greyson retrieved his sword and aimed it for the giant, whose wrath transformed the golden blade into a glowing rod of fire.

Tay shot at him again, this time watching his bullets as they flew. His amber beams started off on course, then bent as they approached their mark, veering down into the ground or all around him. "Why can't I hit you!?"

"It's that light!" Greyson answered. From his angle he could see the shots that came closer to the red blade bent more severely.

Itxaro barely flinched at all, locked onto Greyson, who slipped behind the fountain's centerpiece for cover. The giant leapt into the air and splashed down into the pool, slicing through the stone blossom at its stem. *That light could cut through anything!* But Greyson had no choice now. He had to defend himself or die. That sword moved much faster than his pipe. He had no time to dodge Itxaro's next blow, water dragging on his feet.

Greyson raised his sword to block and prayed to whatever god would listen that it stayed in one piece.

Itxaro's blade struck Greyson's block with such force he collapsed, legs buckling underneath him, unable to keep his balance in the water. He splashed down on his ass, chest deep, as Tay sprinted 'round the pool to get a better shot.

And for the first time, Itxaro's face was not angered or pleased, but surprised that he had not sliced Greyson in half. His mirrored blade emerged from the water in one piece. Not a scratch.

Tay opened fire from the opposite side, this time getting a reaction. Itxaro spun to place the red blade between him and the laserfire as Greyson hurried to his feet to take advantage of the only opening they'd had. But it wasn't as much of an opening as he thought. Itxaro leaned away from him and planted his foot in Greyson's chest, knocking him off his feet and to the fountain's rim, where he slammed down against the lip and kept falling backward to the ground.

Itxaro looked back to Tay with an accomplished grin and raised his glowing blade high overhead.

"Big mistake, spit shine." Tay slapped his gun against his leg, turning its amber glow to blue, and in the same motion, plunged it into the fountain. The pool lit up as bands of electricity rippled over Itxaro's contorting body. He screamed for as long as Tay held down his trigger, which was as long as his gun held the charge. About three excruciating seconds.

The electric bands were replaced by smoke as Itxaro went quiet, tipping back like a felled ceptris tree. A tidal wave spread from his body as he laid flat against the bottom of the pool. The water washed over Greyson as it left the fountain, and he poked his head over the lip to see what had happened. "Oh thank gods," he sighed, collapsing against the lip.

Tay breathed deep in relief along with him. "Damn, he was big."

"Can you do me a favor? Let's never split up again. I almost just died right there."

"'Cuz you refuse to carry a gun like a normal person."

"Can you not make it about that?" Greyson stood, glaring across the pool. "Your guns weren't working either."

"Well. They sure ended it."

"Whatever. Can I walk in here now?" Greyson pointed to the water.

"Yeah. You gunna kill him?" Tay asked as Greyson climbed back into the fountain.

The water level was a lot lower now thanks to Itxaro, just low enough to keep his mouth above the water, of course. He almost looked helpless lying there, a scarred and tattooed island in a tiny sea. Part of Greyson did want him dead. But in that moment, he knew to ignore it, having already satisfied his day's quota for blood. "Not if we don't need to."

"So what are you doing? He's not gunna stay down forever."

"Seeing how the hell he did that to the sword." Greyson dipped his hand into the water to retrieve the blade, now returned to its natural gold. And as he lifted it from the pool, its hilt snagged on something. A thin, silver chain was wrapped around it and Itxaro's fist. A quick tug yanked it free of his limp hand, bringing it into view. The strange chain, almost like a necklace, dangled from the sword's pommel, wrapping the grip in a spiral up to the fancy hand guard. It wasn't part of the actual sword, unraveling as Greyson watched. Itxaro must have put it there.

Greyson turned the blade parallel with the ground to keep it from unwrapping any more.

"What is it?" Tay asked.

"No idea," Greyson said with wonder. "But . . . I used something just like this in my dream."

"Your angel dream?" Tay said like *oh, this again.*

"Yes." Greyson curled his hand around the grip of the sword, holding the blade far away from him, squinting his eyes, expecting it to activate.

But nothing happened.

"What are you doing?"

Greyson looked curiously at the sword again. "I don't know."

"Let me see it."

"What, like you know how to work it?" Greyson walked it over to him and climbed out of the pool.

"Well, you clearly don't." Tay looked the blade over, fingering his way along its hilt. "It obviously has something to do with this chain."

"No shit."

Tay glared at him. "Or maybe nothing. Maybe he was just magic." He shoved the sword back in Greyson's face.

"Maybe Sam knows." Greyson said, taking the sword back, and sheathing his dad's.

"Why do you think *she* would know?"

"Because she mentioned Stiqula having something like this. Maybe he gave it to this guy to protect something." Greyson turned back to the keep's alley.

"That's a great theory—Can we go now, before we get left here?" Tay started for the rescue ship.

"Wait. The girl. There was a little girl here. Did you see her?"

"Yeah, I helped her on that ship that's about to leave without us." Tay threw a thumb over his shoulder.

"Okay, good." Greyson turned and ran back toward the keep.

"Where are you going!?"

"To save her mother!"

The stone door was surprisingly well hidden, blending in with the keep's brick foundation. Greyson might not have ever found it if he hadn't seen it shut in front of him. It was obviously meant to be kept secret. So how to open it must have also been a secret.

"She's behind this door," Greyson pointed as Tay rounded the corner. "But I don't know how to open it."

Tay swiped his hand across the door, feeling that it was stone, then knocked to guess its thickness.

"I bet this sword could cut through it. If I could just turn it on."

"Do you remember how you did it in your dream?"

Greyson thought back for a moment, shaking his head. "No."

"And you didn't see how that guy did it either?"

Greyson shook his head again. "He was just . . . really angry. Like it fed off of his emotion."

"That's stupid," Tay dismissed. "I can probably open this door with one of my guns if it's not too thick."

"Really?"

"Yeah, It's easy. I'll just overcharge it . . . But it'll break the gun. And I won't be able to use it 'til I get it fixed."

"Good thing you have two."

"Well, are you sure I'm not gunna need both a them for whatever's inside?"

"No. But we don't have a choice. I'm not leaving 'til I see what's back there."

"What a hero." Tay lifted one of his guns, popped off a piece of its bark shell and fiddled with the dials inside. The gun's yellow circuitry grew more vibrant and faded to white as it rang louder and louder. Tay took a step back, aimed, and looked away as he fired a brilliant plasma into the door, white as a sunbeam. The shot exploded against the stone and sent shards of it flying as the plasma degraded into fire.

When the smoked cleared, there was a crater in the door the shape of a toilet bowl. Only a fist sized chunk had broken through to the darkness behind.

"Great," said Tay. "Can't anything just be easy?"

"Use the other one."

"And be completely defenseless? No."

"Do it again!" Greyson shouted. The gold sword sparked in his hand, shimmering red for just an instant.

Tay recoiled from the shout, and Greyson did the same. That really wasn't like him . . . But he had to get in there. He had to save her. And Tay was just being stubborn as usual.

Without a word, Tay rigged his last gun to blow.

The silence was awkward, neither one of them knowing what to make of his outburst. Neither one of them wanting to talk about how that blade had just sparked, like it reacted to his anger . . . Just like it did with Itxaro when he wanted Greyson dead.

Tay fired again at the door, this time breaking a hole large enough for them to crawl through.

"Good. Thank you." Greyson stepped through the hole.

But Tay didn't move.

Greyson turned back, looking out from the darkness that encircled him. "C'mon."

"Yeah, I'll just stay here." Tay holstered his pistol.

"What? Why?"

"'Cuz now I'm useless."

Greyson sighed quickly. He didn't have time for this. "C'mon. I still need you."

"What for?"

"'Cuz we're a team!"

Tay gave him a look like he didn't really believe him, but followed after him anyway. "I swear to Darkness, if I get murdered in here, I'm gunna be pissed."

Beyond the door was a staircase completely carved of stone, leading down into the dark. The air was thick with must and humidity, quite the contrast to the dusty air outside. Quickly following the grimy stairs, a new smell came to permeate the air. The smell of blood and death. The stink rested at the bottom of the stairs like a stagnant fog. And as they reached the last few steps, they saw why.

The room was small, and intricate. Walls dressed in alcoves, blessed by the Symbol of Fire. But this room was damned. Piled on the floor in every corner, were mangled bodies, stacked so high they reached the ceiling.

They both shielded their mouths from the rot all around them.

"What the fuck is this?" Tay said through his shirt.

It looked like a secret chamber where the believers in this town gathered . . . and died. But Greyson didn't answer, searching desperately for a copper-haired woman among them. If he couldn't save all these people, he would at least save her, and reunite her with her little girl. If he could just do that, then his sanity, his humanity, would be safe.

A familiar scream echoed from another set of doors ahead of them, slightly ajar. And Greyson's fear swelled as he ran up to them—fear that he'd come too late. He peered inside its one-inch opening, and found what he was looking for: the mayor's daughter, held by the neck, quietly struggling. She was looking at someone, unseen behind the door, her last desperate stare. And then, her eyes, bled dry of all regret, fluttered and closed.

Greyson wrenched open the door so fast it nearly knocked him off his feet, and stared upon a startled face: a face so dark and grey, with teeth sharp and stained, black flames for hair, and eyes so deep and empty, their darkness wreaked havoc to his soul.

*Stiqula.*

Every fiber of his being told him to run, but he was too pissed to listen. His fear swelled to its maximum, bursting from his heart to light his gold sword aflame. He raised the glowing blade over him so fast he nearly tore his arm right from its socket, swinging down upon the monster.

Stiqula looked up to the blade, reflecting red against his skin, and raised his arm to block. The flaming sword struck his forearm and disintegrated, splattering into drops of molten gold all down his side and neck.

Stiqula drew back and shouted, clutching his neck as Greyson stumbled forward in leftover momentum. Stiqula's body let out a pulse of air, ejecting the plasma from his skin, and knocking the boys back as he launched into the dark.

Greyson and Tay recovered quickly, frantically searching the dark for where he'd gone. They were in some kind of cave, sharpened stalactites dangling from the ceiling, but it was much larger than any cave could be. It was a goddam hangar. Home to something Stiqula wanted hidden. A ship, gigantic and sinister, made of metal, in the shape of a three-bladed claw. And the hangar floor, another hundred feet below them, was crawling with Stiqula's men, all turning to face the two intruders on the stairs.

Having a better fight or flight response than Greyson, Tay grabbed hold of him and yanked him from the room as the cave glowed orange in laserfire. They slammed the door shut and sprinted for the exit, but instantly the door exploded open again in flames, hurling them onto the steps. Greyson braced himself in time, but Tay, whose arm was stuck behind Greyson, couldn't catch himself, slamming head first into the second step up, splitting his brow wide open on the stone.

"Tay!" Greyson cried. Ears ringing, he flipped him over to see the cut above his closed eyes, pumping blood from his body. He pressed down on the wound and looked to the smoke behind them, dreading to see the face of evil once again.

"Tay, get up!" He shook him.

He wasn't responding, knocked out cold.

Greyson lifted him into his arms with all his strength. Not feeling Tay's full weight until half way up the two-story stairs, dropping him from exhaustion. He dragged him the rest of the way, grabbing him under the arms and hoisting him up each step to the top, then through the hole and to the street.

But he couldn't go any further, gasping for air, arms, legs, and back burning from strain. Greyson's legs folded under him, and he fell to the square with Tay in his arms.

"Taymes!" He tried to wake him, eyes jumping back and forth between Tay's, praying they would open. But they weren't even fluttering. He looked to the streets in search of anyone to help. But they were abandoned. "Help!" He tried to move, crawling forward just a foot. "Help us!" he yelled again, now with a quiver in his voice. He knew those men were close behind.

Greyson looked to the sky in search of their rescue ships, but they'd gone too. They were alone. He was alone. Helpless. Hopeless.

Tears met his eyes, feeling death's cold gaze upon him.

Then, a flicker of movement.

The fountain.

His eyes found Itxaro, rising from the pool, water rolling off his back like he was oil. And in his eyes Greyson could see his thoughts were just as black.

"No!" He dropped the golden hilt, chain still wrapped around his fist, and drew his father's blade. He knew so far that light had melted everything it touched, but he didn't have a choice. This sword meant nothing to him dead. And death was something he was coming to accept. He didn't know what to do, what to think. Was he supposed to reflect on all his failures? What he'd learned throughout his life? Was he supposed to be at peace? Because he wasn't. He wasn't thinking about himself at all. All he could think about was Tay, and how he'd let him down. He had to protect him. He had to protect *everyone*! His own life meant nothing to him, yet his heart screamed out in fear of its end. But not for fear of death, fear that he had failed. Fear that Bail was right about him after all. Destroying all the lives around him. Leaving nothing but a wake of darkness on the world. Just like a demon would.

"Stay back!" He aimed his sword for Itxaro, and its shining steel ignited in a glorious green plasma, sucked from the air, clung to his blade with a sizzling clang.

Stiqula's men filed from the alley, dozens of them, pouring out on to the square, surrounding him. And Greyson aimed his glowing blade at every one, excepting that his destiny had finally come.

# 15

# KYRI

No sooner had he accepted his fate did an explosion rip through the crowd. Then another, each sending those convicts flying. Greyson looked to the sky, into a spotlight that shined down through the clouds. Those weren't explosions, they were cannonfire! A bark ship sank from the smoky sky and continued its barrage of amber rockets as the convicts scattered.

A gale rushed through the square as the ship touched down and opened its mouth. Greyson used what little strength he had left to drag his friend aboard as a few convicts opened fire at the ship. But they could do no real damage with their tiny rifles, useless against its thick bark.

The ground lowered away from them as the ship returned to the clouds. And as the ramp lifted closed, Greyson could finally breathe. Letting the tears break free as he looked down to Tay in his lap. His sword's green light dispelled, dropping from his grasp. The danger was gone. And his heroic mask finally fell . . . It was all just for show anyway.

His mind played back through everything that had just happened again and again, on repeat, highlighting every stupid, vicious move he'd made, drowning him in failure and regret.

If only he'd let Tay stay outside that cave. If only he hadn't forced him to use up both his guns. If only he hadn't taken so long to get to that woman. If only he hadn't stopped to take out his revenge on those prisoners, he would have reached her before she ever disappeared behind the door. But none of it happened that way. He wasn't the hero he pretended to be. He was a killer. Spreading death over life at every turn. Bail's eyes flashed through his mind, alongside Fyren's, and the woman's. Everyone he'd failed to save.

And now Tay . . . He couldn't lose him too.

"Tay." He sniffed back a rush of fluids. "Wake up."

He would have nothing left.

"Tay, please."

Tay moved his head, trying to open up his eyes. "Greyson," he muttered.

That took his breath away. Literally. His body didn't know what to do, sparking with joy that his friend was still alive, but terrified it might not be for long.

Tay tried to sit up from Greyson's lap, getting as close he could to his ear and whispered, "Get . . . me . . . Get me a band-aid."

Greyson couldn't help but smile as Tay fell back into his lap and slapped his hand to his forehead. "My face feels like a vagina."

He was going to be just fine.

Tay pulled his hand away to see it covered in blood. "Oh . . . fuck."

The security door to the rest of the ship opened. "Are you alright?" A woman stepped through, wearing a tan guard uniform like Fyren's.

Tay pointed right at her and yelled, "He needs a tampon for his vagina face . . ."

"Excuse me?"

Tay bent his finger back at Greyson, "is what you're supposed to say." Tay closed his eyes again. "A'right—I'm, g'night." He went limp.

"I'm so sorry." Greyson flashed an awkward shade of red, pressing down on Tay's cut.

"It's okay," she said. But Greyson wasn't sure she meant it. "Is he normally like that?" She opened her first aid kit, taking out a roll of gauze and bandages.

Greyson shook his head. "I—I don't know—Are we leaving the city soon?" He hadn't felt the ship move any direction but up.

"We're holding here for a bit longer, then taking the survivors to Cantidium."

"We need to leave *now*. Stiqula's right below us."

The woman opened her mouth to reply, but was cut off by a sharp inhale, suddenly startled by the invocation of Stiqula. She dropped the gauze and hurried to a door opposite the one she entered from. "Captain!" She slammed against its metal frame, swinging it open to reveal the glowing monitors of the bridge. "Stiqula's down there! We have to go *now*!"

"He is?" Greyson heard the captain say.

"Yes, these men just escaped him." Before she could finish, Greyson felt the ship lift and bank away from the city.

The woman hurried back, staggering from the extra force of the turn. "A battlegroup is converging at Cantidium." She knelt again to continue. "They'll put an end to this."

"How far is it?"

"Ten minutes."

Greyson nodded. That just might be soon enough to make all the difference. Stiqula knew he'd been discovered. He wouldn't stay there for long . . . That ship he had with him . . . It looked strong. Alien. Their only hope was to get back there and destroy it before he had a chance to use it.

The guard finished with Tay's head and helped Greyson move him to another room. They carried him into the ship's main hall, lined with bodies wrapped in blankets and loved ones to keep them warm. There was only just enough room to squeeze by as they traversed the hall in search of a clear space to plop him. Every room they passed was filled, wall-to-wall with bloodied survivors. The air tasted like sweat and tears.

They came to a conference room with a huge window, on their left, and placed Tay down on an open patch of the long table. There was only enough room for his torso, legs dangling over the floor.

"He'll be alright," the guard said. "We'll get him some real stitches when we get to the hospital."

Greyson thanked her has she left, still lost in his own head. He couldn't find his way out. Not without Tay to ground him. Like he'd lost the anchor of his heart. His heart felt like it was missing, gone completely. Left down there in that cave, right next to his mask of confidence.

He slumped against the black window. Weak. Tired. Emptied of all will. He slid to the floor, and rubbed his chest . . .

Where'd his heart go? . . . Did he ever have one to begin with?

If gods were real, and so was fate, and his was supposed to be so much *greater* than everyone else's, then why let him free Stiqula? Why cause all this? What for?

Maybe he was as heartless as Stiqula. As much a demon as Bail had said. It would make sense . . . Death followed him everywhere he went . . . He teetered, delicately balanced over death's valley, casting souls down into the pit, as tribute, to save himself from being swallowed . . . Or maybe he'd already fallen in . . . now the keeper of His gate . . . He could see it . . . behind his eyes. Right out of his mom's stories: a Door to Darkness, tall and black, gaping wide to feed on the hundreds of hopeless and familiar faces that marched by him, in. Everyone he'd failed to save. The soldiers on those ships at the VDC, and everyone in Rock Town, marching . . . through the doors . . . deep, deep, into Darkness. A place the living could not go, and the dead rarely traveled. A place where only demons dwelt. A place so dark and horrible that even nightmares fled from it, in search of sleeping minds to take their refuge.

Then from the darkness shone a light, small but wondrous, dashing in a sea of endless night. Greyson saw it wander toward him, felt its glow upon his face, like starlight.

And then it tugged, gently at his sleeve.

He opened his eyes to find a little girl standing next to him, green eyes nestled into puffy cheeks. Long, wet copper hair all down her back.

"H—hi," he said softly and surprised.

She looked at him like she wanted something, but wasn't sure how to ask.

"Are you . . . all by yourself?"

She nodded.

Greyson felt his bottom lip pull up into a quiver, his eyes warming, suddenly near tears again.

"I'm sorry." His voice hissed and cracked, throat tightening as a sickness spread throughout his body. He couldn't stand it any longer, wrapping his arms around her, tears falling. "I tried."

She cried, buried in his arms.

"I tried," his voice cracked again as he repeated, assuring himself as much as her.

"Wheo is she?" she spoke, not understanding.

"She's . . . gone," he whispered, not knowing what else to say. "She's not coming back."

The vision of her mom's final moments flashed through his mind again and again, seeing her die a thousand times. It was his fault. No one else's.

"I'm sorry."

Her cries were muffled by his body, traveling down inside him. But instead of sinking deeper into despair, somehow, for some crazy reason, she had the opposite effect on him, even as she cried. What darkness had spread across his heart was fleeing, scared off by her light.

At least for now. His hate and fear were gone.

"I'm sorry," he said again, calming, holding her tight.

This poor girl. Everything she'd ever known and loved was gone. Taken from her. It was wrong. So wrong. Something no child should ever have to bear. Who would look after her now? Who would keep her light safe? The light he saw and felt within her.

Greyson knew that all souls, all hearts were born white. Pure, like a blank and glowing canvas for the world to paint on. This he believed, above all else. No heart was ever born dark. But as it navigates the world, and grows, all the colors it collects do make it dim. And without guidance . . . without protection, some can dim too quickly. And their hearts are forever stained.

Like Bail's . . .

But Greyson couldn't let that happen to this girl, so bright. He couldn't let her heart be stained by ash, or fire, or blood . . . He had to keep her safe. For her sake, but also for his own. Because whatever light he felt inside her was so powerful it could cleanse his heart of darkness. And scare away all the horrid thoughts his father told him never to forget.

He couldn't let such a precious thing go out.

Her light might be the only light he had left at all . . . The only ray of hope salvaged from all of his mistakes. Her light was a monument to all of those he could not save.

Stiqula eyed his faded reflection against the surface of a window, looking out onto the dark void of the cave beneath the keep. Slowly, he turned his head to see the dark plasma burns all down his neck, flecks of charred skin crumbling as he moved. His armor was healed again, but his body could not perform the same blessing.

His eyes shifted to see Itxaro's reflection standing behind him, among the control panels of his new ship . . . unceremoniously dubbed: the *Claw*. Built here, beneath Rock Town, commissioned fifty years ago. It was the most powerful ship man had ever seen. A secret, until now.

"You let them in." He turned from the glass to face his bridge. Three control panels lay in front of him, a step down from three more behind them, and the last against the far wall between its doors. Six of his men sat at their stations, ready for orders. Itxaro stood obediently at the last. "You let them beat you." Stiqula stepped toward him. His voice was quiet, like the sound of far off thunder. "You let them *take it*." His face grew tighter as his anger swelled.

There were only three prayer chains on this entire planet, each meaning more to him than the last. And Itxaro had lost Stiqula's. Given to him at his birth, over three hundred years ago.

Itxaro looked down to Stiqula, standing dangerously close, a hellish twinkle in the depths of his eyes. Stiqula kneed him in the groin, bringing the giant to his knees, and wrapped Aliqula's second chain around his neck.

"Shall I kill you for what you've done?" He spoke calmly, but tense, strained from holding his black giant still.

Itxaro clawed at his neck, trying to slide his fingers between the sharp chain and his splitting flesh. He gasped for air and reached for Stiqula's leg, but his great hands were not strong enough to crush his curséd armor.

Stiqula pulled Itxaro closer to his face, lifting him right off his knees, the full weight of his body hanging by his neck. "My *dio* was *not given easily!*" He tore the giant down, bashing his head against the metal corner of a control panel, and released him before he died.

"And this one, even less."

Itxaro coughed and gasped, rolling on the floor, plucking the bladed chain from his bleeding throat.

"Do not lose it. Or I will deepen those cuts down to your bones." Stiqula turned away from him. "Take off," he ordered. "The king's men will be here soon in search of this ship those boys discovered."

His convicts jumped to work, each one of them a former guard, with much experience commanding bark ships, of which the controls were built to mirror.

Stiqula left his bridge as the *Claw* breathed its first breath, like a bow, freshly strung. And Stiqula shivered just the same, alone in the thin, metal hall. A rage blew through him. A maelstrom matched only by his grief. He'd given Itxaro her chain. Her *dio*. A relic, so intimate and holy. He clutched the other, her first, wrapped tight 'round his fist. There was nothing more sacred to an angel than their *dio*. It was their link to Light. To fate. To love. The conduit through which their soul could be harnessed to protect themselves: the lerité . . . And giving such a thing to Itxaro . . . was like giving part of Aliqula's soul away. The only thing that still made her feel real to him. Near to him. Something he could hold, and touch . . . Much more so than tattered memories . . . Not just a lie, conjured by a God to make him do Their bidding.

Stiqula raised his hand, open and shaking, and clenched it closed on her chain with a spark of static in his fingertips. He would find the boy that took it from him. That boy who stole his chain. He would find him. He would find him and rip the air right from his lungs, strip his heart of all humanity, and feed his dark soul to the devil.

Stiqula roared, flexing his entire body, and laid his fist into the wall.

"She's in a better place now," Greyson said, still cradling her. Thinking of anything that would console her. Anything to make her smile instead of cry. "She's in a better place," he said again, not even sure he knew what he was talking about. His mom used to tell him all kinds of things about heaven, and the Realm of Light. But, at this point, he couldn't tell which parts were real and which parts weren't. They all seemed real at the time. They all made death seem not so scary, hopeful even . . . and that's all that really mattered.

"Did she ever tell you about heaven?"

She let up on the crying a bit, curious of this new and unfamiliar word. She shook her head, still nuzzled in his chest.

"Well, heaven is the place we go to when we die. Our soul grows wings and flies across the stars, following their light to the very edge of darkness, where there's no more pain . . . and no more . . . bad things," he smiled, simplifying all "bad things" into something a three-year-old could understand. "And there's a city there, called . . ." *What was it called?* He tried to remember, back to nights when someone died in Wellington. His mom would tell him this story, tucked in bed, afraid his soul would somehow loosen in the night and he'd die before morning . . . It was . . . "Leiaru," he said. "A city made of silver roads and crystal towers. Where the sun is always shining, and haloed by a rainbow." He let go of her to draw a circle in the air so she could see what a halo looked like. "It's the city of angels, where all souls go to when they die. To live together and be happy 'til the end of time."

The girl pushed on Greyson's chest, leaning back to check his eyes for truth.

"And Momma's theo?"

Greyson nodded and smiled. "Yep. She's waiting for you—" He quickly looked away. He couldn't say those words into her eyes without completely breaking down again. "She's looking down on you from the stars." He looked back.

She looked up to the window behind them in search of the precious star light. The black and smoky skies over her town had gone, replaced now by the rich blue glow of the moon against the clouds.

"And whenever you miss her, all you have to do is think of her, and be happy." He tried to keep it together for her. But it was just too damn hard to explain without crying. The tide of sadness rose again under his eyes, and a single tear escaped, which he quickly swept away, and tapped her on the chest. "Because that happiness is a little bit of heaven that you share with her." Greyson swallowed the next rise of the tide, waiting for her to cry again. But she didn't. She stayed strong. His story worked. She looked at him with those big eyes of hers, waiting to hear more of the magical place where spirits lived.

"Here, let's wipe those tears." He pulled his shirt up to wipe her cheeks, gently brushing left, then right. "What's your name?"

"Kyri," she said softly.

"Hi, Kyri. That's a real pretty name. My name's Greyson. It's very nice to meet you." He extended his hand to her in the tiny space between them, wrist tucked up against his chest.

She verged on a smile, seeing his cramped hand stretched between them, and brought hers against his palm. He closed around her arm, and shook up and down exaggeratedly. Then a smile spread across her face. Which, in that moment . . . was the most beautiful thing.

"Do you feel her?" He tapped her chest again.

She nodded very lightly just to agree with him, then bigger when she realized that the growing calm and warmth was what he meant.

"I do too." He smiled, just as big.

A ping over the ship's intercom interrupted their moment, and they both looked up to the speaker on the ceiling, waiting for an announcement. The ship must have been getting close to Cantidium. And Greyson waited to hear the captain tell them to prepare for arrival . . . But after a short span of silence, the intercom just pinged again.

"What's dat?" Kyri asked.

The alarm pinged again, quicker than before.

"I'm not sure." Greyson placed her down as the ship rang again . . . Then again. Faster. And faster.

A woman screamed from the hall as the captain shouted over the loudspeaker. "Ship incoming! Brace yourselves!"

What brief peace Kyri had found was quickly lost as she regressed to tears again. Greyson spun to the window behind him. The moon had turned the sand dunes into ocean waves, with islands of cotton clouds against a deep navy sky. And lurking far behind them, he could clearly make the outline of a ship, ever growing. It was following them. Chasing, twice as fast. Then from behind it, even further through the blue horizon, two red beams fired up into the sky, glowing as bright as Itxaro's blade, and as solid as two straight bolts of lightning, lasting just as long.

Greyson's face wrinkled in confusion, but there was no time to try and make sense of it. The black outline of that ship was growing closer, slicing through the moon beams like bladed tentacles.

"Stay here," he said as firmly as he could without scaring Kyri, then burst into the hall. He turned right and bound over people, pushing off the walls to dodge the traffic. Flying through the loading bay, he reached the bridge, only slightly larger than a two-pilot cockpit. "It's the *Aliqula*! Pull back!"

Without a second thought, the pilot slammed on the brakes as a single anti-aircraft round exploded in front of them. Unable to stop completely, the bark ship dove into the fire as it blackened to smoke, emerging unharmed, into the long limbs of the *Aliqula*, blurring by their starboard side. But they were not its target. It stayed true to its course, driving dead ahead, to the City of Cantidium, and the fleet of seven ships that hovered over it.

"Dear gods," the pilot whispered.

The city glowed beneath them, its streets sprawling like a grid that'd been cut to pieces and reassembled in no ordered fashion. Bright highways wound their way between each gridded neighborhood, sprawled in a crescent from the Desun Sea, black as the dark side of the moon. And in the city's center was a spire, rising almost a mile over the shore, like a planetary lighthouse, large enough to ward off meteors instead of ships.

The *Aliqula* sped over the city, and as it approached the fleet, the sky ignited like a minefield, pulsing in the fire of anti-air shells. But they were not coming from the *Aliqula*. Explosions bloomed from the sides of each bark ship, streaming their glowing shells to converge upon the stick.

From Greyson's vantage outside the fog of battle, the *Aliqula* didn't appear to be defending itself at all. "They're not fighting back."

The stick ship tore through the battlegroup, leaving a trail of flashing fireballs in its wake. It stood no chance, losing one of its limbs and main engines, and its elevation along with it. The *Aliqula* rolled across the sky, out of control. And more shots landed, peeling back its thin shell of bark, which rained down to the beach as it sped past the spire.

The *Aliqula*'s twisting limbs collided with a bark ship, which was too massive to evade in time. Her limbs snapped against the bark's hull. And the thrashed bark ship was sent wavering to the earth. With hardly any engines left, the *Aliqula*'s nose plunged into the sea, hitting hard against the sea floor, half submerged, shaking loose many more of its damaged branches, nearly balancing on its nose like a flaming tree. That's when the rest of its engines detonated, and the *Aliqula* tipped, lying down into the water on the smoking ripples of its waves.

"Holy shit." Greyson couldn't believe it. That just happened.

"Yeah," the pilot agreed.

He stood there, staring, as the surf rushed over the stick ship, slowly extinguishing the last of its fires. And he kept staring, waiting to feel any sort of relief. But it never came. His body stayed as tense as ever . . . The *Aliqula* . . . was not destroyed . . . It'd killed itself.

# 16

# TWENTY HOURS LATER

Tay stirred under his sheets, tucked tight as a friggen cocoon. He could barely move in the damn things. And his brain . . . felt like it was one sneeze away from exploding out his ears. He lifted his hands, heavy, weighed down by a bunch a extra shit strapped to his fingers, imbedded in his arms. Finally he opened his eyes to see what torture device he'd gotten tangled up in. But it was worse than that. He was inside the white, plastered walls of a hospital.

The lights were always so goddam bright in here. Curtains separated the beds, like 30 of 'um, all crammed into this big, circular, holding pen, with one nurse's desk in the middle, and five nurses that would *only* pay attention to you if you're dying.

Tay turned to the chair next to him, Greyson draped over it like a drunken starfish, mouth wide open, head hanging off his shoulders, out cold. He was cut, bruised, and dirty, made the whole room smell like sweat and soot. Hadn't seen a real bed in . . . longer than he'd ever been without a bed for, Tay figured.

Tay flashed a smile and cleared his throat. "Hope I look better than you do."

Greyson didn't even flinch.

"Hey," Tay coughed. "I'm bein' funny over here." His voice was dry.

Greyson gave a little bit of a jolt this time, cutting his snore short and blinking his eyes open. "You're alive."

"Sure feels like it."

"Do you need some meds er something?"

"That'd be greeeeeeat," he dragged out, keeping his head very still. The slightest anything felt like a hammer to his temples.

"I think your thing's right here." Greyson stood and pushed the little red button on the call buzzer next to Tay's hand.

"What time is it?"

Greyson leaned around the curtain to check. "It's uh . . . 8:62. At night." He leaned back. "You've been out for like, twenty hours."

"Have you been here the whole time?" Tay said, almost offended.

Greyson shrugged. "Pretty much."

"Dude, go home. Wait, where are we?"

"Well, we were in Cantidium. But I transferred you to Darakin a few hours ago."

"Yeah then, go home. They didn't give us a room for nothin'."

Greyson sighed and sank back into his chair. "I know. I should. I just . . . don't wanna be alone."

Tay scrunched his face. He'd never heard Greyson say those words before. "Why?"

"I don't know." He looked away. He knew. He just didn't wanna say it. "I just feel like shit."

"'Cuz you haven't slept in a week," Tay said as the nurse arrived.

Greyson didn't give any kind of response.

"How are we feeling tonight, Mr. Hooker?" She was hot.

"Other than my head about to explode, I'm fantastic."

She looked at her clipboard, then to her watch. "Yes, it's probably time to re-admin your pain meds."

"Yes, please. I'll take those to go."

"Well, right now your brain is swollen. It'll make walking almost impossible. But I'll see what I can do." She walked away, but that didn't sound too promising.

"They said you're gunna be in here for at least another day."

Tay sighed like a horse. "Awesome." He shifted his delicate head back to Greyson, friction tugging on the bandages around his head. "So what's *really* wrong with you?"

Greyson met his eyes, studying them before he spoke. "I just . . . don't get you."

Tay smiled, happy to be the subject. "What?"

"Even now, you're, same-old you. Like you always are. Like nothing's happened."

"I've seen better days, Grey."

"That's not what I mean." He grunted, not sure how to explain. "How do you not let anything get to you? Like everything that's been going on." He leaned in and lowered his voice to just above a whisper. "Stiqula, and . . . almost dying. All the people we've seen die . . . All the people we've . . ." He couldn't said the word. "How do you deal with it?"

Tay lowered his sarcasm levels to match Greyson. Or at least as close as he could get. "I . . . don't think about it like you do. I don't let it bother me."

"But how?"

"No, I *literally* don't think about it, so it *can't* bother me."

"I try not to think about it . . . But it's like, I'm two people. Every time my soft side says *hey, don't think about this one thing*, my asshole side does the exact opposite to fuck with me and splays their faces all over my brain."

"Really? *Ugh.* That doesn't happen to me." Thank gods. "That would suck."

"Great. Yeah, it does." Greyson sat back down.

Tay laughed to himself. Trying to think of a different way to put it. "This is some tough shit we're dealing with here. You can't beat yourself up about it." He looked to the ceiling in search of the right words. Something philosophical that he knew Greyson would like. "Sometimes . . . there isn't always a right or wrong choice . . . there's just the *best* choice."

"How do you know what's best?"

Tay shrugged his shoulders, very weakly. "Take that guy, when we first got to Rock Town. Your back was turned. He was gunna kill you. I had to do something. I didn't want to beat around the bush and knick his shoulder or something. I had to be sure he wouldn't get you. So I put him down . . . and then, as inhuman as it sounds, I forget about him." He shrugged again. "Until your sappy ass makes me think about it."

Greyson nodded, fake-smiling.

Tay had one last idea to try and make him see. "You're always worried about what's coming or what's been. I just worry about what's happening right now. And right then you needed help."

"You make it sound so easy," Greyson said, smiling for real this time, but more of a *this-is-funny-because-I'll-never-get-it* smile, rather than an *actually*-funny smile.

"Well. I've had a lot more practice than you . . . It's kinda one a those things you eventually get, or go insane."

"Yup. Yup, I'm definitely one of those." Greyson nodded.

Okay, *now* he had one last idea. "You were this same way when it happened the first time."

He nodded again. "I remember."

"Well, do you remember how you got over it?"

"I stuffed it away . . . and pretended it didn't happen," he spoke slowly, like Tay had finally gotten to him. "But is that right?"

"Stop with the right and wrong crap. What other choice do we have?"

Greyson was quiet.

"Just take a day. While I'm in here, take the day, to chill. Try stuffing, or just not thinking about it. See how you feel. Then ask yourself what's better: feeling like shit, or ready to keep being a guard and keeping people safe . . . Think about all the people you're doing it for. Find *something* to look forward to. And stop wallowing."

Greyson finally flashed a true smile.

For saying the wrong thing so much, he sure knew how to say the right thing sometimes.

"Deal." Greyson stood, fast as a kid before recess. "Thanks for the pep-talk, vagina face."

Tay verged on a laugh as Greyson turned to leave. "What did you call me?"

"You don't remember? You called yourself that after we got rescued. And you also fumbled over a tampon joke to the guard that tried to help us. Who was a girl, by the way."

Tay's smile quickly melted. "Oh god." He deflated in his bed, looking up to the ceiling. "Just unplug me now."

"I can't believe you don't remember it. You tried the same joke on this nurse too."

"I what?" Tay's heart rate monitor sharply spiked as the nurse returned with his meds and Greyson giggled out the door.

# 17

# AN ENEMY OF REASON

Before Tay had woken up, as soon as they'd arrived in Darakin, Greyson climbed to the highest level of the tree, to warn his king about the ship he'd seen beneath Rock Town, and report the unfortunately high probability that Stiqula was still out there.

"Greyson," Megan said as he entered the lobby, surprised to see him so early.

"Good morning, Ms. McBride." He pulled up to her desk. "I have some news I need to discuss with the king about what happened in Rock Town."

"A'right, um. He's been in a meeting for a long time now. But I think they might be talking about that same thing—I'll let you in." She reached under her desk to find the button.

"Thanks." He turned to the opening doors, as morning light flooded through them.

"Where's that friend of yours? Did he get fired?"

"He's in the hospital." He looked back at her. "He cracked his skull open, dragging me to cover."

"Oh," she said, staying very still, like she was surprised to hear Tay was capable of it.

Greyson continued into the light.

The king was meeting with just one person, and as Greyson approached, he recognized the outline of his general.

General Brown turned to face him as he arrived at the dais. "Mr. Wight?" He had a few scratches on his face, and his left arm was wrapped up in a sling.

"Good morning, general." He nodded, then turned to the king. "I'm sorry to interrupt, Your Highness, but I have news about Rock Town."

"Yes, we were just discussing the wonderful news."

Greyson took a double take. "The what?"

"Stiqula has finally been slain," the king said proudly.

"You were there?" Brown asked.

"Yes. And also the battle over Cantidium," said Greyson.

"It's marvelous! I wish I could have seen it myself. The *Aliqula* in flames, plummeting into the sea." Laughter bubbled up from Huey's gut.

"But, sir, how do you know Stiqula was on that ship?"

The king's giddy smile shattered. "And where else would he have been?"

"I saw him, sir. I—hit him." Greyson breathed deeply as he claimed his king's full attention. "In a cave under Rock Town. He had another ship."

"You *hit* him?" The king asked, focusing on the wrong part of Greyson's sentence.

"Yes, Your Highness. But I don't think it did anything. He leapt away."

"Well *where* did he go!?" Huey screamed, beating his armrest.

"I—I don't know, sir. It was dark and I couldn't see much of anything before Tay pulled me out."

"Then you don't know *what* you saw," the king decided.

"I do, sir. I know—"

"*Stiqula,*" he interrupted, "*died* at the hands of *my* fleet and General Brown. Long putting to rest my family's tortured souls. And his *death* shall be *celebrated*. I have called for a ball, this Fardeis, to be televised to the world, that *I* have finally *slain* the monster. And *you* will attend and *contest* to this *undebatable* truth."

The king's words blanketed Greyson in a silent disbelief. *Contest?* That was the exact opposite of what he meant. *Contend,* or *comply* was more like it. And in that moment Greyson finally realized that Huey was a fool. A living contradiction. He tried to hide it with big fancy words, but that only made it more obvious. He was lying to himself. And too stupid to remember he was lying. Always used to getting his way, so that even when matters were out of his control, he still believed his word was law. He was a child on the throne.

Not a shred of the great leader he pretended to be. Not a single goddam shred . . . But Greyson couldn't tell him that. All he could do was stand there, fake a smile, and nod, as much as that smile stung his cheeks, and that nodding strained his neck. "Yes. Your Highness."

"Good," the king said, very seriously. Then faced his general. "I think we're done here, Theodore."

Brown was still looking at Greyson, watching the way he moved, and his reactions to the king. He nodded to Huey and motioned for Greyson to walk with him down the great hall.

Greyson was relieved to see the general again. At least *he* actually understood the seriousness of things. He could hardly keep his mouth shut on the long walk to the doors, hoping whatever hard feelings the general felt for him about releasing Stiqula could be pushed aside so they could work together on locking him up again.

"This isn't over, sir," Greyson said quietly as they passed into the lobby.

Brown slowed his pace, but did not respond in any other way.

"Didn't you see the lights?"

That stopped him. "What lights?" He caught Greyson's eyes.

"Just before the *Aliqula* attacked, there were red beams shooting up from Rock Town. I think they were from that other ship I saw."

Brown was silent again, staring. Waiting to respond. Begging Greyson to say something of worth. A lead that could actually be followed. Something more than flickering lights and shadowy ships.

"Stiqula's not an idiot," Greyson said with some kick. "Why would he fly right into a battle he *knows* he can't win? It's too easy!"

Brown tensed his shoulders, looking to the gawking secretaries on either side of them. He turned and clapped his hand against the back of Greyson's neck, walking him from the lobby like an outspoken child. Outside, he shoved him into the corner of the hall. A place no one could hear them. "Don't you ever talk to me like that in front of *anyone*." He came two inches from his face.

Greyson recoiled, almost afraid of the old man. But really he just regretted pissing off the only person in the whole damn kingdom he respected. Then something Sam said crossed his mind . . . maybe Brown wasn't as virtuous as he'd thought.

"I opened up to you, speaking about Vertuém Destiny and Stiqula. Because I thought you needed to know. Do *not* make me regret it. You will not speak against the king so publicly. There is much more going on here than you realize, Greyson . . . I am not Huey. I try to guide his choices, but I am not the only one. And whatever choice he makes, I must obey."

Maybe that's what Sam meant—that he didn't know he was on the wrong side. He thought he was doing the right thing by obeying the king, trying to sway his opinion whenever possible, but . . . at the end of the day, he had no other choice than to obey. And Brown was only as "good" as the king commanded.

Brown's eyes left their lock on Greyson's, dropping to his waist. To the tail end of the chain that dangled from Greyson's pocket. The general shot a breath out of his mouth, instantly backing away. "What . . . is that?" he asked, though it sounded like he already knew.

Greyson looked down, pulling the chain from his pocket. It clung to his skin, holding him as tightly as he held onto it. Even unactivated, he could feel it tingling. There was something very unsettling about this piece of alien metal. "I'm not sure. Something of Stiqula's."

"How did you get it?"

"One of his men in Rock Town had it. Eat-Sorrow, er something."

"*Itxaro?*" Brown's eyes bulged.

Greyson nodded carefully. "You know him?"

"I'm the one that put him in that prison. Good Lords, how many more vertuém has he released?" Brown turned away.

*Vertuém*. If Brown was so afraid of them, he must believe. "Please, sir. What are the vertuém? You have to tell me. So I know what to be afraid of."

Their eyes met again. Locked while Brown deliberated. "The king knows I believe. And part of me knows that he must as well. But the fact that you *are* one . . . is the only reason I will tell you."

Greyson swallowed, opening his ears as wide as they'd go, clearing his mind like a blank sheet of paper. Ready to finally learn the truth that'd been taunting him so long.

"They are prophets," he said firmly. "Able to hear, to see, and speak to the Lords of this world. And sometimes, with events strong enough, they can see the future."

Crystal, teeth, and blood flashed through Greyson's mind.

The *future*? What kind of fucked up future had he seen?

Greyson looked down to himself, no longer wearing his clothes, but a silk-white robe, torn at the chest. His flesh was missing there too. A fist-sized hole down to his sternum, which was not bone, but a dark, grey crystal.

"The trouble is knowing which god to listen to," the general continued. "Sometimes it drives them mad. And those we hold . . . *held* in the maximum security branch of the detention center, were the worst of them. They pose one of the greatest threats to mankind. They are that powerful."

Greyson felt sick, still staring at his own insides. "I've seen something, general." He spoke very slow, deliberately, terrified the consequence these words would bring.

The demon was dead. But the danger was not gone. The window burst as Greyson leapt from it, sucking the black monster out into the stars. But space's vacuous claws showed no prejudice toward evil, and pulled Greyson back upon a torrent of escaping air.

Then, just before he disappeared through the broken pane, the window's safety shutter slammed shut over the shattered glass, and Greyson slammed into it, instead of following the demon into space.

He panted and slid to the floor as the room filled with oxygen, equalizing once again. And as the air returned, so did the ship's alarm.

Greyson looked left, to a glowing wire outline of his ship, suspended in the middle of the dark room. It was made of a dim, blue light, and looked just like a weighty chandelier. Its main body was tiered in concentric cylinders, from which hung an array of spikes, like icicles, the three largest dangling from its lowest point. And surrounding its main body were four arms, stemming from its crown, further dressed in even more crystal spikes.

The entire model was poxed with red, pulsing spots. Infected.

The demons. Greyson knew it. Because the angel knew it. Their ship was lost to them.

"We should not have left our place. We should not have gone to Læ! Stiqula was not there! Only Darkness." The words came out of the angel's mouth, though Greyson had not spoken them, himself. He was not controlling this body he envisioned. He was just along for the ride. Yet everything that angel felt, so could he. Including the deep drum of his heart, the chilling air upon his sweat, and the dripping of his own blood as it left his body through the cuts upon his arms, and the hole within his chest. It would have been a fatal wound to any man.

But he was no man.

The angel sprang at once and drew his heavenly blade, cutting through the darkness as he sprinted down a crystal hallway before him. The light was following him, sticking to the clear and rippled walls, leaving a wake of white behind him as he ran. But his wings remained folded. The hall was too narrow for them to spread. Instead, to speed his momentum through the near weightlessness, Greyson grabbed hold of a U-shaped handle adhered to the wall. And the moment his fingers wrapped its grip, it took off along an invisible track in the wall, pulling him off his feet, speeding down the white hall.

In no time the white hall ended, intersecting with a grander hall of gold. Enormous. Over twenty feet in diameter, and seemingly infinite in either direction. Here, Greyson's angel released the fast handle and spread his wings wide, nearly fourteen feet in all. Catching the air, he banked left and flew down the gold hall, which glowed like a tubular sun around him. And standing up ahead, there was another. An angel, like him. But a girl.

He landed before her, but she did not see him. She stood, still as stone, staring past him to the shadows at the very end of the hall, far past the white passage he'd come from. Almost half a mile away.

"Sister!" Greyson said to her. "What are you doing here?" She wore a silver halo on her crown, and her robes were torn and bloodied just the same as his.

"Refsiel's progeny," she spoke, still watching the shadows far ahead. "They have killed us all." She finally turned to Greyson. Her eyes. So deep and full of sorrow. An arctic blue. Like two grieving oceans. Tears fell from them, and instantly froze upon her cheeks. "Why would Oyopa let this happen?"

Greyson breathed deep, and placed a hand upon her shoulder. "Speak not ill of our Lady, Nevrine. This was our doing. We should not have left our place. And we must destroy this ship to make certain Her Creation is kept safe from our actions."

The young angel nodded at Greyson's words. "It is already begun. What few of us are left are headed to the bridge now." She pointed down the hall again, this time opposite the shadows. "You must follow after, and see it through to the end. Destroy this ship by self-detonation, and all the sins we carry with us will be cleansed."

"And what will you do?" Greyson asked.

"The demons must not reach the bridge," she wagged her head. "I will see to it this axis hall is severed, so that they cannot reach it easily."

But, as if to deny her plan, the far shadows at their back began to stir, and cry. And like the cold finger of space had stroked their winged spines, Greyson and his sister turned to look upon them.

The demons were already on their way. Dragging darkness ever closer, blotting out the gold light of the hallway. They flew, they flowed, like black water toward the angels, hissing, crying, roaring.

"Was it a vision of Stiqula?" Brown asked, as if he expected it.

Greyson shook the darkness from his mind, and focused on the general again.

"You saw how to defeat him?" Brown assumed.

"No, sir. Stiqula had something to do with it, but I'm not sure what."

Brown deflated slightly.

"I was an angel," Greyson continued. "On a ship, in space. Shaped like a chandelier. And it was overrun with . . . demons."

Brown's eyes widened.

"It terrified me, sir. Enough to order Tay to fire on that tanker . . . Because, I try to destroy the ship by self-destruct." Greyson swallowed. "I thought it was a sign. To blow that tanker up before it had a chance to free Stiqula."

Brown nodded like it finally all made sense, but there was one part Greyson was still leaving out: "But," he said. "It doesn't feel like it's the future, sir. It feels like . . . like that ship is up above us right now." Greyson could feel it. Floating out there in the dark. Drawing ever closer. Like someone holding a finger an inch from his skin ever since he first had the dream, the day he arrived in Viæden.

General Brown's eyes drifted from Greyson's, giving a shudder. But he did not say a word.

"What does it mean?" Greyson had to know.

"I'm not sure. It doesn't sound to me like any vertuém vision I've ever heard of."

"Does that mean . . ." Greyson couldn't help but fear all the death and darkness that he'd spread was a side effect of the true color of his heart . . . a dark Vertuém Destiny, now awakening. He saw his sword again, enter the long-haired, scruffy convict, and silence the life in his eyes. He saw Bail again, as he pulled the trigger on his life. Greyson swallowed once more, trying to keep his churning stomach down. ". . . that I'm not one of the good ones?"

Brown looked at him and breathed deep. "Greyson." He placed his hand on his shoulder. "You are," he said, so plainly.

His stomach settled.

"I saw it in your eyes, the moment we met. And regardless of what's happened from then 'til now, I still see it."

Greyson's chest fluttered. If he didn't believe in himself, at least someone did. "So then . . . what does it mean?"

"I'm not sure what to make of it. But time has a way of making all things clear." Brown backed away from him again. Standing up straight. "And in the end, the only one who will know how to interpret this vision, is you."

# 18

# The Ball Announcement

The fissure of the mirror room had been mended, boarded up so tight no light could enter. Stiqula knelt before the chasm, having lit a single candle that was resting on a raised lip of the pit. A makeshift altar. The candlelight reflected in the mirror, and against Stiqula's focused eyes as he gazed upon the altar, only a foot higher than the floor. Aliqula's chain was lain across it.

He dragged his blade over his middle finger, slicing it deep. Hardly any pain at all, compared to the unrest of his heart.

Then, he dragged his finger down along the wood, leaving a straight line of black blood behind. "Half an empty heart." He drew as he spoke. "Marked by the cross of angels. Crowned by the horns of demons." He pressed his finger down, until his crystal bone touched wood. "Give sight to Refsiel."

Stiqula blew his candle out, and let the darkness take him, wrapped around him fully like a Father's love.

"I have given You death," he spoke. "Surely their souls number in the thousands . . . But still You are unsatisfied . . . You remain silent."

The silence . . . it was powerful now. Like Darkness Himself was all around him, absorbing the words as they left Stiqula's mouth. The silence was listening. Lingering. Threatening.

"How many more must die?" Stiqula continued. "Or is this number endless? . . . Are my actions Your means, or Your end? . . . Surely the lives I've taken are for something." Stiqula's anger grew as the silence deepened further. "*Speak!*"

But nothing replied.

"The riddle of Your Gate has never been solved. Tell me what must be done to free You!"

Just then, the chamber door slid open, like stone dragged over wood, and the torchlight of the hall spilt in. "Sir!"

Stiqula turned to his man.

"You told us to wake you for the news."

Sam stood in her kitchen, scrambling two cosabro eggs as she sipped honey tea from a mug. Her hair was a mess, pulled back in a tail. But she didn't care this early in the morning. The only people she had to impress were her dad and Audris.

"Good morning Samanta," Audris greeted, reaching for a mug in the cabinet next to the stove. She had warm honey-colored skin, and long, silk hair, black and braided. She was from a land far to the south, on the other side of the world. A refugee her father took in when Sam was just a girl. She came to the kingdom, like so many other immigrants, without understanding the king was such a xenophobe, and would arrest anyone who wasn't as white as him. Her dad offered to pay for a trip back home but . . . Audris refused. She wanted to stay. In the hopes that one day things would change. Even if it meant she couldn't set foot safely outside the O'Nasi estate until that dream came true.

"Good morning Audris." Sam stirred her eggs.

Nash was sitting forward on his brown leather couch, looking over a mess of papers fanned across the coffee table in front of him, glasses clinging to the edge of his nose. He sat in the center of a spacious living room, lined with bookshelves and tall windows that looked out onto an endless lawn. His morning tea was in one hand, a blue pen in the other. The television played in front of him, though very softly, as it did every morning. Sam could see him out of the corner of her eye, over the counter to her left.

And she saw when he lurched forward, choking on his tea. She turned to him, concerned, then looked to the TV to find out what had startled him. On screen was a woman with black and curly hair sat behind a glass desk, wearing a rosy blazer as bright as her excited cheeks. The headline in front of her read: *STIQULA DEFEATED.*

Sam's eyes pinned open wide as she stepped round the counter, and Nash turned up the volume.

"As of this morning, King Huey has confirmed that the rumors of the villain's return are in fact true. For fifty years he has remained in hiding, speculated somewhere deep in the Biazlé Mountains. And this Viædeis he made his return, descending upon the city of Kabdrey in the same crooked ship he appeared in, all those years ago. True villain that he was, he destroyed the Museum of Animallia, desecrating the monument to all those lives he ended fifty years ago. From there, he attacked the Detention Center, freeing 3,000 of its prisoners, and releasing them into the nearby grass forests. The area around the tree has since been evacuated and checkpoints are in effect to contain the escaped convicts that did not join him.

"And last night, he struck his final blow, setting fire to a town in the Canted Desert, completely destroying it. It's estimated that over 600 people have died in this attack, and thousands more injured. Hundreds are still unaccounted for. But in a brilliant move, the King's Army ambushed the *Aliqula* at Cantidium, before he had a chance to strike again, and brought his infamous ship down in a ball of fire."

Amateur footage played behind her, taken from the ground. A black sky with grainy pops of light and delayed booms tore across the sky.

"His ship crash landed in the Desun Sea, drowning any chance of his survival. Divers are inspecting the wreckage today in search of answers as to why he chose now to return. Perhaps the last effort of a dying man to seek revenge. Or perhaps we'll never know. But regardless, King Huey would like to personally assure everyone that the Kingdom of Viæden has never been safer. And this Fardeis he will be inviting us all into his great hall via live-stream for a cordial celebration of Stiqula's demise."

Nash turned to find Sam standing right behind him, fixed on the screen. "You think that boy you met knows anything about this?"

Stiqula stood on the bridge of his *Claw*, the entire front windshield, which doubled as a television, was paused on the newscaster's excited expression. He turned away from the screen in thought, his men looking on. "Perhaps I was mistaken to destroy the *Aliqula*."

"It worked, sir. They think you're dead," his pilot encouraged.

"It has brought them security," he denounced. "And in their certainty of my demise, I have brought hope to their hearts. I have weakened Refsiel. So that He cannot tell me my next move." Stiqula gritted his sharp teeth. "I have wasted those lives."

"I don't understand."

"Because you are human," Stiqula glared at them. "You do not understand the world is built of Darkness and Light, together. And every emotion is tied to their war. So mankind's *hope* erased my work. And must be crushed again."

# 19

# Cantidium knockout

It was cold here. So cold, and dark here in this place. A black veil hung ten feet from him in all directions. And nothing else. Nothing but a grey, featureless pond beneath him.

But he could feel something behind him, soundless, motionless. A presence, commanding him to turn and face it. He looked over his shoulder, listening for any signs of life. But all he heard were the whispers of his breath, and the echoes of his feet on frozen ground.

But he could feel her, looking at him.

He could feel them *all* looking at him. Everyone that he'd let die . . . standing just beyond his sight, a little ways inside the veil. Bail. Ellis, Lawson. The nameless convict. Fyren, and the men that killed him. Crowded in the depths of the dark mob of souls, stretching back into infinity, the souls of all Stiqula had slain. An army of dark souls, waiting for their orders.

But there was one, standing with him in the light. Her hair was copper-brown. And her eyes were heavy. Filled with grief and questions. But also acceptance. Her dress . . . so strange. Flowing down her body, clear and rippling, a curtain of water springing from a fountain at her collar, clinging to her skin as it rolled down her body to the floor, spreading across the ice to him.

She raised her hand, inviting him to take it. To save her, or come closer, he didn't know. But before his mind was made, her clear dress turned to black, flowing now like ink instead of water, crawling to the floor. The sea no longer clothed her, but darkness instead. Because he did not act. He did not take her hand. He did not save her!

And the darkness grew to drown him.

He was choking on it, coughing up the darkness in his lungs. Then air kissed them again, and woke him. Greyson gulped down a shallow breath, opening his eyes to find himself beneath a tree, just like the one back home, growing sideways over the wheat fields. For a second he thought he *was* back home . . . But that didn't last long.

He was all wet, lying in a few inches of water. And someone had him under the arms, dragging him along a floor, as smooth as marble. He splashed, throwing his hands down to sit up. It looked like he was in the middle of the friggen ocean, water rippling out in all directions. The *Aliqula* wasn't far off, less than a mile in front of him, half sunken in the sea, like a kraken's wooden tentacles reaching from the deep. A fleet of guard boats circled it in the water. And a small bark ship hovered above, that looked a lot like General Brown's.

"Are you alright?"

He spun to the voice. It was Sam, wearing nothing but a wetsuit, haloed in the sun.

"Sam?" he said, hoarsely.

"Are you okay?" She asked again, out of breath.

"Where are we?"

"I got us to the sunken tree."

Greyson looked down. "The what?" It was bark below him, sanded smooth by the tide. The sideways tree over them was just one of its branches. And looking to his right, he saw many more like it, sprouting from the water for miles along the sunken tree's trunk, until its head rose from the water like a green mountain. Each leaf glowing gold in the sun.

She looked a little concerned. "In Cantidium, remember?"

Greyson looked left to find the shore in the distance, and an enormous wooden spire, looming almost a mile high, like a spike that anchored land to sky. It looked vaguely familiar, different lighting, and a much different angle, but it was the same spire he saw from the sky when the *Aliqula* attacked Cantidium.

"Oh . . . yeah." He wasn't too sure. All he knew was he still couldn't breathe too well, unzipping his wetsuit and curling it off his bare chest.

"That bastard gave you a concussion didn't he?"

Greyson raised an eyebrow. Since he didn't know who she was talking about, "I'm gunna say, yes."

She nodded. "I was afraid of that. What do you remember?"

He thought back.

He remembered answering the door of his apartment to find her and her dad had come to visit. And that stood out to him because he'd fallen asleep, face-down on his couch after he'd left Tay at the hospital, and slept through the night like that. So when the doorbell rang at 8:75 in the morning, he had all kinds of red lines streaked down his face from the cushions, lookin' real cute.

When he invited them in, they were acting real sketchy, avoiding his questions, and grilling him on if he thought the king had forgiven him for Stiqula or not . . . Well, her dad was the one doing most of the talking. She kinda just stood there. Anyway, he answered yes, since the king hadn't thrown him in jail or had him killed yet, even though Greyson still hadn't forgiven himself.

He remembered Nash was watching him real closely, then hummed when he found what he was looking for, and dragged him out of his apartment.

The old man was testing him, to see where his loyalties lay, to see if he could be trusted. In the hall, they dropped their games and told him his room was probably being bugged, and that the king would likely be watching his every move . . . That was not a pleasant surprise. But he believed it.

Then they asked him the real question they'd come to find out. So important, Nash grabbed him by the collar to let him know he wasn't fucking around. "Is Stiqula alive?"

Greyson didn't know the answer to that question. But his heart was plenty sure. "Yes."

Nash's grip loosened, pulling back.

"Probably." Greyson softened as Nash did. ". . . I don't know."

Nash released him completely. "You were there, when the *Aliqula* crashed."

Greyson scrunched his face. "How do you know that?"

"I didn't." He smiled. "But vertui have a remarkable knack for being in the right place at the right time. And I recall giving you one of my ships to head back in that direction the other night."

*Shit.* Greyson totally forgot about the ship he'd left in Rock Town. "Oh . . . your ship—"

"I don't care about the ship." He waved it off. "What did you see?"

"Stiqula had another ship, in Rock Town. Something I've never seen before. Metal, like a claw . . . I think he used the *Aliqula* as a diversion. To get the king off of his back."

"Well it worked," said Sam.

"I told the king, but he, basically ignored me."

"Huey only sees what he wants to," Nash explained.

"I'm starting to realize that."

Nash nodded. "Then we must take it upon ourselves to discover what he's up to."

Greyson's vision focused back on Sam kneeling in the ocean as she pulled the tassel on her back to unzip her wet suit, peeling it off her body, rolling it down to her waist. She had on a bright blue bikini top underneath, and her dewy skin mingled with the sun beams. But her eyes loved the light most of all, reflecting the sparkling rays as they undulated on the surf around them.

"I remember you coming to get me. But not a whole lot after that." He rubbed the side of his tender head. "Who knocked me out?"

"I think you said his name was Riese."

Suddenly it hit him. Literally. The memory smacked him upside the head.

Nash had landed their little O'Nasi transport—an exact copy of the others he'd lost—just outside the city harbor. The boat harbor, not the sky harbor. He was very concerned with the time, nervous the City Guard would contaminate the crash site before they had a chance to look at it themselves. It was just a few minutes to one. And that's when Greyson noticed that the bark ship floating above the sunken *Aliqula* was Brown's.

"Is it?" Nash squinted through his glasses, humming in agreement. He was always humming in agreement. "Well it looks like you two are on your own then."

"What? Why?"

"They have a bit of a history," Sam answered.

"Like how?"

Sam looked to her dad, not about to answer for him.

"I wasn't always the shining samaritan I am now."

"Brown went on a bit of a witch hunt for him, back in the day."

"What did you do?"

"I was a pirate," Nash said proudly.

Greyson wrinkled his brow and leaned away from him, the situation suddenly becoming so much more complicated he needed to take a step back to comprehend it.

"Best the world has ever seen," Nash continued. "First, and *only* air-pirate, to this day. I stole more trades, tech, and gold than any other river pirate ever could. More hueys than I knew what to do with. It was back when airships were a new thing, defenses were minimal. No one ever expected to be boarded fifteen thousand feet off the ground."

"Alright, Dad. We get it."

Nash smiled. "Sorry, dear. Not every day I get to talk about it."

A *pirate*, Greyson laughed in his head. A friggen *pirate*? "For real?"

Sam just looked at him, wondering what was so funny.

"Oh gods, you're serious."

Sam nodded like, *duh, just said that.*

"I trust you can keep this a secret." Nash slapped him on the shoulder. "I retired a long time ago, disappearing into the populous as *Nash O'Nasi.*" He waved his hands in the air, spinning in his seat. "Entrepreneur, extraordinaire."

Greyson looked back and forth between him and his daughter, putting it together. That actually made a lot of sense. It explained why Sam was such a badass, and as good a shot as Tay. She got it from her ex-pirate, rebel of a dad. He nodded, laughing for real this time. "As if this couldn't get any more complicated! Let's just throw this into the mix. Why not?"

"Good." Nash stood, pleased with himself. "Sam, get the wet suits."

"Are we going swimming?" Greyson asked as Sam disappeared into the back room.

"*You* are." Nash smiled. "Let's try to use your relationship with Brown to our advantage, shall we?"

"Ah, so I'm your inside guy, huh?"

"That's the idea." Sam said, handing him his suit with a cheeky smile.

Greyson nodded, accepting the situation for what it was. Though part of him couldn't help but feel a little disappointed. When Sam had shown up at his door that morning, he didn't know what to think. But getting used by her and her dad certainly was not on the short list of ideas.

Oh well, though. He shrugged it off.

He kinda felt like Tay, right then . . . So used to having him around, maybe Greyson's subconscious was taking over for the both of them. Or maybe he'd actually taken Tay's advice to let go. Whatever the reason, it sure was going to hit hard when he started over analyzing things again.

After that, they went to the harbor. Brown's guys had closed off one of its piers and set up a makeshift HQ at the end of it to investigate the crash: a big white tent filled with all sorts of folding tables, recovered debris, and scanning equipment. They hadn't found anything useful yet, except that Stiqula had gotten all his ammo from the VDC.

General Brown was standing, at the end of the pier, overseeing everything. The *Aliqula*'s wooden tentacles rose out of the water less than a mile away from them, in the shadow of Cantidium's spire, standing at the southern edge of the harbor.

Brown was actually glad to see Greyson. Which was a relief. He gave him and Sam permission to enter the ship and try their hand at uncovering anything more useful. Anything that could prove Stiqula was still alive. Even though Brown already knew it . . . He told Greyson that before arriving at Cantidium, he'd diverted to Rock Town, to see if Greyson's story about that secret ship hidden below the city held up. And all he found there was a giant hole in the ground. The entire city had fallen into the cave Greyson had found. And whatever ship he'd seen was long gone.

But at least the general trusted him again. At least a little.

A guard boat pulled up to take them to the *Aliqula* after that. Just a little dingy with a few places to sit and an open wheelhouse. And who else would be behind the wheel but good-old Riese. Greyson couldn't remember anything after that.

"Riese." Greyson nodded.

"What country is he from?" Sam asked.

"Mohavik."

"That explains a lot."

"Like what—Where'd he go by the way?" Greyson looked both ways down the tree, then back to the *Aliqula*. "And how'd we get here?"

"He drove off after he tried to kill us. Too much of a bitch to finish the job."

"He tried to kill us!?" Greyson spun back to her.

"Well, yeah." She didn't sound nearly shocked enough. "As soon as he realized it was you, he got a *crazy* look in his eye, drove us out to the middle of the sea, and tried to shoot us."

"How are we not dead?"

"You saw it coming and ran to tackle him while he was turning with his gun raised. Clocked you right in the head, and you flipped over the side of the boat."

Greyson felt the side of his head. "That sounds about right." Real heroic.

He tried to stand. But as soon as he did, all the blood rushed from his head. "Whoa."

Sam sprang to help him before he fell, grabbing hold of his arm, and wrapping hers around his waist. His skin tingled at her touch. Though that was probably only because he was so dizzy. "Don't try to stand," she said, shuffling him to the trunk of the sideways tree branch. "Let's just stay here for a little while."

"Okay." He wasn't about to argue with that, since she'd pretty much have to carry him at that point. They both slid down into place, resting their bare backs against the tree. Which normally would have been excruciating. But this particular tree had all its sharp bits sanded smooth by the sea.

"We're safe here." She sat next to him, pressing her shoulder against his, just in case he needed the extra support. He didn't, but . . . he wasn't about to pull away. She was warm against him. Soft. Soothing.

With her opposite hand, she wrung the water from her dark hair, combing her fingers through its waves, and pulling it taught. The water trickled from her curls and ran down her shoulder. He could smell her shampoo. Like freshly cleaned strawberries, and the smell of thunderclouds before the rain.

"So what's his problem? Why does he hate me so much? He knows Stiqula was an accident, he was there."

"It's not about Stiqula—well, maybe a little. But it's mostly about your eyes."

"What about them?" Greyson was getting a little tired of hearing that.

"In Mohavik they think all vertuém are evil servants of the devil."

Greyson's eyes got all wide. "Why would they think that?" The sting in his chest began to swell again, taken by a sickly feeling.

"A lot of people think a lot of stupid things about us."

Bail flashed through his mind. He could almost even see him standing in front of them, clutching a rock as big as his head, all the other kids behind him, screaming and egging him on. Not hard to imagine, leaning against that crooked tree like he was nine again. Especially having almost just been killed by Riese for the very same reason . . .

So if that many people believed it . . . did that mean there had to be some truth to it? Why they hated him so much . . . Could he really be some kind of demon?

He killed people just like one.

Sam must have seen the nervousness in his eyes. "Let's back up. How much do you even know about being a vertui?"

He thought for a second. There wasn't much. "General Brown said we were prophets . . . and that sometimes we see visions. And my mom said we're some kind of blessed by the Goddess of Earth."

"That's all?" She looked at him, one eye bigger than the other.

He gave an uncertain nod.

"Okay. Let me start over then." She looked away, wondering where exactly to begin, Greyson supposed. "So this religion, that's now illegal to believe in . . . One of its main doctrines is that the Goddess of Light created the universe with a Grand Destiny in mind."

"Okay, yeah. I know about that," he said obviously.

"Okay, good. And this Grand Destiny is made up of everyone's individual fates." She looked to make sure he was still following.

He nodded.

"But, seeded throughout humanity, likely by the Goddess of Earth—who is the guardian of all life—are a handful of these . . . *special* people, with fates that are stronger than the rest. And these people—*the vertuém*—have the ability to see things others can't. More supernatural things, glimpses of the future, maybe. Because their souls . . ." She held her hands out in front of her. "Are closer to the gods." She swept them away from her body. "I don't know. I'm not really sure the technical reason, or even if there is one. But this belief, as a whole, is called Vertuém Destiny. Because, while it's still part of Her Grand Destiny, it's . . . also different." She dropped her hands. "Its own thing."

Greyson could tell she wasn't completely clear on how it all worked. But it was the clearest explanation he'd heard so far. It made sense with what he'd seen in his vision, and what Brown had told him . . . and the king . . . it even matched his mom's stories too. The boy who would be king was looked after . . . *protected* by the Goddess of Earth.

Maybe his mom was trying to tell him all along that he was special. That all those legends were real . . . Trying to guide him to the light. But his dad also tried to guide him. In a very different way. And none of what Sam was saying fit in with *his* ideas of the world.

So, constantly being pulled in opposite directions, Greyson felt unsatisfied with both of his parents' ideologies, yet forced to pick one. "So do you believe it?" he asked. "You believe that everybody really has a destiny written for them?"

Sam smiled. "It certainly is a comforting thought, to know that everything happens for a reason, and we all have this beautiful plan ahead of us." Her smile lessened. "Most days I do. My *dad* certainly does, but . . ."

Greyson gave a single chuckle.

And Sam looked at him, smile widening again. "What?"

"My dad's the exact opposite. He doesn't believe any of it."

"It's funny." She chuckled with him. "Sometimes it feels like our destinies are written by our parents instead of Oyopa."

"I was just thinking that *exact*. Same. Thing."

That made her laugh for real.

"It's like," he continued, "I didn't even want to be a guard. Not really . . . I just thought I had to be one because my dad, and Tay, wanted me to be."

Her smile softened, looking at him. "So why don't you stop?"

He looked at her like she'd just made a sound he'd never heard before. "Never really thought a that." He looked away. To the infinite sea. "All my life I've wanted to do something exciting. Something worthwhile. And, in Wellington, I guess being a guard was the closest I could come to that. But all the downsides are . . ." He breathed deep. "I don't know if they're worth it."

She nodded. She knew what he meant.

"I love helping people. But. Lately I haven't been very good at it. And . . . it hurts." he rubbed his chest. "Like, literally."

"Well . . . I don't envy you. But I think what you're doing is very noble. And selfless. We need people like you to protect the rest of us."

He didn't really understand, shaking his head. "But if we all have destinies, why should we need protecting? I thought Oyopa and Trigana were doing all the protecting for us? . . . Most days, especially lately, it just feels like I've been spreading darkness, instead of protecting anyone from it. No matter how hard I try."

"If that's how it really worked, you'd be right. But it's more complicated than that."

"What do you mean?"

"Well, Oyopa isn't the only one that made us . . . We're the progeny of gods, not *god*," she said, so simply. But still her words had such a power to them. Such a casual truth. This was a part of the story he hadn't heard before. "Oyopa couldn't do it on her own. She needed Darkness too. Which means that Darkness plays almost as integral a part in our lives as Light. And while our hearts are spiritual, our bodies are still biological. And each of us is different. Each of us has a different tolerance for darkness. Some of us can stay true to our fates. But others are dragged down by the darkness in the world, and can get derailed from whatever destiny Oyopa gave to us . . . Which means that we need people like you to protect us, from those who've lost their way."

*Whoa*, Greyson thought.

"Darkness . . . *Refsiel*, cannot write fates. He can only destroy them. And He loves doing it. He is the *absence* of fate. And life is a constant struggle, for everyone, to find their path, their destiny, and stay on it."

"*Whoa*," Greyson thought again, this time out loud, as everything he ever learned about the world, from *both* his parents, became entangled: children, born with pure white hearts and a clear destiny, enter the world, which is made of all the colors of the gods, including darkness. And as they grow, their hearts become colored and stained to reflect the world they live in. And where darkness stains those hearts, it's like an eraser, blotting out little bits of their destiny, deforming it.

Finally his dad's words made sense to him. He could see him, standing over that dead ferret, telling young Greyson that every heart had darkness in it. And that it was safer to recognize this than deny it. He finally understood. He didn't have to choose between his mom's stories or his dad's . . . Because they were both true.

And what stood out most to him right then was the boy who would be king. Knowing that boy's destiny held such a weight on the world, Trigana had blessed him. Protected him, so that his destiny could be saved from Darkness. Acted out. And if *his* destiny was that important, then that meant Greyson's was too. And Trigana was his guardian.

"Wow," he breathed out. And the stinging pressure in his chest melted away.

Everything he'd done. All the darkness he thought he'd spilt . . . Maybe it wasn't as bad as he believed . . . If it was part of Light's plan all along.

He looked to Sam, right in her green eyes. There was so much light in them. And not just dancing on their surface, but deep inside. So much beauty. And wisdom. And even though she didn't have all the answers, she had every answer *he* was looking for. And he could feel that light, that *clarity* in him, erasing all uncertainty. And growing. Energizing him. Transforming him. He smiled so hard he had to fight it, to not seem like a crazy person.

He couldn't sit any longer. He had to stand, and look upon this world that was no longer black and white, but painted by Sam's light in every hue he never knew existed.

"How'd you figure all this out?"

She smiled just as brightly, joining him on her feet. "Well, I can't take credit for it. This sort of thing's been studied forever. Some of the oldest writings ever found were . . . ruminations on the soul and its destiny. Ever since we've had a soul, we've been trying to unlock its secrets . . . It might be the greatest mystery we'll ever know of . . . And it's all I think about . . . I think that's *my* destiny. Because it's certainly the reason I wake up each morning. Hoping one day I'll learn the truth, the secret, that will unify my faith to all the facts I've ever learned. And prove the gods exist."

She was on a journey of her own, just like him, navigating through the world in search of its secrets, and its truths. In search of her meaning. Her destiny.

He wanted to know so much more. About the world. But especially about her. "So you just sit around and try to prove the king wrong all day?"

"I—" She laughed. "Basically, yes."

"A'right, tell me something weird. Something he can't explain." He started to stroll in the direction of the shore, kicking through the shallow water.

"Lords, where do I start?" She followed after him.

"How 'bout the trees," he motioned below them. "Why are they so big here?"

She gave a nervous laugh. "Starting easy."

"Really?"

"That's one of the true mysteries." She thought of how to explain. "You remember Jacob?"

He nodded heavily.

"He believes they evolved over time like most everything else on the planet, starting in the Great Ceptris Forest, competing against the trees around them for height. Leading to only the tallest trees surviving. But I don't buy it. Don't get me wrong, evolution's a real process. But not in this case. Another in my team—an actual botanist—has done far more field research than Jacob, and discovered that, due to our gravity, at a certain point," she wavered her hands, "around a hundred yards, it becomes counter-productive for a tree to lug all that water from the ground up to its leaves. Meaning it has to put more energy out than it's receiving. Which is no good way to survive. Which means there's no scientific reason for these trees to be so large. The king's scientists say that the ceptris trees collect all the water they need from the atmosphere." She shook her head. "But if that were true, it'd mean there'd be so much water in the air we'd drown every time we took a breath."

"So what's the reason?"

She looked at him. "The reason is that there is a Goddess of Earth, who planted these trees, and her power maintains them . . . At least that's what I believe. What I want to prove." She spoke with much more uncertainty, separating her belief from fact. "And that's not the only mystery like it. Each god has one. Without a Goddess of Water, how can our freshwater seas be explained? And without a God of Air, how can this kingdom's lack of any sort of weather be explained, when the rest of the world has everything from fog to hurricanes?"

"What's a hurricane?"

"It's not important. Does it rain in Wellington?"

"Yeah, a few times a year. It's a big deal."

"Same here. But only on the very edges of the kingdom."

"That's not normal?"

"Not at all. In some places, further south. It rains every day."

"Whoa."

"The rain cycle is what's supposed to keep everything green—what *does* keep everything green. Except here. It's just perpetually green, for no reason beyond magic."

"How do the king's men explain that?"

"Underground aquifers," she answered. "Which is partly true, but again, it's not enough."

"And what'd you say about the oceans?"

"They're fresh water."

"So?"

"Well, if the planet's really four billion years old—which it is—that's four billion years of erosion by rivers, cutting through the land and picking up all its sediment, depositing it into the sea. In that amount of time, the entire sea should be *salt* water. But it's not. And of course the king's men don't even mention that—because it never rains here, therefore aren't many rivers." She started talking really fast, like she'd said it all a thousand times. "They attribute the fresh water as the reason the trees are so large, and attribute the trees for higher levels of oxygen in the air, which results in a more static climate . . . and also giant insects."

"Both sound pretty compelling." He shrugged.

She glared at him.

"I—I mean, they're good at coming up with excuses."

"M'hm."

"What about Fire? You didn't mention him," he moved right along.

"Yes, well, he's dead. So whatever mystery he governed is long gone."

"He's dead—?" he started in shock, then stopped to think. "Oh, right. I remember my mom telling me that." Then he remembered something else about the God of Fire. "But she said his mystery was still around." He looked back at her. "Parts of his soul, hiding in our hearts . . . disguised as *love*," he said playfully, like it was a pretty cheesy thing to say, which it was. But good cheesy. Pretty much the perfect thing to say.

"That's right," she agreed, just as playful. "If you believe in that sort of thing."

# 20

# A Mirrored Blade

It took almost an hour to get back to the shore, walking along the sunken tree. And as they walked Sam explained all about it. Turns out, Cantidium meant *slanted* in Old Anethan, the language spoken in this land while the tree still stood. But, growing so near the shore, the weak soil slowly eroded, and it tipped, taking the name. It was only recently it fell all the way into the water, leaving only the spire left standing: a massive chunk of its trunk, too stubborn to fall.

The sun sank low as they neared the city, gilding its light as it draped across the sandy facades of Cantidium. Its buildings were short, all around five or six stories tall, and none over seven but for the random bell towers, which normally would have made a city look too uniform and boring. But not this one. This town rolled with hills, making the ancient metropolis look like a collection of tiered cities that once used to war with each other for dominance, now joined together in unity. Or so his active mind supposed. It was all tragically romantic.

When they'd returned to the ship, they found Nash, kicked back in the pilot's chair, feet up on the control panel, newspaper draped over his face like a tent.

"Dad," Sam announced, stepping up into the ship.

Nash gave a snort and dropped his feet, sitting up in the chair and letting the paper fall from his face. "Oh, good, you're back. What'd you find?"

"Nothing," Sam answered as she stepped into the back room to change out of her wetsuit. "We got thrown into the sea by a friend of Greyson's."

"A friend?" Nash asked him, entering behind her.

"Just some Mohaviken, pissed I took his job."

"Hmm." Nash quickly accepted the new situation. "Just as well. If the *Aliqula* was destroyed on purpose, we weren't likely to find anything anyway."

"So, what were you hoping to find?" Greyson asked. "A spare napkin with his plan written on it?"

Nash gave a chuckle, then turned back to the window. "No."

"What then?"

He held back his response, for no other reason than to build suspense. "Proof."

Not exactly what Greyson was expecting to hear. "That he's alive?"

Nash didn't respond.

"That he's an angel," Sam answered.

Greyson turned to her as she emerged from the back room in her street clothes.

"If we can prove that, we can prove that the king's view of the universe—what he's forced us all to accept as truth—is wrong. Ignoring evidence because it doesn't fit your theory is bad science. He should not have the right to tell people what to believe in. Especially if it's wrong. And if *we're* right, I'm hoping it will trigger a movement to get rid of him altogether."

"Get rid of him?"

Nash finally spoke. "He's the last in his line. The worst king Viæden's ever known. You probably aren't aware, but the reason he's been hiring guards like yourself from the outer territories is because crime across the kingdom has begun to escalate. People are outraged, some starving. In his fifty years of rule, he's done nothing to further this kingdom. We're stagnant as the rest of the world marches on. Our population is growing, and our needs are changing. Our culture is in a constant state of evolution, and its outgrown him."

"Whoa," Greyson said. Guess there was still more *rebel* in Nash than he'd thought.

"Sorry, this might be a lot for you all at once," said Sam. "You've only just got here. Haven't really experienced Viæden fully yet. But I assure you, our golden age has long since past."

"Well, what kind of proof would you need exactly?" Greyson took a step toward the pile of his clothes on the ground.

"Something that cannot be explained by scientific means," Sam said. "Like the things we talked about, but more obvious. Tangible."

Greyson bent down to find his pants' pocket, slipping his hand in, and touching the cold coil of metal that was hidden there. "Would this work?" He pulled the silver chain out for them to see.

Sam stared blankly at it, the tendons in her neck rising to the surface.

Nash stood slowly with his cane to get a better look. To be certain what he saw was real. "Did you *take* it from him?" he barely whispered.

"Not him. A man named Itxaro." Greyson extended his arm for Nash to take it.

"No, no." He waved.

Greyson lowered his arm an inch.

"Can you activate it?" Nash asked.

"Um," Greyson retracted his hand, looking at the chain across his fingertips. "I did on accident, once." He pulled his sword from the corner of the room and unsheathed it slowly, careful not to hit anything in the confined space.

He wrapped the chain around its hilt, just like before, gripping it firm. It felt uncomfortable beneath his hand, unused to the extra metal in his grip. But more than that, it tingled, like his hand was falling asleep.

He held the sword away from him and imagined the starlight of the angel's blade in his dream, and the brilliant green light that had clung to his on the streets of Rock Town, attempting to show the O'Nasies the truth of their beliefs.

But nothing happened.

Greyson looked up to them, both staring eagerly, jumpy, waiting for it to happen any moment. But still nothing happened. He couldn't do it. For whatever reason the blade activated before, he couldn't re-create it. Greyson gave them an awkward smile and jiggled the hilt a bit. The chain clinked and tinkled, draping from between his hilt and fist like a trail of sand, but still no light came.

"Well, I did before."

"That's alright," Nash encouraged. "Your blade remained intact?"

"Yeah," Greyson answered, not too sure. "It even blocked Itxaro's laser blade."

Nash cocked his head, surprised for the first time. "*What* . . . kind of blade is it?"

"Just . . ." Greyson stopped to think, looking down at it. "Just a regular sword." He handed it to Nash for inspection, holding on to the chain. "It's an old family sword. But, I don't think there's anything special about it."

Nash took it by the hilt, turning to inspect it in the daylight of the windshield. It only took him a moment to realize. He flipped the flat of the blade toward them, sharpened edge to the ground, length running parallel with the floor. And in its silver glint was each of their faces, clearly, gazing back.

"This is a *mirror* blade." He turned, handing Greyson back his sword, hilt first. "An incredibly rare breed. They are not hard to confuse with stainless steel blades, which is why you might not have noticed. But this sword is far superior. And far more difficult to make. Only a handful of smiths throughout all history have ever been able to craft one. Its strength is comparable to high-carbon steel, but it's lighter, and since it reflects its surroundings, that makes it damn hard to see."

Greyson grasped the black hilt of his heirloom, but it no longer felt familiar. It was the same sword he saw day in, day out, on display in his father's office, racked on a shelf all to itself, among his family's books. The toy he dreamt of playing with each day after school, and longed to one day call his own. But it was new to him now, with a different meaning than before. A secret no one had ever spoken of 'til now.

"Is there a risk to using the chain with it? I've seen it melt through a gold sword and a big iron pipe in just a few minutes."

Nash thought for a moment. "That's something I don't know the answer to." He pinched his chin. "This light was only intended to be used with angelic blades, like Stiqula's. Made of some other element entirely. But I suspect your sword's reflective properties are the same. Its molecules may be so tightly arranged that it not only reflects light, but *heat* as well. Meaning you may be able to keep it activated for quite some time without any worry of damage . . . I'd happily run some tests, if you'll allow me."

"Of course," Greyson handed him the sword again, this time with its chain. "When I saw what that chain could do, the first thing I thought of was Sam." *That sounded awkward.* "Um, because she mentioned you'd seen something like it before," he elaborated quickly.

Nash smiled at his redness.

"What color was it?" Sam finally broke her silence, speaking meekly.

Greyson turned to her.

"The light. What color?" She repeated, more like herself.

"Mine was green," he answered delicately. "But when Itxaro used it, it was red."

"Fascinating," said Nash.

"Green?" Sam repeated. "How?"

"I . . . don't—"

"Every angel ever heard of has always had a white blade. Except for Stiqula's, which is black. How in the world did you get an actual *color*?"

Greyson shrugged his shoulders.

"I'll find out, dear. Don't worry." Nash slipped back into place behind the wheel. "I'll need to go to my lab in Ivy City," he said as the engines fired. "Do you want to come along?"

"Um." Greyson thought for a moment.

"You can see your new ship," Nash added.

"No, actually. I think I'll stay," he answered.

"Stay, *here*? Why?" Sam asked.

"I've got . . . a promise I have to keep."

"To who?" Sam asked, confusion mixing with a bit of jealousy in her voice.

"A little girl I met in Rock Town."

"Rock Town?" The jealousy flash-burnt into sympathy. "Is she okay?"

Greyson turned from Sam, staring at his clothes on the ground. "She lost her mother."

Sam's lips slowly parted, eyes weighed down.

"You could come with me . . . It might be good for her."

She hardly waited to answer. "Of course."

# 21

# EYES OF AN ORPHAN

The old, uneven stones paving the road to the orphanage were bathed in evening light. The road was thin, traveled only by foot, like many of the streets in this ancient town. The buildings on either side were stacked flush with one another, faces ornate with ledges and exposed brick beneath an aging sandstone plaster. Shuttered windows marked their floors, most reaching four stories, some higher on occasion, topped with light blue shingles to reflect the desert's heat. But ahead of them, on the left side of the street was an old temple, even more intricate in its design. Its domed tower was the highest building all around, stemming from the peak of Cantidium's highest hill.

This was the city's orphanage, repurposed after all worship was banned.

The main entrance, a high and rounded wooden door, was blocked by two thick stone flowerpots. Greyson and Sam entered through a smaller door beside it. The old thing creaked on its metal hinges, leading them to a small, unlit room: one of the chapel's offshoots, arched buttresses high overhead. It held only a few chairs, and a desk, fanned with brochures on adoption. Behind it, a middle-age woman greeted them, dark hair braided into a crown.

"Hello, how can I help you?"

"Hi. I brought a little girl in the other day, from Rock Town. Her name is Kyri?"

"Oh, yes, I remember."

"How's she doing?"

"She's quiet, to be expected. Not socializing yet. But this is only her second day. I think she'll need a little more time before she feels ready."

"Are we allowed to see her?"

"Of course." She smiled, leading them through a door to their right, into what was once the main chapel, now a play room. The pews had all been replaced by toys and tables, around which many tiny chairs were placed. Colorful carpets covered the stone floors, further littered by children's toys and board games with half their pieces missing. The room was empty though, everyone crowded at the opposite end of the chapel, where long tables were lined with chatty kids, the smell of supper in the air.

"It's so nice here," Sam said, lost in the vaulted ceilings.

"Yes. The king is very generous to his lost children."

Sam gave a weird expression, a sort of unhappy smile.

Greyson knew she didn't like the king. And he didn't much care for him either, so selfish and brash. But the fact that he took such care of all these orphans seemed so contradictory . . . It made him harder to hate completely. Made him seem more like a real person, instead of just a heavy crown.

The caretaker led them across the short width of the room, and up a spiral staircase to the second level.

"Were you able to find out anything else about her?" Greyson asked as they climbed.

"I was." She looked to her clipboard. "Her name is Kyri Amarine, born Camuel 23rd, 1370. Her mother's name was Adria, and her grandfather was the mayor of Rock Town. But a father was never recorded in her birth certificate."

The stairs led them to where the children slept. Twelve little iron-frame beds lined the left wall. The floor was tile. And the right side of the room was open with large arched windows that let the sunset in.

"Still sleeping," said the woman. "I'll let you have some time alone." She backed out of the room with a modest smile.

Sam poked her head out from behind Greyson, spotting a lump in the sheets, fourth bed from the end. "Oh Goddess," she whispered, leading the way to her.

Greyson was slow to follow, instantly feeling the weight of regret dragging on his body, like it had turned his blood to lead. She was alone in the room. Alone in the world. She had nothing. No one. And it was all because of him.

*Adria . . . I'm sorry . . . I'm so sorry.*

But this crippling grief . . . he didn't want it to define Kyri's life too, forever lingering between the dust and sunbeams. He had to protect her light—But wait . . . She was vertui too. So her destiny was just as strong as his, protected by the goddess.

. . . Did that mean her mom was always meant to die? That if he lived his life a thousand times, he'd always be too slow to save her? . . . Was it *not* his fault?

He didn't like that idea. Because if nothing was his fault . . . then nothing was his doing either. And if that was right, then what's the point? He was useless. But Kyri didn't make him feel useless. She made him feel needed. Responsible. And comforted . . . knowing he could be there for her. Because he needed her right back.

Sam stopped at the foot of her bed, grabbing the iron frame as she watched Kyri sleep. But Greyson went right up and sat down next to her, head poking from the covers, copper hair floating in the static. She woke quickly, rolling over to see who sat beside her, opening her brilliant green eyes, still red with tears.

"Hi, Kyri," he whispered, placing his hand on her back, just like his mom used to do for him.

"Greysom?" She crawled from the covers and wrapped her arms around him.

"Oh," Greyson cooed, holding her just as tight as she squeezed. She must have been relieved to finally see a face she recognized, even from the brief time that they'd spent together. He looked up to Sam, wagging her head slowly as the tears welled. "I brought someone to see you."

Kyri sprang back, looking him in the eye with shock and joy. "Momma?" She looked to Sam. But her brittle happiness crumbled again.

Sam's face wrinkled from sorrow to tragedy as she realized she wasn't at all who Kyri wanted. "My name's Sam," she said, reaching to pluck her from the bed. "I lost my momma too."

"What?" Greyson said slowly as Kyri slipped away from him, realizing he'd made a terrible mistake.

"It's okay," she said to both of them. "You didn't know."

Sam turned to the open archways, and walked with Kyri hugged against her shoulder. She looked out to a small courtyard below them, a few brick gardens in each corner, and a bubbling fountain in the center. Its walls were covered by a blue-tiled overhang, creating pillared halls connected more children's rooms across the way. And beyond was the city, sloping down to the golden sea.

"My momma's in heaven," Kyri said to Sam. "Is your momma dare too?"

Sam couldn't help but smile at her, pinching the tears from her eyes. She looked to Greyson as he joined them in the sunset.

"We had some story time on the way here." He rubbed her back again. "I told her all about heaven, and how happiness connects us to those we've lost."

"Yes. My momma's there too," Sam whispered.

Greyson couldn't imagine. It must have been like looking in a mirror.

"But she also never left me. I always feel her when I smile."

"Me too." Kyri grinned. "But . . ." Her smile faded, looking down in search of words she couldn't grasp.

But Sam knew what she was thinking. "I miss mine too."

Greyson came unraveled. This was heartbreaking. He couldn't stand it. How could the gods do this to them? How could they take their moms away from them and leave him his? It wasn't fair. Not one bit. Kyri and Sam . . . were so much more deserving than he was.

He cried, quickly wiping his face and turning to the sun to breathe. This wasn't about him. They needed their moment together. Kyri needed to see that Sam had made it through. So she knew that she could too. That she could overcome this horrible fate he'd made for her.

Another wave punched him from within, spilling tears and hissing out his mouth. He covered his face again.

"You okay over there?" Sam asked.

"Yeah," he turned back, a complete wreck. "It's just . . ." He kept his eyes covered. Trying to dam the tears. Trying to hide Kyri and Sam from his sight.

Seeing him like that started Kyri back up again.

Hearing her cry, he had to do something, uncovering his eyes and wrapping his arms around them both. "I'm just so sorry," he whispered, head resting against both Kyri and Sam's. "I'm so sorry."

Then he cleared his throat, collected his thoughts, blinked the tears from his eyes, and pulled back, still holding onto them. "I don't know who wrote this destiny for you." He looked Kyri in the eyes. "I don't know, and I don't care. Because *I'm* the one that feels it." He grabbed his chest, balling his shirt up in his fist. "And I promise you, Kyri. I promise *I'll* look after you. No matter what. I *promise*." He could barely speak. But he had to. These words were painful, cutting at his tongue. But he needed to bleed. This darkness needed to be bled from him so that he could heal. "I don't know how. But I promise, I'll get you out of here." For the sake of his heart, and hers, he had to.

Kyri didn't say anything, staring at him with those beautiful eyes. But he saw in them, deep in her grieving expression, a primal understanding. Some part of her knew the gravity of his words, and trusted him to make good on that promise.

"How is everything in here?" The caretaker spoke softly from the doorway.

Greyson locked eyes with Sam, his wet cheeks grinning at how perfectly awkward the woman's timing was.

"We're fine, thank you," Sam said over her shoulder as Greyson tried to pull himself together again.

He blew a raspberry with his lips and shook his head and flailed his arms at his side to shake it off.

Kyri let up a bit, seeing him so silly.

Then he took another breath and found himself. "Okay. Let's be happy from now on." He smiled, looking to Sam. But she wasn't smiling. She was lost, staring at Greyson like she didn't know who he was. And her eyes were glistening, like he'd said something horrible.

That got rid of his smile pretty quick. But on they stared, exploring deep into the emerald forests of their eyes, in search of what wonders they could find within.

"You . . ." she whispered, voice breaking. She looked away to blink and clear her vision. Then she began again. "I lost her when I was nine."

Greyson felt the punching waves return. "Sam, you don't have to explain."

"Yes. I do." She sniffed. "Because I knew I should have smiled and been happy that she'd returned to Light, but I wasn't. Because I would never get to see her again. Not with my own eyes." She paused to wipe her cheeks. "So I put all that grief into one place. One project. And turned it all to hope. Hope that I would see her again one day . . . Because that project was a ship. One that could take me all the way to the edge of the universe, in search of the Door to Light. Which I could use to free my mom's soul from heaven, and bring her back to life."

Greyson's mouth dropped, eyes opening just as wide, as Sam's words sank into his mind.

Kyri pulled back to look at her. Trying to understand what she'd just said.

"That ship," Greyson said. "Did you make it?"

Sam smiled. "Yes. And it still needs a name . . . I thought you could do the honors."

"Why me?" He was nervous of the answer.

"Because it's yours," she said simply.

"No." He shook his head. That's why she was so hesitant. She didn't want to give it up . . . The one thing she'd put all her grief into. He couldn't take it from her. Like taking all her dreams away. He couldn't do it. He'd taken so much already. "I can't. You . . . you can't."

"It's already done."

"But if I take it, it won't ever be used for why you built it."

"I'm still not sure where the line between belief and reality is drawn, Greyson. That dream might be impossible. And I'd rather keep it a dream than ruin it by learning the truth . . . The greatest thing my mom ever taught me was to give. To give until I had nothing left." She took a deep breath. "So I'm giving it to *you*. Because as bad a person you think you are . . . I know you're not. I know your destiny is bound for greatness, to save as many people as you hope you can. And my ship will help you . . . It will be a far better use to you than it would for my selfish dreams."

"Sam . . . I—"

"Just shut up, okay?" she said, very politely. "It wasn't an easy decision. But it's done."

The weight of responsibility was too much for Greyson's legs to carry. He fell into her, wrapping his arms around them again. She believed in him so much more than he did in himself. Everyone did. But that almost made no sense to him, growing up fearing he was some kind of demon . . . Maybe that meant he really was a good person after all. And maybe he needed to stop focusing on the darkness like his dad said, and start focusing on *light*, so he could see whatever it was that made everyone believe in him so much.

"Thank you," he exhaled his doubt, letting her certainty take him over . . . He needed that. He really did. "I'll take good care of it. And I'll try my hardest to live up to all the great things you built it for."

"I know you will."

He let her go.

"What should we call it, then?" she asked Kyri, playfully.

Then, staring at them both in the pink light, Greyson knew the perfect name. "How about . . ." He turned to face the sun. "*Leiaru.*"

"The highest light?" Sam translated.

"The name of the city, in heaven, where both your mommas live," he turned back to them. "It'll be my promise to you both, that once all this is over, we'll use that ship to go there, and bring them back with us."

"Yea!" Kyri cried, so purely. Her joy was contagious.

Both Greyson and Sam smiled, as brightly as the sun. And when their eyes met again, Greyson could see such a comfort in them, like he'd given her all the satisfaction and confidence she'd given him, that the choice she'd made to give her ship to him was the right one. Beyond any shadow of a doubt.

He felt so close to them both in that moment. Entangled. Like the sunlight draped between them linked the lights of all their hearts.

He knew he wouldn't let them down. He couldn't.

# 22

# Thank the Gods its Fardeis

Head stitched and wrapped in gauze, Tay pushed through the glass doors into the Office of His Royal Secretaries. Not much of a headache anymore with all the pain meds he was on. He clocked Megan looking up to see who it was, then quickly back to her monitor in a horrible attempt at looking too busy to notice him.

He flashed a sly smile, accepting the challenge, and stepped to the other secretary instead.

"Hello, *Stephanie*," he announced.

"How can I help you, Mr. Hooker?" she asked, politely.

"I was just wondering if you've seen Greyson around anywhere."

"I haven't, sorry," she said, way too emotionally, like she'd personally let him down.

Tay didn't really care that much where he was. He could just call to find out if he wanted.

"Have you checked your room?"

"Yeah." He snuck a look at Megan to see if she was listening. "Aren't you gunna ask about my head?" he whispered.

"What happened to your head?" Stephanie asked, like it was her idea.

"You wanna see it?" He lifted his bandage to reveal the sewn cut above his left eyebrow.

"Ooo, that looks like it hurt."

"Yeah, got it from Stiqula," he bragged.

"Oh, wow!" Her eyes went all doughy.

Megan scoffed.

He turned to her with his stitched brow raised, all inquisitively.

She scoffed again, more obnoxiously to his face. She knew what he was doing.

He turned back to Stephanie with a grin. "So anyway, we were infiltrating his base in Rock Town and came face-to-face with him."

"Oh, gosh! Weren't you scared?"

"Nah, I've handled chumps like him before."

"Really?"

"Oh yeah, all the time."

Megan started typing spastically loud on her keyboard.

Tay raised his voice in response. "So then there was an explosion that blew up in my face as I pulled Greyson to safety."

Megan stopped typing.

Tay turned to find her staring, she had a glint of concern in her eye.

He had her. He abandoned Steph all together, walking over and leaning his weight against Megan's desk. "So what're you doin' tonight?"

"Knitting sweaters for my cats."

"What's a cat?" He plopped his elbows down on her desk and rested his cheeks in his hands, pretending to be fascinated.

"I have a lot of work to do. And you're drooling all over it." She shooed him off her desk, straightening the papers he leaned on.

"C'mon, it's Fardeis. You coming to the ball? They'll be celebrating my bravery," he said as smug as possible.

"Seriously, I have plans."

"We do?" Stephanie chimed in.

Tay looked to Steph, then back to Megan. "I seriously don't believe you."

Megan looked up to him with a dull scowl, then picked up her phone.

Sam and Greyson somehow managed to snuggle into the tiny bed with Kyri, both of them half hanging off the sides, reading through a watered-down version of *The Fable of Faehill*. Sam and Greyson had heard it many times.

A very old story. One of the first ever written, and one of the few to survive Huey's banning. Greyson hadn't heard it in a long time, and with all that'd happened to him lately, he read it through a different lens completely, trying to decipher what parts could possibly be true from what parts were obviously fiction . . . he was having a hard time deciding. But Kyri loved it, each page adorned by an epic painting of giant eagles, talking turtles, flaming horses, or vicious beasts that dwelt in dark places. She had to touch them all, pointing and making the sound of every animal she knew.

"*Art thou Queen of the Fae?*" Sam read aloud. "*Try as they might, none could see her form through the light. 'She is,' Micael said as he stepped forward to stand at the queen's side. 'Does she not speak?' asked Fyriel. 'She does, though you cannot hear,' Micael replied. 'Though perhaps in time you may. Her tongue is not of sound, her words unknown by ears. Instead she speaks to the heart. Her voice is awe incarnate, emotion to the soul.'*" Sam's phone began to ring as she finished the last sentence, some popy-sounding song. "Sorry." She saw who it was and put the phone to her ear. "Hello."

"Hi, Sam." Greyson could hear Megan's voice through the phone. "We've still got plans tonight, right?"

Sam opened her mouth, leaning her head back. "Oh . . . I completely forgot. I'm kind of stuck in Cantidium right now."

A very loud growl came through the phone.

"But, I'm sure we can find something to do here," she said quickly.

"Ugh. Fine." Megan accepted.

Sam looked to Greyson for approval. "You wanna come?"

"Sure." He shrugged as his stomach did a backflip.

"Okay. Bring me a dress 'er something."

Just then, Greyson's guard badge chimed. He leaned over to pluck it from his jacket on the floor and brought it to his mouth. "Hello?"

"Tell her to invite me," a familiar voice demanded.

"Tay? Aren't you in the hospital?"

"I'm out. Tell her to invite me," he stressed in a whisper.

"Tay wants to come," he said to Sam.

"Okay, you have to bring Taymes with you too," she told Megan.

"Oh, *god dammit!*" Megan screamed.

She slammed the phone down and looked across the room to Tay whispering into his badge before he hid it in his jacket again. A completely innocent look on his face.

"You know, normally I'd warn someone with a head injury about getting trashed, but in this case I hope it fucking kills you."

"You could just not go." He called her bluff.

"I get *one* day off every two weeks. I'm not wasting it. Even if you're going to make it absolutely miserable."

"I'll try not to disappoint." He smiled.

General Brown stood just outside his makeshift HQ, left arm still cradled in a sling. He looked down to the black water, sloshing up against the jagged end of his stone pier. "Where are you?" he whispered. "For fifty years I've chased you. And fifty years I've failed. But now. Now that I'm at your heels . . . I've never been further away." He looked up. The sun had sunk below the sea, but the sky still glowed in purple twilight, with a band of orange along the horizon. It made the *Aliqula* look as black as the waters it bathed in, drawing thin rivers of night, up into the sky. "What a coward you are, to use the shadows as your shield. Surprise as your weapon."

"General," Knight called from behind, stepping out from the darkness of the tent.

Brown looked over his shoulder, but didn't face him.

"We've searched every known passage and chamber we could find within the *Aliqula*. There are no signs of his whereabouts, or what he might be planning next."

Brown nodded. He knew the conclusion to this story before it ever started. Greyson was right. "What of the pilot?"

"No sign of him. Chances are, he leapt before it hit the water."

Again Brown nodded, then looked to Cantidium's spire. It stood, soaring from the sand, just a little ways from them, stretching up into infinity. Its very tip still glowed pink in the sun. "And if he was right about this, what else could he foresee?" He shivered as he spoke, recalling Greyson's dream of dying angels floating at the edge of space.

He spun to his lieutenant, marching past him, through the tent and the faint glow of computer screens. "Tell the king I will be late for his ball. There's one last thing I have to do."

# 23

# Water Ball

It was the perfect night. Almost seven o'clock, a dry seventy degrees, not weighed down by humidity, even though they could smell the sea was near. Party lights swayed at the breeze, strung across the street in celebration. The air was charged with a rare excitement. People cheered, howling up into the sky, screaming their praises that at long last, Stiqula was dead . . . And even though Greyson knew it wasn't true, for that brief moment, he didn't let it bother him. For some reason, some magic still unknown, he felt an elusive confidence that everything he'd ruined, all the darkness that he'd spilt, would soon be gone. Sam made him feel like he could do anything.

"Okay. Alright, we'll meet you there. We're getting in line now," she said into her phone.

He couldn't take his eyes off her as she lit up, passing by windowed storefronts, then dimmed again as they stepped between street lights.

She closed her phone. "They're just landing at the spire port. Megan's really pissed," she giggled.

"He's not *that* bad," said Greyson. "He just doesn't know how to act around girls. He's still in that teasing phase from elementary school."

"Has that ever worked for him?"

"Actually, yeah," he was surprised to say. "He's had a lot of girlfriends— er, whatever . . . I guess the girls are just more sophisticated here."

She smiled at that. A not-so-hidden compliment. But more than just flattery, he was serious. No one could hold a candle to someone like Sam back home. She made this new world of his seem a little less terrifying. Like she took all the disorganized blurs of color it was made of and harnessed them into figures he could understand.

"Thanks for coming with me, I think she really needed that."

"No," she said in a high voice. "I'm glad I did. She's amazing. So strong."

"She is," he grinned, Kyri's smiling eyes still lingering in his head.

Passing through the blinding pool of a streetlight, they nearly collided with someone in the dark. He was young, head down, in a hurry, dressed in a fancy green doublet.

"Oh, excuse me," he said.

But Greyson recognized him. "Xander?"

Xander looked up, brown eyes softening. "Greyson! What are you doing here?"

"What are *you* doing here?" Greyson almost laughed.

"King's business, you know." He smiled. "Are you coming to the ball?"

"Mno." He shook his head. "I think we're going to find a party here instead."

"Ah," Xander nodded. "Just as well." He continued past them. "It was good to see you, Greyson. Have a good night."

"Yeah, you too," Greyson called after him.

"Who was that?" Sam asked, continuing on.

"Just one of the king's aides. He's nice. The king's kinda mean to him though."

"The king? Nooo," she played.

Nearing the shore, the crowds grew thicker, and the bass got louder. People spilt into the streets in masses, hovering outside of pubs on either side of the street. This was clearly the nighttime district of town. It became a little claustrophobic even, getting pushed around by the scrambled current of the hordes. But finally they broke through to the beach thoroughfare, looking out onto the sand and blackened sea across the road.

There was a big stone arch built on the beach, four stories high, squared on top where spotlights shined, and rounded underneath where turquoise lights reflected off its intricate carvings. The arch had a large space around it that was completely enclosed by a hedge, with the roar of people and hypnotic lights projecting from within.

"That looks like a party," he said.

"It's usually a park. They must have turned it into a club for the night," she said, growing a smile.

"Well, let's go then." Greyson took her by the hand for the first time, diving into the crowded street, dodging loose elbows and straggling feet to the opposite sidewalk, and the end of the club's line along the hedges.

Sam's phone rang as they arrived. But their hands stayed together for a moment longer than they needed to. "Hello?" she answered, covering her other ear.

Greyson's hand stayed charged, nerves lighting up where their skin had met.

"We just got in line at the Anethan arch," she said.

He searched the busy road for any familiar faces, anxious to see Tay again. They hadn't been apart for this long in forever.

"Oh, you are?" Sam looked up to search the street, waving at the air.

"Greyson!" Tay shouted, jumping out of the crowd, poking him in the ribs like rapid-fire.

"Ow! Stop it!" He laughed, dodging to protect himself.

"It's a madhouse out here." Megan emerged behind him, wearing a tight, black dress, with slits across her chest and all down both her sleeves to reveal pale skin beneath.

"I know, right?" Sam gave her a happy, one handed hug.

"How's your head?" Greyson eyed the obvious bandage in the middle of Tay's forehead.

"They gave me a bunch a drugs, I'll be fine."

"They might not let you drink with that on your face."

"Fuck that. That's discrimination. I'll arrest them."

Greyson laughed at his determination.

Megan glared at him, having had quite enough already. "I brought your dress." She turned and raised her bag to Sam.

"Oh, great! Let's go across the street." She eyed a retail store.

"We'll hold our place," Greyson said.

"We'll be right back." Sam led Megan into the street.

"I don't know what to do. That girl hates me," Tay confessed.

"Maybe try a different approach?" Greyson said quickly, like it was waiting on the tip of his tongue for an excuse to jump. "Or better yet, why do you even like her if she hates you?"

"'Cuz she's hot, and funny. What's not to like?"

"Well, maybe it's 'cuz you kinda come off as a dick?"

"How am I a dick?" Tay winced.

Greyson glared back like, *really?*

Tay relaxed. "Fine."

"Just act *normal*. Show her your soft side, like you do around me."

"You sure she'd go for that? She doesn't seem like that kinda girl."

"Well anything's better than your current approach."

"Fine, but I better not get friend-zoned."

"You won't, I promise."

Tay gave an unassured grunt.

He didn't open up to many people. Like, Greyson, and that's about it. And he probably wasn't going to start now. Greyson almost laughed at the thought of Tay actually being himself around anyone else but him . . . But anything was possible.

Meanwhile, in the world's tiniest changing room, Sam was squeezing into her dress as Megan waited on the other side of a short, yellow curtain.

"How come *you* get Greyson, and I get stuck with *the incredible talking dick*?"

"Just give him a chance, Megan. You gotta stop scaring off all the guys that try to flirt with you."

She could hear Megan rolling her eyes on the other side of the curtain. "Ugh, I know. It just seems like they're all douchebags."

"A lot of them seem like that at first. But you gotta break through their outer, macho layer to find out who they really are underneath. Greyson says he's actually a really good guy. He just doesn't know how to flirt."

"What a winner."

"Oh, stop it." Sam pulled back the curtain, revealing her curves in a tight, metallic dress. "Just be a bro for me tonight, okay? If you still hate him in the morning, I won't put you through it again." She slapped Megan on the shoulder as she walked to the exit.

Megan followed her out. "Whatever. But if some hot guy starts dancing with me, I'm not sticking with the walking boner."

"Deal," she said over her shoulder, striding between round racks of clothing in the harsh light of the store. "Thank you," she called to the man behind the counter as she pushed through the glass door onto the hot and loud street.

They found the boys right where they'd left them. The line hadn't moved an inch. Sam and Greyson locked eyes for a moment, trading something intimate before they looked away with grins pulling at their lips.

"You guys haven't moved?"

"Nope," Tay answered.

"Well I'm not standing here all night." Sam leaned around to check how far the line went. "C'mon." She started for the front. The line bent around the corner of the park, following the hedge down a covered walkway, lit by dim, dangling light bulbs. But just to the side of the line, there was another roped off path that was completely empty, guarded by a big, tan man with a tiny mustache. "What's this line for?"

"VIP," he said.

"And how much does it cost to be a VIP?" Sam asked.

"An *H*. Each."

"Sam, we can wait—" Greyson started.

"I'm not waiting," she said over her shoulder, reaching into her handbag to withdraw a translucent blue card, slightly larger than a credit card, with the same magnetic strip on one end. But on its face were numbered keys, and two scanners in the bottom corners. With her thumbs she typed in *400.00*, digitally registering on the magnetic strip, then placed her thumbs down on the scanners to confirm her bank account. Only a moment later, the *400.00* flashed and scrolled off-screen, replaced by the word *accepted*.

She handed the card to the guy, now worth four hundred hueys. "There you are, sir."

"Here you are, ma'am," he said as he removed the velvet rope for them to enter.

They passed at least a hundred people before they reached the start of the line, Tay cockily smiling at each one, waving like a princess.

Then, passing through an archway in the hedge, the music became exponentially louder, carried into the night by blue and green laser lights, strobing to the stars.

Beneath the arching monument was the DJ booth, built overtop a square fountain, whose waterfalls collected into a river that halved the park, flowing a short distance to a tide pool, connected to the sea. Two bridges joined the two halves of the park. On the far side, a stage was set, with dancers in skimpy outfits, and blinding lights flashing to the beat. And on the near side, booths were built into the surrounding hedge, with a few rows of tables around them, covered by square umbrellas and twinkling lights. There had to be at least a few thousand people all crammed in there together, mostly huddled by the stage, or around the various bars spread throughout.

"Holy shit!" Tay gasped.

"I take it you don't have parties like this in Wellington?" Sam asked.

"Not even close," Greyson answered.

But suddenly the music silenced, and the spotlights dimmed.

"What the fuck? What's happening?" Tay sputtered as the party died.

A projection screen lowered from the face of the Anethan arch.

"The king's ball is about to start," Megan explained.

"Oh. Greyson, weren't we supposed to go to that?" Tay asked.

"Yeah, I didn't feel like it."

The screen flickered onto an image of King Huey, sitting on his throne, wearing the most egregious costume. Just layers and layers of green, white, and gold, with a thick and heavy necklace of pure emeralds, about a hundred of them, all knitted together in silver, like fish scales.

"Good evening, Viæden," his voice boomed in stereo. "Tonight we celebrate the conclusion of over fifty years of unrest. Fifty years of uncertainty as to when evil would strike again. Fifty years of unfulfilled revenge. We hunted him, a *terrorist* responsible for the murder of one hundred thousand innocent men, women, and children. A man responsible for the eradication of our greatest city, and the murder of our former monarch . . . But. Tonight . . . I can gladly say that our unrest is *over*. Our uncertainty is *gone*. And our *revenge* is now satisfied."

Dull cheers and hoots came from the crowd.

"Thanks to the valiant efforts of our Kingdom Guard and its general, I say, with a glad heart, that at long last, *Stiqula is dead*!"

The dull cheers erupted into a cacophonous roar. Leaving Sam, Greyson, and Tay the only ones that stayed silent.

The king raised his crimson glass. "*Tonight*, we celebrate those lost to senseless violence. We celebrate those lost to keep us safe. *Tonight*, we celebrate *life*, and remind ourselves what *evils* belief in deities can brew . . . To Viæden, and her people." He raised his glass higher still. "May our future remain as bright as it is today."

Again the crowd cheered. And as they toasted, the screen turned blank, and the lights and sound of celebration returned.

"He might be an idiot, but that guy knows how to write a speech." Tay broke their silence.

"He doesn't write his speeches," Megan laughed. "He's got a whole department writing his speeches. All he has to do is say the words right."

Sam spotted a group leaving a table in front to them to go dance. Quickly she slid through the crowd to steal it before anyone else could.

"How can he get away with calling Stiqula a man?" Greyson asked as everyone pulled up to the table.

"For two reasons," Sam started. "They let you pick and choose which one makes more sense to you, even though they're both bullshit. The first, and craziest idea, is that a man, calling himself *Stiqula* to sound exotic, used the arrival of the Rock as an omen to prey on the weak-minded and begin his violent overthrow of the monarch. But only cracked-out conspiracy theorists believe that one."

They all giggled at that.

"The more logical approach—which makes so much sense I'm forced to consider it—is that life evolved on Nævah, in parallel with Viæden. Except, due to drastically different environments, the humanoids of Nævah found it evolutionarily advantageous to grow wings."

"Well, that one makes sense to me," said Tay.

"Do you believe everything the king tells you?" Sam asked.

"The king didn't need to tell me, it just makes more sense."

"You know Wellington's curriculum is under the same education system as Viæden's right? So, he kinda did."

Tay suddenly looked terribly let down. "I need a drink." He left to find a bar.

"He doesn't like it when he's wrong," Greyson said into Sam's ear. And she could hear in his smooth voice that he was smiling.

"Oh. Something him and Megan have in common," she said loud enough for Megan to hear.

"What?" Megan asked, irritated.

"Nothing," she played.

"I better go make sure he brings back enough for everyone," Greyson excused himself.

"Seriously, what did you say?" Megan moved closer.

"Nothing," she laughed. "Just that you and Tay both hate being wrong."

"Oh, *gods*." She rolled her eyes.

"He also doesn't believe in those either." Sam poked her in the shoulder repeatedly. "You guys have so much in common!"

"I'd literally rather make out with anything else. Like *anything* else. Like the floor before I let his tongue anywhere near me." She opened up her blush to see how her face was holding up in the tiny mirror.

The boys returned a few minutes later, drinks in hand.

Tay pulled up to the table with his chest all puffed up, slid Megan's glass down in front of her and turned to Sam like he had a great rebuttal. "Okay, *Sam*."

"This should be good," Greyson said quickly in her ear.

She smiled and engaged him fully, ready for anything.

"If all this religion business is legit, and there are these two all-powerful Gods, One's good, and the other One's a total asshole, and all the Asshole wants is for the world to end, what's stopping Him? And what's stopping Her from taking Him out altogether?"

Finally, Megan's ears perked up.

"If a Goddess made the world," he continued, "with literally infinite resources at Her disposal, why would She put a bunch a bad shit in it? And where the hell *are* They? Why don't we see Them shooting down beams from the sky, or blowing up mountains like They used to do in all the stories?"

"That's a great question." Sam smiled, smugly. "And the answer is, it's all about *balance*. The key is that Light and Darkness made the world *together*. She couldn't do it alone. So in a sense, She isn't all powerful, as most believe. Each god is restricted in their actions, in a sort of checks and balances. Each move they make must be calculated, because they know there will be repercussions for it. It's an eternal tug-of-war for the souls of man, and the fate of the universe. They probably do interact with the world on a daily basis, but those actions are so small that we don't even notice them. Because the more people that notice, the stronger the action would have to be. And the stronger the action, the more power they'd be expending and putting into the world, and since the world must remain in balance . . . another god will be inclined to counter. Perhaps undoing or even making worse whatever the first god was trying to do. So you see, they are certainly powerful, it's just that they *all* are powerful. Each one of them."

Tay didn't have anything to say to that.

"Make sense?" Sam twisted the knife.

"Whatever," he turned to Megan. "So you're like, her spy, aren't you?"

"How am I a spy?"

"'Cuz you work for the king, and tell her everything he's doing."

"I mean, I guess. The king doesn't tell me all that much though. It's mostly only what I hear in passing."

It was subtle, Tay definitely didn't see it, but Sam could tell Megan liked the idea of being a spy.

"Sounds like you're a pretty shitty spy," he teased.

"I'm not a spy!" She faked an outburst to hide a smile.

"Does he talk about us all behind our backs?" Tay prodded.

"Well, I mean, yeah. He hates you guys."

"*What*?" The boys sputtered together.

She laughed. "No, he doesn't talk about you."

They sighed in relief.

"The only thing he's been talking about lately is this damn ball."

"I'm pretty sure he hates us anyway," said Greyson.

"And . . . well, I did hear something else," she continued. "Or, Steph did. She said she heard some guards leaving the throne room talking about a new princess."

"What?" Sam lurched in.

"Yeah. But that's all. I didn't hear anything else."

"A new princess," Sam repeated. "He's supposed to be the end of his line. Where'd he get a daughter from?" It looked like the words tasted bad leaving her mouth.

Megan shrugged.

*Well, shit*, Sam thought. *That kinda fucks with my plan.*

She could feel Greyson's eyes on her, worried for her. But she didn't want to ruin the night. If her plans weren't meant to be . . . then they weren't meant to be.

Just then a waitress came up to the table, carrying a tray with four shots. "Oh, gods, what is this?" Sam asked.

"Thank you," Greyson smiled, moving them from the tray to the table. "You ordered these?" she asked.

"Yes," he handed her one, and raised his between them. "To new friends." Megan scoffed at him. "Don't be a pussy, Greyson." She held up her shot and recited, "If this shit was water, and I were a rock, I'd sink to the bottom and blow up the dock. But this shit ain't water, and I ain't a rock, so shut the fuck up, and let's take this shot."

The girls threw their shots back as Greyson and Tay laughed in astonishment at Megan's toast, then did the same.

Sam slammed her empty glass down on the table, taking a swig of her sweet cocktail for a chaser. "A'right," she announced. "Let's dance."

The city below him was alive, rhythmic, and pulsing, celebrating a victory that had not yet been won. The spire at Cantidium was more than just a landmark, more than just a fragment of an ancient tree. At its peak, far away from the glow of the city, was the kingdom's largest and most powerful telescope. General Brown's ship pulled up to dock with a small platform, hovering just outside the domed roof of the observatory.

The general disembarked, trailed by Berinhard, Riese, and twenty others, who hurried out of the wind, and in through the dome's double doors. The observatory's lobby was marbled and extravagant, built of the same stone as the throne room, with two symmetrical stairways curving up along the walls to the second floor. Spared no expense for the betterment of science.

There, waiting for the general, was an incredibly petite man, with short, thinning hair, and small, rectangular spectacles. He barely made five-foot tall, and he couldn't have weighed more than a-hundred-and-two pounds.

"General Brown." The man took his hand. "Robin Kalte. It's an honor." They shook. "What can I do for you this fine evening?"

"I need you to search the sky for me, Robin."

"Well, that's my job," he smiled, turning to lead him up the stairs. "What part of the sky were you hoping to view?"

"I'm not sure." Brown chugged up the stairs in a hurry, forcing Robin to follow.

"Well, what is it you're looking for?"

"Something very near to us. Low orbit, perhaps. I don't know."

"Something in orbit?" A twinge of excitement struck his voice. Viæden had never sent anything into orbit before, meaning whatever it was had to be a craft from another kingdom, or another planet entirely.

They passed through another set of doors into the dome, a giant telescope before them, hanging by a complicated network of metal arms and scaffolds. It was the size of a city bus.

"Maybe not. Maybe just very near to us," Brown said as Robin reached one of the computers controlling the telescope.

"Well, we can zoom out, take a picture of the sky, then another a few moments later and see what changes. How 'bout that?" He rattled at his keyboard.

"If you think it will work."

"Perhaps not on the first try, but I can keep looking for you."

The dome cracked and whirred as it opened to the blackness beyond, telescope rising to meet it.

"I'm not certain if this is a time-sensitive case," Brown admitted.

"You don't seem to know much about this at all." Robin looked to him with concern in his brown eyes. "What makes you think anything's up there to begin with?"

Brown didn't answer for a moment, not sure what to tell him. "I don't."

"Right." Robin looked back to his screen, oddly. "It will only take a few moments."

The men looked up to the telescope, settling into place.

"If it is hidden by the shadow of our planet, it will make it impossible to see. But since the sun set not too long ago, we should be alright . . . There's the first picture," he said as he clicked.

A large monitor in front of them both went white, and soon the picture loaded, crawling down the screen, a thousand tiny black dots.

"This is a negative, to make the stars easier to see."

Brown scanned the picture for anything ship-like or out of the ordinary. But he couldn't find anything in the field of dots, some large, some small, all round or crossed from glare. He scanned and re-scanned it again and again. For six minutes he stared at those dots, to no avail.

"And here's the second shot," said Robin.

A monitor right next to the first went white as the second image loaded, identical to the first in every way. Brown's eyes flicked back and forth furiously, terrified to find one star out of place. But the harder he scanned, the more all those dots blurred together.

"Oh," said Robin.

Brown freed his eyes of the torture and looked to the little man rising from his seat next to him. "What is it?"

"Here." Robin placed his finger on the screen. His eyes, trained for this sort of thing, found the only oddity. The single point of darkness that had moved in the moments between shots. "And on the first try too."

"What is it?" Brown asked, more gravely.

"It could an asteroid," he answered calmly. "Distance . . . is hard to tell at this point." He stroked his keys. "Let's zoom in. See if we can't distinguish some features."

The telescope moved just an inch to keep up with the object's movement, and took one more picture. It loaded over both screens this time. A jagged mass of blackness floating through a void of white.

"What *is that*?" Robin's level head suddenly faded.

And Brown looked to the screen in horror. All the blood rushed from his body, leaving him chilled and shaken. He stepped back, to be certain what his eyes were seeing was not an illusion. It was no asteroid . . . It looked almost like . . . *a chandelier.*

He turned and hurried for the door, Robin still silently staring. But he stopped in the doorframe, suddenly thinking of something. He reached into his pocket and withdrew his phone. He had to be certain this is what Greyson had seen. He needed confirmation, even though it would change nothing . . . He needed to hear it.

But Greyson didn't answer. "Greyson, it's Brown. I need you to come to the Spire Observatory, immediately. *Immediately*, Greyson. We've found something."

His words echoed through the lobby, down to his men, and Riese's ears.

The party raged to the music, booming with the leaping crowd. Greyson and Sam had made their way as close to the stage as they could, standing on one of those bridges in the center of it all. Tay and Megan were close by, just at the foot of the bridge, kind of dancing together, but also kind of not.

Sam lingered tantalizingly close to Greyson, brushing up against his arm, his hip, his chest, repeatedly, each time leaving a tingling mark on his skin. She wanted him closer, but he was nervous. Because once he touched her back, there was no turning back. And he loved this new place he'd found, on the brink of something greater, the height of tension between them. He wanted to let it ride for as long as he could. They had the whole night ahead of them.

Then a new song rose in the background of the one playing. And Sam knew it instantly, screaming in excitement. She turned to face him as the music built, stirring her hips and raising her arms in slow motion as the song grew in volume and complexity. Then finally the bass hit, and she leapt for the sky as water cannons fired all around the stage, raining down on them as blue lasers beamed overhead. She froze as she returned to earth with the rain, shocked to be so suddenly soaked. Then she smiled, and laughed, looking right at Greyson, and singing with the words, so passionately. Greyson didn't know the words, but he pretended to, just making sounds along with her, screaming up into the rain and stars, leaping with her as the bass began again.

Every moment richened, and time, and gravity no longer held them down. They were on an island of light, drifting freely in an ocean of night. Even though they'd only known each other for a few days, it felt like so much longer, like they'd known each other forever, a warm sort of comfort that only forever could create.

He had plenty to worry about. But none of it could bother him right then. Like Sam had put a spell on him, and all he felt was light. He'd heard people say they "wouldn't rather be anywhere else" before, but he never really understood if fully until now. He was at peace here, more than just loving who he was with, he felt peace in his soul. A long overdue confidence in himself that where he was, and what he was doing, finally felt right.

She was beautiful, inside and out, and he never wanted to kiss anyone more. The music quieted, song coming to an end. And instead of jumping, they swayed. Swayed side to side, and stole each other's gaze. They stayed in close, neither backing away. Their faces lingered near each other. Dangerously close. Close enough to touch. Close enough to taste.

He leaned in, turning his head ever so slightly, closed his eyes . . . and then the music stopped.

He opened his eyes to see why, expecting Sam to do the same, but she didn't. She stood still as a wet stone, eyes closed, lips nearly pursed.

Then he realized . . . everyone was as still as her. Even the rain, and the light. Completely frozen. He stepped back to make sure he wasn't crazy. He'd heard of getting lost in the moment, but this was a little freaking ridiculous.

"Sam," he said, reaching to touch her. But his hand moved right through her, like a cloud of dust through water. He sucked down a breath, recoiling as her skin, her dust, rolled away. And his heart nearly fucking stopped at what he saw beneath. He saw her heart, her soul, and her mind, each like glowing veins, red, yellow, and blue, like lightning in her shape. The ground beneath him began to soften as her cloud of dust grew larger and accelerated outward, colliding with the people around him, adding their dust to hers. Revealing everyone had insides as colorful as hers. Then the reds and yellows faded, and all that remained was blue, so bright, each mind became a star, encircling him.

He couldn't breathe, the air was fading as he rose up from where the ground used to be. What little of it left there was, condensed against his skin, like water, becoming an ocean all around. His legs drifted over him in weightlessness as gravity was erased. Below him, where once was the sky, now was the surface of a sea, raging from a storm. But he was safe, far beneath the waves, lightning flashing, rolling through the grey sky beyond. There was no end to it. An inverted sea in all directions, but for above his head, where light could not penetrate the ocean's depths. Up there, the sea was black as space. And just as beautiful, sparkling with blue stars, as plentiful as sand.

*"Greyson,"* a voice called out from the dark, smooth and soothing. He could have sworn it was his mom's.

But he was too afraid to speak.

*"Greyson,"* she came again, gently, sending ripples through the blue, which brightened each star as they passed.

Then he noticed, looming right behind him, a massive door, blue as sapphire, thirty feet high, fourteen feet wide. It looked just like the one in the throne room. But instead of Viæden's symbol in its center, this one held the Seal of Water. And this door rested on no floor, or in any wall. It floated there, as freely as he did.

235

Greyson could only think of one reply for the disembodied voice. "I . . . died?"

*"You are not dead."*

But her words brought no relief. "Where am I?"

*"My realm, my soul, in all its power. I am Wisdom. I am Foresight. I am Anetha Wae Witaru, Goddess of Water."*

The stars began to sink past him, like snow . . . down . . . down . . . to the surface of the sea. *"It was exceptionally difficult to bring you here. To peel away the layers of reality, so that this realm was all that remained. And exceptionally dangerous . . . I doubt I shall recover."*

That's when Greyson noticed the inky cloud emitting from his chest. Small, but growing. Like a tiny hole was punctured in his skin, it bled from him, this blackness, thicker than blood, drifting through the weightless water. "What is this!?" It poured from him as his fear grew.

*"It is the darkness in your heart. This realm is pure. Bringing your soul here has stained it."*

"I'm sorry!" he cried. "Why did you bring me here?"

*"It must be done, young vertui. For in all the ages of the world, the truth must now be known. Of all destinies created by myself and Light, the vertuém are the greatest."*

He knew it. Sam was right. Their destinies were stronger.

But the goddess was not done. *"For your destinies are your own. Unwritten. Thus unknown to even us."*

A wave of electricity swept over him, a bodily chill with such a bite it stung every inch of his skin. "My destiny?" he whispered, so confused.

*"You do not have one."* She couldn't have been more clear than that. *"It is the greatest gift Oyopa has ever given. Every action, every choice you've ever made, and will, are yours to make. And because of this, vertuém are guardians of fate, and also its undoing."*

He had no destiny?

So all that certainty, all that clarity, and confidence he thought he'd found . . . was all for nothing? After all he'd learned. All he'd done and fought for. He knew nothing . . . He had no idea the true impact he had on the world. Which meant Stiqula, Bail, and Kyri's mom . . . truly were his fault, and no one else's.

And as he realized what he was, that cloud of darkness sprouting from his heart grew ever larger, ever darker. "Its undoing?" he whispered. "How?"

*"Your actions are so powerful, they send out ripples through the world, which distort the fates of all they touch. I have seen it, time and time again. Thus it is imperative you keep this secret locked away. For not even I know what fate will come if it is known to anyone but you."*

"But, why are you telling *me* this? Why not Sam? Surely she's a better choice. She knows so much already!"

*"She knows much of us, and yearns for more. But, her mind is made up in the end. Within you lies a vital uncertainty. Naivety. And this vacillation of your heart grants you a strength far beyond what she can achieve."*

Greyson shook his head. "I don't understand . . . Why risk so much to tell me?"

*"I see but a shallow way into fate's inconstant sea before the darkness clouds me. But His dark veil grows ever closer as of late. And I fear it means a coming cataclysm, beyond which lies uncertainty. You must remove this veil, whatever it may be. And return it to its proper place, so that my sight may be restored."*

"What veil? What cataclysm?"

*"I cannot see it. I do not know."*

"Then how can you expect *me* to figure it all out on my own?!"

*"You will know it, young vertui. Something is changing in the world. Something only vertuém can see. I can feel it, beyond my waves, growing stronger by the day, and by the night."*

"Stiqula?" He knew. ". . . Am I the one who's caused all this?"

*"He is a grave threat to mankind, and the world, riding on the crest of His dark tide. And tonight he will strike again. Hurry to the castle tree, Greyson. The lives of all that live there are at stake."*

"What? Why? What's going to happen?!" Greyson's next breath was a mouthful of water, and he clamped his lips shut tight as the darkness pouring from his heart attacked him, consumed him, and all that he could see.

He screamed in trepidation, tearing from the black water, gulping down a breath of air, and choking on what little water snuck into his lungs.

"Greyson!" He heard Sam's voice, opening his eyes.

The music was still blaring, lights still firing across the sky, party still raging on. But he had moved. Fallen from the bridge into the tide pool of the Desun Sea. He found the sandy bottom and stood, water only to his chest.

Sam pushed her way from the bridge and to the edge of the dance floor, which cut down into the steps of the pool. They were both in just about the same amount of shock.

"How did you fall?" she demanded to know as she reached the last step, a few inches underwater.

"I—" He coughed. "I don't know."

"Are you okay?" She held her hand out to him.

"Nn—I." He had no idea how to answer that, taking her hand and climbing from the inky liquid.

"What happened?" she asked again. "You were standing right next to me."

He had no fucking *idea* what happened. "I think I . . . had a vision," the words sort of just fell out of his mouth without him knowing. But *was* that a vertui vision? Because if it was, then what the *hell* did he have before?

"What? Really?" She suddenly turned up the excitement, switching back to scientist mode.

"I don't know. Can we get out of here?" His words were slow, almost inaudible in the roar of the party. He was still deep in shock, eyes wide, unable to shake the blue stars from them.

"Yeah." She helped him up the last few steps and through the crowd to their table. "Where's Tay?" His and Megan's things were missing.

"He probably left because of the water," Greyson said, taking his Wellington jacket from the back of his chair, and sliding it over his shoulders.

Sam grabbed her bag, scanning for Tay or Megan quickly before walking with Greyson to the street, where it was quiet enough to think at least.

"What did you see?" she asked.

Greyson didn't know what to tell her, so ignored her and stuck his hands in his jacket pockets with a shiver. He found his badge in one of them, and pulled it out to call Tay. But he noticed he had a missed call from an unknown number, and a message. He put the badge to his ear as Sam waited patiently for an answer.

"*Greyson, it's Brown. I need you to come to the Spire Observatory, immediately. Immediately, Greyson. We've found something.*"

Observatory?

Darkness flooded his mind.

*Observatory?*

And from the darkness crawled the hideous figure of a demon, soaked in angel's blood.

"No . . . *No!*" He ripped the phone from his ear, like it just bit him, gasping deep.

The ship . . . was here. Coming. Just a little ways above their heads. Growing ever closer. He looked up, to the lights across the sky, eyes stinging . . . *That* was the cataclysm. The coming darkness Water couldn't see. The *Chandelier*.

He clapped his hand over his gaping mouth to keep from screaming. But he couldn't keep it in. He only muffled it.

"What is it!?" Sam asked, just as terrified.

He dropped his hand. "Everything," he choked. "Everything." Coming to Viæden had rewritten his understanding of the world. And now, this new world was coming crashing down.

Sam had had enough. She grabbed him by the shoulders, locking in on his green eyes. "Greyson, who was it?!"

"Brown," he panted. "He's at the observatory. He wants us to come."

"The observatory? Here?" She looked up to the spire, lit sparsely in the night.

"I think so." He put the badge to his ear and started down the street in a hurry. "Tay . . . It's me. If you get this, meet us at the top of the spire. Brown said he's found something."

Sam hurried to catch up.

They walked down the beach side of the road, along a sidewalk that was bordered by a metal railing, separating them from a few foot drop down to the sand.

"Greyson, what's going on? You *have* to tell me. What did he find? What did you see?"

He wanted to tell her. *So* bad. It was everything she'd ever wanted to hear. The gods were *real*. He'd seen one, *spoken* to one! And she'd told him the *truth* about Vertuém Destiny, kept secret for eternity. *They had no destiny.* Blank agents, carving their own paths through the world. He had to tell her. He didn't know what else to do, where else to turn. He needed her help.

He had to tell her! "I—"

The road suddenly shuddered as a wave crashed into its sea wall, blasting white water straight up, thirty feet into the air next to them. The shock of sound scared Greyson right off his feet, falling into the street as the water rained down over them.

"Holy shit!" Sam brushed the water from her face. She looked out at the sea, slowly receding. It'd rushed at them, over fifty yards of sand, in complete silence, for seemingly no reason whatsoever.

Greyson stayed on the ground, dumbfounded and terrified to his core. He knew it was the goddess. She wasn't kidding about him not telling anyone. She'd silenced him before he'd even known what he was going to say. Could she really be that powerful? Could she really see that far? Even inside his own head?

Sam gave him a hand, standing him up. "Are you okay?"

"Yeah." He so was not.

"Wae's really pissed at you today for some reason."

Greyson eyed her nervously. She'd said it as a joke. But . . . joke's on her.

"What were you about to tell me?" She continued walking. Completely oblivious to the fact that a goddess had practically just touched her.

Greyson followed her, having no idea what to tell her now. And frankly he didn't even know if that *was* a vision, and not some sort of divine intervention. "What's *supposed* to happen in our visions?"

"It's different for everyone. Mostly they're of the future though. Some might be goals, aspirations, or even dreams."

"Dreams?" That one stuck out. "Like nightmare dreams?"

"Yes."

That was good enough for him. He hadn't told her about his angel dream yet, and now was the perfect time. Hopefully she'd buy it. He didn't really have any other choice. He'd already told Brown and nothing bad had happened . . . at least not that he knew of.

"Then, yes. I had one. I was an angel. On a dying ship. Overrun with demons."

Her face glistened with awe. So far, so good.

"It was *so* real, Sam. I could feel everything. Every tense of his muscles. Every gust under his wings. Every scrape. Every cut. And *all* his fear. For some reason I kept blaming Stiqula for our ship going to hell. And when I made it to the bridge, I saw a single green planet in the distance. We were in space, and the planet was this one. And I would die to make sure it was safe, to save it from the demons. I tried to destroy the ship. But I was too late . . . I died just before I could."

That silenced her. Almost in as much shock as him now.

He just hoped she wouldn't put the two together, and just keep on assuming he had absolutely nothing to do with Brown finding the *Chandelier*.

# 24

# The Observatory

They picked up the pace, practically sprinting the rest of the way to the spire. Both soaking wet, Sam's feet started to blister in her heels, and Greyson's jeans were chafing in a particularly excruciating place. She led the way to a lift that would take them up to the observatory. And once inside, they could finally catch their breath, and their thoughts.

But Greyson didn't like the thoughts he was catching. He could deal with not having a destiny—or maybe that just hadn't sunken in yet—but the part he couldn't get over, the part that kept replaying in his head, was the thought that he—that *vertuém*—were the guardians of fate, and also its undoing. That was way more freaking responsibility than he was comfortable with. And what did it even mean? . . . He had no destiny and he was also the undoing of everyone else's destiny?

That sounded . . . exactly like what *Darkness* did.

Bail's brown eyes flashed through his mind. And Ellis', and Lawson's, and the prisoner at the Rock, and Fyren's, and Adria's, and all the faceless dark souls that Stiqula'd claimed since his release. Every soul. Every destiny Greyson's actions had brought to its end. His heart stung with the weights of all their souls. And he clutched his chest in pain, squeezing his eyes tight in disbelief . . . He truly was a demon, who'd cut a trail of death and darkness all across this world.

"Are you okay?" Sam asked. She stepped right up to him in that tiny elevator, putting one hand on his shoulder, and the other on his heart, as if to feel it screaming through his chest.

"No. No, I'm not."

"What is it?"

He opened his eyes to find hers. "You never told me why Riese hates vertuém."

"What does that have to do with anything?"

"You said he thought we were servants of the devil. Why?"

"It's just some superstition. It's not real."

"Please, tell me, Sam!"

She stepped back, taking her hands with her. "In Mohavik they believe that vertuém destinies are not only stronger, but somehow powerful enough to affect the lives of those the vertuém come into contact with. In effect, derailing people from their destinies, and making them susceptible to Refsiel."

Greyson breathed long and deep listening to her, never blinking from her gaze. She already knew half of what the goddess had told him . . . If only he could tell her how true it really was.

"In other words they think we leave a trail of darkness everywhere we go. But it's not true, Greyson," she pleaded with him as the lift came to a stop.

"Maybe not for you," he said as the doors opened.

"Right on time," Riese boomed.

Greyson and Sam spun to the voice, to the five men standing in the middle of a marble lobby. The largest one with a growing grin across his face . . . more giant than man.

Instinctively, Greyson reached for his sword.

But it wasn't there! He'd given it to Nash!

Defenseless.

"Where's Brown?" he asked, barely hiding his shock.

"Oh, he left. You took too long."

Greyson took a step back, having no intention of leaving the safety of the lift. But as the doors closed, Berinhard appeared, reaching in and wrapping his fingers around Sam's arm, tearing her right from the goddam elevator. She stumbled to stay on her feet, then fell to her hands and knees, halfway across the room, rolling the rest of the way to the opposite wall.

"Sam!" Greyson leapt after her.

"I'm okay." She lifted her head, keeping her eyes on each one of their rifles as Greyson sidestepped around the lobby to her.

"He found your ship, *grunbick*." Riese approached them. "It's coming." He raised his four-foot long rifle to them. "And it's *your* evil that draws it here."

"You won't get away with this, Riese," Greyson threatened as Sam found her feet.

"I will return to Mohavik a hero."

"Don't do this! She's done nothing wrong!"

"She will. You all do." He leveled his thick and glowing barrel to Greyson's head. "You will not escape this, beast. Either you kill me and prove what darkness lies in you, or I kill you, and rid the world of it, myself!"

There really was no escape. Nowhere to run, and no way to talk him out of it.

Was this really the end?

Greyson thought his destiny was great, strong. Protected. But in reality, it was nothing at all. His life had no purpose. No meaning. No climax it was driving toward . . . It *could* end. Right here. Right now.

Then the room began to shake, and the roar of engines resonated from above, quickly settling beyond the open doorway to their left. To a landing pad, outside.

"Is it Brown?" Riese asked, looking to the door.

He was distracted, but still standing too far away for Greyson to make a move. And even if he did, one of the five other assholes standing next to him could just as easily take him out.

The guards shifted uneasily, not sure what to do as a light shined in on them from the docked ship and the sound of someone neared, their shadow growing on the floor. He was old, limping through the doorway on a blue, metallic cane.

*Nash! Thank fucking Light!* Or better yet . . . thank *him*. Gods couldn't save them. But they could save each other.

"What's all this?" Nash said, like they were all just rowdy school kids, settling a score.

"Go away, old man. This isn't your business," Riese told him off.

"Oh, I believe it is." He lowered his glasses, giving them a look like they had no idea what they'd gotten themselves into. Then, he pulled back his white coat to reveal Greyson's blade, unsheathing it in his left hand. Stiqula's chain spiraled down its grip, adhered to it beneath his hand, a few inches dangling off the hilt. And all the men swung their aim to him.

"Are you fucking kidding me, guy?" Riese shouted.

"Let's find out." He aimed the blade right for them.

They looked on, more amused than threatened.

Then Nash threw the sword to Greyson. And as they watched it float across the room, their grins faded into scowls.

Greyson caught the blade out of the air and looked to them with sharp and heavy eyes.

"Protect us, Greyson," Nash said as he limped to him.

The guards returned their aim to all three vertuém standing back-to-back.

"Enough!" Riese screamed, flexing in frustration, and finally pulling the trigger.

Greyson cried as the lasers fired, holding his blade like a shield in front of him. And from within him came the power to protect. A green field of electric light swirled around the blade and collapsed onto it with a clang, just as the first beams of red whizzed by and bent away. The entire volley curved around them. Not a single bullet landing on its mark.

The guards ceased fire in confusion, eyeing the hundreds of scorch-marks in the wall all around the vertuém. The marble cracked from the heat of their beams, lighting tiny fires in the ancient wood beneath. They were dumb-founded at this magic, unsettled by it.

Then, it was the vertuém's turn to strike.

Sam whipped a pistol from her bag and took aim for their weapons. She fired, piercing one guard's rifle and reducing it to shrapnel. She fired again, this time aiming for Berinhard's gun, but missed by half an inch and struck his arm instead. The metal bullet entered at the wrist and shattered his entire radius as it traveled up his arm into his elbow. Berinhard screamed and dropped to the floor as Sam bound to him, punting his giant, blond head.

With his cane, Nash slapped a guard's rifle right out of his hands, then in the same motion, lunged forward, elbow first, and planted it right in the guard's exposed chest to knock the wind out of him. Then he gripped his cane with both fists and cracked him over the head.

Meanwhile, Greyson sliced through Riese's gun and reared his sword back to plant its hilt firmly in the giant's nose, which exploded in a spray of blood and knocked the giant to the ground. But there was another guard behind him. Greyson launched himself off Riese and lunged for his new target, being careful to swing his glowing blade for the man's rifle only. But the guard lunged away and dodged as the hot blade arced by.

Sam's disarmed guard grabbed for her gun, clutching her forearm so she couldn't use it, then wrapped his arm around her waist to keep her still. But her other arm was still free, and with it, she elbowed him in the face again and again, three times until he let her go and fell on his ass with a busted eye-socket and bruised brain.

Nash looked up to his last man only to find the barrel of a rifle staring him in the face. But Nash grabbed the gun and pointed it to the ceiling before it could fire. Then as the guard tried to force it down again, he wrapped the hook-shaped handle of his cane round his neck and yanked his head down into his rising knee.

Greyson's last guard dodged back and bumped up against the far wall, sliding along it as Greyson swung for him, slicing through the marble. Then, just to keep him still, Greyson stabbed him in the shoulder, pinning him against the wall. But the intense heat of the blade burned right through his muscle and bone as he pulled away, melting his arm clear off his body. Greyson cringed and pulled the sword free as the guard fell to his side, unconscious.

He hadn't meant to do that. This sword was a lot stronger than he thought. Greyson looked around to see that Sam and Nash had handled themselves just fine. And took in a quick breath, realizing that they'd won. Nash couldn't have had any better timing if he tried.

Greyson looked to Riese, still lying on the ground, clutching his broken face and grunting as he tried not to choke on his own blood. He stepped to him and lowered the blade to his neck.

Feeling the heat, Riese uncovered his face. It was a mess of blood and bone-fragments, poking from his skin like white quills.

Greyson wanted to kill him. Move that blade an inch closer to his throat, and end the misery. Riese was just like his ferret. Crippled and beaten. Pathetic, and full of a creeping darkness . . . His dad had taught him that lesson so that when the time came, Greyson would know when to pull the trigger, and not think twice about it. But Greyson never saw it that way. To Greyson, his dad had done a horrible thing. And he'd always wondered what that poor creature's life would have been like if his dad hadn't shot it from that tree. His dad changed its destiny, and sent it into darkness. An irreversible thing, he'd said. But Greyson never believed it was the truth.

And if being a vertui meant he had those same powers over people . . . He couldn't. He couldn't believe that the darkness he'd spread upon the world was irreversible. All the lives he'd changed for the worst . . . He had to believe that he could make it right again. Or at least make up for it somehow.

He *wanted* to kill Riese. If nothing for the sake of his own protection. But maybe by sparing him, that'd be enough to prove he was no demon.

"I can't help what I am," he said. "Just like you can't help it either. I can't blame you for being what you are. Believing what you do. But I can give you the chance to change it. To realize we aren't the monsters that you think." His blade's light dispelled, diffusing in an instant, fading into the invisible realm from which it came.

Riese said nothing, expression hardening as he swallowed a mouthful of blood . . .

Was that enough? Greyson had the choice to spread either light and spare him, or darkness by killing him. And he chose light . . . But was that enough to change this man? Put him back on track with the destiny that Greyson'd knocked him from.

There was something in his brown eyes . . . Something Greyson had seen before. The epiphany of a man about to die, and the realization of all the mistakes he'd made that led him to his death. But this time the life was spared. And this realization of his wrongdoings would not go to waste. Riese was baptized in his own blood. And a new destiny was born for him. One that did not end in darkness . . . Greyson could feel it. And he smiled, knowing Riese could feel it too. "Have a good life, Riese."

"Oh!" Nash moaned as he put weight on his leg again. "I think I just blew my knee out." He limped around with his cane. "Yep, definitely blew my knee out."

"How did you find us?" Sam asked, collecting herself.

"I have a tracker in your phone. Obviously," he hissed in pain.

"Obviously." She winced, clearly not in love with the idea of him watching her.

"Darakin's in trouble," Greyson said like he'd just remembered, heading to the door. "We've got to go *now*." He took his scabbard from Nash and sheathed his sword as he stepped out to the platform.

"How do you know that?" Nash limped after him.

"I—" Again he swallowed the real answer, "saw it."

Docked outside was a bark ship, lit only by the light of the observatory, and the underglow of the city. But Greyson didn't need good lighting to tell this was no ordinary bark ship. For one, its bark was lighter than a standard capital ship, made from a different wood entirely. And it was enormous: three levels high, just over thirty feet, with a long nose that stretched its total length to . . . exactly seven hundred sixty-four feet. He knew this ship, and froze when he realized.

"What are we going to be up against? This ship is still being tested," Nash warned.

"This is . . . "

"The *Leiaru.*" Sam joined them outside.

He looked to her in surprise, now knowing its true worth to her.

"I was going to surprise you with it."

"I am surprised. But I don't know what's waiting for us." Now he was worried. He didn't want to destroy such a beautiful creation. "How much can it handle?"

"The shields are not online yet," Nash advised.

"With the three of us, she can handle anything. With or without shields," Sam asserted, taking the lead toward the glowing portal of the docking bridge.

"Are you sure?" Greyson watched her pass, following slowly. "I haven't had the best track record with ships lately."

She stopped, one step inside its white halls. "I trust you," she spoke aloud, to Greyson, and the ship. Then turned to face him. "What about Tay?"

"He's going to hate me." Greyson looked to his badge, blank of any notifications. "But we really don't have time to wait." He hurried to join Sam in the *Leiaru*, afraid Riese had made them too late already.

# 25

# THE LEIARU

The *Leiaru's* bridge was the most impressive control room Greyson had ever seen in all his life. It was shiny and new. A gem, untouched by human hands. Fourteen plasma touch screens mounted into fourteen control panels lining the horizon of a panoramic window, looking out at the long nose of the ship, stretching far over the lights of the city below. It had two laser hologram displays at either side of the entrance and one in front of the dual piloting stations, between the window and the helm. And below their feet was painted the green Emblem of Viæden. Normally, Greyson would have wanted to run around the room and play with absolutely everything, but he was too on edge to focus on anything other than getting to Darakin as fast as this ship could take them, terrified he and the O'Nasies would not be enough to stop whatever force the goddess feared so much to break through the fabric of reality and warn him of.

He approached the two pilot chairs, noticing only one of them had a wheel. "What's this one for?"

"The left is for the pilot, the other is weapons command."

"Voice-print accepted. Welcome, Samantha O'Nasi." A voice that sounded a lot like Sam's greeted her, and the lights of the room illuminated in hues of blue and green.

"This ship has an AI?" Greyson gave a nerdy gasp.

"She's not an AI. She just helps run on a skeleton crew. Computer, input new user: Greyson Wight." Sam commanded, then whispered to Greyson. "Say hello."

"Hello?"

"Voice-print accepted. Welcome, Greyson Wight."

"She'll let you pilot now."

"Thanks." Greyson took the chair on the left, looking to the empty one at his side . . . That was *Tay's* chair. He should have been there with them.

Greyson grunted, reaching for his badge. "Tay," he spoke into it. "Tay, come on!"

He inspected the golden gadget. None of the lights that were usually lit were working anymore. "Is it broken?"

Nash slid into Tay's seat. "That may be a result of activating your lerité."

"What do you mean?"

"I mean, he's not coming."

He didn't have to be so damn blunt about it.

Sam took a seat on the far side of her dad. Each one of their monitors switched on as they placed their hands on the controls, displaying a wire frame of the ship's networks that pertained to their specific consol. Greyson's showed altitude, speed, pitch, yaw, and roll. Nash's showed the weapon arrays as well as side and rearview displays. And Sam monitored the ship's energy output, and integrity.

"Greyson, hit the red engage button on your screen to take command of the engines."

Greyson did as she said, tapping his screen. The large red button then shrunk to the corner of his screen and changed its label to *disengage*, and a larger *anchor* button above it.

"Computer, Darakin onscreen," she said, showing off her creation.

A waypoint appeared at the left edge of the bridge's smartglass. And Greyson shifted the helm in its direction. The *Leiaru* handled much more sensitively than any other ship he'd flown, and much more accurately, with incredible response time. As the nose of the ship panned across the western sky, the waypoint crawled to the very center of the bridge window.

"Darakin," the computer said. "Five, seven, three, miles to destination."

Greyson accepted the challenge with a roaring throttle, and the *Leiaru* boomed from zero to six hundred. It rattled as it cut through the air, not the most aerodynamic thing he'd ever flown. Its asymmetric shape was adding some uneven drag.

"If the shields were active, it wouldn't be this bumpy," Sam assured, reading his mind. "And we haven't really stretched her legs yet. So try to keep it at a thousand. I don't want to break the sound barrier yet."

"A *thousand*," he almost laughed. It hadn't even occurred to him that a ship this size could go that fast. He'd never gone faster than eight forty-five during flight training in Wellington. He glanced down to his speed, just as it passed *845*. "What's the speed of sound again?"

"Thousand fifty-six." She didn't sound too sure of herself. Like a mom afraid to let her kid explore and find his true limits. He let off the throttle as the *Leiaru* crested over one thousand miles an hour.

"Is there any way to see what's going on at the castle tree?" Greyson asked.

Sam thought for a moment. "The ball." She stood, stepping to the communications chair. "Huey said it would have a live feed all night." She leaned over the terminal and found the broadcast. "Here." She slid it up to a corner of the main smart glass.

The shot was of the throne room, at a high angle. Dozens of round tables with white table cloths lined the marble floor, swarmed by guests in black suits and light dresses. The king's dais was visible in the upper left corner, where Huey sat, mingling with his people.

Greyson breathed a mini sigh of relief. At least they were all still safe. They weren't too late. They could make it.

"Everything's okay," said Sam, standing easy again.

"Maybe my vision was wrong," Greyson said, unconvincingly.

"I highly doubt that." Sam took her seat again, then looked at him, realizing she'd said that out loud. "Sorry." Not wanting to sound like she was rooting for something bad to happen, she quickly changed subjects. "While we have a minute, Dad. What'd you find out about the chain?"

He smiled, looking at her. "Inconclusive."

Her face lit up.

But Greyson didn't get why. "Wait, why is that good?"

"An inconclusive result is what we were looking for," Nash explained. "If it were conclusive, then we would understand its mechanics completely in physical terms. But the chain works for inexplicable reasons."

"Just like all those things we talked about," said Sam. "The unexplained mysteries of the world."

"What I *did* learn is fascinating though," Nash continued. "When active, the chain produces a short-range, but incredibly powerful magnetic field—which is probably what broke your phone—simultaneously ionizing and attracting the gas around the blade, creating a layer of plasma which coats the entire surface of the weapon. Excluding the area nearest the chain, of course. It will work with any material the chain can make a closed circuit around. However, if the object is not a conductor, the magnetic field will have nothing to adhere to, and the plasma will not take a shape, dripping off. The durability of the weapon is also a factor. Iron, for instance, is magnetic but cannot withstand the intense heat of the plasma, only lasting a few moments. A stainless steel blade is a bit stronger, and due to the chromium in the metal, more reflective, resistant to the heat for longer. It will last a few minutes or so. But the best blade I've tested is yours, Greyson. It is almost one hundred percent reflective of all heat and visible light. Meaning you can use it almost indefinitely. Though I wouldn't go longer than say, twenty minutes, without giving it time to cool again."

"I don't think that'll be a problem." *Twenty* minutes. What a crazy fight that would be.

"Mirror blades are man's best attempt at duplicating the alloy of angelic blades, and likewise, an angelic blade is the only thing that can maintain its leretic form indefinitely, with no risk of degradation. And, because of this, an angelic blade is the only weapon that poses a threat of breaking your sword."

"Well, it sure sounds like you know everything about it. What was inconclusive?" Greyson asked.

"What's inconclusive is *how* this chain produces such an effect."

"Were you able to see what it's made of?" Sam asked.

"Yes. Though I had a hell of a time with it. The chain is incredibly durable. But by heating it to *twice* the temperature of the active blade—that wasn't easy—I was able to vaporize just a sliver of a single link, submitting it through our mass spectrometer to determine it was made of mostly carbon—I suspect carbon nanotubes—grafted to trace amounts of silver and silicon. All elements are accounted for, and none are behaving as they should."

"Why aren't they behaving as they should?" Greyson asked.

"Because producing the plasma requires a staggering amount of energy. Too much to just be coming from the chain alone."

"You think it's coming *through* the chain, from its wielder?" Sam proposed.

"Exactly. But the human body cannot produce that much energy either."

"What about the heart?" she asked.

"The heart is my only explanation, creating a link to the Realm of Light, through which the energy flows. Because, through my tests, I've discovered the lerité will only activate through the emotions of fear or a strong confidence in one's self. It would make sense that upon feeling such emotions, Oyopa lends Her power to the wielder as a blessing of protection, or an endorsement to carry out a righteous act." He turned to Greyson. "This is how I knew you'd be able to protect us back there. If you didn't trust yourself, your fear would have activated the blade, regardless."

Greyson gave a nervous giggle.

"In time, I'm sure you'll learn how to activate it even without using such intense emotions."

"This is unbelievable." Sam beamed. "We need to start testing this theory right away. We need to be absolutely certain we aren't missing anything before we report it to the Ministry of Science." She looked to the live feed of the ball.

Greyson smiled as he watched her grinning to herself. Maybe he didn't even have to tell her about the Goddess of Water at all. Maybe her dream of proving the king wrong could be fulfilled by this chain alone.

But then her glee quickly faded. "Something's happening."

She stood and stepped back to the com terminal, turning the volume up on the feed.

The congregation had all begun to head back to their seats. And one of Huey's aides stood to his right, addressing them. "If you'll all be seated. The king has one more very special announcement to make on this wonderful night."

# 26

# THE CLAW

General Brown hurried down the highest hall of Darakin, star charts and photographs clutched in one hand, and with the other, he checked the time: 9:99. One minute to midnight. He entered the throne room lobby, traversing it in nearly a jog. "Stephanie, open the doors." He came to a stop before the massive, ancient portal, looking to the secretary in frustration. "Stephanie, now."

"I'm trying, sir, they aren't opening," she squeaked, rapping at the button under her desk.

Sam, Greyson, and Nash looked on intently as the king began to speak.

"Thank you. Thank you, all," he addressed their applause, waiting for them to quiet. He took in a deep breath, as if this speech were from his heart and not his crown. "Today marks a momentous day. A great battle has been won, yes. *But*, an even greater end has now been mended.

"As you know, since I took this throne, fifty years ago, I have not produced any heir, of any kind. And due to the horrific deeds Stiqula inflicted upon my family, I am the last of my line. A dynasty that has stood for over thirteen hundred years. Doomed to end with *me*."

Light booing came from the crowd. Very light.

"But no more."

The room was silent.

"Fifty years ago, I lost my family. I became an orphan king. And in my mind, all orphans are royalty. And in this recent tragedy, many orphans have been made. But there is one, above all the rest, I could not deny."

Greyson *really* didn't like where this was going, chest suddenly tightening.

"People of Viæden. Your new heir has been found." The king stood and motioned to his right, where two aides led a little girl up to this throne, copper hair all dressed in jewels. "I present to you, on the night of her adoption. Princess Kyri Amarine."

"*What!*" Greyson shrieked, jerking forward on the wheel.

"Kyri?" Sam looked at her. The camera zoomed far in to see her nervous expression, her emerald eyes in perfect clarity. All the crowd was in an uproar, cheering with pride, or howling in anger, hard to tell.

"No!" Greyson slammed his fist down on his control panel. "*No!*"

His heart burned. His skin burned. And fury shook his bones, tensing all the muscles in his arms as he slammed down on the panel again, realizing his purest light had just been taken from him. Stolen by the king. And all the colors that she'd added to his heart began to fade. Draining, dripping, melted by his rage. "*You can't!*"

And suddenly the feed was cut.

* * *

The castle tree went black as pitch.

Stephanie yelped at the sudden darkness.

And, inside, General Brown was screaming too. He lunged for the Viæden Doors, slamming against them. "Your Highness!" Brown laid into the door, but it wouldn't budge. "Stephanie, help me!"

Eyes adjusting to the dark, the secretary ran around her desk to help push on the massive slabs of jade. And a crack resonated from them as the two pushed with all their strength, finally budging, just an inch.

"Your Highness!" Brown screamed, feeling the cool air rush through the tiny part in the door. He could hear the guests stirring, chattering uneasily in the dark. And he could hear the king's voice shouting something in frustration. Then with one final thrust of his weight, Brown slid the doors open large enough to see into room, lit only by the dim, orange light of torches on the walls.

He spotted the king still on his dais, clinging to the throne, aides fighting to pull him to safety. But as Brown watched, that orange light turned to red. Everyone spun to the room's right, to see what caused such radiance, their fear briefly calmed by curiosity. The red glow shone in through the stained glass, drifting over each window.

But their docile calm had been misplaced. And when their fear returned, it came with all the power of its God.

A single soul let out a scream as the stained glass exploded inward on them. The throne room's wall erupted with a bone-splintering pulse of sound. Tables, chairs, and stone blasted across the hall and disappeared behind a thick and constant beam of burning death that fired in through the smoke.

Huey stared, mouth agape at the flickering light as his aides rushed him, yanking him to safety. "No!" He latched onto the throne's golden arm. He couldn't leave it. "No!" They pulled him again, tipping the chair over and sending it tumbling down the steps. "Kyri! Get Kyri!" he screamed before he disappeared behind the dais.

The beam rose, lifting straight up to the ceiling, cleaving the throne room in half like a plasma knife, erasing everything it touched in an instant, then disappeared, as quickly as it came. Smoke rose from the gash, and molten debris rained from above as the survivors ran for the door, slamming up against it, closing it again.

The general backed away from the door, eyes wide at what he'd seen. Unable to believe it.

The light flickered as it returned. And Viæden's doors swung wide, releasing the hundreds that survived in a current of well-dressed fear that washed past Brown, bumping up against him as he stood and stared in awe of the destruction.

The throne room. The heart of the kingdom. Torn in two.

"Hero," he uttered. "You god-forsaken fool." This didn't have to happen.

Brown could have stopped this, prevented it from ever coming. If only he'd been brave enough to open his mouth when he *knew* the king was wrong. Brave enough to call him out when he ignored the truth. He could have saved them. Instead of condemning the world to the king's misguided logic. "This will be the last mistake I ever let you make." He turned with the flow of the crowd, crumpling the papers in his fist.

He headed for the lifts, down to Castle Control. Where Huey's word meant nothing, and Brown's was absolute. Darakin's military control room looked like the three-tiered bridge of a massive ship, with display screens along its circumference, in place of windows, revealing the events unfolding outside.

"Why aren't the shields up?" he yelled as he entered the dim room, full of men, faces buried in the green glow of their monitors.

"They are operational, sir."

"Then why was the throne room torn apart!?" he screamed.

"There was a power failure, general."

"I've noticed! What caused it?!"

"We still don't know."

"Well, get on it! Scramble the fighters. And *all* available bark ships."

"That's only three at this hour, sir."

Brown shook his head. So disappointed. So unprepared. He stepped to a window at the side of the room, sliding back its shades to reveal the tree's military hangar, three stories down. His men dispersed, frantically, to their ships, some still in their dress clothes from the ball above. He prayed he was not sending them all to their doom. "Do we have a visual?"

"Not yet, sir. It's dark out there. And radar's not picking anything up."

"Try infrared." Brown took his place in the middle of the room.

"There," a man said. "Picking something up. But it's not moving."

"Onscreen."

The black wall at the front of the room suddenly flashed red as the infrared scanner came on. Then the red blur condensed, shrinking into the very center of the screen, leaving the sky a dark black and blue. The red blob turned white with heat as it took form, in the shape of a long body, thick around its trunk, and at its head, three forward-facing talons.

Brown fell silent, voice chained to his sinking heart, recalling instantly Greyson's warning of a ship shaped like a claw.

*Stiqula.*

A swarm of fifty splinter ships jetted from the hangar, diffusing from the tree's branches, shortly joined by three bark ships. From their distribution pattern it was clear they could not see what was right in front of them.

Brown choked. "T—tell them to switch to infrared!"

"All ships, all ships. Use infrared filters to view the enemy. I repeat, infrared filters."

"That's going to confuse the missile locks."

"Everything's playing out just as it did before." Brown shook his head again. "Don't waste the rockets, or risk locking onto our own men. Anti-aircraft shells only," he ordered.

Now able to see, the battlegroup made their move, bark ships separating to encircle the craft, splinter ships charging forward in an amber fury of laserfire.

The *Claw's* talons spread wider, in a triangular formation, and fired itself down into the swarm of fighters, colliding with them as though it were swatting at flies. Six splinters instantly exploded on the *Claw's* metal surface. And its two bottom talons lowered further, sparking white with engine-fire, arcing the ship back into battle before it came any closer to the tree. As it rounded back into the fight, Brown's bark ships opened fire, engulfing the *Claw* in a cloud of a hundred small explosions. But the horrid ship appeared from the fire unscathed. Its metal hull was too strong for anti-aircraft shells alone. It would withstand anything that wasn't a direct hit.

"Hull surface is dropping, sir," an inmate shouted on the *Claw's* bridge.

Stiqula stood in the middle of the room, arms folded, one hand on his chin. Ever calculating. "We're faster than they are. Rise above them. Clear them out."

The *Claw* sped up, over the swarm of splinters, broadsiding a bark ship as it climbed. The wooden ship had two levels, and twice as many laser cannons, each one firing a barrage of plasma into the *Claw's* port-side, stripping away the metal exterior, down to its glowing circuits underneath.

Stiqula braced himself on the back of his pilot's chair. "Pull *up!*" He reached over the pilot's shoulder and yanked back on the helm, launching the ship into the sky at nearly eight g's. "Prepare to fire!" The ship continued to arc until the stars fell past the forward glass, and the curve of the dark horizon came into view again. "Hold! Reverse thrust!" He let go of the wheel, still using the pilot's chair to stand at the awkward angle, almost a full ninety degrees from the surface of the planet. And through the glass, the tips of each claw—shaped more like blades at the corners of the glass—began to glow a brilliant red, hanging over the splinters, their tiny engine lights like fireflies.

The *Claw* fired straight down as the splinters rose to meet the tri-beam head-on, piercing their formation and igniting any ship it touched. The fighters scattered from the light. But as they fled, the lasers followed, all three moving independently of the other, rotating around each other in a cyclonic display, taking out as many ships as they could with every sweep.

Two bark ships came at the *Claw* from either side, firing everything they had in an attempt to save their fighters. But the *Claw's* steady beams continued to rise as they spun, meeting the bark ships' underbellies, tearing them in half. The bark ships split down the middle, unzipped at their newly molten seams, and exploded as the fading lasers struck their engines.

But Stiqula did not celebrate halving their battlegroup with ease. His entire ship was one giant weapon. Built to play against Viæden's weaknesses. Sharp and jagged, to confuse their radar, strong and metal, to resist their weapons, and with three main cannons powerful enough to eviscerate their wooden ships in moments. It was a slaughter. They didn't stand a chance. And he would soon have all the souls He needed.

The ship leveled out again as he looked to the three gauges above the bridge window. Each one displaying a slowly growing red bar, representing each of the lasers' cool-down gages. And when the bars neared full, a high pitch ring grew louder as the lasers charged again.

"Those beams," said Brown. "They're too strong. Can our shield hold against them?"

"We won't know until we're hit, sir."

He watched the heinous talons charge, glowing again, with such heat their infrared monitor could not compute, appearing as three black holes, haloed in rainbows.

"Switch to dynamic shielding. Focus power on lake-side branches."

"Aye!"

"We've got a fourth ship ready to launch, sir!"

"Send it. Missiles live. Bring it down any way you can!" Brown ordered.

Another bark ship rose from Darakin's branches.

"One more ship coming, sir," Stiqula's radarman brought to attention as the *Claw's* lasers sounded their readiness to fire.

"Destroy it, and whatever hole it came from."

The *Claw* dropped to the ship's level, its talons' tips glowing red as it faced the bark, head-on. The bark ship spotted them, firing everything it had, but the *Claw's* beams energized before their rockets could strike, igniting them in mid air as all three beams burnt past, eviscerating the bark ship in a fiery wreck that bounced against the castle's shield. The outermost lasers then swept around to use up their charge on what splinters remained.

Stiqula stepped toward the forward glass, watching as the beams struck the tree's forcefield. Their shield was comprised of a network of flat polygons, each of their corners stemming from the tips of a branch. And each shielded surface lit up, a pale blue, as the *Claw's* laser passed over it.

"Their shield is dynamic, feeding power to what quadrants need it most. How very primitive." Stiqula turned to one of his men at a terminal in the very back, which had no purpose until now. "Increase, full power."

"We're burning through our power, sir. We'll only get two more shots off if we raise to full."

"Do it. I only need one to tear it down." He turned back to the tree.

The man nodded and fiddled with his controls. "Full power."

Stiqula eyed the gages as they rang louder. "Spread the beams, widest distribution pattern."

"Are we holding?" Brown demanded to know.

"All three beams struck at over two hundred thousand degrees, sir. We are holding, but we won't last long!"

"Light, almighty." Brown whispered. "Are we at maximum?"

"Aye, sir. We can only do so much! We've never seen anything this powerful before."

Brown looked to the *Claw*, glowing in the darkness, like the red hand of Refsiel. He could not win. Lost already. And he would lose this city, to the same monster that stole Animallia from them . . . After all he'd been through, all he'd done to avoid this very moment, his fate was inescapable.

The *Claw's* talons glowed red through its bridge window, obscuring the two-layered bark ship as it swung in for another attack, broadsiding the *Claw* on the opposite side as before, dealing just as much damage. The bridge was rocked as the charge-alarm rang again.

"Ignore it! Fire!" Stiqula pointed to the tree.

The *Claw* fired, like three points of a triangle, spreading its beams to the furthest reaches of the shield, each one over twice as thick and bright as before.

The tree's shields quickly reallocated their charge to keep up, radiating out across the forcefield in blue ripples, to the very edges. But it was too much. Spread too thin. The shields flashed as they overloaded, overcompensating for the insane amount of energy bombarding them.

"Now! Draw them together!" Stiqula roared. And the *Claw's* blades slammed together in front of him, joining their beams upon a single point in the center of the shield, exactly where the power had just been drained from.

"No!" Brown screamed, monitors and control panels sparking around him. The shield generators nearest the beam exploded from the surge of energy and a hole was torn right through the forcefield. Free of obstruction, the laser fired into Darakin's branches. And Brown could see it, out the hangar window, flashing into the docking bay, torching all it touched, flipping bark ships, disintegrating fighters, and vaporizing men, before it slammed into the opposite end of the hollow, right below his window, rocking the entire city.

But for all the beam had burnt through, its power was exhausted, only burrowing a few feet into the trunk before it dissipated.

The *Claw's* talons opened to cool, clearing the way for Stiqula to see the glowing edges of a polygon, missing from the shield. He bared his sharp teeth in accomplishment, though short-lived it was. Their ship was rocked again by laserfire. The last bark ship was still circling them.

"Target that ship," he pointed off the port bow.

The *Claw* swung up out of the line of fire, and twisted as its talons came down to line up with their target. The metal ship blasted downward at full speed, colliding with the two-story bark ship, and tearing it to splinters.

Stiqula braced himself against the frame of the bridge window as the *Claw* swung back into position, talons aimed for the hole in the shield, like a raptor ready to strike.

This was it. "Draw them together."

His men followed his command as the charge ring built to a final crescendo.

Brown searched the smoke of his control room for the *Claw*. And as the grey cloud cleared, he found his adversary in the forward monitor, charging its talons once again.

The tree, and all its three million inhabitants, were now completely helpless. He'd failed as general. He'd failed as guardian of this city, this kingdom. He'd failed to keep his people safe from an incompetent king. From a heartless beast. He'd failed . . . Light knows he tried.

"Evacuate the city," he fought his pride to say. "He can't kill us all."

"Fire," Stiqula said. And as if the God of Fire, himself, had heard him, his wish was granted.

Three missiles collided with the *Claw's* glowing talons and erupted in a violent cloud of fire. The cloud grew in Stiqula's eyes, no time to act before the window shattered and the explosion rained inside. The shockwave caught him in its fiery arms and hurled him across the bridge, slamming into the back wall as the fires wreaked their havoc on his men and their controls. The *Claw* lurched back from the blow, and with the loss of its pilot, spun, plummeting from the sky.

"We got it!" Sam cheered, watching the fire-cloud fade in the distance.

"That was way too close," said Greyson as the *Claw* sank to the grass forests, cutting a trail of black smoke behind it.

The grass, the lake, the castle tree, and the ceptris forest beyond were all suddenly bathed in light as the full moon rose over the battlefield, casting its wise, blue glow upon everything it saw.

Brown's tense body went limp. Stiqula was hit! "Hold the evacuation!" he screamed. "Who's still out there?"

"Unknown ship, sir!"

The view-screen zoomed out to show an unidentified bark ship, slowing to a halt, long-nosed and three floored, like no ship he'd ever seen before.

But still, some familiar light came to his mind as a victorious grin pulled at his lips.

Stiqula woke to furious wind howling in from the night, sparks and flames spinning all around him as his ship corkscrewed through the dark.

Fury boiled in his blood. *This* was not how it would end. Not after fifty years of tortured slumber, and *all* the darkness that he'd spilt. *It would not be for nothing!* He would right this ship, and wrong the world to see his love again!

His eyes glowed yellow in his rage, and with his talons he climbed through warped metal and rattling debris, across the spinning bridge to the wheel. He ripped the charred pilot from his chair, and with all his might and screams, he fought the helm for control.

Seeing the blue grass, like an infinite, spinning wall, headed straight for him.

"*Come on!*" He pulled back so hard on the wheel, its metal bent in his claws.

Then, finally it responded.

The stabilizers blasted, jerking the ship upright again, so hard it felt like he'd slammed into the ground. But through the broken windshield, he saw the wall of earth fall below him. Grass forests, painted in the new light of the moon. And his engine-fires grazed their tips as he arced back into the sky.

The bridge was almost completely destroyed, littered with the corpses of his men, now jiggling in the turbulence of his ascension. Not one left alive. And he could see that one of the *Claw's* talons had been blown off in the explosion. Only two main lasers left.

He looked to the laser intensity controls behind him, spotting their operator dead on the floor. He had no choice but to release the helm, spinning out of his chair to alter their power. The *Claw* began to fall again as he lowered their intensity to half of standard wattage, knowing that in their lesser state their beams could stay constant, taking much longer to overheat, but at the cost of reduced damage. He had no other choice. He couldn't aim and fly at the same time. He couldn't run this ship alone!

"There's no explosion," Greyson said, searching the grass for any sign of impact. The *Claw* had fallen too far to see. Everything below him blurred together in the moon's light.

"Let's not let him escape again," said Nash.

"I wasn't planning on it." Greyson drove the *Leiaru* down, flying as quickly as he could after the *Claw's* thinning smoke trail.

Then from the hazy blue, two beams of solid red fired past.

"Whoa!" Greyson screamed as the beams swung in closer. He pulled up and spun between them to save the ship. But he couldn't escape them all together. The lasers swept across their engines, completely destroying some of them as the *Claw* blurred past. The whole ship lurched forward as he leveled out, Great Ceptris Forest right in front of them.

"Shit!" Sam yelled. "Engines 17-21 are gone, and the power's not re-routing." She unbuckled herself and braced to stand. "We'll never outrun him without full power."

"We're not running, we're fighting!" Greyson declared.

"He just tore through an entire battlegroup!" Sam screamed. "Without shields, we're just as vulnerable. We have no choice!"

"She's right," Nash agreed.

Greyson accepted with a grunt.

"We can't play by his rules. Take him into the forest!" Nash shouted as Sam rushed from the bridge.

Greyson punched it for the wall of trees ahead as Nash switched his monitor to rear display. The *Claw* twisted as it turned back for them. Following, just as planned. But its red beams followed too, cutting through the sky, blazing a path across the face of the forest until the beams came parallel with the *Leiaru*, shining red on either side of them like the fiery edges of an invisible highway.

"No!" Greyson saw them begin to spin, corkscrewing around the *Leiaru* to increase the chance of landing a blow. He jerked at the helm, sending the ship into a barrel roll, spinning right along with them to evade and stay between the beams.

Sprinting down the ship's main hall, Sam was flung from her feet, into the wall, just a few steps outside the engine room. She couldn't move, pinned down by four times gravity, smashed so tightly up against her ship, she could feel where the lasers struck, port, then starboard. Greyson's maneuvers weren't fast enough. The lasers grazed her ship on either side, burning through its bark and pouring smoke into the sky.

But still onward it flew. The *Leiaru* was strong. Stronger than any ship this kingdom had ever seen. And it would survive. Greyson leveled out again, as the *Claw*'s barrage ended, and they plunged into the darkness of the ceptris forest, through a tiny gap in the curtain of its leaves. And beyond was a cavernous void, like the cave of a hollow mountain, seven miles tall, lofted to the sky on pillars of mangled bark. But the trees were so far spaced at this height—miles apart—that Stiqula had no problem keeping up.

The *Claw* slammed into the back of them, lurching Greyson and Nash back into their seats, and Sam into the engine room's controls as the *Leiaru* took a fishtailing dive.

"We're losing altitude!" Greyson screamed, shaking the dead helm.

"Sam, hurry!" Nash belted into the intercom.

Quickly, she killed the power to the broken engines, and rerouted it to all the rest, multiplying their power. Instantly, she was hurled against the controls again as the ship boosted back to speed. "Done!"

Greyson adjusted to the burst, riding the air again, smooth as rails. He climbed, aiming the nose for the canopy, still three miles overhead. Patches of blue light trickled down between the sparse gaps in its tightly woven branches. If they were ever going to lose him, it'd be up there.

"Stay back there, Sam! Take an aft turret to him!" Nash barked.

Sam pushed off her controls and entered the hall again, fighting against the steep incline and heavy gravity to reach the next door over: a large, white, empty room she'd labeled *training*. She slid down the floor on her back, using the ship's incline to reach the far corner, catching a door with her feet and entering a small storage room with a single, mounted turret, facing aft.

If Stiqula wanted to chase them, he'd have to work for it. The monitor lit up as soon as she sat down, automatically switching green in night vision and targeting the *Claw* in a yellow square as it followed them into the sky. The *Leiaru* was now almost completely vertical, and beginning to shake as it blasted through the atmosphere, approaching the limits of its aerodynamics again.

Sam let out a trail of amber beams after the *Claw*, and in response, the *Claw* screamed, firing straight up for them. Its lasers lit a path through the branches of the canopy as the *Leiaru* dove in. Greyson spun the helm to avoid the red lasers. But again the *Claw* followed, spinning to strike them. They were trapped within its beams, unable to divert. And above them, a fat branch, fast-approaching, illuminated by the laser light circling on its surface.

"Oh, Gods!" Greyson didn't know what to do. If he pulled away the beams would hit them! And if they stayed, they'd slam straight into that branch! "We're trapped!"

"Samantha!" Nash shouted.

Sam heard her father's voice over the intercom, and Greyson screaming in the background, never gaining more focus than in that moment, honing the skills her father had taught her. The secret to hitting anything. Moving target or not. This wasn't like shooting a pistol, where keeping calm was key. This was a heavy, two-handed turret, and it took all the concentration she had. She held her breath, tensing every muscle, sharpening her aim down to the millimeter, and pulling the trigger. Her red trail of plasma fired down at the *Claw*, mixing with Stiqula's beams, following the line back to its talon. The beam fell to darkness as the *Claw's* port blade exploded in a pop of fire. Just in time for Greyson to dodge the mammoth branch to one side.

Finally, Sam could breathe again, sucking the air down with a smile as she felt the *Leiaru* turn hard right past the branch. The *Claw* mirrored it to the left.

Greyson bolted through the canopy, now flying parallel to the ground— he hoped—dodging limb after limb, as well as the *Claw's* remaining beam as it crisscrossed through the leaves, cutting a trail of fire. Sam did her best to land another blow, but the two ships weaved so dramatically through the trees, it was damn near impossible.

"I can't keep this up!" Greyson's heart was about to burst into flames itself, palms working up so much sweat the helm was getting hard to hold on to, slipping out of his hands if he loosened his death-grip whatsoever. His hands burned, cramped shut, not used to crazy shit like this!

But Nash was. "Pull in, close to a trunk, and climb!"

Greyson turned along the nearest branch, following it in to find its trunk, arcing up again to climb even higher. The branches were less chaotic here, only slightly easier to dodge back and forth. Greyson noticed Nash prepare something on his terminal, queuing up an order. The trunk thinned as they rose, breaking off into tiny branches itself. Then, finally they crashed through the top layer: the gigantic leaves at the forest's ceiling, out into a sky as black as space, twinkling in starlight.

"Pull back!" Nash screamed. "Hold engines!"

Greyson did exactly as he said, yanking back on the wheel before slamming the throttle down to zero. Nash smashed the enter key, releasing a barrage of lights from beneath the *Leiaru*, flaring out both sides of the ship as it did a backflip through the air. Its nose came around almost a one-eighty to face the forest again, and the canopy lit up in the light of their flares, giving them a clear view of it for miles. The plumes of its leaves were so vast at this height they looked like living mountains, with rivers of darkness between their leaves, which streamed from their domed summits to their clouded valleys.

"Come on!" Nash yelled as the *Leiaru's* momentum slowed. His hand hovered over his terminal, waiting for the *Claw* to break through the leavéd ceiling, and be blinded by the light.

But, even in his rage, Stiqula knew not to follow after them. He knew not to fall for such an obvious ploy. And instead of the *Claw*, only its laser burst through the green, firing blindly, striking the *Leiaru* all the way across its bow, only a few feet from the bridge window.

"Shit!" Nash slammed his hand down and fired everything they had at where the laser came from, colliding with the forest's leaves in a swelling burst of flame as the *Leiaru* began to fall. It sank, straight down toward the yellow cloud. And as the wind rushed past, the smoke and fire rising from the bow's gash grew to blind them.

"I can't see!" Greyson screamed, fire splashing up against the windshield.

Nash grunted, looking past Greyson to a door off to the side of the bridge. "Reverse thrust, Greyson! If we hit that canopy, we'll be torn apart!" He unbuckled himself and wrangled his cane.

Greyson laid on the reverse, tripping Nash up as he stood. "Where are you going!?"

"I've got to vent these flames!" He rounded his chair, holding the back of Greyson's to stay on his feet in the leaping turbulence.

"I should be the one to go!" Greyson screamed, as the old man struggled to the door.

"Shut up and drive!" Nash threw his cane to the ground and leapt for the open doorway, colliding with its frame and pulling himself through it in the lessened pull of gravity.

But the reverse engines couldn't stop them altogether, and leaves and branches rattled against their hull as the ship plummeted into the flaming canopy. All the bits of tree that Nash had destroyed were falling all around them, blazing as they passed. They tumbled blindly through the fiery trees, diving closer to their deaths with every blind collision, limbs and cinders bouncing from the hull.

But Sam could see just fine from the back, watching as the flaring branches of the trees fell upward, past her. And among them was the *Claw*, hiding, waiting. It lit up as the *Leiaru* passed, engines firing, pulling out in pursuit. And as it turned, Sam noticed something. The sides of its hull were exposed, glowing blue with fragile circuitry as the final talon glowed.

The *Claw's* beam blasted down at the *Leiaru* as it spun out of control, completely annihilating all of its rear engines in a single sweep. Sam screamed as they exploded next to her, warping the wall of the storage room she was in, whirling everything on the shelves into the air.

"That's *my* ship, you *mother fucker!*" She pinned down her triggers and sent a trail of red, twisting through the branches at the *Claw*.

Sirens blared on the bridge, a giant *engine failure* sign, strobing on Greyson's control screen. "The engines are gone!" he screamed, helplessly, as Nash finally made it to the splinter bay controls.

The *Leiaru* was capable of carrying a small fireteam of splinter ships in its hold. And though the bay was empty now, its heavy door could save them. Nash knew every corner of this ship like his own home. And he knew that bay was directly below the bridge, now breached by the laser that had torn into its hull. At his command, the bay door slid open wide along the port side of the ship. And immediately, the wind feeding the flames that blinded the bridge were sucked down into the gash, through the splinter bay, and out the hangar door.

But all Greyson knew was that he could see again. "It worked!" he screamed. Just in time for him to avoid a massive branch. He pulled the helm with all his strength to get the ship to evade, having hardly any engines left to work with.

"Come on!" Sam screamed, every muscle in her body flexed to the max, giving everything she had to land a blow on the exposed circuitry. But the *Claw* was moving so erratically, and there was just too much shit in the way to do it!

The *Leiaru's* engines were gone. The ship couldn't turn to face the *Claw* and fire its rockets. And the target lock would never work with all this debris. She had no choice. She had to take it down. Or it would take *them* down. There was no other way. She yelled in frustration, switching rounds from laser to anti-air, praying the explosions that they made would be enough to crack those power lines. Her cannon rotated from a thin laser barrel to a much larger, perforated, AA cannon, and she let loose an eruption of tiny explosions, striking everything in sight. All the sticks and debris between their two ships exploded, clouding her view as she continued to fire. But as they fell, the cloud of fire that she'd made stayed still, and the Claw plunged into it, emerging from the black smoke just as its main laser lit again and blasted down at them. Aimed right for Sam. But she was honed in on her target, and refused to lift her fingers from the triggers. She saw the shells leave her cannon in slow motion, her perforated cannon flashing with light as it sent the rounds, streamlined through her crosshairs, passing the *Claw's* laser as it struck at her feet, igniting what shells remained in her gun's cache, causing the whole turret to exploded, and start a chain reaction, detonating the line of AA shells she'd fired, leaving a trail of orange, fiery spheres all the way back to the *Claw*, and right into the breach on its starboard side.

In a safety measure, Sam's seat ripped away from her gun, along a short track, saving her from the explosion that blasted a hole through the wall of her ship. She covered her eyes from the light, then opened them to see that she'd finally struck her mark!

The *Claw's* beam ceased, and its blue power lines exploded from its side, kicking it sideways into an oncoming branch, which it bounced off of, recoiling back into another. Then another. The metal ship warped from each blow, lighting tiny fires in the fissures of its steel as it ragdolled through the canopy behind them.

"I did it!"

"The *Claw's* been hit!" Nash yelled, returning to his seat to find it clambering through the brush behind them.

"Great, but we're still screwed!" Greyson screamed, jiggling the useless helm.

Nash leaned to the integrity console next to his. "We've still got full ventral engines, they're just not strong enough to stop us. *Sam!* Reroute the power again!"

The *Claw* crashed through the canopy, slamming into branch after branch, launching Stiqula from his pilot's chair. He bounced from one wall of the bridge to the other as the ship rocked back and forth, then finally broke through the canopy into the void below.

The siren faded as his ship lost all power, barreling through wind and whipping flame. He could see the *Leiaru* below him as his ship cartwheeled end over end. And his heart became nothing but rage and lust. For blood. *Their* blood.

*They were dead. He would kill them all! If it was the last thing he ever did! Such arrogance! Such ignorance! Such wasted lives!*

He screamed so loud and wide his mouth became unhinged, and his eyes burned yellow with the wind. Stiqula launched himself from his dead ship and down into the night upon a sonic boom. He fell like a yellow comet as the *Claw* detonated behind him in a sphere of pure red light that lit the forest, giving him a clear sight to his target. He held his blade behind him as the wind tore at his cheeks, ready to strike.

*One more millisecond and he'd have them.*

But then, the engines on the bark ship's underside glowed, white hot, lifting the ship, and changing its descent. It slowed, and blew right past Stiqula as he fell.

"No," he whispered, reaching for it as it blurred by. He turned, facing the sky, watching them jet into the distance. And above him, the glowing fires of all the limbs their battle had broken free, falling down to him like strings of fire streaking from the stars. Below him, as he turned, he saw eternal darkness. The forest floor was too deep for any shred of moonlight to reach, trees growing up from the dark like they were born of it . . . just like him.

And now . . . *finally* . . . He was returning.

Returning to the shadows whence he'd come.

His fury left him, washed away by the soothing current of the air, just as it had moments after his rebirth. He welcomed his end. He welcomed Darkness, like an old friend.

Death . . . was all he wanted. And in His realm, he would once again be with her.

He closed his eyes, breathing easy.

"Aliqula."

It was the most peace he'd felt since his awakening . . . The only peace, in fifty years of torment, knowing death would take him soon . . . And for the first time, the slightest sign of peace curled at the edges of his blood-stained lips.

He slammed down into the black water at the bottom of the ceptris trees, but did not feel the impact. And as the flaming boughs crashed down around him, he could not feel them either, like he'd phased out of the world and all its senses.

Darkness . . . was all that remained.

Was this death?

Excitedly he opened his eyes to see Aliqula, at any moment, emerge from the blackness.

But there was nothing out there.

Nothing but a void, and shadows.

He accepted death with open arms . . . but Death did not welcome him.

Stiqula was lain down upon a rippled stone: the only visible thing in an endless dark. The stone was black as well, though nearly grey compared to the abyss in which it floated. There was no light in this place, no illumination whatsoever. No way for him to be seeing this thing below him, yet there it was. Black and terrible.

*The Door to Darkness.* Cursed with Refsiel's Seal. The signature of evil.

Fear wrapped him fully as he stood and stared upon it, thirty feet long, fourteen feet wide. And it was then he realized he was no longer at the bottom of that forest. He had not found the door after millennia of being lost. But instead he had been brought through it.

Refsiel had brought him to the Realm of Darkness.

Then at once, the Darkness struck his skin like acid, burning to his bones, sensing the faint glint of light still in his splintered heart, boring down inside of him to snuff it out. He lurched back in agony, muscles writhing as he screamed—or at least tried. There was no sound here in this place. Only the high and numbing ring of the abyss. His body could not stay for long.

Such *pain*! Such *fear*! Such *brutality*, and *hatred* swimming in the devil's soul. Stiqula could feel it, as if it were his own.

Then, finally a sound, a crash, a hiss, a roar, like death shot through his brain, implanting a vision. Refsiel's voice was monstrous, sick, and damned. But deep within it lay His plan. He saw the ship—the curséd ark of angels— plummet from the sky to Viæden's plains.

Stiqula saw the *Chandelier* wreathed in black and flame.

Stiqula's ears pooled with blood as gravity struck him again, falling back to the hard wood of his mirror chamber within Gardeón. He convulsed against the floor, his body going through a fit as all life's sense overwhelmed him once again.

He had returned from Death's Realm, quivering in shallow breaths. His body nearly did not make the journey, and for certain would not have if Refsiel had not made it so, rejecting his dark soul every time it tried to sunder from his heart.

His soul was tired . . . Its grip weak. But Darkness simply would not have it.

Stiqula lay there for a long time still. Slowly adjusting to this cruel world again.

He thought he'd won . . . He thought he'd see her. He thought his fate had come . . . But now there was one *more* thing Refsiel wanted.

Was this forever now his fate? To always be one *more* step from relief . . . but never truly within reach. Did the King of Lies ever truly intend to keep His word . . . and reunite them?

And . . . *Was it worth it . . . in the end?*

Darkness . . . Could he really give the world to Darkness? A God so evil and demented, even Oyopa could not love Him?

# Part 3

# King of Lies

# 27

# CRASHING DOWN

The *Leiaru* shot from the ceptris forest, into the blue light of the plains. The entire engine-bank had been destroyed by the *Claw*. And the only ones Greyson was getting any response from were the five hover thrusters on its underside. With those at least he could keep them from falling straight down like a dead stick. But they were still *falling*, just at a shallow angle, and picking up speed. Greyson could see the speed flashing on his control screen, shaking violently in front of him, *380 mph*.

He pulled back hard on the helm, lifting the nose in front of them. But without rear engines they still couldn't fly. They had no lift at all! His only option was to slow their blistering descent, before they all were turned to fiery dust against the ground.

Keeping the ship's nose up at a forty-five degree angle, he laid on the hover thrusters, trying to use the ship's flat bottom to catch the wind, and hope the friction didn't tear them apart in the process. The helm thrashed in his fists as gravity surged, pressing him and Nash down against their controls. But at least that meant it was working! They were slowing! But the awkward shape of the ship dragged unevenly on the wind, and oscillated side to side, faster and faster. Greyson tried his best to keep the nose up and not flip them back into a death-spiral.

"Hold on, Sam!" Nash yelled as they approached the grass forest.

She was still in the back when the tail end began to skim along the grass, blazing a bright-orange skid mark as they dipped into the moonlit blades.

The *Leiaru* jolted as it struck against the friction of the grass stalks, bouncing from its blue blades like a boat launched from the waves. It fell back down again, almost horizontal, crashing straight into the forest at just over one hundred miles an hour, sweeping along the soft blades, ripping many from the ground, and lodging them firmly in the jagged bow of the ship like food between crooked teeth. Greyson almost broke his freaking ribs against the helm, blood pooling in weird places, like he'd stood on his head too long. But finally the forest's friction dragged them to a halt, and the extra g's released them, flinging Nash and Greyson back against their seats.

*Thankfully* . . . they were not dust.

Greyson unstuck his claws from the wheel, and hung his aching hands down at his sides. His whole body ached, panting heavily to help his blood reallocate. The engines still roared beneath him, vibrating the ship in an omnipresent hum. He strained his arm to reach and press the red *disengage* button on his terminal, then let it swing back to his side again as the hum shook away.

"Well done, Greyson." Nash pat him on the shoulder, equally out of breath.

Greyson looked at him. *Well done?* He'd barely held the ship together. Nash should have been punching him, not patting him, for completely destroying his daughter's beloved invention.

"You guys a'right?" Sam asked, returning to the bridge.

Greyson unbuckled himself, straining to turn and see her. He was relieved she was okay. But also grieved. "I'm so sorry, Sam," he said, hoarse from screaming. "I ruined your ship."

She couldn't accept his apology. "It's *your* ship, Greyson. And it did its job."

"You did a fine job," Nash assured. "And the ship can be fixed."

"Yeah, but *that* ship is not recovering." Sam threw a thumb over her shoulder. "You guys should've seen it." She smashed her hands against each other to mimic the *Claw* bouncing through the canopy and exploding. "So cool."

Nash smiled at her. "Ever the optimist."

"You think he survived?" Greyson quieted her cheer.

Her smile faded, struck with the sobering thought . . . "He's survived worse."

The gash outside the bridge window sparked as its fires started up again.

Nash looked down to the integrity readings, fires were still burning all over the ship. "Come on. Let's get these fires out." He limped for the door. "Greyson, contact command and have them send a rescue. Two carriers should do it."

Darakin's hangar had seen better days. It was halved down the center, scorched by a misshapen, black scar that drove across its floor from mouth to maintenance hold at the back, overturned bark ships on either side. What the laser hadn't completely disintegrated, it'd lit on fire. Ash and white extinguisher residue lined the burn. Grey smoke filled the dome above. And busy men hurried all around to make certain every spark was put out.

The tow-ships set the *Leiaru* down on a clear patch near the hangar's mouth, where at one time, a hundred splinter ships had sat at the ready. Now only a dozen remained. "We're gunna put you down here," they said over the intercom. "General Brown would like to thank you."

"A-alright, thanks again," said Sam, holding a button on the com panel.

Nash's cool demeanor thawed. "Oh. Oh no." He stood from the weapons controls.

"Where are you going?" Greyson stood as Nash limped off the bridge.

"I'm getting off this ship before he gets here."

"You really think he's going to remember what you look like after fifty years?" Greyson and Sam followed him out to the lifts, on either side of the bridge's main entrance.

"I'd rather not take the risk." He limped onto a small, round elevator.

"Neither would I," Sam agreed as they stepped on and descended to the *Leiaru's* first floor.

As they exited the lift, they turned right, to the starboard loading ramp as it opened and sloped from the ship's floor to the hangar floor below it.

And who else would be standing there waiting for them but General Brown.

"Oh. Fuck." Nash said, a little louder than a whisper, stuttering in his step.

"Too late now." Sam pushed him, thinking it way more suspicious to turn back.

The general smiled brightly at Greyson, who led the way down the ramp. "Greyson." He grabbed his hand for an eager shake. "I knew it was you, when this ship came out of nowhere—which is *un*-registered by the way. We should fix that."

Greyson had never seen him so happy. Even with all this destruction around them. His hope shined on. It kinda made him feel like a rockstar for a second.

"Ms. O'Nasi," he greeted her, just as brightly. "A fine ship you've built. We'll get it fixed up, good as new. Compliments of me, personally."

"Thank you, sir. That's very generous of you. But we've already called for the ship to be returned to Ivy City for repairs." She didn't trust the king's men with her ship for a minute.

"That's fair enough." Brown nodded.

Then it was Nash's turn to greet him, donning a smile to match the general's. "Nash O'Nasi." He stuck his hand out between them.

"Ah, Mr. O'Nasi." They shook firmly. "A pleasure to meet you. Especially under such circumstances." He released him. "The king would like to congratulate the saviors of Darakin, personally." He motioned for the elevator core.

"Oh, that's quite alright. I really need to be going." Nash took a step back.

"Nonsense, come." Brown wrapped an arm around his shoulders. "He'll be ecstatic to know that it was you three that saved the city."

Nash forced a chuckle. "I'm sure he will."

The four of them crossed to the elevator core, and rose to the tree's highest level as Sam and Greyson explained to Brown how they'd taken down the *Claw*. Nash stayed as quiet as the wall, not making eye-contact with anyone. But Brown didn't seem to be too interested in him anyway, enthralled with the heroic tale.

"Well, I certainly am glad you arrived when you did," Brown said, stepping out of the lift. "A moment later, and this entire tree would have fallen."

Greyson was suddenly struck by a wave of deja vu as he left the elevator, flashing back to when he'd first arrived to see the king... So much had changed in those few days, for better, and for worse. He'd felt like a different person then. So innocent... Naive to all the lives he was about to change. Blind to the kick he was about to land on the globe, forever shifting its fate... He may have saved the city, but he couldn't forget that it also would not have needed saving if not for him. It did not change the fact that darkness followed everywhere he went. And the only thing that could scare that dark away—or at least make it *feel* like he was rid of it . . . was Kyri.

The green doors boomed as they swung open to the throne room.

But the brilliant light that once lived there was gone, replaced now with dim torchlight. The pristine sanctuary that once was the castle's greatest hall had fallen to ruin. The white tables of the ball had all been shoved against the walls, huddled up like junk. Some resting on their sides, contents slid to the floor, others flipped completely. The marble was littered with silver plates and broken chairs. Piles of rubble lined the long green carpet, stained by drink and blood. The smell of spoiled food and burning wood weighed down the air, wafting on a chilling breeze as they strode to the king.

But Huey was not on his throne. He stood at the edge of the ravine that had been torn through his great hall, staring down into its chasm, lost in his own mind. Next to him was a chandelier, shattered on the marble. And his aides were scattered throughout the hall, beginning the arduous process of cleaning up this catastrophic mess.

Seeing the state of the throne room once again, General Brown's smile quickly fled. Perhaps the king was not going to be in as good a mood as he'd thought.

"The *Claw* did this?" Greyson whispered. But there was really only one thing he cared about right then, darting his eyes across the wreck to find her. "Where's Kyri?" he shouted, stumbling closer to the king. "Is Kyri okay?!"

Huey turned to him, still in his ceremonial robes, disheveled as they were. Shallow tears clung to his eyes. "Kyri?" he spoke softly.

"Where is she?" Greyson demanded to know. He had never been on level footing with the king before. He seemed much smaller this close up. Hardly as intimidating.

"Greyson," Brown tried to quiet him.

"You," the king said, very slowly. "*All* of you." His breath deepened. "*Where were you?!*"

His cries struck them like a sea wave, staggering them back as it hit them in the gut.

"I told you he'd come for me! And you *abandoned* me to him!"

"Your Highness, we did not," Brown tried to calm him. "Greyson has saved this city."

"You think I was not here, *Brown*? You think I did not see it for *myself*!?"

He was untamable, shaking the tears from his eyes. His lips spread from anger to disgust. "This is *your* fault."

"Huey, that's hardly fair. I *was* here. And *still* we were defenseless." Brown tried to keep his own cool now.

Huey zeroed in on Greyson, scrambling to blame *anyone* but himself. "And *you*. You lied to me! You made me believe he was *dead*!"

"I didn't—" Greyson started.

But Nash stepped forward to put a stop to it, pointing right at the king's face. "He tried to warn you, you little *shit*!"

Huey backed up, mouth opened wide, uttering nonsense until he found the words. "Ah—H-how dare you!"

Brown came between them, locking eyes with Nash and trading a determined stare before he pushed him back. "That's quite enough, Mr. O'Nasi."

Huey's aides closed in around them, sensing a threat to their king.

But the king could not pull his eyes from Nash. "How dare you," he said, eyes widening. "How *dare* you," he repeated as Nash's face finally emerged from the back of his mind. "*You*."

Nash kept his eyes locked on the king's, standing proudly in his guilt.

Brown stepped aside, to see the king's fury drip from his eyes.

Huey threw his robes back, uncovering a sword, and drawing its gold blade. He reared back, screaming, aimed right for Nash's green eyes, and thrust to strike.

Sam screamed as her father stayed perfectly still. But, the blade froze, one inch from his nose. Brown caught it, right out of the air, slicing deep into his palm as he tore it from the king's grasp.

"*Brown!*" Huey screamed.

The general dropped it to the ground, blood trickling after. "You're in enough trouble as it is, Huey."

"And don't I know it!" Huey kicked the ground.

"Think of your image. How will you explain that on the night of your victory ball, the castle was attacked by the very creature you claimed to have destroyed," Brown explained.

Huey panted, mouth open, waiting to hear what else his general had to say.

"Let him take the blame, sir." He eyed Nash. "The pirate, *Té Nova*, returned, posing as Stiqula to wreak havoc on our people, and reap the treasures from our pillaged cities. He is worth more alive. As proof." Brown looked to Nash. "He will admit to it, himself. And rid the people of all doubt."

Nash said nothing, clenching his jaw tight.

"You don't want to raise Kyri to lead a kingdom that does not trust her," Brown said finally.

*Kyri.* The only thing Greyson heard out of that sentence. She was alive. He breathed in relief, almost un-noticeably.

And Huey's breathing calmed as well, to an almost manageable intensity as he acknowledged the general's plan. "Fine," he said quickly. "And what about them?" He threw his hand to Greyson and Sam. "What should be done with them?"

Brown didn't understand, eyes twitching. "Nothing, Your Highness?"

"Clearly this criminal has bewitched them. Sculpting them into the heartless *killers* that they are."

*Killers?* Greyson shook his head, like the king had somehow seen into his soul.

"And I cannot have either of you running free throughout my kingdom."

"Who," Greyson uttered. "Who have I killed that *you* have not ordered me to?"

Huey smiled. A horrible, shit-eating grin. "I've just received word that the bodies of *six* royal guards have been found at the Spire Observatory."

"What?" His eyes fluttered, confused.

"Among them were the mutilated corpses of Reintree Berinhard and Kelvan Riese."

A horrid chill crawled down Greyson's chest, like a thousand dagger-legged spiders marched across his skin . . . *Dead? Mutilated?* But he'd left them *alive!*

"As I *recall*, they were your former *peers*. Your *competition*," Huey said as one of his aides handed him a glowing tablet. "Sounds like the perfect motive to me." He presented the tablet to Greyson. Security footage of the observatory lobby. It showed Greyson and Sam both being threatened by Riese and his men, then Nash arriving to throw Greyson his weapon. But as soon as the light of his lerité appeared, the recording pixilated and blacked out.

Greyson was speechless . . . Had he blocked it out? Had he really killed them?

*He was sure he hadn't . . . But then, if he didn't . . . who did?*

Sam wouldn't stand for it. "We had to defend ourselves, Huey. They were threatening our lives. About to kill us because of the prejudice *your* laws have endorsed."

"Be silent!" Huey snapped at her.

But that wasn't enough to shut her up. Not nearly. "We did not kill them!"

The king's aide handed him photographs of the bodies. Bloodied messes, hardly distinguishable. Scarred and cauterized, burnt and molded into vile and unnatural forms.

Huey scattered the images at their feet.

"They were found with wounds matching those of Stiqula's light-blade," Huey said as his aides circled them, grabbing hold of Greyson, Sam, and Nash, removing what weapons they carried, including Greyson's sword and chain.

The king took the blade from his aide, chain wrapping its hilt. "I don't know how you came by this. But the wounds it leaves are unmistakable."

Greyson was dumbfounded, unable to resist the aides fondling his empty pockets and holding his hands clasped behind his back. *He'd left them alive . . . He was sure of it.*

Brown stepped closer to the king, looking on in paralleled disbelief.

"It was me, Huey." Nash spoke up. "I killed them all, myself. Don't punish the boy. And leave my daughter out of it. They are innocent in all of this."

"They are *hardly* innocent," Huey spat. "But the truth is *irrelevant* at this point. They have both *associated* with a known criminal of the realm. Not to mention, he is still responsible for Stiqula's release. And therefore, the lives of *thousands*." He leaned in close to Greyson, staring as deep as he dared into his emerald eyes. "You *belong* in that dungeon."

# 28

# A Ruined Heart

General Brown walked them to the dungeons, far below the castle, in the bowels of the tree. Each was placed in a separate cell, side by side, along a curved hall of barred-off pens. First Greyson, then Sam, then Nash, unable to see each other through the solid walls between them. Brown took Nash's cane from him as he limped inside. And Nash turned to watch the door slide shut, and lock into place. The men stared pensively at each other, for longer than just strangers would. They were nearly the same age, faces weathered like reflections of each other.

"Never thought I'd see the day you ended up behind these bars," Brown said softly, almost to himself. His words lacked any hint of character, stoically pronounced.

"You and I both know who really belongs in here," Nash replied, with all of Brown's missing emotion.

Brown closed his eyes and turned to leave, walking past Sam and Greyson's cells.

"Sir!" Greyson stopped him. "You know I didn't kill them!"

Brown turned his head, ever so slightly, eyes on the floor. "Then who did, Greyson?"

"I don't know," he admitted, meekly. "But I left them alive . . ."

Brown looked forward, on his way again.

"Riese told me you found the ship." Again he stopped him. "The one from my nightmare . . . Is it true?"

"Yes," he spoke over his shoulder.

And Greyson's eyes began to water.

"It's coming. A few hours from now. Bringing with it whatever darkness your destiny foresaw." He walked on without another word.

"Wait, sir! Wait! I can fix it!" Greyson cried, pressing up against the bars. "*General.*" He slumped, falling to his knees, bars in his hands. "I have to."

His heart was broken . . . Its light . . . he could feel it fading. It'd been fading a long time. Strangled by the overwhelming power of his destiny, and all the souls that destiny had cost. His heart . . . felt so heavy. Like the darkness chilled its throbbing flesh to ice. No, heavier than that . . . strangled, squeezed, with such pressure it collapsed to diamond.

He fell back, splayed out on the floor of his cell, unable to move. Encumbered by despair and diamond blood.

Death truly did follow him, everywhere he went. Everyone he'd met in this cursed kingdom had ended up dead or here in jail with him . . . and everyone else wouldn't escape it much longer. That ship was coming—his *Chandelier*—to drown the world in all his fears and Refsiel's darkness.

"The demons must not reach the bridge," the angel wagged her head, white tunic ripped at the sleeves and stained red with her blood. "I will see to it this axis hall is severed, so that they cannot reach it easily."

But, as if to deny her plan, the far shadows at their back began to stir, and cry. And like the cold finger of space had stroked their winged spines, Greyson and his sister turned to look upon them.

The demons were already on their way. Dragging darkness ever closer, blotting out the gold light of the hallway. They flew, they flowed, like black water toward the angels, hissing, crying, roaring.

Greyson looked to his sister. And she back at him. Agreement in her eyes.

They spun into each other, back to back, wings against wings, and drew both of their lerités. In unison they drove their blades into the hall's floor and darted from each other, sprinting up the curved wall of the golden tunnel, dragging their swords behind them, leaving a trail of molten crystal all the way. They met at the roof and leapt back to the floor, hitting hard to dislodge the now severed axis hall, breaking it in half.

Standing at the very edge of the severed hall, they watched as the half they'd cut drifted away from them, into a void of nothingness. But this black beyond the hall, though looking much like space, was not. It was the largest chamber of their ship, where once lived thousands of angels. Now thousands of demons took their place. And still thousands more came flooding toward them down the hall that remained at their back. Too many to count. Too many to fight.

"Take the portal to the bridge," his sister said, waving her hand over the abyss. And as she did, a single star appeared from the nothingness, and grew to the size of a circular doorway.

"Come with me!" Greyson pleaded, feeling the wind swept from the hall by the demons pressing ever closer. Only one hundred feet away now.

"I will slow them." Sixty feet.

"You will die!" Forty feet.

"Go!" His sister spun between him and the wall of demons, striking him, open palmed, right in his bloody chest, and launching him into the void. Right into the portal's light.

Greyson was spit out from the other side of the starlight portal, and fell to a hard steel floor. Quickly he found his feet again and spun to look upon the grand bridge of his ship. Dead silent. Not even the ever-constant alarm rang here. And there were no angels left to make a sound. Nor their demon counterparts. Though there were signs of their presence strewn all around. Blood and the melted steel from lerité burns littered the chamber, floor to ceiling.

The chamber itself was massive. Five hundred feet high, perfectly round. A hollow sphere. The floor on which Greyson stood was but a catwalk along the sphere's equator. And ahead of him, the railed walkway plunged into the sphere's hollow core, running its complete radius, ending in a crystal control terminal, suspended by nothing but the walkway itself. The far side of the spheroid control room was completely made of glass. A five-hundred-foot lens bowed out to the stars, layered with smaller control platforms along its edges, like crystal mushrooms on a tree, blinking red with warning lights.

And beyond the glass was darkness. A sea of diamond stars. But among those diamonds hung an emerald. A planet, half draped in the shadow of its sun.

"Viæden."

The *Chandelier* was on its way. And Greyson was helpless to stop it, imprisoned in that cell. Not that he could do anything about it anyway.

He was a demon. Whether he liked it or not . . . A demon with a diamond heart. Pulling that ship down from space, just like Riese had said.

What did the Goddess of Water see in him anyway? What had Brown seen in him? Or Sam for that matter? Or even Ky—

"Kyri," he whispered. The brightest light of all.

He'd promised to protect her, as she protected him from his own darkness. He'd promised to save at least one soul from all the others that he'd lost: all the souls he'd pushed clear off the tightrope they called destiny, into the abyss below . . . He'd failed her. Let her slip away from him . . . She'd be ruined by the king. Stained by his ignorance.

"Why would he want her? Why *her*, of all the kids to choose from?" he spoke to himself. But there was no sound barrier between him and the others.

Sam looked to the metal wall between them, almost peering through it to the floor where he lay. "I was wondering that myself," she said softly, hearing the frailty in his voice.

"I've got to get her out of there. I've got to give her the life I promised." The tears unstuck from the corners of his eyes, rolling down, through the hair above his ear and dripping to the floor. "The life I robbed her of."

"You didn't rob her of anything, Greyson. Stiqula did."

"You weren't there, Sam. You don't know. You don't know what I felt. Those men that took her mom . . . I wanted them dead. And I stayed back to kill them before I chose to save her. If I hadn't done that . . ." his voice quivered, "she'd still be alive."

Sam paused for a moment, then defended Greyson from himself. "And they were just going to let you run off?"

"I . . . I don't know. It wouldn't matter anyway . . . I *wanted* to do it."

"No. You *needed* to do it. There's a difference."

Greyson turned his head away from her. Even though she couldn't see it . . . She was wrong. She was wrong about him.

But *why*? Why did everyone think he was so damn good? Was he that good at hiding it? Hiding all the rage and violence he felt clawing to escape, always just below the surface. "And how do you explain the thousands Stiqula killed since I freed him? Explain to me how I'm not guilty for their deaths." He closed his eyes to find the red streets of Rock Town burning beneath his lids, and all its people lying on their backs and bloodied, still as stones.

Sam was quiet. She didn't know how to answer that. The whole cell block slipped into silence. Except for the salty drips, patting to the floor. But only Greyson could hear those. "You don't know me, Sam . . . You don't know me."

"Well, yesterday you hardly knew yourself. So enlighten me." She didn't like that.

But all he knew, he could not tell her. He couldn't tell her that a goddess took him to her realm, and showed him the true color of his heart: an inky cloud before him . . . Not a single shred of light.

"When I was young, my dad taught me to focus . . . on all the *horrible* things in this world. And all the pain and suffering that I could cause. He taught me that, as a guard, it was my duty to remember what I fight against, and not lose myself to darkness." His words began to quiver. "But I got lost anyway . . . I was obsessed with it. Addicted to that pain it made me feel . . . And if happiness is light, then this pain is darkness."

More silence followed. But, just barely, he could hear something else. Like Sam's breath, wavering to keep from crying . . . She probably felt sorry for him . . . or afraid of him. Which only made him feel worse.

"Greyson." Nash finally spoke. "Listen to me. I've done many things that I regret in my life. I've killed many people, without hesitation. And I have felt much guilt for it. It weighed me down. It crippled me. But you cannot let it beat you. You have to know that what you fight for is worth that sacrifice. You cannot blame yourself for every life you may have ended. It's too much. One heart cannot support so many others. At some point, you have to draw a line, and on one side, you keep all those you love and want to protect, and on the other is everyone else. But doing that does not make your heart black. It makes it grey like all the rest of ours."

Greyson straightened his head again, rubbing his eyes with the palms of his hands. "So I'm just supposed to pretend I'm not responsible for all those lives?"

"You made a *mistake*, Greyson. We can't fix what's happened. We can't change who we were. But we can mold ourselves into the people we wish to become. And the fact that you *do* regret what you've done is all the proof you need to know your heart is not black. Regret and sadness are negative feelings, yes, but they come from a much better place than hatred and violence. They come from that thin line where your light and dark meet. They come from your heart's light *attacking* and *reacting* to the world's darkness. Not from the darkness itself."

Greyson heard him. He wanted to believe him. But he knew his dad did not teach him wrong. His dad only believed what was real, and certain. And he knew that darkness, like death, was irreversible. Once settled into the heart, it can never be washed away. Never swept clean . . . His innocence was impossible to recover. "But there's so much. There's so much of it. And it can never be erased . . . It's too late. I've *ruined* my heart . . . And that's why I need Kyri so bad. To save her light from that same fate . . . To shine on me, so I can know what light feels like again," he cried.

"That's not how hearts work, Greyson," Sam managed to say. "The black stains are irreversible, yes, but your heart's canvas is *endless*. You might feel that darkness outweighs the light right now, but it's *not* too late. You can always fill it with more light, to outweigh the dark again."

Greyson turned his head to her again. "What do you mean?"

"Remember when I told you the world was made by Light and Dark together? Well our hearts are just like that: born of light, die with darkness, and all the life between is a mix of the two. We move through the world, collecting bits of light and shadows from every place we go, everything we do, and everyone we meet. Our experiences collect in our heart, and make up our soul. But there's no *limit* to how much light it can hold."

Even though he couldn't see her, Greyson knew from her voice how firmly she believed those words.

"And I know because I felt . . . *exactly* the way you do now. When my mom died." She breathed deep. "I felt so lost, in despair. I thought I'd never recover from the scars death left on me . . . But, building the *Leiaru* filled me with hope and light again. And yes, that darkness I felt remains. It always will. But my heart has filled with so much light since then, I hardly feel it anymore."

"Every heart has darkness, Greyson. You can't escape it," Nash added. "You can't prevent it . . . Doing so, can cripple you."

That sounded just like his dad . . . explaining that he couldn't stay in Wellington, because it would *cripple* him . . . He never did understand just what that meant . . . until now.

"This battle between dark and light inside us all is what gives us our strength," Sam continued. "Our will. And if the battle never happens, we'll never grow." He could hear her start to smile. "Which means you probably have more will than any of us."

*Will* . . . he thought. And a naive vacillation between darkness and light . . . Those were the exact same reason the goddess said she'd chosen him.

"She's right, Greyson. I don't care what the king believes, I watched you make the choice to walk away from Riese: the man that tried to kill you *twice* now. That's something I could not have done."

Their words . . . their light, their faith in him, began to thaw the chilled rock in his chest.

Maybe . . . his heart was not as dark as he had thought, if all these horrible feelings and regrets were actually coming from his light's struggle with his darkness like Nash said. "So my heart's not ruined? Not permanently anyway?"

"No." Sam almost laughed. But it didn't sound like it was out of pity, or laughing at his ignorance. More like the relief of finally getting through to him.

"But that doesn't change the fact that it's mostly darkness now." He sat up and dried his eyes for the last time. "And Kyri . . . my only hope of lightening it, isn't mine to protect anymore."

"What do you mean *only*? What about Tay? . . . What about me?"

Greyson . . . hadn't really thought about that. Whenever he was around Tay he definitely felt more alive, more light. But it was so commonplace, such a part of him . . . he never really noticed until now. And Sam . . . well she made him feel like that too, but even stronger. Like her light amplified his, and gave it color, and clarity. But Kyri . . . her light was different. Bathing . . . Absolving.

But even though he felt these things . . . he still didn't know what to say to Sam. He couldn't just tell her how he really felt! "I . . ."

"Kyri will be fine." Sam spared him the awkward explanation. "No matter how ignorant and evil Huey may be. So long as you stay in her life, her heart will *never* fall to darkness."

Her voice brought him so much comfort. Because he knew she spoke the truth . . . If there was anything he'd learned of Sam these past few days, it was that she cherished truth, above all else. Which meant he could be certain she was not lying just to dull the pain.

"She's going to be okay," she said again, like she knew how good it felt to hear. "The aide who searched me, he saw how scared you were for her, and he whispered in my ear. He wanted me to tell you that he would take good care of her too."

Greyson thought back to who had patted Sam down in the throne room, tearing up again. "Xander." He smiled.

"I know you want Kyri back. And if we get the chance, we'll take it. But if we don't, she'll be okay. I know you want to protect her, but she's stronger than you think. And she's a lot more like you than you think." Sam lowered her tone. "That feeling she gives you. That innocence, and light . . . I get the same from you."

"I saw it, Itxaro. I saw everything." Stiqula spoke into the candlelight of his altar.

Itxaro was leaning against the light of the doorway behind him.

"Darkness took me to His realm, and showed me the answer to six thousand years of secrecy. He showed me the keys to His Gate. The door Oyopa sealed Him behind at the dawn of humanity. He showed me how He should be free." Stiqula rested his hands against his head. "I can still hear His voice. Unrelenting. Like acid flowing down the valleys of my brain. I can't escape it." He stood to rip down the papers from the wall, the blueprints of the *Claw*, and took a pen to them. Writing the words he'd heard the devil speak: a horrid rhyme, burned into his mind, an endless loop.

*Oyopa made this Gate to close . . .* he wrote down quickly. Writing took the pain away, at least until he was finished. Then he would start again. He could never forget the words the devil spoke. "Never before have all its keys aligned. Until now. Until today."

# 29

# THE DAY OF DESTINY

"Why don't you ever answer your goddam phone?" Tay said, stuffing his badge back into his pocket, and taking a big bite out of his shitty apple. He hated fruit. But there was nothing else to eat in their stupid apartment.

The midmorning sun shined straight through the windows in the Hall of Kings, damn-near blinding him as he made his way to the throne room. He hadn't heard a word from Greyson since he'd left a message on Tay's phone, telling him to meet him at the observatory. Then he wasn't even there . . . But something super fucked up was instead.

The hall was way more cluttered than normal.

There were a lot less people in fancy get-ups, and a lot more dirty, like . . . *construction* people. Tay guessed, based on their fluorescent vests and hard-hats. And a bunch a crates lying around, filled with white stones and wooden planks.

Then, once he pushed through the glass doors of the secretary lobby, he knew why. He froze, still clutching the door. The Viæden doors were open wide, revealing the throne room beyond, almost completely destroyed. Cut, right down the middle, short-ways, not long-ways. And the construction men were climbing all over it, inspecting the gash, loading in materials, or carrying rubble out by the wheelbarrow.

"Holy shit." He almost choked on that fucking apple. "What happened?"

"Oh, Taymes," Stephanie said, cleaning off her desk. "You weren't here?"

He turned to her, letting the glass door slide out of his hand. "No?"

"The throne room was struck during the king's ball by some *Claw* ship," she explained. "They're saying it was the old pirate, *Té Nova*."

"What the fuck?" he said very slowly, looking back to the mess. "Where's Greyson? Was he here?"

"Yes, he fought the ship away."

"He *did*?" He whipped his head back at her. "Well where the hell is he?"

"He was arrested," she deflated.

"What the fuck? Why?"

"Um." She clattered on her keys, pulling up the file. "It says here, murder . . ."

"Whatthefuck?"

". . . and harboring a fugitive . . . and treason."

"What the *actual* fuck. It's only been, like *nine* hours. How did he manage to fuck his life like that?"

Steph shrugged. "I—"

So *not* at all the same kinda night Tay had had. When all the water cannons started firing at the ball, Tay freaked out, as usual. Which sucked because he was actually having a great freaking time, and he was pretty sure Megan was too. At least she liked him enough to follow after him when he ran screaming out of the party. Then they just walked around and talked about his issues for like an hour. Bein' all sensitive and shit. Then he hooked a shuttle home. And apparently missed all the action completely.

"Where are they holding him?" Tay sighed.

Stephanie looked to her screen again. "He's . . . in the Castle Control block. Level 595d."

The faucet in his cell was leaking. Like a constant tapping on the shoulder of his brain, keeping him awake, all through the night. Like the eyes of the water goddess, ever watching, wide-eyed and dumbfounded that the boy she'd chosen to save the world had been locked in a cage.

He could still see those blue stars, and the ripples of her voice that made them twinkle. *"In all the ages of the world, the truth must now be known,"* she'd said.

The truth that Vertuém Destiny really meant his fate was his own.

And *now* that ship, that cataclysm, the *Chandelier* was on its way. And whatever darkness lay within posed such a grave threat to the goddess, and the world, that she had no choice but to rip the very fabric of reality to warn him of it.

He breathed in a nervous sigh. It made sense to him now, but he was still tortured not being able to share that truth with a single other soul. What a cruel thing the goddess was making him do. Keeping her existence from Sam. And all the secrets that she'd shared. Most of what the goddess had told him Sam was already on the track to solving. But without confirmation, without proof, her theories meant nothing . . . He *had* to tell her. It would bring her so much light, and him such relief. Why was Water so afraid of her knowing anyway? She was a vertui. She didn't have a destiny that would get messed up by him telling her. And neither did Nash. He *could* tell them! They'd be the only ones to ever know—*Oh . . . They'd be the only ones to ever know . . .* They couldn't tell anyone else. Because if they went public with it, like they planned to . . . then the whole world would know . . . and the whole world would be derailed from its destiny.

Greyson shuddered at the thought.

But they wouldn't do that. They'd understand how dangerous that would be, and they'd keep it a secret, just like him . . . Tortured, just like him.

He couldn't do that to them . . . To Sam.

He had to keep this burden for himself, just as the Blue Goddess had decreed.

The clang of metal doors rang through the hall. And Greyson shot from the ground, peering out between his bars to see who was coming.

The others did the same.

"Greyson!"

He'd recognize that voice anywhere. "Tay!" The last sliver of cold diamond melted from his heart as Tay came into view. He would have cried if he had any tears left.

"How the hell'd you manage to get yourself in here?"

"Clearly I'm useless without you."

"'Bout time you realized." He nodded, unlocking the cell.

"Wait, how are you doing this?" Greyson stepped back from the door.

"By my orders." General Brown came into view.

"General? Why?" Greyson sputtered. He'd seemed so hardened last night.

"Taymes here has come forth as a witness, attesting to your innocence. At least on one account."

Greyson looked to Tay. "How?"

"I got your back," he smirked.

"Does the king know about this?" Greyson asked, stepping from his cell.

"Not yet." Brown moved to Sam's door. "And I have a bargaining chip that may just be strong enough to free the O'Nasies as well."

"Seriously?" Sam stepped into the hall as Brown opened her door.

"Yes. Though it may come at a heavy price."

"Samantha," a meek voice called from behind Tay.

Sam turned to him, "Jacob?"

"Oh, yeah. Ran into this guy on the way here too," Tay said.

"What price?" Nash asked as Brown freed him.

"You're not going to like it." Brown turned and stepped through them to the exit. "The ship's almost here. We have to hurry."

Greyson, Tay, Sam, Nash, Brown, and Jacob all returned to the throne room, which was busy with construction crews. They moved in formation, like a line of soldiers marching to battle, crossing a fresh, wooden bridge that spanned the throne room's ravine.

The king was standing on his dais, watching over Xander as he knelt to straighten Kyri's little gowns. Greyson's heart skipped when he saw her, jolted by the shock of her light, so near again.

"Kyri," he whispered.

There was no way she could have heard him, but even so, she turned to find him, joining their emerald gazes.

"Greysom!" She ran from Xander, bounding down the steps, and across the green carpet to his arms.

He knelt to catch her, finding a few more tears he'd saved just for her. "Kyri."

Huey was appalled, clambering down after her. "No! Kyri, get away from him. That man is a criminal!" He spotted Brown on his march to them. "*General!* What is the meaning of this?"

"Greyson is innocent, Your Highness."

Huey looked away from them, grunting, tired of this outplayed game. "On what account? He wasn't the one that released Stiqula? He wasn't conspiring with this man?" He waved his fingers at Nash. "He didn't *slaughter* six men, single handedly?"

"Don't listen to him, Kyri," Greyson whispered, covering her ears.

"Get away from him, Kyri!" Huey sputtered, but would not retrieve her himself. He wouldn't come near the pack of rebels that had barged into his hall, looking for a fight.

"He has defeated Stiqula, Huey. By your own words, his debt is paid. And he did not kill those men."

"Says who!?"

Brown looked to Tay.

"I was at the observatory . . . sir. I got there just after Greyson left. He didn't kill them."

"Then who did? *You?*"

The king's furious tone was scaring Kyri, a pout growing on her face. Greyson looked to Sam, handing Kyri off so she didn't have to be right in the middle of all the screaming. "Go with Sam," he said softly. Sam took her gently by the hand and walked her back to watch the men work down in the ravine.

"No, sir," Tay looked to Greyson. "It was that big black guy, from Rock Town."

"Itxaro?" Greyson gasped.

"Yeah," Tay nodded. "He had another one of those laser blades. And he was chopping all those guys up when my elevator opened. It was really effed up. He stared me down. Smiling at me. I tried to shoot him, but. You know how useful that is. He ran outside and jumped onto a bark ship waiting for him."

"What was he doing there?" Greyson couldn't figure it out.

"The pilot of the *Aliqula* was never found," said Brown. "I suspect *he* was its pilot, and parachuted out before the crash. He must have been waiting to be picked up at the spire. Likely there the whole time. Watching us. Which means he knows about the falling ship as well."

"What falling ship? What are you talking about?" Huey tried to follow.

Brown turned to him. "We've spotted an object, Your Highness. In space."

He took the wrinkled pictures from his pocket and handed them to the king.

Huey snatched them from Brown's hand, glancing at them quickly. His eyes darted about the pictures like they didn't know what part to focus on. "And you're just telling me this *now*?"

"It was only discovered last night."

"When will it fall?" He looked up from the pictures.

"Very soon, sir."

"Can we . . . stop it?" Huey looked confused and horrified all at once. The thought of some unknown object falling from space no doubt triggering parallels to Stiqula's Rock in his mind, as well as all the darkness that followed.

"There's nothing we can do."

"Well, whose ship is it!? Where's it from?"

"Unknown, sir." Brown threw his eyes in Greyson's direction. "Though we have a theory you won't like."

Huey's state of shock hardened as he looked to Greyson.

This was his chance—though he was afraid to speak—to explain to the king of disbelief the nightmare that had haunted him ever since he'd first arrived. But surrounded by his friends, he found his courage. "The ship is from Nævah, Your Highness. Once piloted by angels, in search of Stiqula. Now, somehow, overrun with demons."

"Heresy," Huey growled. "*Heresy!*"

"Huey," Brown barked.

"How could you know!?" The king demanded of Greyson. "Did you *see* it," he mocked. "In a *dream*, from some make-believe goddess in the *sky*!?"

"Yes! Sir, I did!" Greyson practically shouted, accepting what he was, fighting for himself and what he saw. "You must believe, Your Highness. You're a vertui! You must know. Haven't you seen a vision for yourself?"

"*Never*," Huey spat. "And how *dare* you accuse me of such a thing! Vertuém Destiny is a *fairytale*! If it were true, my father would have seen him coming! It would have *saved* them!"

Huey gasped for air, red in the face, verging on tears, just as Greyson had seen him on the night they'd told him of Stiqula's release . . . And then Greyson knew, that's what this really was about. The reason the king didn't believe, and banned all religion. Not because Stiqula was an angel, but because Vertuém Destiny did not save his family. No god had warned them of Stiqula. Neither he nor his green-eyed father had ever seen a vision of his coming.

Betrayed by the gods . . . in his eyes.

"Huey." Brown stepped forward, resting a hand on his shoulder. "I loved your parents as dearly as my own." He tried to keep his voice calm, but Greyson could tell his words were bending in fear, or sadness, or rage, or all. "But he speaks the truth. I would not have found the ship without him telling me where to look."

Huey looked up to his general, a withering conceit in his eyes.

"There are certain truths we must come to accept. No matter what our faith tells us."

Huey breathed and exhaled sharply, looking to Kyri. His faith was too strong to be broken so quickly. "Kyri." He pushed Brown's hand from him and headed to Sam. "I won't ask you again. Get *away* from her!"

Sam's eyes burnt into him.

"Pull her away from me like I'm some wild animal," he muttered. "I have *saved* her from an orphan's life."

"No you didn't." Sam loved those words. "Greyson did. *He* saved her life."

Huey froze, a foot from her, turning back to Greyson, eyes as sharp and wide as bastard swords. "*You.* You want to take my princess from me?! What gives you the right!?" He turned and ripped Kyri from Sam. "She is perfectly happy *here*, with me!" He clutched his crying princess tightly.

Greyson was about to tackle him for yanking her so hard. But a roll of thunder stopped him, stopped everyone, seeping in through the *Claw's* fissure, from far, far, away. Building, growing like an echo in reverse, swelling to cacophony: an explosion beyond sound. Everyone jumped, screaming as the glass panes rattled in their frames, and the throne room shuddered. The trembling faded slowly, but the sound of the explosion was gone in an instant. Like it'd grown beyond what ears could hear.

Greyson rushed to Sam and Kyri at the crag, looking out onto the silent planes beyond.

But it was all very wrong. The sky was broken. Falling. *Collapsing.* As literally as it could. Like it was made of blue glass, and the clouds were only paint. The dome splintered, crumbling at its highest point, letting all its pieces fall inside, streaming down like shooting stars. The hole tore larger, stretching its black fissures across the sky like Refsiel's crooked claws. And then the black of space poured in, stars and all. A geyser of darkness, plunged down to the earth, spinning as it fell, twisting to a vortex, seven miles wide.

It was unbelievable, incomprehensible. Making as much sense as a nightmare.

But this was real.

Greyson's destiny had come.

From the bridge of his stolen bark ship, Stiqula witnessed the calamity approach the heart of Viæden's planes, piercing through the sky.

He had not anticipated Refsiel to put on such a show. They were almost right below the vortex as it plunged. Too close. "Pull back!"

Instantly his ship slowed to a halt as the inky curtain fell before them. The darkness was impenetrable, coagulating in the air to form a skin of grey clouds. It was falling much slower than it should have been. Refsiel was slowing its descent. Catching it to save whatever keys it held from being destroyed on impact. "So this is what I've worked so hard for," he spoke gravely. "The power of one hundred thousand souls in Refsiel's claws." Refsiel would never have the strength for such a feat as this without the extra power that Stiqula had provided Him.

But still that power was not enough. The vortex dissipated, unable to reach the earth, three miles from it still. Then out of its black veil fell a ship, wreathed in flame. A godly, crystal, chandelier, three miles tall. The largest ever built by man or angel.

It was the *Metaleiru*. Stiqula knew it well. A ship, in part, Aliqula had helped create.

It crashed into the ground, but did not shatter, shedding only the weakest of its shards, flattening the grass forest in a shockwave of fire and air as it buried itself in the ground.

A flash of fire. That's all they could see before darkness took the plains. They couldn't even hear the crash. Nothing since the sky had shattered . . . as if the world mourned the coming of its death. Grey clouds spilt in from beyond the sky, draping over the plains almost as far as they could see.

Greyson's skin chilled at the sight of it. His journey finally coming full circle.

As terrifying as it was, he felt drawn to that evil place: the darkness in him, stirring. Yearning for it.

His hand hurt. Sam was grabbing it. Crushing it. Her eyes fixed on the sky, and the clouded vortex. Kyri was just as hypnotized as her, clinging to Sam's leg.

"I've never seen clouds like that before." Sam broke the silence.

"No one has," Nash spoke. "No one living anyway."

"What are they?"

"Refsiel is protecting that ship. Whatever's on board, He wants it."

"Refsiel?" The king spun to Nash. "How dare you speak His name?! Why are we listening to this man? *Brown!* Send your ships. I don't care *who* thinks they can protect it, we will destroy it!"

Brown nodded and headed for the door. But Nash, the old pirate, planted a hand on the general's chest. "That ship just fell from *space*, Brown. Made of angelic steel. You really think your rockets are going to affect it?"

Brown turned to the vortex, hearing Nash's words. This realm of the supernatural was beyond his understanding. He knew enough to admit that much.

"Don't you listen to that man." Huey stumbled over his robes as he stepped forward, pulling them up and out of the way to walk to his general. "We have enough ships, a *kingdom* of ships! There will be nothing left of it!"

"And what if you're wrong, Huey?" Nash said. "What if you only scratch the surface, and release those demons in every direction?"

"*There's no such thing!*" He stomped his feet.

"Look at you." Nash gave him a disgusted sneer. "You've lived in your own world so long you've forgotten it was built on lies. Is *that* imaginary too!?" Nash flung his finger to the clouds.

"Enough." Brown stopped him. "Your Highness. If Darkness is protecting that ship, He will not let it be destroyed. He will have anticipated our attack already."

Huey stewed silently, listening.

"But there is one thing He cannot see coming." Brown looked to Greyson.

"And what is that?" Huey snapped.

All the blood drained from Greyson's head. He'd been waiting for that look. Afraid that it was coming. "Me." He stepped forward, letting go of Sam's hand.

Huey spun to face him. "*You?* Why you?"

"His vision ended with him destroying the ship by self-detonation." Brown assured the king.

But it didn't assure Greyson. Because that's *not* how his vision ended.

Greyson looked away from his planet, and the stars outside, back to the glowing portal that he'd come from: a sphere of white light, suspended a foot from the ground. But, brilliant as it was, it did not hurt to look upon. At least it did not hurt his eyes. It was a much deeper pain looking at it knowing that his sister chose to stay behind.

He could not let her sacrifice be in vain. Greyson spun to face the forward glass again, and the long stem of steel leading to the primary controls in the very center of the spheroid room. Along the railing to the control terminal, there was another of the U-shaped handles, which Greyson grabbed immediately, and was pulled down the two-hundred-foot walkway to the terminal.

Arriving at the crystal controls, he stroked its angelic keys, drawing up the command for self-detonation. It was a long process, to prevent accidents, and his time was running out.

The sirens blared now within the bridge, lights dimming to red as the detonation command took a few moments to prepare. And at the same time, the bridge door began to boom, deep and echoed.

Greyson spun to face it, just beyond the portal that he'd come from. An enormous silver disk, over twenty feet wide. The exact diameter of the golden axis hall on the other side of it. It was endowed with Oyopa's Seal of Light.

But like a Door to Darkness, it held behind it only evil.

The demons had come. Banging, rattling, screaming, scratching, resounded their demonic fury.

"These demons will not take my life!" Greyson cried. "And I pray forgiveness, my Lady, for the sin of taking it myself." He turned back to the command console. There was only one more key he needed to touch. One last command to be given. The last thing he would ever do.

It flashed at him, on the console screen. The Symbol of Light. Which, once pressed, would cleanse the ship of all sin, and send every one of those creatures back to the hell from whence they came.

But Darkness did not intend on being defeated so easily.

And from behind the terminal crawled a single demon, black and terrible. It had been hiding beneath the platform, waiting until now to strike, slinking slowly over the top of the terminal with its wings spread wide, hissing in a fury that this angel dare defy it.

Greyson tried to raise his blade, but as he did, the demon leapt and latched onto his sword arm. Greyson fell to his back with the creature on top of him, arm pinned across his body. And out of fear, his blade ignited, burning through his own wing on the floor. He cried, a scream of pain and anguish as his hope all but vanished.

The bridge door burst, and darkness swarmed him. One million razor claws, ten million razor teeth, biting, snapping, gnawing, tearing at his flesh to find the soul that lay beneath.

Greyson had seen the sequence of keys he needed to touch to detonate the ship, sure. But that didn't mean he was confident enough to carry out such an ultimate responsibility.

But then, if he didn't do it . . . no one would. As much as it terrified him, he was the only one capable of doing what needed to be done. He had to go inside that god-forsaken thing. And destroy it from the inside . . . to mend the world, and lift this veil of darkness the goddess had foreseen.

Huey breathed deep, focus fading from Greyson, to the black clouds behind him. "You trust this boy, Theodore?"

"Greyson is our only hope," Brown said swiftly.

The king looked down to Kyri, taking her in with the smallest glimmer of a smile. As if only by her light, could he see reason. "Fine," he spoke. "Destroy that ship, and consider yourself a free man."

"I will, on one condition, Your Highness."

Huey locked onto Greyson with a scowl, as though disgusted he would thicken this plot.

But for the first time in his life, he finally had the leverage. "You let Sam and Nash go too."

Huey looked to Nash, then back to Greyson. "Nash will go with *you*. To *help* you. And if he dies in the process, then well done." He looked to Sam. "But Ms. O'Nasi will stay *here* with me. To insure that *you* return. Or at least finish whatever *destiny* commands of you."

# 30

# INTO DARKNESS

It was time to go. But he didn't want to leave. He didn't want to leave his light behind. Having a good feeling he would never see them again. He stalled for just a few more moments with them, on his knees, in the throne room lobby, holding Kyri's hands in front of him. "Do you like it here? Is everyone nice to you?"

"Uh-huh." She nodded.

"Anything's got to be better than that orphanage, all by yourself." He pushed a loose strand of hair out of her face, and tucked it behind her ear. "I just wish I could have taken you, myself."

"Why not?"

"Because you belong here, with the king now. You get to be a real princess . . . I guess that's better than anything I could have given you . . . And I'll still come visit you, all the time."

"Okay." She wasn't sure whether to be happy or sad about that.

"You have to promise me something though." He pressed her hands against her chest. "Don't lose your light, okay?"

She didn't really know what that meant. Not saying anything.

"Don't forget that as long as you're happy, Momma's happy too."

She smiled at that. "I know, Greysom." She snuck her hands out from under his, reaching to touch his chest. "You too."

He gave an inverted smile. "I will." He stood before things got too emotional.

But she wouldn't let go of his hand. "Stay here."

She sure wasn't making it easy. "I can't, Kyri. I have to go." He knelt again to hug her one more time. "But I'll come back . . . I promise."

"Kyri," Huey called, lingering in the doorway of his hall. Xander stood next to him, waving her over playfully.

She pulled away from Greyson, looking at him one last time. Not an ounce of sadness. She ran to Xander with a smile. And that smile cleared all doubt from Greyson. Whatever happened to him, he knew she'd be okay. Just like Sam had said, she was stronger than he gave her credit for. Stronger than he could imagine.

Greyson stood as Sam released her father from a hug. She was already broken up, knowing full well it would be the last time she would ever see her dad. And Greyson's chances of survival were hardly any better.

"You better come back," she said to him—more demanded, really, coming closer. "Come back to me." She wrapped her arms around him.

Greyson coughed out a nervous laugh, and breathed her in. Just like home, the strawberry fields, a moment before the rain. Their hearts beat hard against one another.

"You'll do it. You can stop Him. I know you can. Or else you would never have had that dream . . . It's your destiny." She squeezed him.

"But, Sam . . ." He had no destiny. No god had written this moment for them. Whatever outcome came of this, it was all up to him . . . And if he wasn't enough . . . then he'd never come back. And whatever darkness dwelt within the *Chandelier* would escape. Then it would be up to Sam to fight. But he couldn't leave her so empty handed. She had to know what the goddess had told him. She had to know how powerful she really was. He had to tell her, now. Before it was too late.

She pulled back, looking as far into his eyes as she dared.

"If I don't come back . . ."

She pulled in as he spoke, turned her head, and kissed him. Silenced him. Lips pressed against his. Warm and soft.

But she pulled away just as fast to say, "You will."

Sam stepped away from him, wiping the tears from her eyes. She was done crying. Ready to believe. And await his victorious return.

They stole one last glance at each other before she turned to the throne room, and to Kyri, stepping inside as the Viæden doors closed behind her.

Greyson's heart bubbled, tiny fragile spheres of elation bounced around inside a cave of dread and anxiety. He didn't know how to feel. Feeling everything at once. He rubbed his chest, feeling light headed. Almost too much to handle. He wanted to jump, laugh, scream, cry, punch the king right in his face, and run screaming into the dark, blade drawn. Everything. Which balanced out into a stoic stare, focusing on the green symbol in the center of the door. The Insignia of Viæden. The Symbol of Earth. Goddess of Growth and Protection . . . She was always his favorite, in his mom's old stories.

He nodded to it, to her. As if to ask for her protection, and his safe return, just like the boy who would be king.

He turned to face Tay, Brown, Nash, and Jacob standing in the hall. Tay giving him a very subtle thumbs up, proud look on his face.

"Are we ready?" Brown asked.

Greyson nodded stepping forward, falling in line next to Tay as the group started down the hall. The black vortex could be seen through every window on their way.

"What's with you and that little girl?" Tay said to Greyson.

Greyson looked at him, a little confused. Forgetting Tay was knocked out when she'd wandered into their room aboard the rescue ship to Cantidium. "Kyri? She's the one we saved from Rock Town."

"Oh, whoa." Tay looked back as they walked. "She's a princess?"

"She is now." Too soon.

The group turned down the hall to the elevator core.

"So," Jacob said. "I'll just be taking the *Leiaru* and heading back then?"

"Oh, no. You're coming with us," Nash assured.

"What? Sir, it sounds dangerous. And I haven't yet recovered from the *last* expedition I was on with those two."

"We're going to need a biologist to take a look at these demons up close."

"But, sir, you know I don't believe in them."

"Then I'm sure you'll come up with a biological reason for their existence."

Jacob gave an uncertain grunt as they all packed onto a lift.

The ride down was dead silent, due to a mix of nerves and Greyson's awkwardness for having just made out with Nash's daughter right in front of him. Luckily, his awkwardness was outshined by Tay's as the lift pulled down into the docking bay.

Megan was standing right there when the doors slid open. "Oh." She was quite surprised. "Hi . . . everyone."

"Good morning, Ms. McBride." Brown strode right by her to the bay. Everyone following, except Tay.

"So . . . I had a good time, last night."

"Yeah," she said, quickly, then held back a little. "It was okay."

"So . . . I might not be coming back." He tried to squeeze a goodbye kiss out of her, feeling left out after Greyson's. He leaned in, completely uninvited.

"Whoa-kay." Megan planted her hand on his face, palming his pursed lips. "Make it back and maybe we'll talk." She pushed him away, circling around to the lift. But she didn't leave him empty handed. She gave him a nice slap on the butt as she walked by. "See you later, Tubby."

Tay jumped from the spank and turned to see her grinning playfully as the doors closed.

He gave a giddy laugh and skipped over to Greyson. "I'll take it."

Stiqula stood at the rim of *Metaleiru's* crater, a massive scar upon the earth, two miles wide. The once-bléssed ship protruded from it like a splintered dagger, two miles high. Only its outline could be seen against the silver sky, far beyond. Its black body was textured by smoldering filaments, like hairs plucked from the dead god's head.

The world was silent now, after the crash, as if all the winds were blown away, and fire had lost its strength to burn. Even the footsteps of his men approaching from behind were hardly heard. The air was stagnant, dead.

Refsiel had fallen to the world, decaying all into an absent nothingness . . . even *time*, it felt like. The God of Darkness was not even freed yet, but already His power took its toll upon the world . . . Witnessing Oyopa's beauty muted so . . . stirred something in him. The slightest whisper of a doubt, made louder in the silence. Something deep within the ruins of Stiqula's heart . . . A single star in his black night.

"*Aliqula.*"

So close to her now.

Finding the keys to Refsiel's gate meant also the keys to Aliqula.

He could not waiver. This was all for her. To free her from that devil's claws.

The old engines of General Brown's ship boomed as they ignited, lifting the craft, and rotating to the open exit of the hangar. Two more ships, twice the size of Brown's, rose to flank it, flying in formation from Darakin's branches.

Greyson and Tay stumbled to catch themselves as the ship blasted forward, pushing their way through the overcrowded hall, to the bridge. The whole ship was packed with Royal Guards, all dressed in the same deep blue uniform, a silver pauldron over their left shoulders.

"Greyson," Brown called from beside them. The boys turned to see him shuffle through the crowd. In his hands was Greyson's sword, angelic chain still wrapped around its hilt. "You'll be needing this."

"Thank you, sir." He took the sword, squeezing it tight, hating how powerful it made him feel to be reunited with it.

"I hope you've mastered how to use it," Brown said.

Greyson nodded, trying not to spoil the moment. He had no idea what he was doing.

Brown's lieutenant, Knight, came around behind them, eyeing them both, still not fond of the rookies, now graduated to the same rank as him.

"Pretty full boat, huh?" said Tay.

"Yes," Brown answered. "I know we wanted to keep the numbers low, but I'm also not taking any chances. If Greyson is our only shot at this, I want to give him the most protection I can. You've got nine fireteams at your disposal. That's over two hundred guards."

Greyson nodded. "I'll do my best, sir."

Brown left them, moving through the crowd to the helmsman.

Greyson looked past him, to the growing darkness outside the bridge window. He took in a big, uneasy breath.

"You scared?" Tay asked.

Greyson looked at him. "You're not?"

"I mean, I'm *nervous*, but . . . I don't really know what for."

"And I'm scared because I *do*." He swallowed. "I've seen what's waiting for us."

Tay scratched the side of his face. "So we're just accepting all this vertuém stuff is real?"

"Do we have a choice?"

"What if we get in there and it's not like your dream at all?"

"You still don't believe it, do you?"

"Believe that you're better than me in every way? No. *Some* things, maaaaybe. But not everything."

"It's not like that, Tay."

"Uh, that's what it sounds like, Mr. *Only Hope*."

Greyson glanced away, giving a soft, frustrated scoff.

"Really though, how many times have I saved your ass?"

"A lot," Greyson admitted.

"So if your destiny is so important, how could *I*, a mere *human*, save your life so many times? It just doesn't make sense."

Greyson's eyebrows sank, wondering what Sam would say about that. Tay kinda had a point. And what's worse . . . if Greyson's lack of a destiny was really so disruptive, why hadn't Tay's destiny faded into darkness yet? That kinda . . . went against everything the goddess had told him . . . But she couldn't have been wrong. She wouldn't have lied to him . . . would she?

"I don't know, Tay. I guess there's still some mysteries we'll never understand." He played it off as a joke, but ambiguously, not wanting to state one way or the other who was right, because while Greyson knew the truth about his destiny . . . Tay still made a good point.

"Psh." Tay rolled his eyes, but lightly, glad to see Greyson wasn't taking himself too seriously, for once.

Greyson spotted Nash and Jacob standing up by the forward window, and started for them. The busy chatter of the bridge quieted as they approached, and the ship neared its target. The vortex had formed only a hundred miles from Darakin. And everyone just stared at it with dread as the last moments of sunlight streamed in through the window. Greyson stepped into the veil of golden dust, which warmed him as he moved deeper into its rays. He took in its brilliance, for as long as he could, fearing it would be the last time he would ever get the chance . . . Then the bark ship drove into the shadows, and Oyopa slipped behind the clouds. There was no silver lining.

As his eyes adjusted, the vortex appeared ahead of them, clearer than ever. Like black smoke, rising, twisting from the ground, six miles wide. But the vortex did not reach the ground, hovering three miles from the earth, a ring of glowing flames in the forest below.

The bark ship shuddered in an air pocket as it descended.

"How's He doing this?" Greyson asked.

"Refsiel?" Nash answered. "I'm not certain. Events like this were commonplace before He was locked behind the Door to Darkness . . . I can only dare to fathom what it means." He really knew how to make everyone as uncomfortable as possible. "Perhaps the door is . . . prying open. Or perhaps man's soul has become so dark now that its seal is weakening."

The ship shuddered again.

"Fifteen miles to target," a guard said.

The Door to Darkness, Greyson thought. His mom had only ever spoken of it once. When she'd told him of Light's triumph over Darkness, locking Refsiel behind an impenetrable door, to keep man safe. A door through which only dark souls could pass. The gate to hell itself.

He'd felt so close to it lately . . . Like that's what was making his darkness stir. Excited. Agitated. And then it dawned on him: the door he'd seen in the Water Realm, nearly identical to the one in the throne room, though marked by a different symbol. *Each* of the gods' realms was linked to the world by a door. And that meant that the Door to Darkness had a physical location too, instead of just poetic imagery for passing into the afterlife. It was somewhere in the world. But *where*?

"Where is the Door to Darkness?"

"It's lost. Unaccounted for, like all the rest," Nash answered. "Except for the Door to Earth, of course."

Greyson thought back to his angel. He never did see exactly *how* those demons had gotten onboard the *Chandelier*. But he knew they'd come from hell. "Is there a chance . . ." He felt light-headed again. "It's on that ship?"

Nash looked at him, like he'd been waiting for him to say it. "It very well may be."

The bark ship hit the wind, a violent torrent that threw them all forward as the ship kicked up and veered right. Greyson braced himself against the window as all the guards behind him piled forward. The stabilizer alarm rang as the ship was thrown about by the storm, nearly colliding with the bark ship to starboard.

"Pull back!" Brown shouted as the other bark ship dove past the bridge.

"Five miles to target!"

"Get down below the storm, Brown!" Nash screamed, trying to keep himself on his feet.

They could see the earth rushing below them now, with bands of fire feeding off the grass. Slowly, the pivoting plain of burning fields flattened out as they dipped below the vortex and leveled again. The skies were instantly quieted here. And the bark ship that had dived in front of them regained its balance.

And beyond, the craft could finally be seen. The *Chandelier*.

Greyson hadn't named it that for no reason. It looked just like an inverted crystal castle, high towers driven into the ground, and shattered all around the crater's bowl. Its core was cylindrical, sprouting four arms from its top, which bent down to surround the cylinder.

Other than a wire-frame model, Greyson had never seen the ship from the outside before, and wasn't sure if it was supposed to look like that, like shattered ice, mixed with steel, or if the crash had mangled it beyond all recognition. Like a fractured, spiked cigar, two miles high, snuffed but still glowing.

"Ship on radar, sir! Just outside the crater."

"Someone's already here? What's the ID?" Brown asked.

"It's unregistered!"

"Stolen?" Then he remembered. "Itxaro."

A golden flare shot up from the crater's rim, firing straight for them.

"Look out!"

It exploded right in front of them, sprinkling the sky in a dozen more explosions along their flight path. Greyson pushed off the glass, as they plowed into the flames and slammed into the burst of air, hard as a wall, cracking the windshield in a spidered lattice. The fire swirled around them like a glowing fog, infused with invisible boulders that rocked their ship from every angle.

"Take it down!" Brown ordered as they emerged from the other side. His ship, and the two that accompanied it, opened fire in an amber rain aimed for where the rocket had come from. But their laser shower couldn't find its target fast enough. Six yellow flares fired from the dark earth just as the lasers struck and reduced the stolen bark to a pool of plasma.

The flares followed the line of fire, headed straight for General Brown's ship! But, in a selfless move, the foremost bark ship swung up and caught all six of them in the belly, erasing it in a golden cloud. Brown's bark dove below, but found that there was not much air left to dive through. The crater was much wider than the *Chandelier*, and fast approaching. Brown's ship pulled up, nearly skimming the curve of the crater's wall as it leveled out again. But their troubles were far from over. The entire floor of the crater's bowl lit up with small-arms fire, dotting trails of yellow bullets as it tracked their ship across the sky.

The bullets could do no real harm to them, but it would complicate their landing.

"Take us in as close as you can get to the craft," Nash said as everyone regained their balance. "We'll keep it to our back and use our bark ships as cover to search for an entrance."

Greyson noted how he took charge of the situation, even though he had no power here. He seemed almost more tactically adept than the general.

Brown nodded to the helmsman to confirm. "Use our cannons against them," he added.

"How the hell did Itxaro get here so fast?" Greyson asked.

"You don't think Stiqula's with him, do you?" said Tay.

Greyson looked to Nash, as if the thought had never crossed his mind.

Nash didn't respond at all, leaning away from the glass as the men began to shuffle to the exit. He managed not to lose his cane in the turbulence, but he was favoring it more than usual. Even though his face wasn't showing it, Greyson could tell . . . He still hadn't recovered from that fight at the observatory.

The bark ship's cannons fired out onto the walls of the crater as it touched down within the bowl. But the opposing fire wasn't letting up. It grew. A few dozen scattered men were a hard target compared to two massive, wooden ships. The second ship circled once before it landed, firing down into the dark to try and pull some of the attention off of Brown. But Itxaro's men weren't falling for it. Two rockets screamed out of the deep, and impacted Brown's ship, destroying two of its laser cannons, leaving only two left to defend them.

The ship lurched from the hit as its loading ramp opened to the night.

"Man, they are *serious*," Tay said, catching himself as the first of Brown's men filed out.

Greyson and Tay rushed after them, weapons drawn, into the crackle of compact explosions, and the rhythmic ping of laserfire. The soil was hot, steaming in the chill of the dark, a thin fog in their flashlights. The ship had landed right next to the wreck, so close that the *Chandelier's* enormous, cylindrical core seemed to unravel into a flat and solid wall of a strange silver-grey alloy. It leaned over Greyson as his eyes followed it to the sky, now glowing grey from the sun beyond. Lightened, ever so slightly. Either that, or Greyson's eyes had finally adjusted to the dark.

The surviving bark ship flew low overhead, landing just next to Brown's and laying down a suppressive fire as guards spilt from each ship to set up a perimeter.

"Great Goddess," Jacob said as he descended the ramp, starstruck by the wall before him. "We can't even get a single manned ship into space, yet somehow this mountain flies. Remarkable." It inspired such wonder in him.

Nash followed Jacob down the ramp, Brown behind him.

"I'm not seeing any way in over here," said Tay, lights traversing the ship where it met the raised and rocky soil.

"We may have to try blasting our way in," said Nash.

Tay turned to him. "It'd be a lot easier if these assholes weren't shooting at us."

"My men will take care of it," Brown assured.

A spray of bullets arced over their heads, and by instinct everyone dropped to the dirt, finding cover behind the rough terrain. Everyone except Jacob, who just stood there as one of Brown's guards took out the charging shooter.

Greyson's grip on his sword tightened as fear attacked his muscles. His blade ignited in green light, startling him. He hadn't done it on purpose. He and Tay shared an odd look, like he'd just popped a fear boner in front of everyone.

"It's the prisoners," Brown's guard confirmed as his men rose from cover again.

"How?" Brown asked the same question as Greyson. "How did they know?"

"Isn't it obvious?" Nash spoke, sitting up from cover to rest against a boulder. "Refsiel told them." They all looked at him. Greyson, Tay, Brown, Jacob, and the twenty-five men that surrounded them, as if he'd just cursed them all. "His motives are always the same . . . He wants out. The door must be on this ship. And they're here to open it." For the first time that Greyson had known him, Nash sounded tired. Defeated almost.

Brown shook his head. "How could He be so strong?"

"Because you've fed right into His plan. And let all your men die."

"Don't you blame this all on me." Brown puffed up. "This cannot be on *my* head alone. Just because I'm man, and you're vertui, does not mean that you can do no wrong."

Nash looked right at him. "I don't command anyone, Brown. I've locked myself away from the world where He can't get to me. While you stand center-stage."

"You're a *coward*, Nash! I have stood and *fought* for *all* these years!"

"The only way to win is not to play."

Brown was quiet, taken aback by Nash's words. "I don't believe that for a second. I can't . . . And there was a time when you didn't either." He turned away from him. "Greyson. You have to get in there." He grabbed his shoulder, firm. "I believe the vertuém are our greatest ally against the Darkness. If only they choose to act." He threw his eyes to Nash. "Go. Take this fireteam. It's all I can spare. The rest of us will hold the line, and make sure they don't close in behind you."

Greyson nodded to the general, then looked to Nash. If Refsiel really was as strong as he described, he wouldn't stand a chance. None of them did . . . And he couldn't bear the thought of turning Sam into an orphan too. "Nash. You're in no shape to come with us," he said, as much as he wanted him there. Nash knew so much more about all this than he did. Maybe too much, Greyson thought . . . Nash knew how the world worked already. He knew how thick the devil's plot could go, and that the only way to avoid it completely was to take himself out of the game. But that also meant one less player for the Light.

"I want you to stay here. I've been responsible for so much death already, I can't add one more to the list. Especially you . . . I don't know exactly what you two see differently. But I do know that you're still in this, whether you like it or not. You're still important to Sam. And I can't let you die, just because the king says so." His lerité disappeared. Making it pretty obvious how much he didn't want to say those words. To cut the tether, and venture off alone.

Nash leaned forward, sensing that. He tried to stand. But his old body wouldn't let him. He didn't want to be the coward Brown painted him as. "Nonsense." He threw his cane down, grabbing the much sturdier rock behind him, and wobbled to his feet. "If I'm going to die, it will be here."

Greyson shrank as he stood, wishing Nash would have just stayed on the ground. Wishing he would have just kept his mouth shut instead of egging Nash on. But Brown intervened. He pushed Nash back, sitting him down on the rock and putting a rifle in his hands.

"Don't be stupid, old man. You're staying here where I can use you. Instead of getting in his way."

Nash gave a chuckle. "It took all my strength to stand up, you bastard."

"I would still like to go," Jacob said to Nash, then turned to Greyson. "If that's alright?"

"Sure." Greyson nodded. A fair trade. "But keep up." He backed away from them.

"I'll send more men when we're through here," said Brown.

"Don't, general. I need you to keep anything *in* that might wander out. And if we're not back by sundown . . ." Greyson took in a deep breath. "Find a way to destroy this ship. Use the whole Kingdom Guard if you have to." He knew Nash had said their weapons probably couldn't make a dent in the ship, but . . . It was better than nothing.

Greyson was sure he'd be dead by then no matter what, seeing himself lying on his back with a bloody hole in his chest, surrounded by a thousand demons, just like his angel . . . For being able to have a fate of his own design, that one sure seemed pretty unavoidable right now.

Brown nodded, throwing Greyson his gold badge. "Take this then. Call Knight if you need me."

Greyson put it in his jacket pocket, turning to Tay with heavy eyes, and taking in a long breath to speak. But Tay spoke up before Greyson had a chance.

"Don't even think about asking me to stay here too, idiot. Somebody's gotta look after you," he said without a grin.

But Greyson smiled for both of them, slapping him on the arm and starting on his way along the wreck's wall to find a way in. Tay, Jacob, and the rest of the fireteam following after.

"That's an awful lot of faith you have in him." Nash stood next to Brown as they watched Greyson leave.

Brown turned to him. "Where's yours?"

"Oh, I've got plenty. But it's unlike you to trust someone so completely."

Brown turned from Nash, raising a rifle to the volley of laser light behind them. "Then you never really knew me at all."

# 31

# The Chandelier

For looking like such a wreck, the *Chandelier* had very few fractures in its hull, most too thin to even stick a finger in, not that Greyson wanted to. But after a few minutes of searching, they'd found one, tall and jagged, just barely wide enough to slide through, single-file, turned to the side, with their gut sucked in.

It was a contorted and demented gateway into never-ending darkness.

Greyson shielded his eyes from the cold wind coursing through it. And the smell that rode along the breeze was like stale death: a sour rot of blood, and grease, carried on the shallow taste of recycled air. It was damp, clinging to his skin, weighing down his clothes, and lingering on the hairs inside his nose.

"What is that *smell*!?" Tay covered his mouth, sliding through the passage behind Greyson.

"Angel blood, I think." Greyson focused on the dark ahead. His flashlight seemingly useless in the overwhelming shadows. The crack they were crawling through seemed to go on forever, constantly snagging their clothes on jagged bits of steel and wire. And it felt like the passage was narrowing even more. Closing in around them.

Tay nodded. "That's great. Why don't you freak us out a little more?"

"You asked," Greyson said over his shoulder. But as he faced forward again, he ran into a bundle of sharp wire that scared the shit out of him, dragging across his face, not enough room for him to bend and duck under them.

Then he jerked to a stop altogether. Stuck. His jacket was caught on something.

Something had him!

No. No. *Focus*. Nothing had him. It was just a bit of broken metal.

"Shit, is it too late to go back?" Tay whined.

"Yes!" Greyson tried to scream, but couldn't get enough air into his lungs, compressed by the thinning passage. "I'm stuck!"

Instantly a hand hit him on the back, and he burst free from the crevice, falling flat on his stomach into someplace just as dark, just as cold, but wide open and echoing with the sound of trickling water. His light lay on the floor next to his face, shining in his eyes, but also illuminating whatever surface he was lying on. It was a translucent, silver-blue, with clouded streaks like white marble . . . or . . . *crystal*.

He was back. Inside his nightmare. Unable to distinguish what was real from what was not. The darkness here shrouded everything. Because this was where it lived. An abyss his light could not break.

Tay and the others began to file in behind him as he stood, trying to make sense of the crystal ledge they stood upon. It looked to be about sixty feet long, maybe twenty feet wide, mostly rectangular, and canted at about twenty degrees, higher on the left than the right. The ceiling was low, only about nine feet high, at the same angle as the floor, but it ended in about forty feet. And then there was nothing overhead. And absolutely nothing could be made out beyond the edges of the floor, even with their eyes fully adjusted, pupils dilated so wide they ached. The floor just ended. Greyson kept blinking to make sure his eyes were even open.

"Where," Tay whispered, panning his lights in search of anything, "the fuck . . ."

"I'm afraid to find out."

All of their men searched the void with Tay, shining the lights at the ends of their guns every which way. But none of it did any good.

"We need a flare," Greyson said to them. "I need to know which way to go. But if we do this, there's a good chance either Itxaro . . . or something worse could see it too."

"Sounds like we don't have a choice," Jacob answered quickly, readying the flare gun Greyson had given him.

"Hold up, *Eager Eddy*." Tay pulled Jacob's aim back down. "What if we *are* spotted?"

"The flare will last for a little while. We can run back through the crevice and use that as a bottleneck." Greyson nodded to the hole in the wall.

Tay looked at him, holding Jacob's arms down a second longer, then let go.

Jacob took aim over their heads, and pulled the trigger. A white light popped from the pistol, shooting up over two hundred yards, and exploded in magnesium flame, illuminating the void like a pale sun.

This room, this void . . . was colossal. Endless, almost. Greyson couldn't even tell how tall it was. A mile? Maybe more? And they weren't even standing at the bottom. They were right in the middle of it. A cylinder. The whole of the ship's core, hollow. And almost another mile in diameter . . . A full mile of nothingness between them and the opposite wall . . . which was . . . *strange*. There were things on it. Buildings. *Towers*. Of ice . . . or crystal, plunging toward them, into the void. At a perfect ninety degree angle from the cylinder's wall. And all the towers were arranged on grids like . . . *streets*. It was a city. One massive city, wrapping the entire curved part of the cylinder. There was even a dark ring around the cylinder's middle, right below them, where it looked like there used to be a lake—or rather, a thick canal—separating the upper half of the city from the lower . . . Or maybe right from left? Bow from stern? He couldn't tell. Normal directions didn't seem to mean a whole lot in here, where there really was no up or down. Of course, there was no up or down in space . . . so Greyson supposed it did make at least a little sense. But there *was* a down now, here on the planet, and looking down he found all the water that once filled that ring-lake, pooled at the bottom of the cylinder, along with all the city's rubble from the crash. The cylinder had lost its shape down there. Busted apart and now flooded with dirt and water to form a muddy sea.

"Okay, I don't remember *any* of this."

An all-consuming light flared up to challenge Refsiel's darkness. Out in the void, just below Stiqula and his men as they traversed high along the city streets. Even though they could not stand on the actual streets at this angle. Instead they leapt from building to building over the thin alleys between them.

Stiqula turned to face the orb, which slowly drifted downward, dragging the shadows of the city up along the walls. He scanned the shifting landscape for its origins. Finding them at the same place he'd used to enter, a mile across the void from him. A small collection of men, no more than twenty-five.

"They're here. Fewer than I thought they'd send." He drew a finger. "Kill them."

Itxaro moved in beside him, aiming his shoulder-mounted rocket launcher down to the intruders, and fired all three of its shells across the sky.

The flare masked the rockets behind its light. They couldn't see them coming until it was too late.

"Move!" Greyson screamed, diving right as one slammed into the ice ledge and knocked them all back on a wave of heat. The other two exploded against the walls above and below them. Greyson didn't know exactly where, but he could feel their concussions hit his body. Dizzy as hell, he looked up to see if there was anything else coming at them. There wasn't. But whatever-the-fuck they were lying on was falling apart. It cracked down the middle where the rocket had hit. And across that crack, was Tay.

He raised an arm for Greyson, and Greyson reached back. But the crystal split and fell before their fingers touched.

"*No*," Greyson barely whispered, no air in his lungs, watching as Tay's brown eyes . . . his scared, regretful eyes, sunk down into the darkness, then disappeared completely as the flare's light ended.

Greyson's hand stayed, stretched into the dark, the sound of icy crystals smashing as they fell further and further away from him. He couldn't see anything, couldn't *feel* anything. But for the swelling pain inside his chest. He stayed, frozen, suspended as it grew into a bitter, burning, bite. Acid in his lungs. He needed air, and gulped down the freezing oxygen, then let go of his hot, acid breath, panting as the heat of his blood sweat through his skin. "*Tay!*" He gasped again. The air refused to stay in him. "*Tay!*"

Someone grabbed him, shining a light over the cliff's edge. It was Jacob.

"Tay!" Greyson wailed, voice cracking. He lurched forward to follow after. He had to follow. *He had to find him!* He was still down there! Just out of sight.

"No, Greyson." Jacob fought to hold him back. "Greyson, he's gone."

He came between Greyson and the void, kneeling to plant both hands on Greyson's chest. "He's gone."

Greyson looked at him, now illuminated by the scattered lights of the guards, his eyes flickering back and forth between Jacob's thin, brown irises.

"No!" he growled, pushing past Jacob and stealing his flashlight.

Greyson splayed out on the ground, arms hanging over the sharp cliff, and cast the flashlight down the cliff, following its translucent, shattered wall almost fifty yards below him, to the brown and bumpy rubble of the sideways lakebed before the light faded into nothing.

It was way too far to jump. So his eyes followed the lakebed sideways, as far as his pathetic light could reach, looking for a way down. *Anything.* But there was nothing.

Behind him, his guards collected themselves, rifles high, searching for whatever it was that had fired at them. "The fuck was that?" "Keep your eyes open."

Greyson couldn't have cared less about that. Almost wishing more rockets would come finish him off.

Still panting, he rolled over to his back, remembering the badge Brown had given him. He ripped it from his jacket. "Tay! Tay come in! . . . Please," he whimpered. He should never have let Tay come in here with him. He knew it could have only ended like this. "Tay."

Only static replied.

But it was something. "Tay?" Greyson asked, pulling it away from his mouth to listen.

The badge gave a grumbled static again. Then kind of a moan. Then, finally, a voice. "Holy. Fuck."

Greyson couldn't help but cry and laugh at the same time, breathing easy as Tay's voice soothed his tormented heart. He rolled over again, peering into the dark for his friend. "Yes. Thank Holy Fuck you're alright. Where are you?"

"I don't know." Tay sounded strained.

"You're okay, right?" He was afraid to ask.

"Dude, I just fell a hundred feet, gimmi a second."

"Can you see my light?" Greyson shined his flashlight down again.

"Uhm. Yeah. I think."

"How far is it?"

"I don't fucking know. Really far. Like this far." Tay shined his light back.

It appeared far below Greyson, deep in the dark, barely brighter than a star. But it wasn't *right* below him. It looked like the ship was on an incline. Somewhere between seventy and sixty degrees. And Tay had slid down it for almost four hundred yards.

"God dammit." Greyson shook his head, pulling his arm back in.

"Yeah."

"We have to get back together. Can you walk?"

"Yeah," he strained again. "But, um. A couple of my guys didn't make it."

"How many?" Greyson looked to his own guards, nine of them.

"There's six here with me . . . Wait . . . One of um's dead. Five."

That meant six men were still missing altogether. Greyson cringed, standing back up. "I don't see any way down. Do you see anywhere you can climb?"

"You gotta be kidding me. That's like climbing a fuckin' mountain."

"Just try! We have to stick together!" Greyson shouted, more afraid than angry.

Tay didn't reply for a while. "I don't know what to tell you, Grey . . . I'll try."

Greyson dropped the badge from his mouth, letting his arm swing limp.

Jacob came up behind him. "Perhaps it's for the best," he said. "Now that we're split up, we'll have a larger chance of finding the control room."

Greyson turned to him with dead eyes.

"He'll be alright," Jacob assured. But in a weird, heartless way. Like he was just saying it because that's what a normal person would say in that situation. "We should get moving." He turned his back to Greyson. "Since Taymes is down there, we should progress this way."

How easily Jacob brushed off their separation, like he didn't understand real emotion. Okay, fine, him and Tay weren't on the best terms but, regardless, this *entire* situation didn't bother him the least!

Jacob shined his light on the structure right above them. From this angle . . . and knowing they were standing in a city now, it was clearly a sideways building, protruding from the wall they'd passed through to get in here. It had pillars at its edges and everything, "holding up" its slightly peaked roof. In fact, there was a whole line of buildings beyond it . . . *above* it that they hadn't even seen before. Greyson could see all their roofs up the ship's incline like they were standing on the roof of an adjacent building, looking out across the rooftops at night . . . Except that they were actually on the *side* of the building, just a little taller than all the other ones, which gave them a clear view.

Jacob walked all the way back to the crevice, which now looked like a hole in the floor of an alleyway between these crystal buildings, in Greyson's shifted perspective. And as Jacob touched the floor, still standing on the wall of their building, it made Greyson's stomach turn.

"Fascinating." Jacob almost shouted, so they could all hear his discovery. "It appears whoever built this ship used this chamber to simulate an artificial gravity. This city must have spun along a central axis, using the centripetal force to turn this curved wall into the actual floor."

His chipper tone was not sitting well with anyone. Least of all, Greyson.

"I don't know what to tell you, Grey . . . I'll try." Tay said, looking up into the dark, to where he'd last seen Greyson's light. Then he looked to the five men around him. "Let's take a look around."

The ship was all kinds of fucked up down here. Obviously the part that'd buried itself in the ground. The place they stood still had a slope to it, but nowhere near as dramatic as it was up there. And instead of full buildings the only thing around them was the rubbled outlines of foundations. Likely because all the shit that broke free in the crash all fell in this direction, wiping out whatever structures used to be here.

As Tay's men fanned out uphill, he turned to see how far they were from the actual bottom of the chamber. In just a few steps, he had his answer. They were on the edge of another cliff. Not the edge of a building this time, a literal cliff, where the wall of this enormous ship was bent in and broken. And 100 feet down was a dark, rippling shore, with crystal islands jutting from it. Tay's light sat stagnant on the ripples, unable to break through its oily murk, floating like a ghostly cloth along the surface. The chills hit his back so fast and hard, the shudders raised him to his toes. He stumbled back. *"Whoa."* They'd almost ended up down there . . . And that's probably where the rest of his guys *did* end up. "Well, we're not goin' that way." He turned back to his men.

"Lieutenant, look at this," one said, shining his light on a hole in the floor. It looked kinda like a manhole, but square, and just a little bit wider. Peering his light inside, Tay could see the floor of a tunnel in there, only about eight feet down. The tunnel looked like it ran along the outside of this huge cylinder's wall . . . er *floor*. Whatever.

"Should we try it?" another asked.

Immediately, Tay jumped inside, wanting to get as far away from that water as fast as he could. But aside from that, he didn't see a good reason why not. It'd be much easier to defend themselves in this tunnel vers out there in the open. Besides, there was even a ladder to climb out if it ended up being a dead-end. The only awkward part was that, because of the slant of the ship, the square-shaped tunnel was tipped so that one of its corners was the floor, instead of a nice flat surface. So that was gunna be a bitch on the ankles. But luckily Tay at least had some experience with awkward angles, hiding out in all those trees as a kid. He shined his light both ways down the dark, metal, corridor, then back up to his guys. "Looks good to me."

Sam had been waiting for this day, since before she could remember. The day the angels returned to Viæden. She'd always wanted to see the mythic creatures from her mother's stories. So young, she'd fallen in love with every word, believing those wives tales and legends were the extravagant truth beyond this frightening world . . . Then when her mother passed, and no wings grew from her soul to carry her light to Leiaru, the frightening world Sam saw became all of her reality. Or at least most . . . because somewhere inside her, that innocent girl still lived, fighting for her hopeful voice to still be heard over the cold drone of facts and worldly limitations. While she was still a skeptic, and very critical, deep down Sam desperately wanted to believe the gods and all their myths had just as much truth in them as magic.

The real truth of the world *had* to exist somewhere between science and religion. And Greyson's *Chandelier* was proof. The angels' return was not "delivered on a light-beam of power and glory," but with a *spaceship*. Not exactly how she'd envisioned it, but it made more sense at least. A *lot* more sense. Enough sense to prove the king's word was not absolute . . . But of course, life was never as clear-cut as you'd hope. It never made it easy for you. It was dirty, and grey. Darkness left His mark on the *Chandelier* too. And any proof she'd hoped to gain by its arrival may very well be lost in the depths of its shadows . . . Just like Greyson.

Sam breathed in nervously, thinking about him, and wringing her hands. Praying to Light and Trigana to keep him safe. To complete his mission, and save the world from what unimaginable terrors had come down on that ship. She sat on her legs, in front of the high, arching windows of Kyri's new royal chambers, looking out onto the black clouds circling in the distance. Still in her metallic dress from *two* nights ago.

"Here," a sweet voice said.

Sam turned to Kyri, sitting next to her, little white gown fanned out on the floor, and all her new jewels spread between them, glinting in every hue the sun could offer. Kyri presented her with a tiara made of pink and lavender flowers.

Graciously, Sam bowed as Kyri placed the crown on her head.

"Now, *you're* a princess," she decreed.

Sam smiled. "Oh, *thank you*, Your Majesty."

Kyri nodded regally, mimicking the way she'd seen Huey do it. Then she plucked another tiara from the pile, silver this time. "Zaand," she called, scampering to the door, where Xander was watching. The king had assigned him to keep an eye on them both. "You're a princess too."

He grinned widely, kneeling as she arrived.

"Here you go." She placed it on his head.

"Thank you very much, Your Majesty. You're too kind."

"You're welcome," she smiled.

It was just playful now, thinking these things were toys, Sam thought. But soon she'd learn the power she had over people. And, growing up like that, learning from the king, she might not develop any sort of empathy, *Lords know Huey doesn't have a shred of it.* She'd grow up not knowing just how privileged this life really was . . . becoming entitled to it, instead of humbled by it. This easy living, getting everything she wanted, having everything done for her . . . it would weaken her light, her goodness. Sam could see it. She could see her life play out before her, no different than Huey's, who'd taken the crown at only ten.

Vertuém hearts were stronger, less susceptible to Refsiel, which was why most were destined to lead. But the king supposedly did not believe that. Yet he chose Kyri as his heir. What a hypocrite. He didn't deserve her. And she didn't deserve to be raised by his ignorance. Sam wanted to stop this, to save her, just as much as Greyson. But, with so many competing vertuém, whose heart was strongest? Whose fate was greatest? Who would win out in the end?

Was it Kyri's fate to be a princess? . . . Or was it Sam's fate to free her? . . .

Somehow convince the king to take her as her own?

She sighed again. *It's useless to ask such questions. The confounded thing about fate is that you never see it coming 'til it's gone.* Unless you're a vertui with a vision . . . a dream. A desire.

Maybe she did have the power after all. What if this was her own Vertuém Destiny?

She could do it. She was as strong as her desire. And right then, she desired nothing more than to free Kyri from that golden prison.

Greyson and his team had found their way precariously across the curved and canted city to one of its main streets, which was oriented as flat as they were going to get. In areal terms, there was no roll or yaw, like all the other streets on the walls of the cylinder-city, only a steep, seventy degree pitch, which made it extremely hard to climb. But it was the best they were going to get.

If the city had still been pristine, it would have been impossible to climb, but luckily the crystal road was fractured in many places, revealing a hard steel beneath, which made for better footholds. But it was still like climbing a thousand story staircase. So progress was slow.

Tay was right, it basically *was* like climbing a mountain, but even more nauseating than that, because at least on a mountain you knew which way was up. Here, in this darkness, what little bits of buildings they could see with their flashlights were all at that seventy degree angle, messing with their heads, so off from the direction of gravity's pull. Even the buildings themselves were hard to fathom, built of semi-translucent stone, sometimes with silver metal shining through from beneath. Like the crystal was grafted to a metal skeleton. And, even stranger . . . the architecture was not all that different from Viæden's. But more like Wellington, he supposed, where there were more brick and mortar buildings than leaf-moulded ones.

But the worst part about it was a feeling Greyson couldn't shake. The feeling of an eyeless gaze upon him. The demons of his nightmare lurked in every dark corner of his mind, and played tricks with his eyes. The longer they went without running into one, the more Greyson wondered why. Where were they all? He'd seen thousands in his vision. Had they all died in the crash? Or were they just waiting for the right moment to strike?

Compared to those things, running into Itxaro didn't seem so bad. At least they'd share a common enemy in here . . . He hoped.

His team came to a halt, flashlights panning over the steep road ahead. Blank and smooth. They'd run out of cracks to climb on, and would have to find another road, and hope for better luck. Greyson didn't know exactly where the control room was, but if he was going to find it and activate that self-destruct, he had to get out of this city. He had to find some part of the ship he remembered, just to get his bearings. And since the cylinder was an endless loop, up was their only option, with Tay already down near the bottom of the ship.

Greyson shined his light to the right, to a building next to them. There was an alley above it, just at eye level, and another, even bigger building hanging over it. Probably the biggest building they'd seen yet, stretching fifty yards in every direction, until the shadows became too much to see any further. But that alley was definitely climbable, and they could use it to get to the next street over.

Greyson jumped and pulled himself up into the alley, with the giant building hanging just three feet over his head. The alley wall he stood on was, for the most part, flat, just tilted at the same twenty degree angle as the structure they'd first entered onto. But the wall above him was slotted with crystal pillars every ten feet or so, looking more like a ceiling's crossbeams at that angle. Between each of the pillars were tall windows. And one of their panes was broken. A pile of something rested below it, on the wall of his building. It looked almost like a pile of . . . *books*?

Jacob followed Greyson into the alley, needing a hand to help pull himself up. He spotted the pile of books instantly as he stood. "Look at this." He stepped to it as the guards climbed up behind him, plucking one from the pile. It was definitely a book. Hard leather binding, paper pages, and everything. It looked so weird on this ship from outer space, where everything was steel and crystal.

Greyson huddled close to see inside as Jacob flipped through its pages, inked with tiny hieroglyphics. All curvy, dotted, and crossed, very similar to the symbols of earth, water, air, and fire . . . In fact, in the short time the pages fanned past his eyes, Greyson spotted the Symbol of Fire, exactly as he knew it.

"It's all in Vínesíren," Jacob said.

Greyson blinked at him. "I thought this was called Ancient Viædonic."

"No," Jacob said simply. "That might be what the king is calling it. But as far as the historians are concerned, it's Vínesíren."

Greyson remembered the name. Not from his vision, but from his mom's stories. *Vinesíri.* The land Viæden was called, long before it was Viæden. The land where all her stories took place. "So what's it doing here?"

Jacob looked to the broken window above them. "Let's find out." He closed the book and climbed.

Too weak to lift his own body, Greyson had to give him a boost, then jumped and pulled himself up after. The building *was* enormous, inside and out. And there was hardly any room to stand on the inside wall. Only enough for Greyson, Jacob, and two other guards. Beyond that were piles, upon hills, upon mountains of books, across which their flashlights panned. Some enormous, some tiny, all varied in color and age. All thrown from their shelves in the crash.

"Wow." Jacob marveled at it. "A *library*. On a spaceship," he laughed. "Who would have thought?" He bent to inspect a few more texts. All of them were written in the same familiar language. "Remarkable. Samantha always advocated for the shared lineage of man and angel . . . I never thought it could be true. But this shared language certainly works in her favor. Vínesíren is said to be the language from which all others on our planet originated."

"She's right about a lot more than just that," Greyson said.

But Jacob ignored him, shining his light over a rampart of books to a line of six pillars beyond. But they were not tilted on their side like the rest of the library, they looked like they were standing almost perfectly straight up and down. And above them, it looked like the library's ceiling was missing . . . crashed through by . . . something large, and gold.

Greyson took off up the rampart of books, climbing as fast as he could to get a better look, stumbling as the books shifted and opened underfoot. Jacob and the others followed after.

As he reached the pillars he found them attached to a cracked, marble floor, perhaps a second story that had fallen—or maybe a mezzanine—that now lay relatively flat upon the books and rubble. But the flat surface was surrounded by devastation. The entire back wall of the library, as well has half the roof had collapsed, plunged through by a round, golden tower . . . But it wasn't *really* a tower.

Greyson's angel flashed through his mind, flying down a golden hall, glowing like a tubular sun. *That* was it. The axis hall he and his sister cut to save themselves a few moments more. It must have fallen into the library from higher up in the ship. At least this end of it did. It looked like the vast majority of it still stemmed up into the dark.

*Finally*, they were getting somewhere. One step closer to finding the bridge, and ridding himself of this darkness.

Greyson stepped onto the marble floor, and walked the short span to the base of the golden hall, its round opening hanging over him like the mouth of a twenty-foot-wide trash shoot. And this close up, it was obvious it was not gold, but yellow crystal. Not glowing at all like he remembered.

The floor on which the shattered lip of the hall had landed was ornate, marbled, translucent stone, configured in many detailed, concentric circles. To the left of this mezzanine were broken stairs down to the front entrance of the library. And to the right was a thin, metal strip of wall, twenty feet wide, that went straight up to what was left of the ceiling, five stories overhead. Open space on either side of it to the rest of the library. On it was an enormous picture frame, thirty feet high, gilded and carved of a white wood. And on its inside edge were the charred remains of a canvas. Its picture had been burnt away, rather recently by the look of it. The frame only outlined the metal wall behind it now . . . And also a jagged inscription, burnt into the metal.

Jacob walked toward the deeply carved words, but Greyson couldn't take his eyes off of the crashed axis hall. Its dark, yellow barrel was angled almost straight up, eighty degrees. And so smooth . . . there was no way they could ever use it to climb higher.

Greyson's hopes fell again.

"I wonder who has written this?" Jacob said.

Greyson finally turned to the frame as the guards formed a perimeter around them. Jacob touched the letters. Their molten cuts looked just like the scorches of a lerité. And they were written in *Modern* Viædonic.

"Oyopa made this Gate to close," Greyson read the first line.

"But it will open by My throes," Jacob read the second.

Unmistakably a reference to the Door to Darkness. Greyson knew immediately, zapped with fear. If his dad's sword were unsheathed, it would have lit up with every shade of terror.

"The door is here," he whispered.

"What door?" Jacob snapped.

"To Darkness."

"There's no such thing," Jacob said with such certainty.

"Really? You're going to sit here, in this crystal city and tell me it's not real?"

"*This* is all explainable. It has been theorized that a civilization evolved to sentience on Nævah. And just because that may be true does not mean that all myths are suddenly true as well."

Greyson tensed his jaw and ground his teeth to keep from screaming. He knew the truth. But could not speak a word of it. He'd *seen* a goddess, *spoken* to her. And he'd seen the door she brought him through to do so. It was torture standing there and staying silent with that prick running his mouth like he had all the answers.

"We've been in here for," Jacob checked his watch, "*two* hours now, and there is still no sign of your demons. If they are as supernatural as you say, don't you think they would have found us by now?"

Greyson balled his fist, squeezing 'til it hurt. How could he be so *fucking stupid*!? Not believing what was *right in front of his face*? Jacob was no better than the king.

Part of him wished the demons *would* come, show themselves, and prove him right.

*Wait.* He shook his head. No. What was he thinking? *That's horrible!* He brought his fist up to his chest. Was the darkness in him *growing*? Making him more brash and violent?

Something was wrong.

*Tay.*

He could feel it. In that weird, vertui way his heart tensed up when something horrible was near. He looked down to the window they'd come through, and to the dark beyond, searching for Tay's light anywhere. But there was nothing out there.

Nothing good anyway.

Tay and his five men hobbled through the crooked sewers, ankles rolled out as they walked along the jacked-up floor shaped like a V. After two hours a *that* bullshit, it was really starting to hurt. And now especially because the tunnel had started to tip up at an unbearable angle. Basically too steep to keep going without constantly slipping back.

"This isn't working, lieutenant. We're not getting anywhere," a guard said. "And this place smells like shit."

"Oh, is that what that smell is? I had no idea. Thanks for clearing it up." Tay was over this place too, but he wasn't about to walk another two hours back through this shit. There was one turn-off a while back, which they probly should have taken, but he'd just figured there'd be another one . . . *somewhere.*

"Hey, shut up!" another guard shouted from the back.

Tay craned his head as far as he could without losing his balance. "*You* shut up. I'm in charge here, shit-burger."

"No, I hear something," said the guard.

Everyone quieted to take in the soft, drippy dark around them. There was something else out there, echoing ahead. A muted whirr, like a tiny motor still left running.

"What is that?" Tay asked, shining his light at all angles, stepping carefully forward, using the pressure of his spread legs lodged between the narrow walls to help him climb.

In a few tense steps, he saw the flicker of something move. Something small and thin dipped into the hall and disappeared. Then another. And another. As he neared he saw the flickers of movement were coming from an adjacent passage. *Finally* they'd found another one. The new hall cut right through theirs, leading above and below them. But below was covered by a closed aperture door.

The whirring sound was coming from . . . like, little handles, shaped like U's—or n's, he supposed. A whole bunch of them, moving along the wall, tracking down out of the dark, dipping into their hall, then turning and heading back up again. They looked like they should have been riding on some kind of track in the wall, but they weren't. At least no track Tay could see.

Why this was the only thing still working on this goddam ship he didn't know, but he didn't care either. "I'll take it."

"But we don't know where it goes."

"Then stay here." Tay holstered one of his guns and stretched for the next handle as it swung down. As soon as he wrapped his fingers around it, it clutched his hand right back, yanking him up off his feet into the dark. The thing sped up as he rose, topping out at 40 miles an hour.

"Whoa," he gave a little shout from the tingle in his gut, shining his light ahead to see where it was taking him. His light bounced and reflected off the speeding metal walls, as he rose high into the ship, ears popping. Then something different flashed past him. An unmistakable shade of red. And instantly the tingle in his gut turned sour. *Where the fuck was he headed?* And what was waiting for him on the other side?

He passed another junction, but wasn't about to let go for that. He wanted to wait 'til he was *out* of these goddam tunnels. Or at least ride this lift to the end. Which came suddenly, just then.

The tunnel opened all at once, mangled, like a hole had been blasted through it. His handle-thing didn't know how to react, spinning back on its invisible track and ripping from his grip. Tay fell about a story to the floor with a crack. It hurt, but he was just relieved to finally be back on solid ground. Or at least as solid as this messed up ship could offer.

Quickly he panned his light around the place to see where he was. Some kind of room, with silvery-white walls. He saw doors, solid white, and wide windows on either side of them, that looked out onto a slanted street. Hard to tell with just his flashlight . . . but something was off about it. Pushing off the ground and getting his feet under him again, he figured it out. The street outside was still at that same awkward 70°, but now everything was *upside-down*. Looking around the room again, he saw pillars in each of the corners, and stairs behind him, but they were upside down too. Taking a step toward the stairs, the floor beneath him gave another crack. And he looked down to see that there was something written in it. Burnt into it.

*What once was locked, may be unbound,*
*once all unholy keys are found.*

Tay didn't have time to make sense of it, because one of his guards had followed after him, and dropped from the hole in the floor-ceiling, right on top of him. And in their combined weight, the floor shattered, dropping them even further into the inverted building.

They both slid down the incline, screaming, and crashing into a bunch of shit they couldn't see.

"Oh, fuck. Oh, fuck. Oh, fuck!" Tay tried to latch hold of anything but it was all fucking crystals! Finally they slammed into the bottom, or at least a slight incline that wedged them to a stop. Tay pushed away from the incline, his back against the wall they'd slid down, kind of standing, kind of not. He couldn't catch his balance anymore, everything was so fucking *wet* and slippery. The light on the end of his gun wasn't working anymore either, covered in . . . "Oh, fuck." It was covered in blood. He wiped that shit off with his jacket as quick as he could and shined it down to see where the hell that blood was coming from.

His new boots were red too. *All* that wet was blood. Pooled here at the bottom of some huge broken-dome tower, hanging from the wall of the city-chamber like a crooked stalactite. But the *vast* majority of the dome was missing completely, a void of nothing beyond. All that supported his feet was the lip of it, which cracked when they'd slammed into it. It was *glass*, like the floor above. And *not* gunna hold forever.

The other guard was coated in blood, next to him, frantically trying to stand as more screams came from behind them. Tay looked up to see another guard flailing as he slid right for them.

"Grab something!" Tay shouted.

The guard slammed into the glass lip just like they had. Another deep crack resonating beneath their feet.

"God dammit!" Tay couldn't move. There was nothing to grab onto, and it was too steep and slippery to stand. *All this blood. It was a trap!*

More screams came from the shaft. Tay shined his light up to the hole they were all flying out of, a small crater in the building's "floor." Quickly, he fiddled with the settings on his gun, as another guard dropped from the hole and slid toward them.

There were still two more coming after him. And they'd never make it with an extra 400 pounds against this thing. The glass was *already* just about to break!

Tay's gun glowed white-hot in his hands as it reached full charge. "Sorry, guys." He took aim at the shaft's crater and fired his overcharge. The plasma slammed into the already warped metal and exploded, cascading chunks of debris down into the shaft. Then a giant slab peeled away from the floor, the perfect size, and fell into the open tunnel to seal it shut.

The glass gave the loudest crack yet as the last guard and a few straggling bits of rubble slid down and hit the rest of them.

But it held.

"You just . . ." a guard started, looking at Tay.

Tay said nothing, looking back at the bloody guard. His eyes said all he needed. He knew what he did. And he did it to save them.

The guard held his tongue.

"Whose blood is this!?" The last guard squealed.

"I don't know. But I don't wanna stick around to find out." Tay tried to stand, very carefully, one foot on the slippery wall, one foot on the glass. He holstered his gun, broken now because of the overcharge, and unholstered the other, using his free hand for balance as he looked down into the black. So much black. Tay imagined that if the flare was still burning, he'd probly be able to see the place they entered the ship from, a mile below them. This might have even been the place those rockets came from.

He turned back to search the inverted room above for any possible way to escape the bloody ledge. The four pillars he'd seen before were holding this dome up . . . or, *anchoring* it to the ground now, he supposed. And just barely out of jumping range, there was another level to the ceiling: lower, normally, higher now, just to the right of the dome's cupola. He might have even been able to reach it if the slope wasn't so damn slippery. He couldn't see exactly where it led to, but those stairs he saw below had to lead *somewhere* up here.

"How the hell do we get out of here?" The guards began to stand and search as well. "We gotta get off this glass."

"I'm working on it!" Tay hissed. "If we could just get up there." He pointed to the lower ceiling, squinting through the shifting light. "It looks like maybe there's a bookshelf or something we can use to get higher."

"You want to go higher?!"

"Back to the ground, idiot!" Tay spun his light back to his stupid guard's scared face. "Unless you feel like jump—"

A scream let out from the deep, but not one any human could make. It was a screeching, fucked-up cry that echoed through the dark. Amplified by it.

"*What* . . . was that?" Tay whispered as he turned to face the void it came from.

Then another sound stroked their ears. A paralyzing noise that shredded any hope they had of escape. The sound of *wings*, goddammit. *Wings*. Dozens of them.

Greyson never mentioned that part.

They all took aim, but they might as well have had their fucking eyes closed. There was nothing out there but that sound. Coming closer. A blur blew past the furthest guard from Tay, snatching him right off his feet, torn into the night, leaving nothing behind but a trail of yellow bullets and his shrieks.

Three men left. They all shot out into the black. But their bullets faded into nothing as the guard opposite Tay let out a scream. Something latched its claws into him, slamming into the glass tower, and blasting off again with a swipe of its wings. Tay and the last guard were blown against their backs by the gust. It kicked them a few feet back from the dome, sliding up the bloody wall, almost in reach of the lower ceiling. The only thing on Tay's mind was getting the fuck out of there. Every man for himself. As he slid back to the dome, he crouched, ready to jump. And as soon as his feet hit the glass he sprang back up, sliding through the slick blood as the dome shattered below him, dropping the last guard into the dark. Tay's fingertips latched onto the ledge of the lower ceiling, just as the guard's screams changed pitch, like one of those—whateverthefuck they were, caught him right out of the air.

Tay pulled his heavy ass up onto the ledge and crawled under the crossbeams to a hidden corner of the roof's underside, just below an empty bookshelf. But he didn't climb it. He curled up as small as he could get, back against the wall, switching off his light and aiming his gun at where he'd come from, gasping for one last breath of air before he held it in and waited, as silent as he could.

The silence was fucking absolute. No more gunshots, no more screams, no more wings. Just him and his pounding heart. He couldn't see a damn thing. But he bet *they* could, snatching a guy right out of the air like that. He'd have to rely on his ears to know when one was coming. But at least they couldn't swoop out of nowhere now. There was only one place they could come from, right fucking here, right where his gun was aimed.

It was only quiet for a moment longer. He felt the roof vibrate again as one landed somewhere near the dome. He could hear the nails of its talons prick into the glass as it walked up the bloody slope, hissing, smelling, searching. He couldn't hold his breath any longer, skin burning from the speed of his blood rushing by beneath. But he had to hold on. A few seconds more.

The footsteps stopped. And so did the hisses.

Should he shoot? Could he breathe? *Where the fuck was that thing!?*

"Tay!" His badge blared. Scared to death, he jumped, gasped, and fired all at once. The roof lit up as his bullets passed, burning into the wall across the dome. And the demon turned to follow where they'd come from, leaping right for him, lodging itself between the roof and its crystal crossbeams, too big to fit. Its black head was long and featureless, except for a snapping jaw and silver teeth. Tay riddled it with amber craters as its long, boney arms slashed at him. It screamed as the bullets entered its head, and went limp, only a little slower than a human would've. Its skull split open, and dumped its brains onto the ceiling, 2 feet in front of him. It stunk and sizzled, bubbling as it burnt a hole right through the crystal.

"Holy fuck!" Tay scampered for the bookshelf, just before the ceiling cracked and fell away, weakened by the acid blood.

"Tay, are you there!?" his badge rang again.

He was a little fucking busy to answer at the moment, pinned between the bookshelf and a window at his back. But he knew Greyson would keep calling. He had to shut him up, ripping the badge from his jacket. "Greyson, shut the fuck up! You're gunna get me killed!"

"Are you okay!?"

"I found your demons. They just killed *all* my guys. And they're coming after me." Tay noticed a flicker on the gold badge in his hand. It was reflecting from something behind him. He shifted to see out the window at his back, seeing the fronts of all the buildings along the upside-down street. The third one down had a glow coming from its windows, a pale silver. All the buildings' facades were at that same 70° angle, too steep to climb. But they all also had balconies beneath each of their windows. Balconies that he might actually be able to stand on the undersides of.

The roof vibrated again as another demon landed somewhere near him.

He was done for. His only chance was to make it to that light. And hope it'd help him kill them, keep them away, or if nothing else, give him a clear shot.

"What?" Greyson hissed.

"Actually, forget that. I need you to yell. Make a shit-ton a noise. You're gunna help me escape."

"Wait, Tay!"

"Do it or I'm dead!" Tay pressed his gun against the glass and fired, shattering it out into the black. And as Greyson's screams came through the badge, he hurled it behind him, hoping to distract the things. Then with all his strength he leapt from the window, and crashed onto the underside of the next building's balcony. That hurt. But he didn't have time to feel it, scrambling to his feet and jumping over to the next balcony, only the light of his pistol to guide him.

But the next jump was further, over a bottomless alley between buildings. He had no choice, jumping from the screeches at his heels. He barely made it to the next building's balcony, tripping forward and jumping immediately to the next window.

He fell that time, hearing those things coming after him. Apparently they weren't falling for his little trick. He fired blindly to the sky behind him as he stood and leapt again to the last balcony of the second building, then quickly drew his gun forward to light his way. Last alley. Last jump. The glowing building was right in front of him. And even though it didn't have any balconies to land on, he leapt anyway, pinning his trigger down.

His bullets poxed one of its windows to weaken it, but as he flew through the air, he could feel the winds change, like slow motion. A black wing swept in front of him and a single talon latched onto his jacket. It yanked him right along the demon's path. But just as fast, his jacket ripped, flipping him through the air and crashing down into his glowing target in a hail of blood and silver glass.

*Answer me, you mother fucker!* Greyson went silent, panting, waiting for a response. Anything, any sign that Tay had made it out alive.

But there was nothing. Not even static.

Fed up, he smashed Brown's badge against the ground, tears in his eyes. His breathing deepened as he paced, mind spinning, contorting with demons tearing his best friend apart. He laced his fingers on his head, opening his airway. He was suffocating, heart and mind burning up his oxygen. Tingling. Dizzy. Sick.

*Did he make it? Was he alive?*

. . . Or had Greyson killed Tay too?

He felt something, rolling up his throat. He bent over to puke, but screamed instead. It just exploded from him, taking every ounce of strength his body had. He crashed to his hands and knees as his wailing echoed through the crystal library and out into the ghostly city.

His fear was gone. Replaced by *pain* and *hate*. If Tay was dead, then he had nothing left to fear. His greatest fear had come and gone. He'd *lost* his light. And in its absence, a wrathful dark consumed him, dripping from his heart like tar. Tar lit aflame by fury. He hated this dark world, this evil place.

He hated his dark soul, his demon heart. But most of all he hated *Darkness*, for tearing down all that he was, all that he loved, and leaving him with nothing but despair.

But his blood-boiling cries were echoed by a sound, far more vile, and distinct. Something only Greyson had heard before, once in a dream.

The demons surrounded them, smashing through the library's windows, hiding in the valleys of its books. The guards pulled together, shuffling into half a ring around the entrance of the broken, yellow axis hall. But there was no place to hide. Nothing between them and the coming darkness but pillars and air. And worst of all, Greyson didn't care. He was ready to die, and ready to take out as many of those motherfuckers as he could before he did.

He drew his blade, expecting it to glow as red as Itxaro's. But all it did was pudder, shimmering lightly with a spark, then falling as dormant as it'd ever been. "Come on!" He swung it down again to try and draw his lerité. But nothing came.

He couldn't even go out fighting.

Darkness had robbed his life of all its dignity . . . So why should his death be any different?

"What was that sound?" Jacob asked, stepping closer to Greyson. They were both directly below the gold hall's broken entrance, in the center of their men.

"Jacob," Greyson whispered. It was the sound of their death approaching. The monsters Jacob didn't believe existed.

It sprang from the dark, sweeping across the marble like a shadow, catching a guard by his legs and skipping him along the floor as he yelped, flying into the unknown again. The guards lit up, all panning their dotted, amber fire for the same target. Then another struck, checking a guard with such raptor speed it snapped his back. That's when the dark closed in around them, and the seven guards that were left fired in every direction as the heaving of two dozen wings approached.

"Greyson!" Jacob cried for him to do something. To be the hero, and save him.

But Greyson was no hero. He was a demon, having led the next meal to his kin. He stepped back, bumping up against the bottom of the golden hall, watching as three guards were taken out at once, then three more disappeared completely but for screams. Only one was left alive, firing blindly into the black. But then the blackness swelled, and flooded through the pillars. A dozen demons black as night, slithered toward them, thirsty for the light within their hearts.

Jacob screamed and turned to the steep hall clawing at its smooth stone in a pitiful attempt to climb and save himself as the last guard disappeared behind a blur of wings.

They were next. This was it.

That vision really was of Greyson's future after all . . . Vertuém Destiny was all a lie . . . He was always meant to die by Refsiel's demons . . . Just like his angel had.

A blaze of light fell from above, slamming down into the marble before them with a glorious flash and boom, arresting every demon in its tracks.

It was . . . It was . . . his angel. Rising from his knees, bloodied, tattered, and one-winged, he drove his heavenly blade into the monsters all around. The demons leapt for him, his light far more attractive than Greyson's or Jacob's. And he slashed at them with blade and wing, turning to face Greyson, throwing something at him. It hit Greyson in the wrist, and pinned him back against the gold hall's inside wall. And looking at it, Greyson recognized it from his dream as well. The U-shaped handle that let him move through zero g's.

The angel was here to save them.

Without a second thought, Greyson clutched the handle, even though it wrapped his wrist already. And with the other hand, he grabbed for Jacob, snatching a wad of his clothes, just as the handle darted up, and jerked them both off their feet.

But Greyson's angel stayed, demons piling on his back. And as he shrunk into the distance, they tore at him, reaching over his shoulders to claw at his chest, knocking him to his knees again. They ripped the wing right from his back like a white weed with red roots before he and his glowing sword vanished completely beneath their darkness.

Greyson had more than a few thoughts about what had just happened, but no time to think them, because it wasn't over. Not nearly. Those demons could never be satisfied, and took wing to follow them up the golden hall. Greyson looked up, nothing but shadows ahead, no end in sight. Those monsters were closing fast. They were going to catch them! The wind rushing by grew colder as they approached, wings heaving, and hungry mouths screaming.

Then a flash came from Jacob and fired down, striking the physical shadows and exploding in a blinding magnesium flare.

"Jacob!" Greyson cheered as the shadows slammed against the light and clotted the twenty-foot hall in a tangle of limbs.

The lift handle sped away from the flair at forty miles an hour, finding the end of the hall a moment later. But it didn't stop, it launched from the hall and arced them a few feet into the air before they hit the floor again. Upon impact the lift fell from Greyson's wrist, and Jacob lost the grip on his flashlight. The tiny light rolled up the inclined plane they'd landed on, where Greyson caught it before it could roll back down again. They were going to need that.

He shined it back on where they'd come from. But its light couldn't find anything to reflect off of. The flashlight was dimming. Dying. He panned it left, finding the familiar yellow crystal of their hallway, and another passage splitting from it.

They must have finally made it to the ship proper, above the hollow cylinder-city.

But the demons' cries could still be heard below. They weren't safe yet.

"Can you run?" Greyson whispered.

"I think so."

"Then run!" He sprang to his feet, grabbing Jacob's shirt again to pull him up as well. They sprinted left into the splitting passage, and into uncharted shadows, though part of Greyson lagged behind, wanting nothing more than to stop altogether. To turn and face his demons, the darkness of his heart, and let it tear him apart. He fucking deserved it. His wake of darkness was so powerful that even an angel could not escape it . . . An *angel*. The purest creature his mother ever spoke of, aside from Light, Herself.

Greyson deserved to die. And he would. But not yet. There was another force that kept him running. Darkness Itself. And his desire to destroy it. To rid the world of this forsaken ship once and for all. Darkness had destroyed his life. But he couldn't let it destroy the world too.

His legs burnt, muscles tired. He didn't know how much longer he could hold out. They slowed, Jacob's shirt still curled in his fingers. This damn hall would not end! And worse yet, his flashlight began to flicker, turning an orangey-yellow. The spark of his laser blade must have ruined it. It wouldn't last much longer. But what would give out first? His legs or his light?

Neither. The hall ended, opening into a lightless room. Greyson slammed

against the inside wall, swinging Jacob in behind him, finally letting him go
and stumble to the floor. Neither had any breath. Greyson felt something
digging into his back, and rolled off the wall to see a tiny control panel. Only
two buttons on it. He slammed them both, so hard he tipped over backwards
as the door slammed shut. He hit the ground, ass first, and laid out flat against
its translucent fractals.

Jacob wheezed, having never run so far in all his life.

Greyson's breath slowed only slightly as he scanned the room with
what little light remained. Looking at it from his back, he saw some kind of
computer terminal, sitting all alone to his left. Just a chair with a very thin
spire for a back, a wide control panel, and a blank piece of glass for a monitor
against the wall. That was all. There was nothing else in there with them.
Greyson checked each corner twice.

"Do you believe me now, Jacob?" he asked, exhausted—mind, body, and
soul.

His angel. He was here. Alive. He'd saved them.

But his vision . . . Greyson saw it again. His angel, on the bridge of this
ship, covered in those demons, tearing into him . . . He couldn't have survived.
He *hadn't* survived . . . Had his vision been cut short? Or was it not even of
*his* future at all? But his angel's instead? Well how would that make any sense?
It *had* to be of his own destiny. There were so many similarities: Stiqula, the
lerité, this ship, those demons. They had all seeped from that nightmare into
his reality. It had to be his own destiny he'd seen.

"Demons, angels, Darkness. It's *all* real, Jacob . . . And I've seen this all
before. It was my destiny to come here . . . and die in this darkness."

"I'm aware," Jacob started, pausing to catch his breath, "of your vision,
Greyson."

"How," Greyson turned his head, shining his dim light right in that
know-it-all's face.

"Samantha told me," Jacob breathed again. "In an attempt to make me see
things the way she does . . . But you and she both already believe you know the
truth . . . And it's this confirmation bias that clouds your further reasoning."

"What is your problem! Did you not see those things out there? That
angel!" Then Greyson let him have it. "The gods are *real*, Jacob! One pulled
me right out of fucking *reality* to talk to me." His skin flushed with fear,
instantly filling with regret. He'd let the goddess' secret out . . . But, did it

really matter now? He'd already changed Jacob's fate so much. And they were both going to die in here anyway. No matter what he told him.

"You what?" Jacob winced.

"I never told Sam. But the night of the ball, the Goddess of Water took me into her realm, and spoke to me. She told me I have no destiny and warned me about the attack on Darakin." It felt good to finally say, and watch the look of confusion finally splash across his face. "You're wrong, Jacob."

Jacob just sat there against the wall, making little noises with his open mouth, trying to come up with any reasonable explanation. "Were you drinking when this happened?"

"No," Greyson said dully. Which wasn't the whole truth, but one drink wasn't enough to give him an out of body experience and hallucinate a whole other dimension.

"You're making this up. You must be." He refused to believe it. But the fear in his voice egged Greyson on.

"I'm really not."

"And she told you you had no destiny?"

"No vertui does."

"But . . . didn't you just say it was your destiny to come here?"

Fear struck Greyson's skin again. His heart realizing some terrible fault in his story, faster than his mind. "I . . . It's complicated."

"You know, there is another theory about the vertuém," Jacob said. "One that links your visions to Darkness, instead of fate."

"I've heard the theory," Greyson turned his head back to the ceiling. "But my vision wasn't from Him, it was from Water."

"You saw it in her realm?"

". . . No."

"Did she mention it at?"

". . . No," Greyson uttered, coming to understand what his heart had already discovered.

"What exactly resulted by you having this dream?" Jacob asked.

"I . . . knew about all this, the ship, the angels, Stiqula . . . before any of it happened."

"And what use would that be to a god for you to know all those things?" He was on to something. "If the gods are all powerful, and their legends are all true, the one certainty is that they never make a move for any arbitrary reason

. . . So what use is it for you to know these things, if you have not—*could not*—have prevented this from happening?"

"I was afraid of it, when it happened. It terrified me. But what scared me most was that it started seeping into the real world . . . Stiqula . . . I'd never heard his name before that day we released him . . . It . . . made me react. And order Tay to fire."

Could it really have been *Darkness* that gave him that vision all along? "No. No, Sam said Darkness can't write destinies, only destroy them!"

"But you have no destiny, Greyson."

Just like Darkness. A breath shot from his tense lungs. "And He used *me* . . . to destroy all those lives . . . and free Stiqula."

"Fascinating." Jacob smiled. "You may turn me into a believer yet."

"I was played." *Tricked.* It was true . . . Bail was right about him all along. And Riese too. Death really did follow him, ever since the beginning. It was always there, behind his every move. A puppet. Vertuém were nothing more than servants of the devil. Whether they liked it or not . . . Their true Vertuém Destiny.

"Now the real question is, is your role complete? Or do you still have some part yet to play?"

Greyson lay there, burning. Heart at its limit. Stricken by the darkest revelation.

And his light finally flickered to its end.

She wasn't ready for a kid, but she was sure as hell more capable than Huey.

The only question was, how would she do it? She couldn't just steal her and run away. Knowing Huey, he'd go to the ends of the world to find her again—well, not himself, of course, but he'd get someone else to, and Sam would be thrown right back into that prison, or worse, done away with on the spot. That would get her nowhere. No. She'd have to trick the king. Make him think he didn't want Kyri anymore, and that it was *his* idea for Sam to take her instead. *But how?* He sure was dumb enough to fall for something like that, but it had to be good. Something that would scare him to his core . . . but also not get her in trouble if it backfired. That was a fine tight-rope to walk. And a long fall if she failed.

But it was already done in her mind. Her fate was already decided.

Greyson had saved Kyri's life. But *she* could save Kyri's heart.

Sam returned from the depths of thought, arriving back in Kyri's room. "Xander." She stood, walking to him in the doorway. "Can you watch her for a moment? I need to have a word with Huey."

Xander squinted uncomfortably. "I'm sorry, miss. I would in a heartbeat if His Highness hadn't told me to keep an eye on you."

She sighed, venting her frustration.

"But I could come with you."

"Right." She nodded. "Well, I don't want to get you in trouble." She turned to Kyri, who was standing at the window. "Kyri'll have to come with us too."

But she didn't respond to Sam's invitation.

"Kyri," Xander called.

Still nothing.

*What was happening out there?* Sam hurried across the room to see for herself. The sun had richened into afternoon light, falling onto the black clouds, now seemingly more grey.

But other than that, she saw no difference.

"What do you see?" Sam looked down at her.

But still, stoically, she stared.

Finally she touched her shoulder, breaking the spell.

"Hi Sam," she squeaked, eyes squinted from smiling cheeks.

"Hi, what did you see out there?" she asked, gently.

Kyri looked back to the window for an answer.

Sam could see her thinking.

"I heared it."

Sam shook her head. "Heard what?"

"The outside."

That wasn't exactly what she was expecting, considering the window was sound-proof. "What . . . does it sound like?" she inquired, slowly.

"Like dis." She pointed to the middle of her chest.

*What?* Sam thought. *Ugh. If only you weren't three years old.*

"Here." Kyri pointed to Sam's chest too.

"You feel it here?"

"Uh-huh." She nodded.

"What's it feel like?"

She shrugged. It was beyond her limited vocabulary.

It must have had something to do with her Vertuém Destiny, Sam guessed. She would often feel things in her chest, a pressure, or a tingling, when something bad was near. And so did her dad. And so did Greyson . . . Maybe this was what she needed to convince the king.

"It'll be okay, Kyri." She picked her up in one arm and marched to the door. "You coming, Xander?"

"Yes, ma'am." He followed her out, through His Royal Chambers, and down to the throne room.

The king had emptied it of all its workers, ever since those clouds had arrived. He wanted complete isolation, to watch and contemplate the truth he could no longer deny . . . Or at least that's what Sam hoped he was doing. But in reality he was probably scheming up some way to swing this in his favor, cramming that jagged peg of a *Chandelier* into his simple, round hole of a belief system.

She found him at the fissure's edge, watching the clouds from the gap blown in the wall. He had only one aide at his side, should he need an emergency glass of water, or some equally important thing.

He glanced at her as she arrived, then immediately returned his attention to the sky.

"Your Highness," Sam said, putting Kyri down between her and Xander.

"What?" he said dully, having had enough of her today.

"I don't want to alarm you, but have you thought about the repercussions of this alien ship?"

"Of *course* I have."

"Even if Greyson succeeds in destroying it?"

"Then life goes back to normal," he shouted, turning his head halfway to her.

"Will it, sir? He is a vertui. And its destruction was predicted by *his* vision."

Huey shut his mouth, waiting for her point.

"If he succeeds, it will prove the existence of a Vertuém Destiny."

His hard, forward face eased back, loosened by nerves.

"Everyone will know."

"*No one* will know, O'Nasi. Because anyone that blabs will be *inprisoned*!"

"Surely that won't go unnoticed."

Huey breathed in, trying to come up with some other excuse, but Sam didn't let him.

"Think about Kyri, sir."

He exhaled. "What *about* her?"

"One day she may have a vision just like Greyson's. And are you going to deny her of fulfilling it? Are you going to *derail* her destiny? And cause even more darkness to propagate across this kingdom?" Even though it was a Mohaviken legend that vertui spread darkness, Sam knew the king was well aware of it. She knew that for all the science that he spit, by the way he reacted to anything he did not understand, he was nothing more than a superstitious old man.

Huey shook his head like a wet dog. "How dare you speak to me of darkness!"

"How long are you going to ignore the truth, Huey!? We are *dangerous*. That's why you've banned belief in such a thing. But just because you don't believe in something anymore, doesn't make it go away—doesn't mean it can't still *hurt* you. The only way to escape it is to understand it, Your Highness. To know how to avoid mistakes like the one Greyson made with Stiqula. If he'd known about Vertuém Destiny, this all might never have happened!"

"Be silent!" he screamed, throwing his fists down, forgetting he was not still in his throne.

This was it. Time to lay it on him. "I saw her future, Huey."

He gasped, so loud he nearly choked on his tongue.

"And it's with *me*. Not you."

Huey's eyes went wide, stepping back, covering his gaping mouth with his old jeweled hand, like she'd just threatened his entire kingdom . . . Because she *had*.

"How dare you," he muttered, regaining his balance. "How *dare* you threaten *me*!"

*Shit*. This wasn't how it was supposed to go. She'd jumped too quick. Losing ground. She had to try something else. An ultimatum was her last chance. "It is my destiny, Huey! You cannot deny me of it. Or else everyone whose fate overlaps with mine will be surrendered to Darkness . . . *Even yours*."

That was it. She had him now. His lips quivered, on the verge of admitting it. On the verge of accepting her demands.

"You *bitch*. You *traitor*!" He cast his bony finger at her eye. "You will not have her! You will not take her from me! You have *no* power here! *I* do!" He beat against his chest. "And I would rather send my kingdom into darkness than give Kyri to you!"

The throne room doors slammed shut like a sonic boom, blasting away the piles of stone and rubble that propped them open. The vibration of the massive doors colliding sent a quaking ripple down the entire hall, knocking Sam, the king, and his aides off balance.

Sam whipped her head to the doors across the ravine, fear flashing through her skin. A little figure stood not thirty feet away from the massive, jade slabs.

"Kyri?" *How'd she get all the way over there without anyone seeing?*

The little figure stood perfectly still, completely unaffected by the sound still ringing in their ears.

"Kyri, come away from there." Sam side-strafed along the ravine, to the bridge in the middle, never taking her eyes off the little girl. She didn't know *what* had caused the door to slam. But she didn't want Kyri anywhere near it.

"Is it happening again?" Huey latched onto Xander.

Then, Kyri's bare foot stepped forward. And all the room began to tremble in her might. The marble fractured underneath her fragile steps as she continued to the doors. And the fractures radiated outward, spitting dust into the air from down below, like she weighed three thousand tons.

As soon as Sam stepped foot on the bridge, it split and tumbled down the gap. She instantly pulled back all her weight and fell to the shivering marble behind her, sitting up again to watch as Kyri's web of fissures stretched out in all directions, even up the pillars and the walls, shattering the stained glass windows.

And when the fractures met the doors, they burst wide again, just as powerfully as they'd closed, obliterating the pillars nearest the door, but the pillars' rubble slowed as it diffused, spreading out like dust through the air, like time was coming to its end. A brilliant green light bathed the throne room from beyond the doors. And sparks, like emerald stars, flooded in at every angle, cascading like a waterfall of light up to the peaked ceiling, out to either wall, and rolling across the marble floor like a billion grains of shimmering sand.

Sam couldn't believe it. What *was* this? What was *happening*? Why was Kyri not listening to her! "Kyri!" Sam sprang from the ground, seeing her outline in the light, still tiptoeing toward the green light like a moth to flame.

She could not let her reach that door!

Sam looked to the ravine in front of her, six-and-a-half feet across. Just short enough to jump. She took two steps back and one bound forward, launching herself over the pit, focusing on the opposite side as she came down again, aiming her toe at the broken marble floor, and landed it, then stumbled to her hands as the floor shook beneath her.

She looked up to the glow, flicking the hair from her eyes. "Kyri!"

Grass began to seed from the emerald stars that rolled across the ground, and great, thick vines sprouted from between the fissures in the floor, stretching straight up to the ceiling like inverted willow boughs.

Sam kicked off the ground, and sprinted through the rising jungle, scraped and lashed by vines and thorns. "Stop!"

The glowing dust swirled around Kyri's little body, pulsing with green light as it blew away from her again with every step she took. Sam was only thirty feet away when another blast of energy erupted from the door like a solar flare from a green sun, thrashing the vines that grew through the air like seaweed beneath a rolling wave. The pulse struck Sam like a powerful wind, tingling against her skin, and halting her momentum. She shouted from the blow, planting her feet and taking off again, tearing through the thickening brush like she had blades for arms. Just ten feet from the door, the thicket ended at a bed of grass and glowing seeds. Sam flew from the vines, but her limbs were tangled in them, jerked to a stop as they tightened around her wrists, legs, and shoulders.

With one free hand she stretched for Kyri, so near she could feel the copper strands of her hair, brushing past her fingers in the wind.

"No!" Sam screamed. But Kyri stepped away, through the threshold of the door, and into the light. Only then did she turn to Sam, eyes widening as their gazes locked, like she'd just realized where she was.

"Momma?"

The doors slammed shut, supersonic, and in the haze of the shock wave, sweeping down the hall, all that had come from the green light disappeared without a trace.

Sam dropped to the floor, throwing her gaze up to the door, spellbound, hardly breathing.

But the sound of the king's screams snapped her out of it.

She gasped, pushing off the ground, and falling against the door. "Kyri!"

The hall was spotless, windows mended, pillars replaced, pristine but for the *Claw's* fissure. The door opened when she pressed against it, automatic sensors re-engaged. They swung slowly inward, pushing her back. Kyri was lying on the ground in the secretaries' office. Sam's heart leapt up into her throat when she saw her there. She squeezed through the doors and slid to her knees, scooping Kyri into her arms.

"Samantha," Stephanie stood from behind her desk. She hadn't even noticed Kyri lying there. "Oh, what happened?" She came around to see for herself.

Sam said nothing, studying Kyri carefully. Feeling her pulse, and listening closely for her breathing. She was unconscious. But alive. Cheeks as red and soft as petals, hair as rich and auburn as the freckles dotting her nose. She had a pure, unnatural beauty.

But what had happened to her?

Sam looked back to the king. He was sitting on the floor, legs spread out in front of him. His aides tried to stand him up, lifting his arms over his head, but there they stayed. He was frozen, staring out across his hall to Sam, strange little sorceress in her arms.

The darkness was eternal here. Omnipresent. Omnipotent. All consuming, and destroying.

And regardless of intent, it was inescapable. Thus was the fate of all vertuém, those unbound by destiny. Since Light and Her daughters were the scribes of fate, it was only fitting that those without purpose were disciples of the Darkness.

He could feel them here, so close to hell. All of those whose lives he'd ended: Bail. Ellis. Lawson. The convict at the Rock. Kyri's mother. Her guard, Fyren. The bastards that killed him. Even Berinhard, and Riese . . . And Tay now too. He thought he'd learned. Tried to change. Fed up with the brutal darkness, he'd chosen to let Riese live . . . even though something in him cried out for his blood. He'd let him live . . . And still he wound up dead. Killed by Itxaro, who Stiqula had freed . . . *Stiqula*. The ever-looming shadow. If Greyson were the stone that disrupted fate's constant stream, Stiqula was his rippling wake, propagating out from every move he made, severing the strings of fate from anyone that dared near him.

The ripples that he made were inescapable. But they weren't simple ripples in a stream, no. They were ripples in space and time itself, creating waves with the deepest valleys, wells of gravity from which nothing could escape. Not even light . . . No matter how hard he tried to do good, to make the *right* choice, Stiqula . . . *Darkness* countered him at every turn.

"Is my part over?" He echoed Jacob's question. "I don't know . . . I don't know anything anymore . . . I don't even know who I am."

He wasn't always like this. This hadn't always happened to him . . . He was not born a demon. He was made one by their King. The King of Lies, Refsiel. Tricked into doing His bidding all along . . . But how? Where did it begin? What changed in Greyson that let Darkness find him? . . . It happened the very night he came to Viæden. He left his home, his sanctuary of light, in search of something greater. And he'd found it. Then, as if he were a new player on some cosmic game board, Darkness planted that nightmare in his mind, and Greyson had become His instrument.

Greyson looked up to the faces of the dead around him. Those he knew and led to die, or killed himself. They'd stayed with him, haunted him. And he'd let them, kept them, as reminders of his humanity. A constant stinging in his heart that let him know what he was fighting for . . . even though Nash—everyone—told him not to blame himself, he couldn't do that. He just couldn't remove all sense of responsibility. Because it *cheapened* the lives he'd taken. Like they weren't worth regretting. But Greyson regretted each one. Blamed himself for them all . . . But he *had* to believe that what he fought for—the *reason* he'd killed them . . . was worth the sacrifice, like Sam and Nash had said.

Greyson was too focused on the repercussions of his actions, instead of the reasons for them. And the reason behind every action he'd ever taken . . . was *good*. He *had* to know that. He had to *believe* that. Because everyone else did . . . Tay would not have followed him in here to die if he hadn't believe in Greyson with all his heart. And if Greyson couldn't trust himself, the least he could do was trust his friends. And their belief in him. They knew he was no demon.

He was vertui . . . The true reason he either inspired or struck fear in so many people. The same reason Refsiel had tricked him. Used him. Because Light and Dark were in a headlock, and the only ones that could make a difference were the vertuém. Greyson knew that now, more so than anything he'd ever known. That's the *real* reason Darkness chose him, and Water too. His destiny was great, and powerful. But most of all: his to decide.

And right then he knew his part was not done.

Greyson rolled to his front, then stood and spoke. "I've spilled so much darkness on this world . . . But I know Your game now, Refsiel. And I will not let You win!" He drew his blade. "You will pay for *every* soul I've given You. And You'll not have *one* more from me!" Greyson panted, heart racing, threatening the Evil Father of all gods. "Not even mine." Greyson would not give Darkness the satisfaction. He would destroy this ship. He would return to tell Sam all he'd learned, and keep his promise to see Kyri again. "Going through all this trouble, leading me here, making me believe I was about to die. You wanted to wring me dry of all I was, then walk right up to Your Door and feed my soul to You. A soul that powerful must be worth *keeping*. Must be bright enough to threaten You. Must be strong enough to *stop You*!"

He felt it coming, from within, the chain tingling in his hand as his fist tightened on his hilt. Then, raising his blade, it ignited. The air clapped to it with a clang, melting into plasma that shone so brightly in the dark that it was white, haloed in green. And all the ghosts that had surrounded him were no more as his white light spilt to the floor, pushing the shadows back as it spread, flashing to the ceiling, and the walls until no darkness remained. The room had come to life, glowing deep, like veins of light beneath its crystal skin.

Greyson's lerité had brought light and power to the room. And with it, the wall before him shuddered and slid up into the ceiling. And he was wrapped in the sun. The blinding light of the outside world shone in, bringing with it a warm, cleansing breeze, with all the scents of life. A deep, fresh smell of wood and grass, and deeper still, the scent of air, pure oxygen. He could smell the rivers too, as they trickled through Viæden's endless fields to the sea. Like sunlight. It smelt just like sunlight to Greyson.

As his eyes adjusted, he saw the brown rim of the crater a mile below him, encircled by the shadows of the clouds. But further still was light. The Great Ceptris Forest, one hundred miles on the horizon, and its crowning gem, Darakin, draped in the low sun.

"Whoa," Greyson gasped, chills bathing him as wholly as the light.

"Fascinating," Jacob said. "As if the lerité works as a power source for this ship."

"Yeah," Greyson said, spotting the bark ships dotting the sky. There were a dozen hovering nearby, encircling the *Chandelier*.

Brown's men. The sun was almost set. Brown was going to try and destroy the ship from the outside . . . But it would never work. This ship, and the darkness in it, was too strong. Their attack would only rupture it, and free the horrors trapped inside.

"Well, at least we've found a way out," Jacob said, rising to his shaky legs.

Greyson turned to him. "We're not leaving."

"What?"

"We still have to find the bridge, and destroy this ship."

"Isn't that what *they're* for?" Jacob pointed to the bark ships.

"It won't be enough," Greyson shook his head, looking to the terminal next to Jacob. "Try that computer. Maybe it can tell us where we need to go."

Reluctantly, Jacob turned to the terminal, sitting down in the tall chair. "What makes you think I know how to use this?"

"You read Vínesíren don't you?" Greyson asked, coming up next to him, green blade still glowing brightly in his hand.

"Not very well," Jacob said with hardly any confidence.

The crystal keys fit naturally beneath his fingers, rising up to meet them. He inspected the black, Vínesíren letters at the finger pads of each key, then looked to the screen, displaying a dim white symbol Greyson didn't recognize.

"Search for a map," said Greyson.

"Um." Jacob's fingers twiddled in place. "I don't know the word for map."

Greyson sighed heavily, looking away from the computer, spotting something on the wall across the room, opposite the window. An inscription, written with the familiar burns of a lerité. This time it was four lines, instead of two. "There's another inscription here."

*Ere into darkness I was cast,*
*wrought solely by the sin Man hast,*
*My Soul was splintered into ten;*
*their hearts are darkest of all men.*

These lines . . . were connected to the first somehow. Connected to the Door to Darkness, behind which Refsiel and all the evils of the world were kept. But who was writing them? And what the hell was this one about?

"Ten?" Jacob muttered. "I'm not sure what ten is referring to, but *darkest of all men*, that's no doubt a reference to the Evil Spirits. But they number seven, not ten . . . strange."

*Evil Spirits.* That legend was only vaguely familiar to Greyson. His mom always cut out all the bad parts . . . and that story was *mostly* bad parts. But Jacob was right, there were only seven of them. So what did this mean? "And what do they have to do with the door?"

"In reference to the first we found, they must have something to do with opening it." Jacob answered. "Strange, I've never heard this rhyme before. It sounds like it would be something quite crucial to our lore."

"Try the Door to Darkness then. Can you search for that? I'm sure that's where Itxaro's headed."

"Yes. That one I know. The words have not changed much." He began to type, slowly finding the symbols on the keys. "*Duru a Deorra.*" The squiggly glyphs appeared on the screen, white on blue.

The screen buzzed and flashed, like it didn't like what Jacob typed. His text was erased, replaced with a flashing horizontal line.

"I guess it doesn't have any information on that." Jacob said.

"Great."

"I could try *carta* for map. It's not as old as Vínesíren, but it's from one of its daughter languages." Jacob typed it in. And as soon as he did, the window slammed shut and the lights dimmed as a blue glow rose up behind them. They both spun to see a three dimensional model of the ship, a wire frame of blue light, forming from thin air.

"That worked." Greyson stepped away from the computer to inspect the image. The ship was just as he remembered from his nightmare. Its main body was tiered in concentric cylinders, city rising from the inside of its curved surface. Three large spikes dangled from the bottom of the city chamber, like icicles. And surrounding its main body were four arms, stemming from its crown, further dressed in even more crystal spikes.

"The bridge is here," he remembered, pointing to a domed tip of the lowest icicle.

"And we must be this light here." Jacob spotted a green speck just outside the rear edge of the city chamber. The complete opposite side of the ship.

So far away.

"Then that means . . ." The image flickered, updating its integrity to reflect the ship as it was now. The entire front end of the ship disappeared. Its outline fading to an almost invisible reddish-purple. "The bridge is gone." Smashed, nose-first into the ground. It didn't survive. And any shot he had at destroying the *Chandelier* faded, just as dim.

"What's all this?" Jacob pointed to a collection of red pulses near the ship's engines.

"The demons," Greyson answered.

"Why are they all gathered here?"

There were random scatters of red specs spread thinly through the ship, but Jacob was right, most of them appeared in an extremely dense mob near the engines.

"It's almost like they're—"

"Protecting something," Greyson finished, pointing to the core of the ship. The central axis hall once stretching all the way from the bridge to the engines, before his angels severed it. It led right back to where the demons huddled. "We can take the axis hall all the way there."

"We're going *toward* them?"

"Something's drawing them. Maybe the door. Maybe Itxaro." Greyson turned for the exit. "And if it's nothing, then we're gunna try everything we can to overload those engines, and destroy the ship that way. We've still got a shot at this." He hit the switch for the door, and it slid open onto the empty hallway. The light crept from the room, not terribly fast, illuminating the oddly angled, silver walls.

"Greyson, it's 4:80." Jacob looked to his watch. "The sun will set in twenty minutes. And that engine room could be half a mile away from here."

"Then we'd better run." Greyson darted from the room, as fast as he could. Heart booming with purpose again, fear tamed by the light of his lerité. He'd seen what it could do to those creatures, and he was ready for them. He ran fast and hard, not caring if Jacob could keep up this time or not. The dark hall came to light around him as he ran, just as it had in his vision, glowing white. But he was done fixating on that stupid dream. This was *his* life now.

The white hall ended, intersecting the golden axis hall, and Greyson stopped, feeling the texture of the floor change, going smoother, and dipping down to form the curved bottom of the cylindrical hall. That's when the light caught up with him, spilling out around him, curving with the walls like a tubular sun.

The axis hall was slanted at the same angle as the ship. Lucky it wasn't that slippery, even though it looked just like ice, or else he would have slid all the way down the thing. The light ended its crawl below him, slammed into darkness where the hall had been broken by his angels, sixty feet away. But, sixty feet in the opposite direction, the light continued on, growing past two shadows that remained.

Like two nocturnal vermin, they hissed in the light, throwing up their wings to try and cover their eyeless heads. Then they caught scent of Greyson's heart, and took wing to find it.

One led before the other, collapsing its wings like a bombing raptor, and Greyson took aim for the kill along the length of its black head. But just then, Jacob burst onto the scene to really fuck things up. The demon spread its wings to slow, and instead of taking Greyson dead-on, it veered left. But he did manage to slice off its wing and tail as it flew by. The wounded demon crashed into the wall and rolled a ways before it dug its claws in to catch itself. Then the other swooped in and snatched Jacob by his leg. Jacob flipped and slammed his head against the glass, dragged down the hall by the demon's claws.

"No!" Greyson threw his legs out in front of him to slide after. "Jacob!" he yelled as he dodged the flailing wing of the wounded demon. He was dropping fast. *Really* fast. And there wasn't a whole lot of hall left! But there at the very edge of the broken hall, he spotted the U-shaped handle, jutting from the floor, still there from when they'd ridden up on it.

"Greyson!" Jacob screamed, grabbing at the glossy surface, lashing out at anything to try and stop. But Greyson couldn't explain in time for him to grab the handle. Jacob had already passed it. The darkness slipped beneath him, and he fell, dragged down into the void of the city chamber.

The air left Greyson's lungs as he stopped himself with the handle, catching it under his heels, which pushed his knees up into his chest. He watched Jacob fall. Seeing his frightened eyes disappear into the dark.

Gone.

All he could see was the fallen section of the axis hall just below him, a dim hollow tube descending into shadows. Nothing else. From up there, the city was a void as dark as a starless space.

Then from the nothingness, came light. A pale warmth glowing in the void. A single star. A sphere of light, six feet wide.

He *knew* that light.

The portal! The portal to the bridge!

The wounded demon cried out for him, and Greyson turned as it found its feet, aiming its eyeless gaze at him again.

He had to reach that light. Even though he knew the bridge had been destroyed, it had to lead somewhere. At least that's what his gut was telling him. But he didn't have wings like his angel. And that portal was at least twenty feet beyond the edge of the axis hall, suspended in the dark. It'd have to be one hell of a jump.

Greyson heard the demon's talons unstick from the floor and take wing as he readied to jump, focusing all his energy into his legs, still squatted.

Greyson leapt, just as the demon crashed into him, meeting claw to face, blade to chest. And they both flew into the void, into the portal.

Greyson was thrown to a hard metal floor, instantly. Disoriented, he shot to his feet, swinging his light-blade wildly in search of the demon. But it wasn't there. Only the big ball of light hung in an alcove, like it was on display. He cocked his head and turned his back on it, searching this new room as it came to light.

The illumination spread from him, just like before, but this room was mostly steel, so its floors and walls did not glow like the others. Instead there was a ring of light around the perimeter of this round room's ceiling, and nineteen other portal alcoves in the walls, at equidistant intervals.

This was not the bridge. It was some sort of hub station for these portals, with empty benches everywhere, bent into circles.

Then, from behind one of those benches, poked the top of someone's head. Someone whose hair was short and messy, brown, just like his eyes.

"Tay," Greyson gasped.

He shot up out of hiding. "Holy shit." Tay leapt over the bench.

Greyson's blade went dark. He wanted to puke and cry at the same time, but instead, he ran in to hug his friend, colliding with him. "You're okay."

Tay stood still as Greyson fell apart on him. Tay didn't know what to do, not used to being so emotional. But right then he needed it, giving Greyson a few good pats on the back. "I mean . . . Probly not. But yeah."

Greyson backed off to have a look at him. "What do you mean?"

Tay's face was trying real hard to crack a smile. But it only added to the torment in his eyes. "I mean, there's some really fucked up shit in here."

Greyson nodded, spotting the dark red stains all up and down Tay's clothes, matted in his hair. They were on the same page when it came to that. No need to explain.

"You, uh, got a piece a your face missing." Tay pointed to his lip.

Greyson hadn't even noticed it stinging 'til right then. The left side of his mouth, where that demon'd clawed him. He touched the deep cut, bleeding over his lips, pulling back to see red on his fingers. "Shit. Is it bad?"

Tay inspected the bloody gash running down his upper lip and chin, a half-inch left of his midline. "Yeah, it's probly gunna leave a scar."

"Fuck, whatever." He dropped his hand. Normally that would have been a devastating wound. But he had bigger things to worry about now. "How'd you get here?"

"I fell through one of those portal things." He pointed to the one next to Greyson's. "But they weren't all lit up like this when I got here. Only one other one. And there's no other way in or outa this room, so I figured I should just stay here instead a wasting my chances out there with those things." A high pitch ring grew as Tay spoke, and suddenly seven of the starlight portals made loud snapping, popping sounds and went out.

"What the hell was that?" Tay said, covering his ears for a second.

Greyson looked to the dead portals across from them, all in a line. Either there wasn't enough power to keep them on, or . . . "Whatever parts of the ship they led to must be destroyed." He focused on Tay again. "Which one was lit when you got here?"

Tay pointed right. To the last light, at the edge of the ones that'd gone out. "That one."

"I think these things are powered by my lerité. Which means they're powered by Itxaro's too." Greyson focused on the last portal. There were burn marks on the ground in front of it. "What's this?" He walked up to them.

"Oh, yeah. I think he wrote that before he left. No clue why."

"*From dark hearts to dark souls, transform, / by way of demon's blood, deform.*" Greyson read. "I found two of these too. But what the hell are they for?"

"I think they're keys to that door you were talking about."

Greyson looked at him. "Why do you say that?"

"'Cuz the one I found before this said they were."

"Oh. Okay. So . . . demon's blood's a key?" Greyson put it together. It made sense. And it sounded just like it could be in one of his mom's stories, which made him extra certain. That's the whole reason Itxaro had come here in the first place. Nice of him to leave bread crumbs for them like that.

"Looks like it," Tay agreed.

"I thought you didn't believe in any of this stuff?"

"It's a little hard to ignore at this point."

Greyson cracked half a smile. It made his face hurt, but he didn't care. "Right." He turned to the portal's light.

"So do we have a game-plan or something?" Tay asked.

"Keep that door closed. And blow this ship up if we can. Hopefully Itxaro along with it."

"So basically we're gunna die."

Greyson looked at him. Maybe for the last time. "I'm not dying unless I'm taking this ship with me."

Tay nodded, an uneasy smile making its way to his face. "Good to see you found your confidence again." He smacked him on the back, pushing him into the light and following after.

# 32

# Refsiels Gate

The boys dropped from the portal, staggering against a crystal floor. The room was dark, and they both were silent as their eyes adjusted to it. Faintly they could see the edges of the room, another rounded chamber, of which they stood in the middle, maybe forty feet from the walls. The portal at their back was just off of center, hovering two feet off the ground. There was a catwalk, a floor above them, a ring around the room, dimly lit by the cyan glow of control panels.

Something sizzled up there. And as their eyes adjusted fully to the dark, they saw where it was coming from. Freshly cut letters glowed on the wall, growing brighter, and more molten as they read from left to right:

*Swing wide the doors of bitter hell,*
*give Life to Father Refsie*

A black figure slashed the final *L* in his inscription, and turned slowly to face them.

"You," his hellish voice rang out.

"Stiqula," Greyson whispered. Terror burnt his skin, so unexpected, sinking down to scatter all the light he'd just collected in his heart. So much for confidence.

But Tay was stronger than that. His heart didn't bend to the world as easily as Greyson's. He whipped his gun up to the grey angel and fired as fast as his little finger could twitch.

Stiqula drew his blade away from his body, pulling Tay's fire with it, sucked into its black rod, then leapt over the rail and fired a clear torrent of air down at them, blasting Greyson and Tay away from each other as it slammed between them. Stiqula struck the ground, boom echoing throughout the room as he strode to Greyson lying on the floor. Greyson could hardly breathe, wind knocked right from his lungs as he watched the shadow come. Stiqula ripped him off the floor by his jacket, spinning him back into the portal's light to see the color of his eyes.

"You," he spoke again, softer.

Greyson was immobile in his claws, studying the gruesome features of his face again, like life had sucked him dry of all he was: a husk of bones and brawn, barely breathing. But his eyes were worst of all. Like two black prisoners, peering out from their grey cage. They trembled and flickered, tearing at their bars to escape. They held such life still in their depths, cold as it was.

"I have felt you before. My shadow's wake. Ever constant. Ever following. Ever mending what darkness I sew into the world." He sounded hurt. His voice near quivering.

That made a little bit of Greyson's light return. Just enough to flash an accomplished smile.

Stiqula cocked his head, ever so slightly, like he wondered if Greyson could somehow have the upper hand, just for a moment.

That made Greyson's smile grow. And as more light came to his heart, his fear bowed to his courage. He knew all Stiqula's plans. And he was strong enough to stop him. It was time to let him know how strong. "Where's the door?"

Stiqula righted his head again. "The door?"

"To Darkness," Greyson spat.

"Greyson!" Tay climbed to his feet, aim steadied on Stiqula.

Stiqula almost smiled. But out of nerves or pity, Greyson couldn't tell. "So, you've been reading my little rhymes? My little curses." He spun Greyson in close, wrapping his arm around his neck in a lock to shield himself from Tay. He held Greyson so tight he couldn't breathe, blood pooling in his head, heartbeat sounding in his ears. But through its drumming he could hear Stiqula hiss, "It's not here."

*Not here?* Greyson tugged at the metal arm around his neck. *But wasn't that the whole point? Hadn't Stiqula come to open it, and free the devil?* "Where is it?!" he coughed.

"Why do you fight? You fool. Don't you realize your constant mending only worsens what darkness I must work. For every soul you save, it's two more I must end."

"*What?*" Stiqula knew the same thing Greyson did: that vertuém— and apparently Stiqula too—were the only ones that could sway the battle between Dark and Light. But the way he said it, he made it sound like *Greyson* was the bad guy.

"Your light cuts Him deep. A wound it is my task to mend before He can grant me what I need."

"Well then He's pretty fucking stupid," Greyson choked. "Because *He's* the one who pulled me into this. *He* made me release you. And brought me here."

Stiqula dropped him, instantly.

Gasping, Greyson collapsed to his knees and elbows.

"Then He has meant for this to happen." Stiqula was quiet. The fury in his voice, burnt out. "An eternity to plot and scheme, moving His pieces into place. Waiting for them all to fall at once." He backed away. Back into the shadows, eyes shining faintly yellow.

Greyson pushed off his arms, looking to where he'd gone.

The clap of a lerité rang from behind the portal. And Itxaro roared as his red blade tore through the dark, right for him. Greyson leapt back from his crouch, just in time to feel its heat swipe past him.

His eyes lit up, surprised to see that red glow again, and by instinct alone, his green blade sprang to life, swinging up to deflect Itxaro's next strike. The colored blades cracked as they connected, and were instantly repelled by their opposing magnetic fields. It stopped Itxaro in his tracks, and pushed Greyson back even further. Neither one of them expected such a recoil.

In the combined light of their lerités, the shadows split, lighting the fogged crystal floor below them, and the translucent-cyan walls around them. But this time, more than just their room was lit. A glow came from far beyond its walls as well. Four giant spheres pulsed in the distance, sparking to life. They were enormous, glowing white hot, appearing as warped moons through the frosted crystal. The spheres encircled their room, an enormous void between them. But the void was not empty. It shone faintly blue in the light of the moons. And, swimming in its blue, were a thousand shadows, with even more lurking in the deep.

*Demons.* Frenzied by the light, swarming it, hurling themselves against their small, glass cage.

"Holy fuck." Tay shivered, looking at them all, losing all concentration.

Greyson was only a little less surprised, having seen their numbers on the map. But being completely surrounded by them now was still terrifying.

Stiqula smirked at their fear. "This is their nest," he said to twist the knife. "Drawn to the heat of the tritium reactors."

Itxaro lunged for Greyson again, their blades bouncing off each other like they were made of rubber instead of steel. The recoil was too much for Greyson to handle. Every time they hit, his sword nearly flew right out of his hands. Itxaro was just as strong as he remembered, but he was still slow. Seemingly, his only weakness.

Greyson kept back out of Itxaro's reach, inspecting the hilt in his giant fist as it swung by. It looked like it was made of crystal, just like the ship . . . *It was angelic!* Fucking great! Nash said that thing would never melt, even if this fight went on for years! And worse yet, it could break his mirror blade if he kept this up. Greyson leapt back again, red blade blazing past his chest. He didn't want to clash his sword with that shit. By the strength of that giant's blows, Greyson figured he only had a few good blocks left in him before his sword was snapped in two.

Tay couldn't take his eyes off the demons outside. And all that fucking water they were swimming in. They were standing in a goddam human fishtank. *What the hell was all that water doing here in the first place!* He was frozen, so scared he could barely even *breathe*, let alone move.

He could hear something going on in the room with him. Muffled cracks and sizzles. Greyson was fighting with Itxaro. But he couldn't see them. All he could see was the backlight of a warped moon through the glass, and a million horrible things swimming between him and it.

What's that? Was he shaking? He was shaking. Great.

He needed to focus. The water was out *there*, not in here. *C'mon!*

Tay's eyes moved, ever so slightly, unfocusing from the glass, dragging slowly across the room. To the catwalk. And Stiqula.

"So, Refsiel has led them here," Stiqula spoke to himself, watching the vertui dodge Itxaro's blade, also keeping an eye on his friend to make sure he didn't move. He'd returned to the catwalk, standing before a small terminal no larger than a podium, housing the controls for the door below. A circular aperture in the middle of the floor, twenty feet wide, which would open to the golden axis tunnel of the ship.

"Why? Why would He do such a thing? Lead such a brilliant light to me?" Stiqula could feel it, he could see it, glowing in his green lerité. A powerful heart for one as young as he. "This boy. This pair. They must be special to Her . . . And Refsiel wishes me to strike their light from the world . . . A heavy loss to Her cause." Stiqula contemplated. Though not for long. What speck of light still clung to him was strong. Fixated on *one* thing. "But I say You are strong *enough*, Refsiel. And our bargain only spoke of *freedom*. Not the eradication of all *light*. So here." He struck a crystal button on his terminal. "*Here* is Your demon's blood. Now You *take it*, and be *satisfied*. *Be free. And return my light to me!*"

Greyson had to do something quick. Dodging that red blade was not going to work forever! *Think!* Was there *anything* from their battle in Rock Town that could help him? Was *speed* all there was? He couldn't think of anything else! *Granted this wasn't the best brainstorming atmosphere.* But he had to think of something!

He leapt back again. Or at least started to, he'd run out of room, smacked up against the crystal wall. Itxaro had had enough already, thrusting straight for Greyson's heart, and pierced the glowing wall as Greyson dodged. The crystal cracked, *loud*, and sprung a leak, spraying water inside at high enough pressure to fly halfway across the room.

*Wait, water? Here?* Greyson thought. *Water was how they beat this guy before!*

"Tay!" Greyson shouted as Itxaro pulled his sword from the wall, worsening the leak.

"Tay!" he finally heard. Snapping out of his spell. Tay looked down from Stiqula to Greyson across the room. And held his aim again . . . But . . . but, his gun still wouldn't work against those laser blades! If he fired now it'd just go around them, and blast a hole right in the freaking wall!

"Tay!" Greyson cried again.

That big black motherfucker just stabbed a hole in the tank! And now water was spraying in. Tay gagged a little. *But the glass didn't shatter.* They were still okay!

Actually, *wait.* That could *help* them! The water is what helped them win before! With his gun's stun! "I got it!" Tay slapped his gun against his leg, switching its setting, and sprinted for them. But as he crossed the center of the room, the white floor sank and split into slices, darkness spreading between their gaps.

"Oh, *shit*," Tay screamed as he slipped and slid down to the center, where the dark grew out like an asterisk. The gap was just fucking wide enough to fall through, but he caught himself on another slice of crystal before he did. And the door held there, not spreading any wider, *thank fuck.* But Tay could feel wind rising from below, growing stronger as a banter of hisses and flapping approached. "Oh, no, no, no, no, no, no, no!" He scrambled to climb the slippery slices, latching onto their edges as the demons slammed into them from below, wingtips and claws springing from the gaps like black, wiggling worms.

"You there," Stiqula called to him.

Tay looked to him on the second level, standing in front of a small control panel. *Probly the one for this goddam floor!*

"Try to lure one out. That's all I need. But a few more couldn't hurt," he said, so fucking smug. "Whatever you can manage."

Tay was bait for these things! "Oh, fuck you!" he screamed back.

A demon's claw hooked around the slice at Tay's feet. He felt it click its talons into the crystal behind his foot, and used it to push himself halfway out of that hell-pit, and crawled the rest of the way out himself.

Tay gave a scream that dropped off into an irritated grunt as he wiggled away from the door and switched his gun back to *kill.* Then he rolled to his back and fired into those demons to his heart's content. The plasma chewed through their thick skin as his bullets piled up, streaming from his gun until it overheated at about 30 rounds.

Maybe some of them died, maybe not. He couldn't tell, it was such a cluster-fuck down there. But finally, one managed to squeeze through those gaps. Probly lubed up from all the water running down it like a gutter.

It looked right at Tay—even though it didn't have any freaking eyes. But it didn't want him. It leapt into the air instead, right for Stiqula, wings stretched wide. But Stiqula didn't flinch at all. He just put his hand up like he was telling it to stop, then fucking blasted the thing with a wind-explosion, breaking all its bones right there on the spot, flinging it, dead, across the room.

"Ho!" Tay put a fist up to his open mouth, almost feeling his own bones breaking too. But he couldn't help but think how badass it was at the same time.

Another one wormed its way out of the hole, flying up to Stiqula. But this time he leapt to meet it. Slicing right through the bitch like it was nothing, then blasting all the rest away from the door as it rose and closed shut again. He landed across the room, right next to the demon he'd broken. Then knelt to collect its blood.

Stiqula's back was turned. *And* he was distracted. If Tay ever had the opportunity to strike, this was it. He fiddled with the charge of his gun, watching the amber grains brighten to white. He didn't care what kind of sword Stiqula had, there was no way it was gunna stop the full charge of his gun. He stood and took aim. But paused. Noticing something weird about the shadows in the water outside the room. Those demons. They followed Stiqula, darkening the glass nearest him. Throwing themselves against it.

They were *attracted* to him . . . And if Tay missed . . . *They* and all that water would come flooding in.

Greyson tried his best to avoid each one of Itxaro's swings, but his reach was just too damn long, and that idiot kept chipping bits out of the walls! "Itxaro! Stop!" Greyson pleaded with him as more geysers sprayed into the room. But the beast's wrath only deepened. His swings became erratic, more desperate to strike. His red blade came down. And Greyson had no choice but to block, or else he'd slice right through the wall and drown them all. He thrust his green blade to meet Itxaro's, and they sizzled as they struck over Greyson's head, so close to his face their heat nearly blinded him. He had to buckle underneath the blow or *both* blades would end up liquefying him.

Greyson fell back against the wall, using his quick swing to slash out at

Itxaro's bulging shoulder, searing his skin before Itxaro could block or dodge, then jumped to miss the red blade as it swung after him. Finally Itxaro leapt for him, fed up with his constant evasion. The giant crashed to the floor, and in his ten-foot reach, wrapped his thick fingers around Greyson's ankle, and yanked him down, pulling him in as Itxaro rose up to his knees. Greyson spun, flailing his blade blindly in an attempt to stop whatever attack Itxaro had coming. But with only one hand on his sword when their blades met, Greyson's ripped from his hand, losing its glow and clattering to the floor. Itxaro arched back with both hands on his blade, held like a dagger over Greyson's heart.

"No!" Greyson cried, holding up his arms to block, as if they could save him.

Itxaro had him.

He was dead.

"Itxaro," Stiqula called. "It's done."

Greyson opened his eyes to see the red blade still hanging over him. Itxaro looking to his master across the room. Stiqula had his prize. A vial, black with demon's blood.

They'd lost . . . They'd fucking lost.

Itxaro rose from his knees. And Greyson scrambled away from him, still nervous he didn't have all his limbs. Because that was probably as close to death as he'd ever been.

But why did Stiqula stop him? To gloat that he'd won? The only possible way Stiqula could lose now was if they somehow managed to kill that sonofabitch. But Greyson couldn't even kill his sidekick, let alone a God-knows-how-old angel with the devil on his side.

"You can stop this, vertui." Stiqula spoke, right to him. He felt his lightless eyes on him, searching deep within his mind and soul . . . But his voice . . . He still made it sound like Greyson was the bad guy. The one with all the power.

"I'm trying to," he replied. He tried to say it as strongly—as pissed—as he could. But he wasn't fooling anyone. He couldn't even look him in the eye when he said it.

He *was* trying. He just knew he couldn't win.

"No. You're not," Stiqula said. "You're making it worse. It's all you've ever done. Losing your hope, then finding it again. This constant tide of light you're causing only makes Him stronger, when I'm forced to eclipse your tide with death . . . What will it take for you to see?"

Greyson finally sat up and looked at him. "So stop killing! It's easy! How can you blame *me* for everything you've done?!" Greyson was over this. He'd already resolved that all those Stiqula killed were on *Stiqula's* head, not his.

"Because, vertui. You are free." Stiqula knew the truth as much as Greyson.

"And you're not?" Greyson inched to his blade.

Then Stiqula said something that arrested him all together. Something he was never expecting to hear come out of that fanged mouth of his. "Don't you see? I hate Him as much as you do."

What? . . . How was that possible? He'd killed so many. He wants Him *freed*! He's *lying*!

Furious, Greyson snatched his blade and leapt to his feet. "Then why are you doing this!?" He drew his lerité.

"Because I have no choice!" Stiqula roared, launching after Greyson.

Greyson screamed, blade aimed like a lance at the angel's heart. And Stiqula bore his chest to the sword, as if to drive it through himself. But when it slammed into his steel, it did no such thing, clanging against his armor like he wore a diamond shield. Greyson's locked joints nearly snapped as he recoiled. Stiqula's chest had not chipped or warped a single atom's worth, resting fully on the tip of Greyson's blade, green plasma peeling back and dripping to the floor.

Stiqula leaned in close to hiss, "He will not let me die."

Greyson met his eyes, wise and terrible.

"So this choice lies with you, vertui." He pulled away from Greyson's blade. "But what man are you? One who would sacrifice his light to save the world's? Or one who would save his light to sacrifice the world?"

Greyson lowered his sword. Useless . . . Beaten.

What man was he? Were those his only options? Both ended with him dead and Darkness free. "What do you mean? I stop fighting, and the world ends, or I keep fighting, and the world ends anyway, but at least my conscience is clear? Knowing I did everything I could to stop it?"

"Refsiel's freedom does not mean the world's destruction," said Stiqula. "It lasted long before He was locked away, and it will stand after His chains are broken."

Greyson remembered from his mom's stories what the world was like when He was free. A dark, chaotic place, without sanctuary, barely holding on to any shred of order. He couldn't do that to the world again . . . But, was his fighting, his constant push-back, really strengthening the Darkness like Stiqula said? For all the light he brought to the world, Stiqula had to counter it, by adding to Refsiel's strength . . . *Balance* . . . Just like Sam had said.

Stiqula . . . was almost just like Greyson. Trapped into doing Darkness' bidding. Now posed against each other. The only difference was that Greyson hadn't realized it, and escaped it. But Stiqula was completely aware . . . and could not change it.

*Why? . . . What did he say earlier? . . . That it was his task to help Darkness, so that Darkness could give him something? . . . What could it be? What could he possibly need so badly that he would risk the whole world to have?*

"What did He take from you?" Greyson asked, barely louder than a whisper.

But Stiqula heard it, reacting more to those few quiet words than anything else Greyson had said. His body tensed, eyes hardening. As if Greyson finally posed a threat to him.

Then suddenly a single plasma round, white as a sunbeam, struck Stiqula in the back of his left shoulder, exploding in an even brighter flash that hurled him across the room. Stiqula slammed into the chamber wall, armor stripped from his back, and grey skin sizzling.

"*Whoa!*" Greyson shouted.

"Ohmygod, it worked!" Tay cheered.

Too soon. Itxaro came to life again, swinging his blade wildly at Tay.

Tay could dodge his swings like Greyson could, but not forever!

"Tay!" Greyson was about to jump in and help when Stiqula let out a gruesome cry. He wasn't dead! He wasn't even down for the count, just really, *really* pissed off, struggling to shake off the blow. Guess that meant they were done talking.

Greyson looked down to the water pooling at his feet. Maybe it could still save them. Or more specifically, maybe *she* could still save them. After all, he knew from experience that she was always watching.

Greyson spun to the crystal wall behind him, seeing the demons swarming in the water on the other side, and activated his lerité, praying it was not the last time. He dug his blade into the wall, as far as it would go, plasma sinking in and sizzling as he dragged it, as fast and far as he could reach before the wall around him shattered.

The water crashed in through the giant hole he'd made, but did not crush him. Instead it bent its flow, hugging the curved wall of the room in one direction, toward Itxaro and Tay.

Just as Itxaro was about to deliver the killing blow, the torrent swept by and struck the giant, carrying him off in its curving wave. Tay fell back from the shock of Itxaro disappearing, only misted by the furious wave as it circled back around the room's edge. The white water hugged the wall with a mind of its own, defying gravity as it slammed into Stiqula and swallowed him too. Then it clapped as it collided with the waters flooding in behind Greyson and completed its loop around the room, still spinning like a vortex.

"Holy shit!" Tay screamed, eyeing the horror all around them. But he and Greyson were kept safe in the eye of the storm. And so was the portal.

"Tay! The light!" Greyson screamed as they locked eyes, then sprinted for it.

The water vortex grew as they ran, grazing their heels as it closed in.

Greyson and Tay bound into the ball of light at once, knocking into each other on the other side, falling to the ground of the portal hub.

"You crazy motherfucker!" Tay sputtered, climbing to his feet as fast as he could. "What the hell was that!?"

"Well I was trying to have a conversation, until you had to go and shoot the guy!"

"Oh, sooo-*rry*. You wanna go back in and ask him a few more questions, *Chatty Kathy*?" Tay pointed to the portal as Greyson pushed off the ground with a grin. The floor was covered in an inch of water. The ball of light was leaking, water pouring from it like a holey dam.

Stiqula could still use it just as sure as they could.

"Oh, shit. He can still get outa there, Tay. *Fire!*"

"Huh?" Tay looked to the light, not really sure if it worked like that. But it didn't matter anyway. "I can't! I used up both my guns!"

Just then, the ball of light glowed brighter and rang louder and louder until it popped, like a water balloon, turning into a sphere of water, Itxaro within.

"Oh fuck," Tay said as Itxaro fell to his knees with a splash.

The portal was destroyed, but Itxaro was here. The giant threw himself off the ground, dripping wet with wrath, and activated his red blade with a vein-swelling war cry.

Greyson still stood no chance of beating him. That water trick was supposed to take care of both those bastards!

The boys ran. They had to. Spun and sprinted for the closest portal, praying it wasn't one they'd been through already. They ran in synchrony, leaping into another light like a hurdle on the track. And it spat them out on the shores of some ungodly sea, dark and frothy, like a-hundred-year-old dishwater.

But it wasn't a sea. It was the puddle at the bottom of the ship, filled with all manner of broken things and blood, maybe some water too. Looking up, they could see the crystal city, wrapping all the way around its walls, like looking down the barrel of a titan's spool, punctured by a thousand icy needles. The whole thing glowed now, in white, cyan, and silver-gold. It must have all turned on when Greyson and Itxaro's fight started the reactors.

It was almost beautiful, for a moment.

Greyson turned back to the portal. Any second Itxaro was gunna come flying out of there. And then what? He'd slaughter them both anyway. They'd taken out Stiqula, and barely escaped with the help of a goddess, just to die here, now? Fuck that. He'd just figured out how live, he wasn't about to let it end now.

Greyson ran for the portal, blade drawn. And out Itxaro flew, right into his emerald swing. He cut right through that fucker's arm, right at the bicep, sliced it clear in half, and even dug into his side, clearing out a space where his ribs used to be too.

The giant roared as he tumbled to the dirt, sword arm rolling limply toward Tay on the shore. Crystal sword and chain lying dormant at his side.

He got him. *Finally.*

It was dirty, and dishonorable . . . but so was Itxaro. It was the only way. The Greyson that concerned himself with solely what was *right* was gone. That Greyson died. This one lived on.

Itxaro's cries echoed out across the sea as he rocked back and forth on his side, clutching his stub, red blood seeping through his fingers. He ground his teeth as he moaned, staring at what remained of his arm, stunned his hand was no longer at the end of it.

Greyson couldn't look away, making sure the giant was down for the count.

"You gunna kill him this time?" Tay asked.

Greyson knew the answer, this time even before his heart. "No. Refsiel's not getting any more souls from me." Itxaro was beaten, and he'd bleed out if Greyson didn't cauterize his arm.

He took a step toward the fallen giant.

But before he reached him, the sky boomed.

Tay spun to the noise, as Greyson looked up to the city, circled overhead.

"No," Greyson whispered.

Darkness was not dead.

Stiqula was not dead.

Slashing, biting, thrashing, crying, he was torn between six dozen mouths, one hundred razor claws, and three thousand silver teeth. Each one searching for the single beam of light still living in his heart. They tore him, ripped him, pulled him, flayed him, feeding on what life remained within his withered, corporeal form. But he offered them none. The deeper they searched, the further down into his onyx soul they crept, the more they fed his fury.

"That *boy*. That cheat. That *vile Light*! No better than these beasts, seeking to steal the *only thing I cherish*. I showed you *mercy*! I showed you *truth*! And you *denied* me! You've chosen your destiny. And you chose *wrong*! You *slave*. You *devil*. Only *you* are keeping us *apart*!" Stiqula burned, his body melting into pain, heart bleeding with despair, soul wracked with fear of never being whole again. All of it unbearable, *all* of it unfair.

He erupted in violence all at once, blade spinning 'round him in an orbit as he writhed back and released a shockwave from every fragment of his heart that still remained. The water and its demons were thrust away from him by a sphere of air that tore the rest of his armor from him, unveiling his charged muscles. He glowed, haloed in yellow lightning as it danced between the black fragments of his armor, peeling back, freezing behind him, as if clinging to the open wings that once resided there.

His feet touched the floor, and the demons bolted from the walls of his twenty-foot air bubble, fighting the raging winds within to reach him. And he spun his black blade through them all, reducing them to fractions of themselves in a wild dance of death. But they were endless, infinite, it seemed, and meaningless to him.

He swept his hand over his blade, and with the power of his Lord, its black lerité glowed yellow, wreathed in the very essence of Wind's power. He circled his body with one final, epic swing. And the sword cut through the air with such force the yellow power was ejected from it, fired outward in a ring around him, which plunged into the water, cutting through its shadows, striking the clear walls of the engine room and shattering them all at once. The ring pushed the water back, long enough for him to break open the door below and drop down into the ship's axis hall as the waves crashed together overhead, chasing after him as he plummeted down the *Metaleiru's* golden hall, a wake of darkness in his path.

The gold hall opened out onto the city, and Stiqula sunk down from its roof, falling past its crystal towers, aiming for the light he felt below. And his angel eyes spotted him, standing on the bank of a dark sea. Itxaro had fallen, and that *dead boy* now had *Aliqula's chain!*

Stiqula sheathed himself in Eir's power as he reached the sea, slowing all of his momentum as a maelstrom of wind fired from his body, parting its waters as he flew to the boy.

"*No!*" he heard him cry as he approached. But the vertui's fear only spurred him, arching back, blade high over his head. Stiqula swung down to destroy him.

But his black blade was met by the power of *two* lerités, lit red and green, crossed over the vertui to protect him. And as their three blades struck, a white flash cracked between them, like a sunburst, firing its white rays out along an invisible plane, separating the vertui from Stiqula like a heavenly shield.

The black plasma of Stiqula's blade was blown back from the blast, ripped right from his sword, and he was flung back, falling to the shallow water of the sea.

The demons dove from above, riding the heavy water as it rained from the broken axis tunnel. But before they could reach him again, Stiqula pulled himself from the water, sitting up and gasping at the light that remained, the sun, burning where the boy once stood. And time slowed to a still as that white sun formed into the face of beauty. The body of an angel.

Serenity radiated from her glow, but in her sapphire eyes Stiqula could find only sadness. Two grieving oceans staring back at him. A look of sorrow that they still were parted. And a look of heartbreak that he would think to end the world to see her one last time.

"Aliqula," he whispered. All he could manage.

All that he had time to say before her likeness collapsed into a sun again, exploding like a nova, whose rays pierced each of the demons raining down around them.

The city folded overhead, collapsing inward as the *Metaleiru* crumbled all around. It glowed brighter as it fell, blazed in Her Light. It *was* light. Disintegrating into weightless beams of dust.

# 33

# HOMEWARD

Greyson and Tay cowered as the light collapsed onto them, striking them with all the force of a breeze. But even that was enough to topple their spent bodies. They fell back against the dirt. And even though their eyes were closed, it was so bright they saw white behind their lids. Then as the breeze fled, that bright light dimmed to red, as if they slept beneath the sun.

Everything was silent.

A peaceful quiet.

Greyson opened his eyes to a clear sky, and the low, amber disk of the sun.

He was certain he was dead. Because he knew Viæden's sky was stained by clouds, and here there were none . . . This sky looked more like *Leiaru's*. The city of the dead. A world away.

"So, we're dead, huh?" Tay asked.

Greyson sat up, off his back, looking down at the both of them, still glazed with dirt and blood. A desert surrounded them. Shaped like the bowl of a crater, two miles wide.

"I don't—"

"Greyson!" they heard shouted from far off.

There were two bark ships, landed in the crater, a few hundred yards away. And standing between them were General Brown and his men.

Tay sat up and looked to the sound. Brown was waving at them, hurrying over with his men. "Oh," Tay said, then looked at the ground, and in the sky, and all around at where the *Chandelier* used to be. "What the . . ."

Greyson looked around too, shaking his head. "I really don't know," he said simply. Was it really over? . . . Was this just another dream?

"I knew you could do it," Brown said as he arrived, a little out of breath. "It was spectacular, Greyson. The whole thing just lit up and scattered to the wind, taking those clouds right along with it."

Greyson was almost shocked to hear him say it, even though he'd seen it for himself. He didn't know what to say.

"Are you alright?" Brown asked the both of them, his men crouching to take a better look. They touched him, shined a light in his eyes, and handed him a cloth to dab his bleeding face.

"I think so." Then he looked back to the barren patch of land, where there once was a sea. And Stiqula . . . He'd disappeared too . . . But why?

*What happened?*

Brown's men helped them to their feet. And the name "Stiqula" fell out of Greyson's bleeding mouth.

"Stiqula?" Brown asked.

"He was here. Right here." Greyson pointed to the nothingness in front of them, staring at it like his heart could still feel him there, but his eyes betrayed him. Like a mirror that didn't reflect.

"Well," Brown said happily, "he's gone now."

Greyson finally looked at him. "Where's Nash?"

Brown sharpened his eyes. "As far as the king is concerned. He's dead."

Greyson's mouth opened, just a little. His emotions were all out of whack, but that still managed to excite him a bit.

"And so long as I never see him again . . . I let him go."

Greyson broke a full-blown smile. It bit at his cut, but he didn't care. A minute ago he thought he'd never smile again. And it was worth the sting.

General Brown said they could take the other bark ship home. But he expected it back, first thing tomorrow. And Nash was waiting for them on the bridge, standing from the captain's chair as they arrived. "You boys look like you've seen hell." He smiled, limping to them.

Greyson and Tay couldn't help but chuckle. It was either that or start to cry.

"I brought this for you." Greyson lifted Itxaro's blade, a solid crystal shard in the shape of a longsword.

Nash pushed the angelic blade away from him, patting Greyson on the shoulder. "You keep it, Greyson. You've given more than anyone could ask of you already."

The bridge shuddered slightly. A small ship was landing out the front window. And on the side it read, *O'Nasi*.

"Sam," he whispered, pushing past Tay, out to the loading ramp, bathed in the setting sun.

The ship set down right next to them. And when its door opened, Sam was standing there in her tight metallic dress, with something in her arms he never thought he'd see . . . Kyri.

She put her down, still dressed in her little princess dress and flower crown. And she ran as fast as she could to him. "Greysom!"

He fell to his knees in the dirt, and scooped her up as she ran into him. "Kyri." He didn't know how. But he didn't care either. She was here. She was safe. And that was all that mattered.

Greyson stood as Sam came to him. She studied his face, and he studied hers. She looked like she had so much to say. So many questions. But when she saw the cut over his lips, she held her words, lips halfway between a smile and a frown, tears running down her cheeks. But her green eyes smiled, fixed to his. He didn't even notice he was crying 'til she wiped a tear away, and rose up on her toes to kiss the wound on his lips, and pulled back just an inch. Then he pulled her close and kissed her harder. It stung, but he wanted it. He barely even felt the pain. He felt like he was flying. As warm and weightless as a sunbeam, and glowing just as bright.